"Heywood is a master of his form."

—*Detroit Free Press*

"Top-notch action scenes, engaging characters both major and minor, masterful dialogue, and a passionate sense of place make this a fine series."

—*Publishers Weekly*

"Joseph Heywood writes with a voice as unique and rugged as Michigan's Upper Peninsula itself."

—Steve Hamilton, Edgar® Award–winning author of *The Lock Artist*

"Well written, suspenseful, and bleakly humorous while moving as quickly as a wolf cutting through the winter woods. In addition to strong characters and . . . compelling romance, Heywood provides vivid, detailed descriptions of the wilderness and the various procedures and techniques of conservation officers and poachers. . . . Highly recommended."

—*Booklist*

"Taut and assured writing that hooked me from the start. Every word builds toward the ending, and along the way some of the writing took my breath away."

—Kirk Russell, author of *Dead Game* and *Redback*

"[A] tightly written mystery/crime novel . . . that offers a nice balance between belly laughs, head-scratching plot lines, and the real grit of modern police work."

—*Petersen's Hunting*

**Praise for the short story collection *Hard Ground***

"Heywood (*Red Jacket*) displays uncommon storytelling versatility in this brilliant collection of 27 tales about the game wardens who patrol Michigan's Upper Peninsula. . . . This volume should be read for pleasure, but would do equally well as an instruction manual for aspiring writers."

—*Publishers Weekly* (starred review)

"Joseph Heywood knows his poachers, deer-baiters, and road-beer-drinking yahoos, as well as his cross-dressing informants and Elvis impersonators, but his most compelling characters are the hardworking and embattled conservation officers, the quietly heroic men and women who enforce the law evenhandedly against a well-armed slice of citizenry. Heywood is at his finest and funniest in these short stories from Michigan's Upper Peninsula, where cold kills and night can be as 'black as the inside of a cow.' These detective stories are a great contribution to the rural American literary tradition, with nods to Mark Twain, Robert Travers, Jim Harrison, Cully Gage, and Dashiell Hammett."
—Bonnie Jo Campbell, author of *Once Upon a River* and *American Salvage*, a National Book Award finalist

"Joseph Heywood has a great ear for the vernacular of some of America's more colorful backwoods 'citizens,' the cast for this wild set of tales. Even more incredible is his ability to see into the wild hearts of a wide range of wonderfully flawed human beings and the cops and conservation officers who try to keep them under control. This is full throttle writing, the kind of stuff you can't put down to pick up the remote. Heywood is a compelling writer who has obviously done his time in the woods and lived to come back to tell us what it's really like out there."
—Michael Delp, author of *As If We Were Prey* and *The Last Good Water*

### Praise for *The Snowfly*

"A truly wonderful, wild, funny and slightly crazy novel about fly fishing. *The Snowfly* ranks with the best this modern era has produced."
—*San Francisco Chronicle*

"A magical whirlwind of a novel, squarely in the tradition of Tim O'Brien's *Going After Cacciato* and Jim Harrison's *Legends of the Fall*."
—Howard Frank Mosher, author of *The Fall of the Year* and others

"*The Snowfly* is as much about fishing as *Moby Dick* is about whaling."
—*Library Journal*

# MOUNTAINS OF THE MISBEGOTTEN

# ALSO BY JOSEPH HEYWOOD

## Fiction
*Taxi Dancer*
*The Berkut*
*The Domino Conspiracy*
*The Snowfly*

## Grady Service Mysteries
*Ice Hunter*
*Blue Wolf in Green Fire*
*Chasing a Blond Moon*
*Running Dark*
*Strike Dog*
*Death Roe*
*Shadow of the Wolf Tree*
*Force of Blood*
*Killing a Cold One*

## Lute Bapcat Mysteries
*Red Jacket*

## Stories
*Hard Ground: Woods Cop Stories*

## Non-Fiction
*Covered Waters: Tempests of a Nomadic Trouter*

# MOUNTAINS OF THE MISBEGOTTEN

## A LUTE BAPCAT MYSTERY

## JOSEPH HEYWOOD

LYONS PRESS
Guilford, Connecticut
*An imprint of Globe Pequot Press*

Lyons Press is an imprint of Globe Pequot Press.

Text design: Sheryl Kober
Layout artist: Melissa Evarts
Project manager: Ellen Urban
Map: Alena Joy Pearce © Morris Book Publishing, LLC

Library of Congress Cataloging-in-Publication Data

Heywood, Joseph.
  Mountains of the misbegotten : a Lute Bapcat mystery / Joseph Heywood.
    pages cm
  Sequel to: Red jacket
  Summary: "Former Rough Rider turned Michigan game warden Lute Bapcat learns that the deputy warden from Ontonagon County has gone missing and must navigate one of the Michigan Upper Peninsula's most lawless places on his search"— Provided by publisher.

  ISBN 978-1-4930-0608-3 (hardback)
  1. Game wardens—Michigan—Fiction. 2. Upper Peninsula (Mich.)—Fiction. I. Title.
  PS3558.E92M68 2014
  813'.54—dc23

                                                                    2014024055

Printed in the United States of America

*For Madelonnie Louise, Heart and Sand*

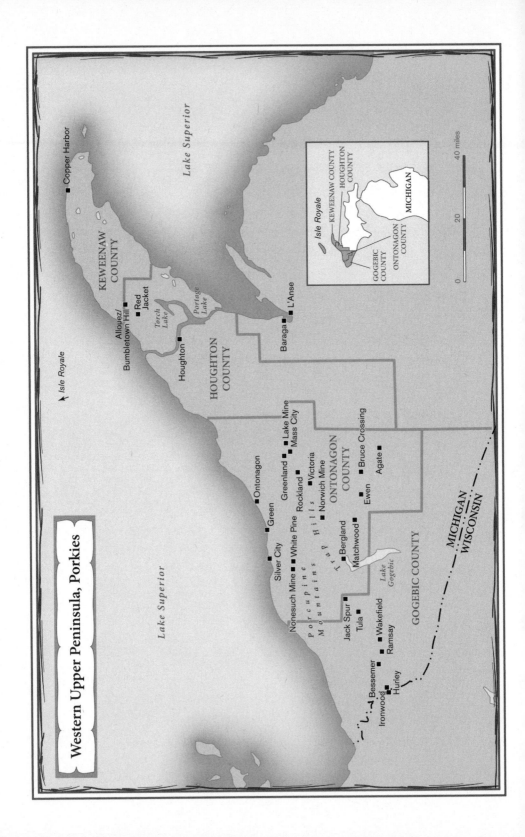

Western Upper Peninsula, Porkies

Lake Superior

Isle Royale

Copper Harbor

KEWEENAW COUNTY

Allouez/
Bumbletown Hill

Red
Jacket

Torch
Lake

Portage
Lake

Houghton

HOUGHTON COUNTY

Baraga

L'Anse

Lake Mine
Mass City

Ontonagon

Greenland

Rockland

Victoria

Norwich Mine

Bruce Crossing

Agate

ONTONAGON COUNTY

Green

Ewen

Silver City

White Pine

Nonesuch Mine

Bergland

Matchwood

Porcupine Mountains

Trap Hills

Lake Gogebic

Jack Spur

Tula

Wakefield

Ramsay

GOGEBIC COUNTY

Bessemer

Ironwood

Hurley

MICHIGAN
WISCONSIN

Lake Superior

Isle Royale

KEWEENAW COUNTY

HOUGHTON COUNTY

MICHIGAN

ONTONAGON COUNTY

GOGEBIC COUNTY

40 miles

20

0

# PART I: BETWIXT AND BETWEEN

One cannot help fancying that he has gone to the ends of the earth, and beyond the boundaries appointed for the residence of man. Every object tells us that it is a region alike unfavorable to the productions of the animal and vegetable kingdoms, and we shudder in casting our eyes over the frightful wreck of trees, and the confused groups of falling-in banks and shattered stones, yet we have only to ascend these bluffs to behold hills more rugged and elevated, and dark hemlock forests, and yawning gulfs more dreary and foreboding to the eye. Such is this frightful region.

*—Henry Rowe Schoolcraft, reflecting on his 1819 visit to Ontonagon*

# CHAPTER 1

## Red Jacket

MONDAY, JUNE 1, 1914

"What say you to the charges, Deputy Warden Bapcat?"

"Why are we even here, Your Honor?" Deputy State Game, Fish and Forestry Warden Lute Bapcat said, although he knew *exactly* why he was in court: He had made an enemy.

Two months ago, Bapcat had been visiting his friend Dominick Vairo in the barkeeper's Red Jacket saloon. When he'd left and swung up into the saddle of his flaming red mule, Joe, he had seen Cruse frantically waving an arm at him. "Get yourself down offen that animal when you talk to a fellow peace officer, boy. Don't you know no better?"

Bapcat had dismounted and stood beside the hulking figure of the Houghton County sheriff.

"It ain't the least dignified nor professional, you riding that four-legged beast into the confines of Michigan's most modern city," the sheriff said. "You oughten to know better, this being the twentieth century. But I s'pose you being a cop way out there in the woods, all this reality has done escaped your notice and undeveloped sensibility for modern life. So, let me help you: This here, Deputy, is a town with *inside* shitters, not ground holes out in the bush, and people take offense at the leavings of an equine nature. Be better for all concerned, you leave that hulking beast outside town and avail yourself of public transport, of which we got plenty. Better yet, drive that Ford you and your Russian partner got out there in Allouez, and at least make yourselves *look* like you belong in this glorious century."

Bapcat had more respect for a drooling rat than the county's sheriff, who was a lawman in title only, having shown his stripes in the recent strike by copper miners. Cruse was bought and paid for by mine owners and operators, and made no bones about it. Bapcat and his partner, Zakov, had sided with the strikers, made the sheriff and his crowd look bad, and Cruse had been stalking them ever since.

"This your idea of April Fish?" Bapcat had asked the man.

"The hell you talking, *fish*?"

"What most of the world calls April Fool's Day, which is today. Kids go 'round trying to stick paper fishes on each other's backs."

"April Fool? You oughten keep your focus on serious law business, not no damn kid foolishness," Cruse had said disgustedly, and stalked away with a paper fish on the back of his jacket.

*Cruse. Bad blood. Need to watch him. Be wary.* Ergo, this episode in court.

Yesterday Bapcat had come to town and been arrested, and Cruse had lodged him in the Houghton jail overnight.

The judge read from a paper in his hand. "It says here the county of Houghton wishes to charge you with violation of the recent ordinance against horses inside the limits of Red Jacket, Hancock, and Houghton. We are here to determine if said charges are justified, and if so, should they be pressed. You see, the two counties in question, out here in the great nowhere south of Canada, are self-anointed technological marvels before the entire world, and it wouldn't do for our collective and carefully nurtured civic image to be sullied by hooved creatures dropping their large, smelly, and unseemly plops on our newly paved and electrically illuminated streets."

The courtroom reeked of chloride of lime, and pinched at Bapcat's nostrils. "I understand that, Your Honor, but I ain't violated nothing. I've been ordered by Lansing to look into the disappearance of a state official that happened west of here, and not knowing how long this business might take us, all I done was that me and my mules, Joe and Kukla, stopped over to Dominick Vairo's saloon to visit our friends on our way south to catch a train out of Houghton. Next thing I know, I am arrested and spent last night in the hoosegow, and today, here I am in court."

Judge O'Brien had a naturally florid complexion and was positively glowing now. "Where are said mules, Joe and—what was that . . . Koala?—now?" the judge asked James A. "Big Jim" Cruse, Houghton County's obese, blatantly political sheriff.

"Kukla, your honor," Bapcat said.

"Shouldn't Your Honor be swearing me in?" Cruse inquired carefully.

The judge's face darkened to crimson. "I decide how things run in my court, Sheriff. You wouldn't dare to be telling me I don't know my own business, would you, sir?"

"No, Your Honor, that *certainly* was not my intent," the fat man said obsequiously.

"Then kindly and promptly reply to my interrogatory. Where are said mules now?"

Cruse pointed. "Out yonder, Your Honor, outside the courthouse, in protective custody."

The judge came out from behind his bench, his gown swirling like a storm-pushed wave of black water as he made his way to the window and peered down. "Remarkably handsome animals," Judge O'Brien announced. "Don't believe I've ever seen a fire-engine-red mule before. Must be Irish, eh, Bapcat?"

To Cruse: "These animals have adequate food and water?"

"They certainly will when you rule for the plaintiff," Cruse said, puffing.

Judge O'Brien picked up a sheaf of paper and rattled it for effect. "This the ordinance in question?" he asked the county's new assistant prosecutor, one Frederick Alward Rockford.

"Indeed it is, Your Honor," the young lawyer answered sharply.

The judge nodded solemnly. "Case dismissed. Mr. Assistant Prosecutor, please make a side note that said animals in the sheriff's custody are mules, not horses, meaning they were sired by a donkey out of a mare, and thus are a hybrid of noble lineage heavily favored in the illustrious Roman Empire, and most great cultures since then. It is a separate species, Mr. Rockford. I assume you *studied* Linnaeus at some point in your shiny education?"

"Not in relation to the law, Your Honor."

"Too bad. Law takes in everything, and as the future unfolds I expect that more and more science will be part and parcel of legal jurisprudence," Judge O'Brien said. "Now, if said ordinance was to require donkeys, mules, *and* horses to be kept out of the city's confines, it should have been specifically written so. Alas, it specifies horses alone, and therefore this case is dismissed.

"Now, if I were Deputy Bapcat, I would no doubt seriously consider engaging an attorney to countersue for what is patently no more than a half-baked attempt to interfere in the state deputy's official duties. Pushing through an ordinance in anticipation of a man coming to town to share a farewell libation with his friends suggests heinous and personal intent. We've got four liveries in this so-called city, and I see nobody from any of them, which makes me think this whole thing is a target on Deputy Bapcat's back. Perhaps even the state attorney general might send one of his legal *coupe-coupe* men north to take the case forward against this poorly conceived, and undoubtedly political, ordinance.

"In any event, Mr. Rockford, you're the shiny new fella around here, and I am surmising that our county sheriff inveigled you into this petty silliness and your bosses don't know about it, so here's what I'll do, lawyer to lawyer, and man to man. This hearing never happened. Therefore, no record is needed, and none shall exist, meaning you can start off without an official loss on your pristine prosecuting record. Further, I hope you'll learn what a political skunk looks and smells like. Mark my words, you follow a skunk around, your own scent will be indistinguishable from the skunk's, and that might just be a toxic thing for a budding legal political career, sir."

"Thank you, Your Honor," Rockford said, sweat glistening on his forehead.

Judge O'Brien banged his gavel once. "Everyone clear out of my courtroom. Deputy Warden Bapcat, see me in my private chambers."

The judge shed his robe, opened a rolltop desk, took out a bottle of whiskey, and tipped a touch into two glasses, offering one to the deputy.

"I'm on duty," Bapcat said, shaking his head.

"We both are. I order you to drink it down," the judge said. "I know you well enough to see your little mule stunt was somehow intended to get Cruse's goat, which you've done, so don't deny it. You've got that fancy Ford truck up on Bumbletown Hill, and no need for mule transportation."

Bapcat handed a telegram to O'Brien:

DEPUTY LUTE BAPCAT TO DEPLOY IMMEDIATELY TO ONTONAGON COUNTY. STOP. DEPUTY FARRELL MACKLEY DEPARTED HIS RESIDENCE IN EARLY MARCH, TELLING HIS SPOUSE HE WOULD RETURN INSIDE OF FOURTEEN DAYS. STOP. PROCEED TO MACKLEY'S RESIDENCE. STOP. FULLY INVESTIGATE DISAPPEARANCE AND PERFORM DEPUTY DUTIES FOR THE COUNTY UNTIL CASE IS CONCLUDED, OR UNTIL SUCH TIME, WHEN NECESSARY, A NEW DEPUTY IS APPOINTED AND REPORTS FOR DUTY. STOP. ALL QUESTIONS TO HARJU IN MARQUETTE. STOP. DAVID JONES. CHIEF DEPUTY, FISH, GAME, FORESTRY, ETC. STATE OF MICHIGAN.

"You know this Mackley?" the judge asked.

"Nossir. Must be new. Last year during the strike the deputy over there was a man named Phillips."

"You know the sheriff over there?"

"Just the undersheriff," Bapcat said, "and only indirectly. Last year during the strike he let us know that his sister and brother-in-law in Chassell were reporting illegal hunting activity. The reports were true. Do you know either man, Your Honor?"

"Can't say I do. All I know is by sheer reputation, which can be quite inaccurate up here. What I know for a fact is that Ontonagon is a damned ugly place over in those mountains, and it takes equally hard men to police it. So why mules over a fine Ford?"

"Rough ground and hills, Your Honor, and I hear there are few roads over in Ontonagon, which I heard ain't the paragon of modernity that graces us here."

The judge burst out laughing. "Paragon of modernity? Let me guess—your Russian partner's creative words."

"Yessir."

"He our man whilst you're man-hunting off to the west?"

"Yessir, Deputy Zakov is in charge."

"And the provenance of said mules?"

Bapcat didn't understand the man's question.

"Where did the animals come from, Lute?"

"They belonged to a couple of Swedish fishermen who died this past winter. The mules showed up to our place and have been with us ever since."

"Why your place?"

"Me and Zakov have known the Swedes for some time, and Joe in particular always seemed to favor me, the way dogs will do sometimes."

"When did this interspecies marriage take place?"

"February, Your Honor."

"And how is the lovely and winsome Widow Frei?"

Jaquelle Frei was his lady friend and sometime companion. "Fine."

"Marriage in the offing for you two?" the judge asked.

Bapcat said, "She ain't mentioned it."

"Mark my words, she will," the judge said. "She will. By the gods that whimsically govern reproduction of our species, 'tis foreordained. Hope you don't have to shoot some hard case over there in Ontonagon, Lute. They're a warlike and savage lot of Irish, French, and Finnish lowlife, all of them hating each other's sheer proximity on earth. Comes down to logic or violence, leave your words holstered, but not your gun, Deputy. Act decisively and do it first."

"I'll remember what you said, sir."

Lute Bapcat had no intention of shooting anyone, and truth be known, this assignment was unwelcome. He, Jaquelle, and their ward Jordy were becoming closer all the time, and Lute Bapcat, who had long been sanguine about such things as family, was finding himself drawn to intimacy and companionship, though certainly not nightly. In his mind it was a real family, without legal fetters.

"Be damn careful over there," Judge O'Brien repeated as Bapcat closed the door to the jurist's private domain. "Ontonagon's the last semicivilized stop for a far piece, and you know the sort of floaters and riffraff that kind of extreme geography seems to pull in."

"Yessir, I do." Fact is, until he had been more or less drafted into being a deputy game warden, he had been a trapper at the tip of the Keweenaw, and assumed he had always been a part of that same riffraff the judge was denouncing. It still struck him as peculiar how a small badge could lift a man from riffraffery to presumed respectability.

• • •

Trial concluded, he telephoned Zakov from the courthouse to pass on the result.

The Russian-born Zakov, a former officer in the Russian army, had been in competition with Bapcat as a trapper in the Keweenaw, and they had not gotten along, but over time Bapcat had begun to trust and respect the man, and had him hired on as another deputy state game warden. They lived in a State-owned cabin on top of Bumbletown Hill, about a mile from the mining town of Allouez.

"I'm leaving for Ontonagon," Bapcat told his partner.

"What of the wardens' survey order?"

Bapcat sighed. Having come on the job last year, he had been faced with a directive from State Game Warden W. R. Oates to estimate deer numbers by county, section, township, and range, and to estimate wolf kills and mortality from other causes. Same for beavers, partridge, quail, ducks, prairie chickens, squirrels, snowshoe hares, cottontails, bears, and a whole menu of game fish, with trout atop the list. In the report, he was to give his opinion at the conclusion of the numbers: population increasing or decreasing. If the latter, why?

Because of the bloody mining strike in Copper Country, neither he nor Zakov had had the time for such work. They had submitted the briefest report and conclusions: All species decreasing, both Houghton and Keweenaw Counties. Cause: the greed of man.

Although they had not been reprimanded, they had promised each other that the 1914 survey would be done in earnest. Now this Ontonagon thing, the latest hitch in their good intentions.

"Do what you can to start it. I hope I ain't gonna be gone that long, and we can both work on it when I get back."

Zakov grunted, said, "With the weather the way it is this year, you may never get back."

Bapcat sighed. The sky was yellow-gray, a winter sky, and here it was June. It had snowed on and off through April and May, and the woods still had snow in shady areas. The problem was that any snowfall this time of year could blink into a blizzard of heavy white stuff, and he was determined to not let weather ever dictate what he did to perform his job for the State.

Horri Harju, his supervisor in Marquette, had emphasized this during training: "Dealing with weather is part of the job. You go out and do what the State pays you to do. All the weather can do is hint at how you might dress."

It had been solid advice during the frigid months of the strike last year.

Deputy Game Warden Bapcat pushed his collar up before stepping outside, and went to fetch his mules. "Let's hope this snow's done while we're on the train," he told the animals.

# CHAPTER 2

## *Ontonagon*

### WEDNESDAY, JUNE 3

The snow turned into a storm and did not end. Bapcat and his animals got stranded two days in the Baraga depot, only thirty miles south of where they had started off. When they were finally able to board the connecting train, the game warden rode in the livestock car with Joe, the flaming red mule looking quite pleased by his company, and occasionally issuing some sort of short braying bark or choked snort as way of language. Equally pleased seemed the square and muscular black mule named Kukla, which Zakov insisted translated from Russian into English as "doll." Kukla was as rare as Joe in her singular behaviors. She needed neither rope nor lead, and followed along, apparently reveling in her pack-animal role within the group. Bapcat had ridden Joe all over the backcountry in Keweenaw in all kinds of weather, Kukla happily following behind; the three of them seemed made for each other.

In some ways, Bapcat thought, being with mules was an improvement over Zakov, who rarely stopped pontificating, or Jaquelle Frei, who was either hurriedly disrobing or jabbering nonstop. "Not sure how long this trip will take, Joe and Kukla. Let's each try to be patient."

Bapcat had packed a month's worth of supplies, intending to live off the land to the extent possible to augment what fit into Kukla's heavy-duty 00-gauge canvas packs. The mules affectionately nuzzled him, and he slipped each a sliver of dried apple.

Bapcat had several choices in routing, and being largely unfamiliar with train travel, he had picked a way that seemed to involve the fewest changes and least amount of discomfort. His confidence in his own intelligence had long been a problem, and sometimes a source of irritation and embarrassment.

The Duluth, South Shore & Atlantic delivered them to Baraga, where he and the mules switched to another DSS&A train out of Marquette bound for Ontonagon, from where it would continue onward to the state line at

Ironwood and Hurley, Wisconsin, the neighboring state's equivalent of the pleasure town up in the Keweenaw called Wyoming on maps, and Helltown by those who knew what it actually offered.

They pulled into Ontonagon at seven in the morning and Bapcat unloaded his partners, got them some water at the rail yard, and walked beside Joe, looking for the house of the missing deputy, Farrell Mackley. Still snowing here, but no apparent accumulation; this was more cold white dust than snow. The telegram said the man's wife had expected her husband to be gone two weeks. He was now long overdue, gone since sometime in March. Why had she waited so long to notify Lansing? Of course, Bapcat couldn't really blame her for not being overly concerned. He knew firsthand how nature or fate could intervene and sometimes confound game wardens' plans, but even then, if you had good-enough woodscraft skills, you could come through all right.

An address given to him at the railway station led Bapcat and his crew to an unusual three-story house with a white wrought-iron fence around the yard, and a widow's walk on top. It looked to Lute Bapcat like an outhouse atop a fancy wedding cake, like the kind Jaquelle had shown him pictures of, in the Hudson's Bay Company catalog. The huge house was painted pure white with pale blue trimmings, and sat on a small hill north of the rebuilt downtown, looking down on the mouth of the Ontonagon River and out at Lake Superior. New house, no doubt; not twenty years ago the entire town had been razed by fire.

Joe and Kukla had behaved admirably the whole trip, neither of them the least bit spooked by delays, new sounds, or sights. Bapcat suspected the months of training had paid off. It sometimes felt like there was not much you could count on in this life, but these mules seemed the exception.

Copper-mining money drove Ontonagon the same as it steered Red Jacket, but there didn't seem to be as much evidence here. Most of the mines were somewhere back up in the hills around Rockland and Greenland, and who knew where else. Presumed money aside, this pretentious new house was not what Bapcat had expected as the domicile of a fellow game warden. Too big and too fancy. Was it possible this was State-owned, like the log dwelling he and Zakov occupied? He doubted it. Horri Harju was forever complaining about the shortage of state funding for deputies' operations, including rents.

The street by the house was paved, as was the main street downtown, and Bapcat wondered momentarily what to do with his companions. There was no livery stable in sight, and he wanted to get on with business, but he couldn't very well tie the mules to the fence and leave them outside, so he opened the gate and ushered them in to snack through the thin snow on the sweet grassy yard. The practicalities of traveling with mules was only now beginning to come home to him, but he also knew that once they were outside civilization, the going would be a lot easier.

From the street he had seen a shadowy figure far up in the widow's walk and felt a lump in his throat, hoping this didn't ordain what lay ahead. The house had a bell contraption, a sort of handle a visitor pulled outward to activate, and after a time a young woman came to the door. She wore a pressed, clean white smock over a dark blue dress and dainty little black shoes which stood her up an inch or two.

"Deputy Warden Bapcat to see Mrs. Mackley."

"Is she expecting you, sir?"

"Yes and no," he said. "She asked the State for help, and here I am. So far as I know, there weren't no times bandied about."

Bapcat was shown into a parlor off the entry hall and asked if he preferred tea or coffee. Tea would be fine, he told the girl, and she left him alone, looking at shelf after shelf of books, wondering how much knowledge lay in those books that might make his life better if he were a better reader, and made time to read. He suspected the books on the shelves weren't getting used on any regular basis. What good was owning so many books if you didn't read them?

The woman who appeared next had light reddish-blonde hair, a long neck, and was dressed in a white dress of silk so fine, he wondered if it might have been spun on her by the silkworms themselves.

"Sir?" the woman said.

Her voice was syrupy and raspy at the same time.

"Deputy Warden Lute Bapcat, ma'am. Are you Mrs. Virginia Mackley?"

"Yes I am. The State moves slowly in support of its men, I see," she said pointedly, all the while with a stiff smile on her perfect lips, the color of ripe plums.

"Ma'am, your telegram was sent ten days ago; I got the word a week ago, and here I am, thanks to the train."

"I did not mean to criticize, Deputy. I must confide to being somewhat unbalanced by my husband's failure to return to the nest."

"Yes, ma'am." He considered telling her about the woods and the unexpected ways of nature, but she was a warden's wife and surely she knew this. "Where exactly did he go?"

The woman looked like she was trying to concentrate, but threw up her hands. "I have not one sliver of a whit of an idea. He said only the high country. Farrell is one of those men who believes in security. That is to say, the less I knew about his work, the less harassment might occur."

"You've had some problems over his job?"

"None, but only because Farrell is a superb planner and thinker. I should tell you, however, that some people around these parts hate your kind. This is surely no secret, but well and loudly established, with criticisms often uttered in public, especially in our town's public liquories, which I would add far outnumber houses of worship."

Bapcat ignored her words: "He say what he might be doing in the high country?"

She pursed her lips. "Certainly not."

"Help me understand the timing of this," Bapcat said. "What I understand is that sometime in March your husband left out on patrol, intending to return in a fortnight, and now he is a couple of months overdue. Is that about right?"

"Yes, I believe that's proximate, if not precise."

"Why did you wait so long to notify the State?"

Her eyebrow arched slightly. "He was in the *woods primeval*, Deputy. Surely I don't have to tell you what sort of things can happen out there, *especially* in the high country."

"No, ma'am, I know," he said, feeling slightly chastised. "He leave any papers or notes that might indicate what his intentions were?"

"None that I know of."

"Does he have a workplace I could see?"

"There is no office in our home. He did his business elsewhere."

"Where might that be?"

"I have no notion, and must repeat that my husband was very secretive in pursuit of his work."

Was *secretive, not* is *secretive. A town this small, and she doesn't know where he's working? Not likely. Something with a stench on it here.* "What if you needed to get hold of him in a hurry?"

She heaved a great sigh. "Because that's not practical, I'd have to work it out and handle whatever it was myself, and that seems perfectly reasonable to me. Why should any woman be accountable to any man? We are not the delicate creatures we are made out to be, though some very much like to entertain that image and live protected in soft cocoons of luxury."

The house sure looked to be exactly what she was saying wasn't so. This dang woman didn't fit any categories, the same way Jaquelle was in a class all *her* own.

"Would you have something to eat?" the woman asked.

*Unexpected hospitality?* "No, ma'am, but thank you just the same."

Bapcat found semiformal ceremony and stifling house manners difficult to deal with.

"You will, of course, remove your *creatures* from my yard?" she said.

"The mules? Yes, ma'am. Guess I can't get too far without them."

She accompanied him to the door where another attractive young woman appeared, handed him his Kromer hat, and curtseyed. Bapcat looked at Virginia Mackley and said, "This is one fine house you have. The State own it?"

"Why in God's heavenly name would you think that?" the woman countered. "We—and by that, of course, I mean Farrell and I—we have no need of welfare housing from the State."

"It's just that deputy wardens don't make a lot of money, and most of us have small, State-owned houses assigned to us."

"There you are, in your own words. 'Most of you,' not all, and though it is none of your business, and I do not wish to be unpleasant, it was *my* money that purchased this place, and it is my personal capital that keeps it going. I would urge you to not generalize in your work, Deputy. It can lead to some very premature and erroneous conclusions."

He wished he had kept his mouth shut. "*Your* money?"

"Yes, through my family."

"You're from around here, then?"

She tensed, and he knew immediately he'd gone too far. "You need to find my husband," she said, smiling, "*not* interrogate me. And may I politely suggest that you attend to your soul while you're at it, and have the time.

Our Creator may call us at any moment, and we must be ready. It is, after all, Sunday, our Lord's Day, and here we are defiling it with our tawdry earthly business."

Bapcat thought, she's got a cold damn attitude for a wife with a missing spouse. "I thought today was Wednesday. Sorry, ma'am, no insults or prying intended. But you know how lawmen are."

"The Lord's Day is every day," she said. "Apparently I don't know how lawmen *are*," she said, nodding him out and emphatically closing the door in his face.

# CHAPTER 3

## *Indian's Farm*

### WEDNESDAY, JUNE 3

The mules came over to him and he rubbed their muzzles. "No help from the lady, and I guess that's my fault. Let's get us a plan, and a place to stay until I can get all this sorted out. Seems like Deputy Mackley didn't say much to the missus about his comings and goings." Bapcat recognized he wouldn't have done much differently, and the starkness of the similarity now stood out.

They took a muddy, slushy, semi-frozen track running southeast out of town. It ran next to a river, through dense, dark-green tamaracks along rocky, boulder-strewn ground, but none of the county's fabled slippery clay. They kept to the crude trail for six miles until coming to a log house set at the end of a cleared stump field. Bapcat swung down from his saddle and went into a small barn and there found a wild-haired man in a faded red flannel shirt.

"Indian," Bapcat greeted the man, whose actual name was Wiley Music, a one-time trapper from Houghton County who had married and settled down here, farming and doing some logging and odd jobs while he hunted and fished. Music owned an Indian motorcycle, which he had ridden to the 1904 St. Louis Exposition. After that he was called "Indian" rather than by his name. Though Indian was not a red man, he'd once told Bapcat there might be a hint of Negro blood somewhere in him, and if so, he didn't know what that made him. If you were a Negro with some drops of Caucasian blood, what were you? And conversely, Caucasian with some Negro blood? Knowing such subjects could bring a lot of heat, and Indian rarely talked about them except with his friend, Lute Bapcat.

"You see Mrs. Mackley down to her palace in town?" Indian asked.

Bapcat had wired his friend of his intentions, and asked if he could stop in for a time, while he got himself oriented and organized.

"I seen her."

"Not much help, I expect," Indian said.

"Seems like her husband don't give her much to go on."

"Lot of men like that," Indian said.

"You and Sara that way?"

"Not usually. How long you staying?"

"Depends. Right now I got a missing man and no notion where he might be. Might take a while to get some direction, and then if I have to traipse up into the high country, I'll probably want to engage me a local guide. Want the job? The State pays good."

Indian said, "Naw—don't be looking to me for such. There's folks around here knows every wrinkle in that nasty backcountry better than I ever will, and they ain't bashful about going up there. But feel free to stay with us long as you need. You sure got you a handsome pair of mules there, Lute."

"Yes, I do," Bapcat said proudly.

"I hope nobody or nothing gets a mind to eat them up in that high country."

Bapcat glanced at his friend to see if this was in jest, but Indian seemed serious. Was the man trying to tell him something about the high country?

"Yari Nordson still the undersheriff of Ontonagon?" Nordson was a friend of Deputy Warden Horri Harju, and had tipped them to illicit deer hunting during the strike last year, down in the Chassell area. Bapcat had never met the man—only his sister Elena Ongin and her farmer husband.

"No, Yari done quit and lit out, and so too did Thell Clay, the sheriff. Yari opted for the life down to Detroit, making them new automobile things, and Thell, who was as close to worthless a public man as one can suffer, well, he's said to have took off for Alaska. How he plans to live up there, I can't say. He's as close to a total incompetent as the Creator ever cobbled together. Good talker, but no action. Yari was the real sheriff, without the title; I think he got tired of carryin' the weight. When he resigned, Clay must've figured the weight would fall back on his shoulders, and he decided to make a break for greener pastures."

"There an acting sheriff now?"

Indian tugged at his chin. "That's all he is, by God, an act. One-time deputy named Hoke Desque, one of them hail-fellow, well-met types, and not much for sticking his nose into sore spots. Pretty much a paper appointment, I think, and no plan to take any action to find a permanent replacement for Thell Clay."

"You saying there's no law in the county?"

Indian reclined his head to the side. "Not sure it's stark as that. All I'm saying is there ain't no sheriff, and the man acting in that role is neither qualified nor emotionally capable of the work. But neither was the last one. Why?"

"I need to start by talking to someone who worked around Farrell Mackley."

"Doubt you'll fill that bill. Mackley is a well-known loner and a top-shelf conniver in his own self-interests, and I mean no offense to you and your colleagues as a group. Your best bet, talk to the justice of the peace, Tecumseh Swoon."

"Swoon?"

"Exalted name, and probably well-intentioned, but a victim of his surrounds, like all of us, Lute. He likes his friends to call him Teedy. Law writ is one thing; followed through on is yet another. But you ain't going to Swoon for legal follow-through, just for information, and if anyone knows of your man Mackley's comings and goings, it could be Tecumseh Swoon, a maestro of gossip, if ever there was one."

"Where do I find this Swoon?"

"Runs a dry goods store, just up the line from downtown, with a little courtroom out back in his warehouse area. He's there most of the time."

"There a livery in town?" Bapcat asked.

"Supposedly. It's run by Romney Archibald, one of those strange Mormon fellas—believes God shows his favor by who accumulates the most money. Far as I can tell, him and his don't snatch and eat Christian children, but who knows. Way his tribe sees things, if you're poor, God's not happy with you, which puts most of us around here in that place. Never mind Archibald. There's a fella up in Greenland, both fair-priced and honest. Archibald is the kind to quote you one price and charge another; believes his religion allows him to lie to get what he thinks is favorable conditions."

"If you ain't up to guiding into the backcountry, who might be?"

"There's a schoolteacher with the subscription school up near Lake Mine, but this is her off time, and she's out in the woods as much as anyone."

"Reliable?"

"I guess I'd follow her," Indian said. "Though she has some peculiar notions about life in general."

"And they let her teach school?"

"Real hard to find people to teach for the pittance citizens want to pay," Indian said as Bapcat walked toward his mule. "Lute, you just got here, and you're in need of slowing down. People in these parts don't like doing business with strangers. If you wait, I can introduce you around."

Bapcat grinned at his friend. "Folks not liking to do business with strangers is exactly why I do. It can catch people off guard."

Indian said, "You become a skepticpalian since pinning on that badge of yours?"

# CHAPTER 4

## *Ontonagon*

### SUNDAY, JUNE 7

Bapcat left Kukla to graze at his friend's homestead and rode Joe back into town to look up the justice of the peace, telling himself that no matter how long he lived and no matter where he went, he continued to encounter the strangest people, which made him wonder how people looked at him. Were all humans strange? What the hell was normal? Did the Bible describe how people looked in the eyes of God? Having never actually read the Holy Book, he didn't know. And though his job put him in contact with all sorts of folk, he felt unqualified to answer his own questions, admitting that maybe he sometimes over-felt or over-thought things. Sometimes it got damn uncomfortable, and yet Jaquelle insisted this was just part of growing and improving one's mind. "No growth without discomfort" she liked to preach.

Tecumseh Swoon was a lanky man with a monk's tonsure and a nervous manner that left him constantly licking his lips like a fox astride a fresh-dead rabbit.

"Sorry to come to your home like this, but I'm Deputy Warden Lute Bapcat, and this is government business, so I guess that makes interruptions permissible. I've been sent by Lansing to find Deputy Warden Farrell Mackley."

"Lansing, eh? You must be pretty good."

Bapcat ignored the comment. "When's the last time you saw Mackley?"

"Well, it ain't like I keep me a record of who I see, unless of course there's money involved—for the store."

"Mackley?"

"Couple of months, maybe. I don't recall precisely."

"He bring a lot of business into your court?"

"No, no, matter of fact, he don't. A lot of people wonder what the heck he *does* do, given that all of us could name a dozen people availing themselves of nature's bounty without license or regard for fair share."

"You got any records on cases and charges the game warden brought before you?"

"Yessir, some."

"Possible for me to see them, develop some names of people Mackley might have had business with?"

"The problem and nekkid truth is that State Deputy Mackley has never actually brought a single individual before my court. I don't know if he's yellow, but what I do know is over in Gogebic and Baraga Counties, the local wardens haul a steady stream of recalcitrant lawbreakers in front of their JPs."

"So you didn't even know he was missing."

"How could I?" the man asked. "He's mostly invisible."

"If not in court, did you see him around town, saloons, wherever?"

"Can't say I did. See the lovely Virginia Mackley everywhere, and don't that make you wonder why she even keeps him around, him being poor and not much to look at?"

"Why would she care what her husband looks like?"

"Did you look at their big house—how pristine it is, the multiple young women employed there, nothing out of place, an establishment of pleasured perfection?"

"It's a nice place," Bapcat said. *This is getting me nowhere.* "If you haven't *seen* him, what have you *heard* about him? Anything about his gambling, or his straying ways?"

Swoon shook his head and crossed his arms. "I'm no gossip."

"'Course not, but this is a legal investigation, which could turn from civil inquiry to criminal, and you sure wouldn't want to stand in the way of that, right, Mr. Justice?"

"I take your point," Swoon said.

"Can you remember any other times he might have gone missing?"

"Well, I don't know this, you understand, but I heard it said in some quarters around town that the man leaves for a couple of months, every June and July."

"Leaves for where?"

The man pointed upward and west. "The hills."

"For what?"

"That information I am not privy to, nor do I want it said that I have been asking questions down that line of inquiry."

"Why's that?"

"Why's what?"

"What you just said?"

"Technically I'm quite certain I said nothing, and could swear to that in a court of law, under the deepest oath."

"You telling me something strange is going on in the hills?" *What's wrong with this fool?* Bapcat turned and saw a woman standing and watching them, her hands on her hips, her elbows sticking out. She looked unhappy, even angry, but Bapcat had only a quick glance and couldn't read her—not that any man could ever read women with any degree of accuracy.

"Where are you staying?" the man asked, pushing him toward the door.

"You know Wiley Music?"

"The Indian? 'Course I do—much as anyone can know a man."

"That's where to find me . . . for now."

The justice of the peace took him by the arm, led him out, and looked away. "Thanks for stopping in. This ain't a town for loose lips," the man whispered when they were on the stoop.

"What's that supposed to mean?" Bapcat inquired.

"Expect you'll find out soon enough. People here got their ways, and they don't like no one from outside poking their noses in."

Bapcat looked at his mule for a long time, rubbing his muzzle. "These people are downright peculiar."

Returning to Indian's, he bedded down with his mules in the barn, hoping for sleep. A deputy didn't just go out on patrol and disappear; someone here had to know something. They had to. Otherwise, how would he know where to start looking?

# CHAPTER 5

*North of Greenland*

MONDAY, JUNE 8

It was not long before daylight, and more snow was falling as Bapcat shared hard-fried hen eggs and smoked ham with his friend's wife. Sara Music was far more gregarious and social than Indian.

Bapcat said, "There's a schoolteacher Indian says might hire out as a guide."

"Could be," Sara said, "if you're man enough to live by her rules."

"Meaning what?"

Indian walked in with coffee, sat down, and intervened. "Jone Gleann's set in her own ways of doing things, in school and in the woods. Her way and no other. She don't abide compromise on nothing. Kind of like you."

"Does she know what she's doing?"

"None better in the hills," Indian said.

"Spends more time up there than most," Sara added. "Alone."

Indian asked, "You find a starting place yet?"

"No, but I thought I'd have a chat with the lady as to her availability."

"Your funeral," Indian said.

Sara smiled and lightly rubbed her husband's hand. "Stop being so gloomy. She's a fine lady. She just scares you and the other men around here because she knows what she's talking about, and she don't feel compelled to hide under her bonnet even when you and the others don't want to hear or acknowledge it."

"I *said* she was good," Indian countered weakly. "I just don't like being preached to when I ain't in a church."

Sara turned to Bapcat. "She's led a very difficult life. Been in America since she was twelve, and showed up in these parts in her late twenties."

"How long ago did she show up here?"

"Five years back, give or take. Don't mind Indian. The students love and respect her. She don't sugarcoat and she talks straight to them—as an equal, not a better. Not many adults have her ability to relate to young'uns."

"Where before these parts?" Bapcat asked.

"She never said," Sara told him.

Bapcat finished breakfast, had a last cup of strong coffee, got directions, and saddled Joe as Indian watched stoically. "I'll be sure to tell the school-marm you send your regards."

"Do that and she might just lop off your head with her cleaver."

"Guess that's my risk to take," Bapcat said.

"Talking tough from afar is easy, chum. You ain't met her yet, up close, eyeball to eyeball."

"I think I heard you say you'd follow her."

"Would, but not too dang close. She seems to draw trouble."

"What kind?"

"He's exaggerating, Lute," Sara said, joining in.

"I ain't," Indian countered. "That woman draws trouble like sugar draws flies."

Bapcat said, "All right to leave Miss Kukla and our gear here for a time? I'm still groping for direction. Should be back in a day or two."

Sara Music smiled. "Long as you like. Our home is your home, Lute."

"Her words, not mine," Indian said.

"You were born a grouch," Bapcat said.

"Wouldn't argue the point," Indian said, nodding to his friend as Bapcat swung up onto the red mule.

Indian and his wife had given him the location of a school at a place called Lake Mine, which seemed to be somewhere near Mass City, and Greenland, another ten miles south of his friend's farm, though the distance was approximate and far from certain. But the road was at least passable to here, even in falling snow, and obviously it was the only road going his way. Indian said to look for a log schoolhouse, denuded of bark and shining like a beacon, the so-called School of Light, because it stood out among the dark forest that surrounded it.

The road soon turned slickery-soft and clayey, and Bapcat edged Joe off it to the east and continued south on a faint trail that slowly separated from the road but seemed mostly to parallel it in the direction he wanted. He decided to stay with it until he had to make another choice, which was pretty much how traveling the few good roads in the Upper Peninsula had to be.

The route grew steep in places, but Joe walked solidly along, unconcerned, and it struck Bapcat as strange that there were so few buildings along the way. Indian said farms were popping up all over the area, but not up this trail. After Indian and Sara's place, few farms were apparent.

Eventually he came to a narrowing of the trail, through a sheer rock funnel. Joe balked momentarily at the sight of it, which was his way of asking Lute if this was really what he had in mind. Bapcat chuckled at his big mule's politeness and good sense, made a couple of clucking sounds with his voice to encourage and reassure the animal, and aimed him ahead into the funnel. Joe's concerns allayed, he stepped lively ahead.

Bapcat found himself looking at a reddish-brown dog ahead on the trail, a largish animal with no right hind leg, and it made him wonder how much a lost limb made life more difficult for animals and people. The state game warden raised his hand to greet the dog coming toward them, and felt almost at peace until something pounded into him and the world went black.

# CHAPTER 6

## Lake Mine

### WEDNESDAY, JUNE 10

"Hello. Halloo-halloo!" a strange voice chirped in the dark. "Steady as she goes, lad, time to chat up the indigeni."

"Who's there?" Lute Bapcat asked, blinking wildly. It seemed he was blind. He felt his head, found a bandage, immediately wondered why everything was a webby swamp, nothing clear or real, lots of things momentarily there and then immediately evaporating.

"I say, old boy, are your oars in the water yet, or are you hopelessly adrift?"

"Who *are* you?" Bapcat challenged, the words out before he could think through what was happening, if anything.

"Wellington Trafalgar Smith-Jones Elphinstone, late of Old Albion, Duke of Greensward Wylde, ex-generalissimo of the Queen's Own, decorated by Queen Vicky Herself for various exploits Beyond The Pale, you know—not a better man in the broil, wot. Thick of it, blood and bone, gristle and the clatter-and-clack, the stark strike of cold steel on the enemy's pate, and wot! My betters and equals call me Duke or sir, but out here among the savage savants, I go by Phin. And who might you be?"

"Bapcat."

"Odd, odd, odd name. Hereabouts it's being told that this stranger encountered the local bangstry. *Absit omen*, no surprise, no surprise! Listen up: This land abounds with borderers. A pox upon them all, a pox, I say, French disease all the way to the end. So you met them and they left you Plato's cock, wot?"

"Plato's *what*?"

"Steady in ranks, lad. Plato's cock, stripped, denuded of feathers—are ye not an English speaker?"

"I guess not your kind."

It was a high and breathy voice, something oddly soothing and yet powerful contained in it. Even so, the game warden found he was faintly tingling with suspicion.

"Stripped you as a bird for the pot, wot. Mind me word, lad: Stay close to your bang-stick in these waters. These lands here are abundant with feculent vapors, queer folk: pleasure jacks, sharkers, scroyles, false sermoners, mawks, and beefs—the whole lot, and you and the sweet Physic, luxurious mutton will draw you into her prickling furze and you'll never away, a siren, sirrah, a siren, I daresay! Necromancer, all of her spells and whatnot, eh. When you've recovered from your endangerment we'll speak again. *Im primus*—get thyself well, lad. The game is ahead."

Bapcat pulled the bandage off his head and found himself alone, the voice gone as suddenly as it had come. Had there been someone present, or just the voice? He could not say. Out in the Dakotas he had done a vision quest, including the fast and haunting sweats. This felt of that. Maybe. Something about the voice rubbed him wrong; his suspicions refused to back away.

In addition to the strange voice, a woman, he assumed, touch as soft as a cloud, came to him twice a day, her speech sweet, her ministrations sweeter.

She wore what appeared through his haze to be the brown habit of a religious sister, clean but wrinkled. She had small, gnarled hands as callused as a logger's, obviously accustomed to physical work, a lot of it, numerous small scars apparent as she ran a damp cloth over his forehead. "Fever's stubborn," she said.

"That a problem?" he wondered out loud, feeling there and not there, sort of floating on a wave of bright heat.

"Duration will determine that."

"What about God and that sort of thing?" Bapcat asked.

"I should think God's got enough on his plate without worrying about one fool gets himself back-shot."

She stopped and looked at him, her eyes burning. "You a shant?"

"What's that?"

"A poor sod from the shanties, the poorest of the Irish."

"Don't know what I am. Orphan."

"That so?"

He nodded. "St. Cazimer's in Lake Linden."

"What order be that?" she asked.

"Weren't religious," he said, not entirely certain what an order was.

"You put there from the poorhouse?" Her brogue was faint, almost clear of it, but his mind still struggled to translate words.

"Left on the doorstep."

"Foundling," she said, nodding. "Where'd the name come from?"

"Way St. Cazimer's did things. Billy Cathist, Paul Orthometh—names like that."

"Yours?"

"Lutheran Baptist Catholic," he said. "Lute." He thought he saw the hint of a smirk, was quickly gone.

"One name good as another. Only matters what you do with it."

He twisted his upper body, feeling a wrinkle cutting into him from below, but she grabbed his shoulders and pinned him. "You daft? Open those stitches and you'll soon be seeing that God you let yourself wonder about."

Bapcat had never known a nun before, but somehow had never imagined them being quite like this woman, who seemed both gentle and ready to attack in an instant.

• • •

Lute Bapcat had no idea how much time had passed, and felt a painful mental juddering as he strained to wake up, struggling hard to emerge, to crawl his way back from a place he could neither remember nor name, splayed on his back, without clothes, a threadbare blanket draped haphazardly over his lower half, leaving half of his skin damp and chilled, his muscles stiff, thick, immovable, like his body had been filled with fire bricks. He used his eyes to check his surrounds: gaudy paintings of the Virgin Mary, and Jesus, glowing bearded folk he presumed sundry saints, all painted in slots of the ceiling directly over his head, hovering close like birds of prey, within reaching distance of his eyes in the semidarkness.

He had a notion, a feeling: *I'm inside a barrel? No sense, that. Too hard to think. No light; everything is moosh. Get to what matters, ignore nonsense and accents . . . damn foreigners.*

"Where's Joe?" he managed, his voice weak and strained.

"So there you are, finally come down to join us. Who be this fella you speak of so much—this Joe?"

Strange voice, croaky-crawly. "My mule, Joe."

"Aye, that great red beastling; loyal as a dog he is, stands right there at the end of the wagon, watching all day long, he does. Have to push him away to eat and drink, that magnificent great red fellow."

"My clothes," Bapcat said.

"The thing is, son, the bloody bullet stuck and embedded near your tick-tick, wide a bit, mostly plowed through. Was found most of it stickin' outten your chest like a dog's snout pokin' up a bitch's butt."

"Bullet?" His brain hurt.

"Your red mule brought you in, son. Bullet never knocked you off the saddle, your legs bein' all wrapped in cordy stuff, and I must add, seen as a miracle by some hereabouts, present company excluded, me being trained to recognize and analyze miracles to separate the real few from the many faux."

"Learned that saddle trick in the Dakotas. If you're night-watch on stock, it don't pay to fall off," the deputy game warden said, straining to be heard. So tired.

"Good for you, and good for your mule. Had you fallen off, you'd likely be croaked and planted down six by now in the eternal dirt sleep awaiting each and all. You were nearly in the ground as it were, and so to speak."

"I don't remember anything," Bapcat mumbled, his head aching, sweat popping under the effort to think clearly.

"To be expected, our dear Jone tells us. You may get some mind-pitchers at some point. Or not. 'Speck don't matter much either way. Done is done. Appears you will pull through and live. Better'n some can claim or hope."

"Where *am* I?" Lute Bapcat moved his eyes, trying to locate the source of the voice.

"They call it Lake Mine, and your mule walked you to us like Cupid sent a dart. Found your blood spatters six or seven miles northwest, when we backtracked to see if you'd been alone. Odd you took the trail instead of the road."

"Snow and clay on the road."

"A reality in these parts, that bloody red clay. You travel alone?"

"Alone," Bapcat said, "except for my mule."

"Nothing can be done here for you," a new voice declared. "Deputy Bapcat, is it?" It was a voice that cottoned no questions and demanded obedience. Bapcat found the new voice too loud, bordering on painful, yet it was familiar. "You know who I am?" *That woman with the soft hands again?*

"Indian sent word we'd be seeing you."

"Told me to ask after the schoolteacher."

"I'd be the only teacher hereabouts, or doctor. My name is Jone Gleann, and you may call me Jone. The misformed creature bending your ear does so, and I can't seem to change it. Damn lucky you're still drawing sweet breath," she said. "But you are not out of the woods yet, boyo, not by a long shite."

Bapcat whispered, "Indian told me you could be difficult."

"Live in a woman's shoes, you'd be no different."

"You an Indian?"

"Better, worse, unimaginable to them nailed to the ground by fate and ignorance—Irish the both of us, you see, adrift in a strange land."

Bapcat felt both tired and confused. "Caliber?" he asked.

"Plenty enough to kill," she said.

"Long distance," he said as his mind began closing down; he couldn't shake the image of the bullet as a dog's nose protruding from his back.

"There's two of you," he managed to say wearily.

The second voice rejoined, close to him. "Fra Goodman, sometimes known as Jimjim."

Bapcat found the initial voice breathing close to his right side, rolled his head to look, found a tiny man with curly, shoulder-length auburn hair, a thick neck, and a child's body. "Fra?" Bapcat asked. "You're a priest?"

"Aye, a man of the so-called cloth. The church told me they only measure a fella's mind, and his vocation, not the size of his body. Yes indeed, fully consecrated and ordained—confessions, communion; I provide the full apostolic service to lost sheep, and I see the all, and watch and smell and hear the world rolling about us. I have the gift for feeling the shite flowing uphill or down-, and the Devil trolling for the weak and lonely."

*Priests are allowed to say* shit? "How long do I have to be in this dang bed?"

"Until you don't have to anymore," Jone Gleann said. "Stop being such a bloody child."

"What about your . . . ?" he asked, groping for a word.

"Order?" she shot back.

"Yeah, that."

"Why?"

"Curious."

"Are you, then? Sisters of Blind Mercy," she added. "Know it?"

He shook his head.

"Then it doesn't much matter, does it? Save your curiosity for matters that count."

The dwarf climbed loudly back into the caravan, grunting with exertion. "Made some exquisitely fine mud, I did. Jone in her usual mood?"

"She's not very friendly," Bapcat said.

"Her usual self then," the dwarf said.

*I'm in an asylum,* Bapcat thought as he drifted back to sleep and into an empty dreamscape, his departing thought, *I'm shot and left in a place I will never leave. Hell is a place where nobody makes sense.*

# CHAPTER 7

## Lake Mine

### SATURDAY, JUNE 13

Time lost meaning, blended and merged with pain, making clear thought impossible. In what he sensed were mornings, Bapcat seemed to remember hearing shots fired, close to him, exactly twenty-four rounds, always in the morning, he thought, but couldn't know for sure. Far from whole, still in some kind of webby pit, dark and sweaty. A licorice skeleton, someone new, helped him sit up and swing his legs over the edge of the raised bed in the rear of the barrel-top wagon.

It was a project. Painful, too much effort, even with help. He was in a long cotton gown, damp from his sweat, which left it sticking to his skin. A woman's plain thing, maybe; he didn't have the focus or interest to figure it out. At least it was cotton.

"You got a name?" he whispered to the skeleton's dark bones.

"Scale," the large creature whispered back in a deep rasping tone.

"Just the one name?"

"Bin plenty for me," his helper said. "You want me point your swipe for you?"

Bapcat bristled at the thought of being touched intimately by a man. "Can do it myself."

"I'll hold the thunder mug, but don't you be pissin' on my hand, boy."

"Don't give me orders," Bapcat said.

"Jes' passin' on what the doctor say; she the boss nigger 'round here."

"She-doctor?"

"Sister Jone."

He searched his memory. *Sister*. "The brown nun?"

The man chuckled. "She white, jes' wear brown. I be brown, and wear white. Now go-wan an' piss straight."

"I think I'll get up," Bapcat said after he urinated into the container.

The bone-man hissed. "Like hail, you gettin' up. She skin my backside."

"Scale, right?"

"Whut I said."

"We in a dream?"

"Not one I'd welcome," the man said in a gush of words. "You don't do what that lady doctor say, we gon' have to face-plant you in a pine box down six feet. And I don't relish diggin' in all this damn clay and rock, my kind always expected to grovel in the menial."

"Okay," Bapcat said. He was exhausted. "Anybody here speak real English?"

"Ev-body ceptin' you, boyo," another man said softly, mirth in his voice. It was the weird little man, the priest.

"I hear shooting every day," Bapcat said.

"Practice," the dwarf said.

"Twenty-four rounds."

"Seven hundred twenty a month, every day, any weather."

"Practicing for what?"

"The inevitable, one might suppose. I see you yourself carry a cannon."

Bapcat allowed himself a sigh. "Krag thirty-forty."

"Me, I'm strictly a thirty-two man, four-inch barrel."

"That won't stop much," Bapcat said.

"Got to hit the eye," the man countered. "One through the window of the world stops all."

# CHAPTER 8

## *Lake Mine*

### SATURDAY, JUNE 13

It was Indian awakening him this time. "Looks like you mebbe ruffled some feathers faster than most. Shot down like a dog on only your third day in the county."

"In the back," Bapcat said. "Is it still snowing?"

"Snow seems done, though I wouldn't yet call what's out there spring. Backshootin's how it's mostly done in these parts. Ain't much face-fightin' in this county; the bushwhack is the attack of choice, and has been for a long time, in towns and in the hills, it don't matter where. You got the hurts?"

"Some."

"Doc says you'll probably make it, but you have to take it easy. Sara talked to her. We wondered what happened, and when you didn't come back, I followed you, found blood just as the teacher's two-legged black creature and that pipsqueak papist reached the same place."

"I can't figure it out," Bapcat said. "The deputy's wife, the JP, you and Sara—you're all I talked to here. Ain't like I gabbed to legions or had time enough to push someone to homicide," he said, then thought: *Not from here, outside—followed from Red Jacket, got to be Cruse's game. Figures. Think about this later, nothing you can do right now; Cruse is the only conclusion, the logic behind it a separate question.* "Teacher, doctor, nun—how many people are wrapped up inside her?" he asked his pal.

"Just one person. She's all three and a heap more, truth be known."

"My mules?"

"Kukla is happy with us, and Joe's making friends here, him and that scauming rumbustical seeksorrow runt. How him and that mule got close is beyond me, and from what we hear, not a bit of skewboggling on Joe's part."

*Nothing registering: I'm trapped in this dang barrel and kept in the dark.* "How long's all this healing business likely to take?" he asked.

"Which part?"

"Me, out of here, getting on with my business."

"Jone seems to want your body to naturally push the lead all the way out, of its own accord. She got some out with her knife, but the main chunk seems to still be there, and you been too dang weak for her to think about any more digging."

"Jone, the nun?"

"Jone Gleann. Me and the wife told you about her. This is where you was headed when you got struck down by an unfortunatism. Jone thinks time's likely to heal you up just fine."

"If the body can do that itself, why do we even need doctors?"

"Don't get owly," Sara Music said, joining them. "You have to trust her and be patient."

"Neither one of those is my strong suit. Tell her I want a parley."

"Can ask," Indian said.

• • •

He was asleep when she came in. No sign of his friends.

"What parley?" she challenged.

"I want you to get all that dang lead out of me."

"It's not that simple."

"I don't care what's simple; I want it done. I've got work."

He saw her staring at him, a tiny figure with long dark hair pulled back. "Sit up," she said.

Bapcat held his hands out for help.

"No deal," she said. "There're no shortcuts in this hospital. When you can sit up on your own, we'll have at the lead. Until then, behave yourself." She eased him down and he was too weak to resist. "In God's time," she said. "His will be done."

# CHAPTER 9

## Lake Mine

### SATURDAY, JUNE 20

Lute Bapcat was sleeping facedown and felt something hard and sharp against his chest. He pushed a leg off the bed, slowly rolled to get a foot on the floor before he groped around the bedding, and came up with something black, ragged-edged. He held it close to his face, saw it was a slug, a substantial heavy thing, maybe from a Winchester .40-72, which threw big lead. Not many rifles like that. The only ones he'd ever seen had been out west in the Dakotas. Had the thing worked its way out of him? And if so, how?

The thought of the chunk of metal tunneling like a worm through his flesh made him queasy, and he took a deep breath and let it out slowly, closing his eyes, steadying himself before sliding the other foot to the floor. Two feet down, he was determined to not return to bed until he could look outside.

The bullet should have gone all the way through, unless the shot had been taken from afar and was losing speed when it struck him. Bapcat shuffled barefoot to the rear of the barrel-top, cracked the door, and was assaulted by bright light he had not seen since he'd been shot. It couldn't have been an extreme light, but after so many days in near-dark, it was still a shock to his system.

If the woman had gotten most of the slug out, how could this much have still been in there?

The deputy game warden eased through the door onto the trailer's rear platform and sat on the edge, with his legs hanging over. The air was soft and sweet and he breathed deeply. The sound of a shot being fired startled him and made him open his eyes again.

A voice yelled, "She wants you to stay in bed."

"Yet here I sit," Bapcat said.

The dwarf laughed darkly. Perched on a wooden keg, he raised a pistol with two hands and fired again. The bullet pounded into the side of a sand hill with a crispy impact. Bapcat saw no target.

"You call this practice, shooting at nothing?"

"Think blue," the dwarf snarled as he aimed again. "Butterflies," the man said. "Blue."

*Pop.*

Bapcat stared at a sky filled with clouds racing over from the southwest, the forest below verdant and thick, the air clean but heavy. He stared at the sand hill, squinted and saw movement, said, "Butterflies?"

"There you have it."

*Pop.* Another round launched.

"You shoot at butterflies and call it practice? For what—museum specimens?" Bapcat wanted to laugh. *The dwarf is odd, and this has to be another dream. I'm dreaming all of this.* But he looked at the bullet with crusted black blood in his hand and realized this was no dream.

"Not *at* butterflies. I kill them, bucko."

"Butterflies can't be killed with bullets," Bapcat said.

"They can when I shoot."

"Go slide," Bapcat said dismissively, meaning the man could go to hell.

More reports, evenly spaced. The dwarf took his time and aimed, his two hands steady, squeezing rounds off with purpose, and when the last had been fired, he jumped down from his perch and scuttled to the sand hill where there was a large patch of gravel, bent down, and picked things up. "Eight," he reported.

"Eight stones?" Bapcat said.

"Butterflies, fool."

"No," Bapcat said. "I think not."

The dwarf brought the butterflies to Bapcat and dumped them on the ledge where he sat. They were pale blue, almost violet, with white dots on the edges of their wings.

"Putting them here don't mean you shot them," Bapcat said. "You'd've hit them there'd be nothing left."

"Contest," the dwarf declared. "I declare a contest to decide the question."

"Ridiculous," Bapcat said with a snigger.

"Sure then, dismiss it. Afraid to be publicly shown up?"

Bapcat winced. "This ain't exactly public. Where's my rifle?"

The dwarf said, "Scale?"

"Fetching," the skeleton called back, and went into the barrel top behind where Bapcat sat, came back with the rifle and a small bag of cartridges.

Bapcat loaded the magazine with four rounds and felt weak, but he was determined to do something other than sit idling like an invalid, even a stupid shooting contest.

As he prepared, the area quickly became public, suddenly filled with children, excited, like something was in the air.

"All them kids need to stay back from here," Bapcat said.

"They've come to see the Lake Mine Lazarus, the fella returned from the dead. You want help limping over here?" the dwarf asked.

"Here will do fine," Bapcat said, looking at the gravel patch and sand hill.

"Suit yourself," the dwarf said. "One shot, alternating, you first as the guest."

"You're a fool."

"I won't deny the charge," the dwarf said cheerily, "but save it for another day and take your shot, bucko."

Bapcat looked for the flutters of blue, and, finally locating a small mass of them, took aim and fired.

The Negro, Scale, went to the area, looked down, and proclaimed, "Ain't nothin'."

The dwarf fired. Scale shouted, "One," picked it up in his left hand, and stepped away.

Bapcat fired again, same result. Scale made a zero with the fingers on his right hand.

The dwarf's turn, Scale shouting, "One," picking it up.

So it went, five shots for each man—no hits for Bapcat, five for the dwarf, who came over to him with Scale and watched the skeletal figure dump the tiny victims on the ground by the trailer.

"What's the trick?" Bapcat asked.

"Accuracy," the man said.

"No," Bapcat said. "I ain't buying them goods."

"The way to think of it," the dwarf said, "is to imagine air as invisible water, all around us. Throw a rock, make a punch, wave your arm, and you move air like you would move water in a wave. With a bullet the wave moves really fast, and its speed makes violence on anything too light to withstand the wave. If the bullet passes close enough to the butterfly, the airwave slams it down and to its eternal death."

*Nonsense—truly a dream.* He answered with a disbelieving grin.

"Accuracy gets you close. There's no trick in this. You try to hit the flutter."

"I don't play snooker," Bapcat said, and the dwarf laughed.

Scale held another cartridge out and Bapcat dropped it into the magazine, took careful aim, erased everything from his mind but butterflies, found his target, filled his mind with it, squeezed.

Scale bent over and held up a kill.

"Accuracy," the dwarf said, holding up his .32. "One in the eye stops any and all."

"What is going on here?" a familiar voice demanded.

For the first time he got a good look at Jone Gleann: auburn hair, shorn short, as if by pinking shears, ends sticking out this way and that, her face long and narrow with a prominent nose and high cheeks and the yellow-green eyes of a rapacious predator. When she looked up, she stopped and stuck out her jaw.

"What the hell is *wrong* with youse scaring all these children!"

Bapcat saw no sign that the kids were frightened. They looked happy and engaged, eager for more shooting. He started to slide off the back of the barrel top but the woman held up her hand and commanded, "Stay right there!"

No longer in brown, she wore a long red skirt she had gathered up to mid-thigh. Long, thin bird legs, and just before she dropped the bunched skirt, he saw that her lower legs were covered with hundreds of marks, like scars, red, like he'd never seen before.

"Just what the hell do you think I can do for you?" she challenged, holding a fist to his face. Her voice was hard and raspy, nothing akin to the soothing tones inside the trailer.

"Ma'am, we ain't even been introduced."

"Of course we have, and I know who you are, Deputy—knew before your mule brought you in. Indian had sent word you'd be coming. I'm Jone Gleann, and you are Deputy Bapcat, and so I ask again, what do you expect me to do for you, and further, what in hell are you doing out of your bed? Are you fey? Lost your minuscule mind?"

Bapcat held up the remains of the bullet. "This was under me, and I thought the largest part was already out."

Jone Gleann rolled her eyes. "They may not sort so easy. Consider this: You don't even have a starting point."

"And you're trying to say *she's* the starting point?"

"Sure be where I'd begin," Jone Gleann said. "You need to understand that the high country stretches most of the way over to *Ous-con-sink*. Big territory that don't entertain much humankind, including red men, if you're of the sort who counts them among humankind, which few do."

*Ous-con-sink* was Ojibwa for Wisconsin. "I guess I am," he said.

She shook her head. "Get back in that bed, Deputy. We can talk more when you're stronger."

She helped him back inside and he eased into the bed and looked at her. "You're a real nun?"

"Why would you doubt that?"

"I didn't say I doubted."

"Your question implies doubt and skepticism."

He pointed at the jars around the caravan, filled with dead creatures, some jars marked with symbols he couldn't read. "You a witch?" he asked.

"Me, a thaumaturgist?" she countered with an amused smile. "More along the lines of an apothecary, self-taught—more precisely, an herbalist, and there's no magic in any of it, only scientific knowledge, which some folk confuse wrongly with black arts. If you and me were to trek off into the hills, and I'm not saying we will, but if we did, there'd be a big condition: I'd have to be the unquestioned leader, and when I gave an order, you'd have to obey, no questions asked, and no exceptions."

Bapcat thought about it momentarily. "Unless and until we find Mackley, at which time I'll be obliged by the law to call the dance."

She made a clucking sound and left him in the dark. He had no idea if they had just made a deal.

His outing had left him exhausted, and he slept easily and quickly, the ragged slug still tight in his fist.

# CHAPTER 10

## Lake Mine

### MONDAY, JUNE 22

His back and chest still hurt, but the wounds seemed to be healing, and the dressing was still being checked and changed daily by Jone Gleann or the Negro, Scale.

Each day Bapcat carefully climbed down from the caravan wagon and walked around behind the school, stretching his leg muscles and exploring his surrounds. Sara Music had called the log building the School of Light, which was the perfect description: white cedar logs, denuded of bark and left natural, the effect of the light wood like a bright beacon set against the black-green forest. At certain times of day, early and late, the light overcame the dark with such drama it stopped his breath momentarily, caused a hitch in his rhythm.

Today he found a couple of children sweeping off the building's front stoop. When he came around the corner, they stared at him with their mouths agape—like he had appeared suddenly out of a hole in the ground. "Where'd *you* come from?" they had squeaked, and fled inside, slamming the heavy door.

He'd seen few dwellings on his ride south the day he'd been shot, and all of them had looked like paint was an unknown concept. No outside paint here either, but the wood glistened and made the place stand out.

Jone Gleann materialized in the wake of the fleeing children, her lantern jaw protruding. "Leave my children be!" she said. But after a moment of what he took to be studying him, she said, "You're sure you're interested in Mackley?"

"Yes, ma'am."

"Dammit, I'm Jone, not no damn fancy 'ma'am,' nor no fancy painted tart either." She held out a cloth sack. "Go on, look."

Bapcat emptied the contents on the freshly swept stoop. There were four pieces of wood inlaid with small, toy-size window screens, four by six inches, perhaps, two ends, both screened, and two axles on which were attached perfectly carved wooden wheels. "A wooden box on wheels," he said. The deputy warden looked up at Gleann and shrugged.

"Are you thick, or slow, or both?" she asked. "The children and I were clearing ground over at the Carlson potato farm, and a fella called Nick Vedder come by and told me a curious story. Nick works for Romney Archibald, and he says his boss got a shipment of a hundred of these toys last week. Catch," she said, flipping a small object in his direction.

He caught it easily from midflight. It was a small, crudely carved wooden black bear. Again he shrugged.

"The slats fit together to make a rolling cage for the animal in your hand," she explained. "They snap together. Either end can be raised and a spring engaged to a small metal platform on which you place bait. When the animal gets inside and takes the bait, the sudden loss of weight causes the spring to release, down comes the door, and the animal is trapped inside."

"This is just a toy for tykes," he pointed out.

"It's a design for a trap to be made of a wood floor and metal frame and bars. Archibald was so pleased that he ordered a hundred copies to give to friends and potential investors."

"This man Vedder told you all that?"

"No, I inferred some from the model and amount ordered. You know what that means?"

"You made a guess?" he said.

She flashed a smile. "An inference is better than a guess, less than a known fact, a theory, or mere premise, you understand?"

"Yes." Horri Harju had talked some of such things during training, especially as they related to seeking search and arrest warrants. Bapcat assembled the toy, surprised at how easily the pieces went together. "Designed by who?"

"Houghton engineer by the name of Beaumont Clewd made the models. He's a Welshman once of Ontonagon, schooled out east, come back to manage the Sullivan Mine, but found inventing machines to be far more lucrative and satisfying. His business is called North Country Iron Works and Machines. Got fifty employees full-time and a forge, on his way to bigger, more profitable things."

Her tone of voice said all he needed to know about her feelings on Clewd. He held up the model. "This alone don't mean, nor prove, nothing."

"We agree. Vedder says Archibald has ordered full-size iron traps from the Iron Works."

"For bears?"

"Based on dimensions and a specification that the floors be capable of holding upward of seven hundred pounds. And he is giving out all those little carved bears, which makes it seem obvious, don't you think?"

Not wanting another prolonged lecture, he answered her with a shrug of indifference. "I guess."

"You know in your heart this is wrong," she said quietly, and sat beside him. "Sometimes I'd compromise everything here for a hot bath and inside toilet, then I see a bear or a wolf, and I know that man-made luxuries will never replace God's best work."

"I thought people were God's finest work," Bapcat said.

"That depends entirely on the agenda of the person declaring that," she said. "But you work in the woods and see what nature is, and you should know better than all the rest of us."

"This has nothing to do with me," he told her. "Killing and taking bears ain't against the law."

"Does it say explicitly in the law that a citizen can capture and sell a bear?"

"It don't say he can't."

"Is that how the law works—anything without a law is allowed, no restrictions?"

"I ain't no lawyer," Bapcat argued. "I got only a few years of school. I just do what I'm told."

"The designer of that trap is none other than your Deputy Farrell Mackley," she said. "And schooling will not instill intelligence that is already there. Schooling only sharpens the point and edge of the spear. It doesn't create the point."

"Who claims Mackley invented the trap?"

"Vedder."

"How does he know?"

"He just does."

"That ain't evidence."

"But it is a clue," she said. "Grant me that."

"*Could* be a clue, I'll give you that much, but it don't put us no further ahead than we was minutes ago."

"Think, dammit."

*I hate feeling ignorant*, he told himself. "Why'd Mackley invent the trap?"

"Catching and selling bears to zoos is his idea."

"When?"

"Last year?"

"He do that last year?"

"No, he failed to raise the money."

"That don't mean he's up to that now, and frankly, I don't give a hoot what he's up to, just so long as I can find him and get him back to work, which he done agreed with the State to do. Besides, the things we got plenty of up in this country is mosquitoes, snow, and bears. You're telling me Mackley wanted to capture and sell bears?"

"Planned an auction in the mountains, a large gathering."

"But it never happened."

"No partners, no finances then, and now he's talked Archibald into financing his insidious plan. You can't see how obvious the conclusions are?"

"I can see 'em, but that don't mean I believe 'em. That requires more than coincidence. How come Mackley couldn't raise the money last year?"

"I'm guessing his reputation preceded him. Most folks hereabouts laughed at him, and when potential investors asked her about the plan, Mackley's wife just shook her head and made an unpleasant sound. She rarely said anything negative and she never said anything positive. She just made disparaging faces and let people draw their own conclusions."

Bapcat rubbed his head. A man inclined to making quick decisions and taking fast action, thinking was often painful, plowing through mental challenges sometimes a lot of work. "It ain't against the law to shoot bears any time of year, so I guess there ain't no laws being broken that I know of." He thought about passages in *Tiffany's Criminal Law* and could recall no bear prohibitions, even on sows with cubs. "Citizens, I believe, can dispose of bruins any way they want."

"And you accept the morality of that?"

"I ain't paid to think about morals. My job's only to enforce the laws passed by our legislature and signed by our governor."

"Absent a law against it, you would allow the wanton slaughter and removal of our bears?"

"Like I said, there ain't no law against such."

"You don't think about morality, is that right?"

"Just law," he said.

She smirked. "Like up north in the Copper Country last year, when the strike was on, hot and bloody, and you and your fancy Russian partner ignored state hunting laws to allow striking miners to feed their families and selves. Like *that*?"

"An exception," he said, trying to hide his embarrassment. *How did she know*? "One-time situations, one-time solutions," he countered weakly.

"Life is the accumulation of one-time situations, the solutions of which can eventually lead to new laws."

His eyes widened. *Who is this woman*?

She glared at him. "You've been in my own personal caravan for going on three weeks. Of course I checked into your background, and what I heard were tales of a man who knows right from wrong and takes moral sides—workers over unfair employers, and so forth. A man who makes choices of that magnitude ought to have an opinion on current state law for all of our various natural riches, and I think *Ursus americanus* ought to be among those thoughts and laws."

"What is it you want?" he asked. "I'm a game warden. I don't make no laws."

"Of course you don't, but what's to stop you from bringing your opinions to politicians, or direct to voters to wake up our fool lawmakers down in Lansing?"

"It ain't my job, and truth be known, I don't even care what happens to the beasts. It ain't like we're gonna run out anytime soon."

"Yet, you ignored laws last year because *you* decided they were wrong. We're talking about black bears, Deputy—or don't they give you people any training in such biology?"

"We get trained just fine," he said defensively.

"It seems like you're trained on the wrong damn things," she said with a snarl. "Why would you *not* put a stop to Deputy Mackley's disreputable and scurrilous plan? It's one thing to contemplate such treachery from a common citizen, but from a deputy game warden? Isn't that much worse—to have him pledge to protect our animals and then wantonly profit from their removal?"

Bapcat was having a hard time thinking. "If this Archibald fella ordered traps from the Clewd fella, how does that make this Mackley's scheme?"

"Maybe it started out as Mackley's, and Archibald's taken it as his own."

"You don't *know* that."

"I know your game warden ain't been seen in some months, and with him nowhere in sight, the traps are still being built, so what's that tell you?"

This was all speculative, not evidence, and he was tired of her harping. "No law is being broke," he repeated. "Dang it."

"You think not? Who owns the animals of our state?"

"I never thought about that, I guess."

"Who employs and pays you?"

"Lansing."

"Wrong. I swear! You're as thick as a rich man's mattress. Pay attention to civics here: The elected state legislature creates a budget, which the appointed state government collects in various tariffs, and from those monies allotted, pays you and your colleagues. Who makes the laws governing plants and animals, and by plants, I include trees and forests? Ain't selling bears the same thing as loggers taking state logs they ain't paid the State to take?"

"The state legislature makes the laws, and there ain't one for bears like there is for forests," he answered.

She kept on. "And who elects those people?"

"The people."

"Not just faceless people generalized," Jone Gleann said. "You and me elect them. So who owns the animals and plants?"

"Us?"

"Yes, bravo—of course, we the people who vote," she said. "*We* own the creatures and fishes and trees, and the minerals in the ground, and the State takes care of our treasures for us. Doesn't it follow that while our fellow citizens may legally kill bears at will, selling them outside the state, dead or alive, is like burgling our state and our private collective property to sell for personal gain? How is that different from stealing timber to render into lumber?"

"I guess I never thought about it in that exact way," he said.

"Maybe you should," Jone Gleann said triumphantly, and urged him toward a small cabin behind the wooden school. "First, the furs got depleted, then the copper got taken; next came the white pine, and now we have a heap of foolish newcomer farmers misusing the land, and soon it won't be able to grow even potatoes. Where does it stop—when all the animals are gone and forgotten?"

She was right. How come he'd never seen how everything connected? Yet more evidence of his deficiencies, he reminded himself.

At the cabin, there were plants in pots on shelves and terraces outside, and inside, jars filled with dead animals staring out dead-eyed, all in a stench of alcohol or something noxious that pinched his nostrils. Long strings of dried morel mushrooms hung from the ceiling like strange gray and brown curtains. "You *are* a witch," he declared.

Gleann laughed and bade him sit at a small table. "I've decided to guide you into the hills on my conditions—that I am the leader of said expedition, and when I give an order, I expect you to do as you are told, no exceptions or questions."

Bapcat considered for a while, said, "Unless and until we find Mackley, at which time it will be my call on the doing that gets done."

Jone Gleann flashed an unexpectedly warm smile. "Why, Deputy, do I detect an open mind, agreeing to take orders from a woman? I accept your proposition."

They shook hands.

"And me yours," he said. Again he felt the scaly calluses of a logger.

"When you're physically ready," she added.

"I'm ready now," he said.

"There's still a lot of snow in the upper hills and valleys. We have to let it melt, and we're still having freezes up high, so let's get through our final freeze first. You got a pack animal besides that tall red mule?"

"Got another mule over to Indian's. Name's Kukla."

"You don't smell like no muleskinner," she said. "Supplies?"

"My mules and me keep clean. Vittles for a month."

"Good. You should make arrangements to gather both animals and move your cache to here. We'll depart when I say the time is right, and not until. Meanwhile, you can help me and my kids do some repairs on the schoolhouse and outbuildings, and that will be my pay for guiding you into the wilderness."

He nodded absentmindedly, suddenly wrestling with a notion he didn't yet fully understand—that while his job might be to protect things the law said to protect, it also might be part of his job to protect things not precisely covered by laws. How did an individual make things happen that weren't yet law, but ought to be—in your own mind, at least? He had no answers, just questions.

But first he had to figure out where the hell Mackley was, and why he wasn't doing his damn duty like he was sworn to do. And he could not shake the vague feeling that he'd just been manipulated by an expert.

# CHAPTER 11

## *Lake Mine*

### MONDAY, JUNE 29

There was a boy of ten or so, a Scot named McIlrath, called only by his last name. The boy was scrawny, towheaded, freckled, hard as steel, and for some reason had attached himself to Bapcat in recent days. Bapcat liked the boy and referred to him as his dogsbody, a term that seemed to please the lad because it sounded like it made their relationship official.

The boy had a poor excuse for a horse, but it seemed to get him around just fine, so Bapcat sent him over to Rockland on Saturday with a telegram for his boss, Deputy Horri Harju in Marquette. He carefully printed out the text but made the boy read it aloud several times with perfection before sending him on his way.

Bapcat had always found bears to be intelligent and resourceful creatures, not to mention downright determined when food was at issue. But generally they were shy of humans, even in small doses, and they surely weren't the vicious vermin some misinformed folk made them out to be. But if the law said killing them was legal, did that include live-trapping and selling? He just didn't know, and wanted help in understanding, which caused him to send the telegram:

ATTENTION HARJU: POSSIBLE ACTIVITY IN ONTONAGON AREA OF TRAPPED BEARS BEING SOLD OUTSIDE THE STATE BY PRIVATE CITIZENS. STOP. ADVISE HOW TO HANDLE. STOP. ARREST AND CHARGE WITH THEFT OF STATE PROPERTY? STOP. WIRE ANSWER C/O TECUMSEH SWOON SOONEST. STOP. SWOON IS JP IN ONTONAGON. STOP. I WILL FETCH ON WAY THROUGH. STOP. HAVE HIRED GUIDE HERE, MISS JONE GLEANN, SCHOOLTEACHER. STOP. WILL SWEAR HER IN AS DEPUTY WARDEN FOR DURATION OF TRAVELS WITH HER. STOP. STANDARD DAILY PAY. STOP. AWAIT YOUR ANSWER REGARDING BEARS. STOP. BAPCAT.

All through his life, until meeting widow and business entrepreneur Jaquelle Frei of Copper Harbor, Bapcat had not thought much about women or their roles in life. The only woman he'd really known had run the orphanage, and she ranked in his mind as a lower-echelon monster, barely qualifying as human. It had been Jaquelle who helped him open his eyes and change his mind, and when he saw the miner's wife Big Annie Clemenc leading the action during the strike, and later a fire-talking old woman called Mother Jones turn rabble into cheering crowds, he began to see women a bit differently.

Now he was confronted by Jone Gleann, who was eternally busy and moving and barking orders like a general, and somehow never seemed excited or confused by all the demands on her. She was a lot like Jaquelle, yet not at all like her. She was impressive. And equally scary.

All weekend they had sorted through their supply and equipment lists, and McIlrath, whom he had taken to calling Mac, had stopped at Indian's to ask that Kukla and the supplies be moved south soon.

Monday morning Wiley and Sara Music had arrived, as requested.

The starting gate barely lifted, Sara's first word were "Here you are gunned down by some cowardly bushwhacker while over there across the Atlantic Ocean a damn yellow-back Serb in Sarajevo killed both Archduke Franz Ferdinand, and his beloved wife Sophie."

"What's a Serb?" Bapcat asked. *Sarajevo. Archduke?*

Sara said, "Near as I can tell from the newspaper, the Serbs are a long line of bushwhackers and cold-blooded assassins. People hereabouts who know about such things are saying the empire of Austria-Hungary won't let this pass, and blood's gonna get spilled soon."

Bapcat knew she expected him to say something, but his mind was empty. *Austria and Hungary. Weren't they two different countries? Holy Pete.*

"Any of this make candles flicker for you?" Sara asked.

"No, ma'am, it's about as dark as it usually is."

"Just as well," she said. "We got enough problems right here without us gettin' ourselves into a state of consternation over goings-on in a place most folk ain't never heard of."

Bapcat tried to concentrate, but his mind was skipping, and between skips he found himself fixated on Jone Gleann, whose own pack animals were Romper, a horse of a mule she rode everywhere, and a small black horse called Quest. Romper was a primo mule, as easygoing as Joe and Kukla, but

Quest was high-strung and jittery without obvious cause, as some horses were wont to be. His main problem seemed to be children and living so close to them. He seemed always on the jagged edge of bolting.

Gleann was a whirlwind and near-dervish, and Bapcat's energy continued to return slowly. She and the schoolkids cut firewood, painted rooms inside the school, and tended various root vegetable gardens. All day yesterday, the woman and her charges had pulled rocks from a neighbor's potato field, and then she had worked well into the night, installing new moss insulation on the school roof, which was built with a steep pitch to help shed the more than twenty feet of white stuff that fell year after year. Snow accumulations of over thirty feet were not uncommon in the high country, Gleann told him.

The deputy warden was now installed in the small house, and quite content there, but that morning Gleann had announced that space was needed, and he was to move back into the caravan.

"What about you?"

"I'll be there too," she said. "Ain't you never slept with a woman?"

"I guess that depends on what you mean by sleep."

She laughed. "Don't worry, I'll be gentle with you. More to the point, I'll be sleeping on the floor, you in the bed. My one rule is that you've got to bathe good every day. Clean mules is one thing, but I don't want no man-stink in my place more than what's already lingering there."

Tonight he was undressed and enjoying a cool night and cold water in the stream when suddenly she appeared beside him, naked as her first day on Earth. She was so horribly scarred he was tempted to look away from her, but he had been a soldier in war and seen soldier's wounds fresh and still killing them slowly and surely, and he willed himself not to react. "We ain't taking no baths together," he chirped at her.

She laughed. "You didn't flinch when I showed up in my altogether. We should do fine out on the trail," she said. "Ain't no privacy up in the hills." She slid into the water near him and dunked her head and came up wringing her hair. "Neither of us need be overly prissy nor constrained by arbitrary rules of privacy. Word is you got a fancy woman. You two do the deed, do you?"

"I expect that's a private matter," he said.

"It don't have to be. Every one of God's creatures does said deed. It's nature's way. What do you think Adam and Eve spent all their time doing in Eden before the expulsion?"

"I guess I never thought about Adam and Eve," he said. He wanted to ask about her scars, but held back. In his experience, people usually talked naturally about their own deformities, including the ones that weren't visible, but her story had to come in her own time. What he didn't expect was her inquiry into his personal affairs; it made him both curious and nervous.

"You're on your own tonight," she announced. "I've got to walk over to Carlson's to help his wife, and I'll spend the night, back in the morning. Enjoy your space for a night."

Later, and deep in sleep, Bapcat heard a voice whispering huskily. "Hullo again. Wellington Trafalgar Smith-Jones Elphinstone, Duke of Greensward Wylde here, whilom general of The King's Own, oft-dined and feted in *Regineosi Atrio*, public-schooled in dear Albion, Oxford, wot? Accomplished deer-stealer in those warm days, served in the *Saus und Braus* of Ireland, fully blooded, yes. Schooled, you see, in book, sword, and lance, possessing equal vigor with words or weapons. I have the finest rhetoric and can shame Michelangelo's stone men and invest paint as da Vinci's better, but above all, as a Gentle should be, my religion is modesty in all things.

"Now hear this: The land hereabouts abounds with rantipolings, borderers, and renegados, murderers and monsters all. I come for the head of the *Die Wilde Jager*, some call the Wild Huntsman, wot, a rousing game of Hoodman Blind 'twill be, me, thee, and our horde on coursers tall. Yes, yes, albeit ill-favored to look upon, I do it all, am a major factotum craving the clangor of combat joined. You may now, at your leave, address me as Phin. Do you remember any of this, dear boy? You see, it's quite tiresome to repeat."

Bapcat opened his eyes and felt them fluttering in the dark. He could make out a form, like a man, tall and gaunt, naked with protruding ribs and a bulging stomach, as if starving. On his drooping head, draped down his forehead to his aquiline nose, lay an otter skin, its tiny eyes turned red and peering with intense vigilance. *Dream?* He decided not to address it, and maybe it would go away. He closed his eyes for a while, but curiosity bested him and he opened them again.

The gaunt one declared, "Don't try my patience or take my time, son. I'm real enough, boyo, and so too is *der Rothbart, hight Die Wilde Jager*— Redbeard, as he is known abroad, and Red Hair in these parts, though he and his familiars are false Babylonians, not supernatural at all—men plain of flesh and blood and bone and guts, same as the rest of us, a bully-rook of the false darkling, wot. I'm led to believe you and the *dominie* soon will launch an expedition, depart the grassplots to run the greenwood, and you'll be needing outriders, gentlemen of the Fancy to jump with and together starve the vagrant varlet. I bid thee take thy vizaments in my words, pray."

*Outriders? What the hell is this strange old bird talking about? Is someone really talking to me, or am I imagining this?*

"You may closeth thine eyes, yet here I'll remain 'til I've finished. Mounted picquets, yes, flankers, yes, to vouchsafe the way in terra incognita. I propose a code only the two of us will know, *comprenez-vous*? Two with the utmost shared estate, dost thou ken? *Être compris une menace*? A green dart means 'move safely on,' red one means 'trouble close,' pull in, stop, and look 'round. Yellow means 'move the lads at the jog-trot,' no rest 'til the next green, wot. The green will point direction, old code, most reliable, never failed my lads. Remember, *Die Wilde Jager* is false, not a specter or child's bogeyman, quite real, no matter how ludicrous the presentation. Believe not what you see, not only what thou think thou know'st."

When Bapcat next opened his eyes, the voice was gone, and it felt like his mind might be next to go. *All of this is outside anything I've ever experienced. War was violent, but mostly direct, little nuance. You met your foe and slugged it out. One side won the day, and the ground. This is something different—so why does my blood run cold the way it did before combat?*

Sleep came slow and hard, mixed with images he had never experienced, incomprehensible.

When he awoke, he was sweating, and Horri Harju, his boss from Marquette, was sitting not six feet away, staring at him. "You got the slug? Good; take this," Harju said.

Bapcat held out his hand and into it Harju placed a leather cord. His boss stared at the ragged bullet. "Forty seventy-two, I'd say. But could be forty eighty-two, something in that neighborhood of heavy lethality. Hang the slug from that as an amulet," his boss said. "Anytime you're injured on the job, take something and add it to the string. Doesn't have to be a bullet. Got ten tokens hanging on mine. Bad luck foiled always regroups to form good luck, if it don't kill you first. Always carry it."

"Bears?" Bapcat said, ignoring the thing in his hand.

Harju rolled his eyes in what Bapcat presumed to be thought. "Law says kill 'em anytime, anywhere," his supervisor said.

"What if they *all* get killed? Won't that be losing something here that belongs to all of us?" Bapcat asked. He had thought hard about this, begun to form the start of an opinion.

Harju grunted. "I'll give you that, for sure, but it don't change nothing regarding the law, and our job's only the law."

"Maybe it should be more?"

"Won't argue that neither."

"There's a beaver-trapping ban to preserve numbers. How is that different from killing too many bears?"

"Different value in furs, mebbe? Don't know the answer."

"Maybe you should," Bapcat suggested to his boss, who grunted without commitment in response.

"You like pushing me, eh?"

"I'm just asking questions," Bapcat said, "so I can understand. Dumb as I am, if I can figure it out, probably everyone can. I'm just a simple lawman."

Harju smiled. "*Dumb* ain't a word I attach to the likes of you, eh. Neither is simple."

Bapcat pressed his argument: "If the people are the State, and the State owns all fish and game and things in the water and woods, and even under the ground, then the people own it all together, and taking it from us is stealing. That's all I'm saying."

"A lawyer might disagree."

To his way of thinking lawyers were *paid* to disagree or agree, based on who was paying them. "Ain't saying they wouldn't, but ain't it our job to get opinions and decisions on things like this?"

"I'm telling you, that's not how laws are *now*."

"I know that, Horri. But ain't it our place to say how we think things ought to be if we truly care about all the things we get paid to take care of?"

"You asking me to make a decision? That's easy: Take care of the damn laws we got. We can't enforce theoreticals."

"I'm asking you to find out what else and how much more we should do, how we can protect more things for the people, in more ways. Who better to see what needs doing than the ones out in the woods all the time?"

Harju said, "You demand a lot of a boss."

"You told me not to hold back, ever."

"You shouldn't take everything I tell you to heart."

"Which things do I ignore?"

Harju was starting to look irritated, said, "If citizens want to trap and sell bears, they can. The law don't forbid it."

"Shouldn't some of that money go to the State, to help pay for what we do?"

Harju said, "Go find Deputy Mackley and I'll talk to Lansing about all these other things, which, I repeat, ain't law now, and therefore ain't our job now."

"Yessir," Bapcat said.

"And carry your amulet. Kept a good many of us alive for a long time."

Bapcat asked, "Ever hear of someone named Elphinstone?"

"Elephant Stone? Nope. Name like that I'd remember if I had. Why?"

"Nothing." *Maybe I did imagine him.*

When he asked the same question regarding Fra Goodman, Scale, and Jone Gleann, he got the identical and immediate answer. Bapcat dismissed the two events as ragged parts of a recurring dream, and resolved to forget all of it.

Meanwhile, he needed to follow up on the bear thing. If capturing and selling bears was Farrell Mackley's brainchild, maybe it would point to his whereabouts. This was the closest he had to a lead, and it felt as thin as a starving man's soup.

# CHAPTER 12

## *Rockland*

### THURSDAY, JULY 2

There were not too many telephones in Rockland, Greenland, and Mass City, except in the mines and in the homes of leading citizens. The one Bapcat used was in the Rockland Hotel and Boardinghouse. He called his partner and housemate in Allouez up on the Keweenaw, Pinkhus Sergeyevich Zakov.

"Ah, my colleague is alive," the Russian greeted him.

"I got shot," Bapcat told his friend.

"We have *not* been informed of this," Zakov said with an edge to his voice.

"In the back."

"Suspects?"

"Not so far."

The Russian said, "When did this happen?"

"June eighth. Do me a favor: Get up to Copper Harbor and look in on Jordy and Jaquelle. Don't say anything about the shooting. Ask her to order me a large copper bathtub and have it delivered to me at the schoolhouse in Lake Mine."

"I infer this is not for your personal use."

"You infer correctly."

"Perhaps you should personally place this order."

"Perhaps you should do what I ask, dammit."

"There is no need for that tone," the Russian said. "It will be done, as instructed, but you must understand she may perceive a competing interest at work."

"I've been shot in the dang back, Zakov. Just do this for me, and we'll let the chips fall where they may."

"Should I bring this thing myself, and join you down there?"

"No. I'll be heading into the mountains soon."

"Mackley?"

"Mackley has disappeared, and it seems it was quite some time ago. No real leads yet on where he went, what happened, or why. Mostly there's just some loose speculation and guesswork. Last year he apparently tried to raise money to capture bears and auction them to zoos."

"I do not believe this is illegal."

"That's the other thing. Would you check *Tiffany's* for me, see what's there?"

"Of course. You have evidence of this alleged bear conspiracy?"

"Not really. I've sent a telegram to Harju and I've talked to him to let him know what's going on."

"The bullet?"

"I have it. Worked its way out, and appears to be no permanent damage left behind."

"It must not have penetrated so deep."

"That's how I read it, too, and I'm thinking somebody might have tried to lazy one over my head, but it was at the end of its powder surge and it dropped."

"But no suspects?"

"None."

"Does the sheriff know?"

"There's only an acting sheriff here, and he's adjudged worthless by all."

"So you *are* alone," Zakov said.

"Not entirely," Bapcat said. "I have Joe and Kukla."

The Russian laughed with genuine amusement. "You are in excellent hooves."

# CHAPTER 13

## On the Road to Ontonagon

FRIDAY, JULY 3

Bapcat tried to get up into the saddle, but the simple act of sitting on it made the wound and muscles around the injury hurt. He got down and talked to Scale about a small carriage, but Scale dissuaded him.

"Wagons ain't no good even on the mos' best roads 'round here, of which there ain't none, 'specially with all this late snow and such. Wouldn't s'prise me none we get snow on Independence Day, and wouldn't that put a damper on the whole whoop-de-do."

Unable to ride because of the pain, Bapcat did what game wardens did best. He made a small lunch, hacked a walking stick off an apple tree, and perambulated northwest, pleased to discover he could maintain a long, stretchy gait and quickstep pace and feel only a little winded.

A mile up the trail Fra Goodman caught up, riding a brown pony. "She told me to go where you go."

Bapcat kept walking, didn't even glance at his unchosen companion. "I'm a grown man."

"A man under agreement, she said to remind you. Her orders, no exceptions."

"Her orders apply only when we sortie into the mountains, which we ain't yet."

"In your mind," the dwarf said. "Her mind is a whole different fish."

"She always in your business?" Bapcat asked.

"Jone Gleann is in every soul's business, all the time."

"And you don't mind?"

Fra Goodman shrugged. "If or how I mind don't seem a consideration from her end, so no point to argue." The man stopped. "Hold on, Deputy."

Bapcat watched the man pull his .30-40 Krag from a saddle scabbard and hold it out to him. "Forgot your partner," the dwarf said.

"Thanks," Bapcat said, slinging the heavy weapon flat across his chest. "She think I'll need this?"

"Didn't seem to do you much good last time, but she insists. She ordered give; I gave. Transaction is now done and out of my mind."

"Where does she think I'm going?"

"To see and rattle Mackley's wife, and to visit Archibald."

"I never said what I'm doing, save I'm going to town."

"Jone don't usually need to talk to a man to know his intentions."

"I didn't talk to nobody," Bapcat said.

Fra Goodman pointed skyward. "*He* always knows our hearts."

"And shares what He knows with Her?"

The small man laughed out loud. "No way to prove He don't."

"Does she claim to talk to Him?"

"Jone don't need to claim nothing."

*Enough about Jone Gleann.* Bapcat changed the subject. "What's Scale's story? I've seen more meat on a mosquito and more conversation from mutes."

The pony walked beside the deputy. "The man's real picky who he palavers with, weighs everything up there in his brain before he lets his lips move, which is how they come to call him Scale. Real name's Quashi Ojnab, of the Bankoli tribe of Southern Africa. His daddy and mama sent him north in 1853, him a newborn carried by his auntie who was his wet nurse, having lost her only child that same day Scale get borned at almost the very same minute.

"Underground Railroad folks got them from Arkansas up to Ann Arbor. Come 1863, he be eight years old and join the Sixteenth Michigan Volunteer Infantry, cute little Negro drummer boy, like a mascot to all those blue-belly soldier boys. Come Gettysburg that night up on Little Round Top, Rebs come squalling up the hill in the darkling, and Quashi, he picked up a dropped rifle and kill two Rebs with a bayonet, damn near as tall as him. His colonel swore him in as a soldier on the spot, put him on the payroll, give him the rifle, and mentioned him in dispatches, which I understood to be a big thing for soldier boys. Got promoted to sergeant eventually. Now he don't talk much about none o' that, and who gonna blame him?"

Bapcat let Fra Goodman talk on.

"Scale and me got likkered up one night and he stared at the moon like it might fall outta the sky on top of us and recited his bona fides: Gaines' Mill, Malvern Hill, Bull Run, Antietam, Fredericksburg, Chancellorsville,

Gettysburg, The Wilderness, Laurel Hill, Totopotomoy, Poplar Springs Church, Dabney's Mill, and, come the end, there he stood, twelve-year-old black sergeant at Appomattox to see Lee strike his colors. Scale said each of them names as if each was a lifetime all its own, said it serious and slow, like old Homer telling his *Odyssey*. I still get chills when I remember, them tones and all those words burned into my brain like God put them there."

Bapcat said, "Thanks for telling me that."

Fra Goodman carried his .32 in a holster on his chest. "Jone says you will do the right thing—that you can't help yourself."

"Does she now?"

"Never wrong, that woman."

"We'll start in town with Mrs. Mackley, then visit Archibald."

Fra Goodman grinned. "See, just what she predicted. You know, people in this town, they give you smiles to your face, bullets to your back."

"I guess I know that better than you," Bapcat said.

"Archibald ain't around; might be good to talk to Helmer Egerd."

"Who?"

"He provisions hunters and trappers."

"This your idea?"

Fra Goodman chuckled and Bapcat knew it was Jone Gleann's controlling hand at work again.

"This Egerd fellow trustworthy?"

"Is anyone around here?"

# CHAPTER 14

## *Ontonagon*

### FRIDAY, JULY 3

Intermediaries speaking for Virginia Mackley and Romney Archibald politely declined to see Bapcat, which made him both cranky and suspicious, but he had Jimjim Goodman lead him to Helmer Egerd's place of business. He stood outside, admiring a fine sign, obviously not homemade, with commendable carpentry and nice paint and clean-line lettering: "H. Egerd, Outfitter, Purveyor of Supplies for the Great North Woods." The whole town was decked out in patriotic bunting. Band members were practicing in a dusty lot, and there were already several blind-drunk miners sprawled on the ground outside some taverns.

It was midafternoon. The store was narrow, organized, and clean, floors mopped and swept. The man wearing a black apron had a well-trimmed sliver of mustache above his upper lip and smelled like something a hummingbird would fly to. The man also wore small round spectacles and had pink, shiny skin that looked freshly polished.

"Mr. Egerd?" Bapcat asked.

"Indeed I am, sir." The man leaned over his counter to stare down at Jimjim. "That Sister Jone's homunculus with you?"

Jimjim answered by touching the handle of his revolver.

"No offense meant," Egerd said quickly, raising his hands. "I just like to know to whom I am talking." The man continued to stare at Bapcat's diminutive companion.

"You're talking to me," Bapcat said, recapturing Egerd's attention. "Deputy State Game, Fish and Forestry Warden." He flashed his badge as punctuation.

"That's sure a long handle. I'm guessing the State don't pay you fellas by the number of letters in your title," the businessman quipped.

Egerd was of a type Bapcat cared little for, always making meaningless oily comments.

"You ever trade with Deputy Warden Mackley?"

"First, if you wouldn't mind," the oily Egerd said, "help me comprehend this. It's my understanding that, under the law and Constitution, I ain't required to answer questions about my customers and records, unless you can get you a subpoena. Ain't that how it works?"

"You just told me he's a customer," Bapcat said. "Therefore, no subpoena is needed now. So, what did he buy, and when?" This was a lie as part of a bluff, and Bapcat was unsure how long he could sustain the game.

"Still not convinced that's your concern," the man said.

"It's 'Deputy,'" Bapcat said, "and it *is* my business, because I am engaged in an official criminal investigation, which means you either talk to me now, or I get a warrant and rip this place apart. When I'm done, it might well take months for you to get it ready for business again."

"There's no need to employ that tone of voice," Egerd said. "I'm a law-abiding citizen, and I know of no JP who'd sign such a writ."

"Your JP Swoon would, quickly and gladly. Him and me talked already."

"Teedy ain't said nothing to me about such conversings," the businessman said, before cutting off his own words.

"The business between the justice of the peace and me ain't none of your concern, sir. What supplies did you provide to Deputy Mackley, and when? I won't ask again."

"You get sent by Lansing to find Mackley, is that it?" the man asked.

"*Find* Mackley?" Bapcat said.

"He's gone missing, ain't he?" Egerd said.

"Why would you think that?"

"'Cause he ain't been coming around is why, and because everybody says the man's long gone."

"Who says this?" Bapcat demanded.

"Everybody in town, including his uppity wife, who'll tell any man jack who'll abide and listen."

"She says he's missing?"

"You talked to her," Egerd said. "Out-of-town game warden comes looking for her husband, asks questions that ain't his business, mebbe gets himself a lesson in lead."

"Lesson in lead?"

Egerd raised an eyebrow. "You know, that thing."

"No idea what you're talking about."

"The thing involving a small projectile of lead, mebbe might have been meant as kind of a message. We're just talking friendly here now, right, man to man?"

Bapcat huffed up. "I'm asking the questions here, not you. One more evasion and I'll place you under arrest for interfering with a legal investigation."

"It ain't such a big deal, the man being gone," Egerd said.

"I'm talking felony charges related to attempted murder."

Egerd's face drained white. "Mackley bought things, but it's been months back, and them records of sales is already stored away. I run me a tight ship here. And I sure ain't shot no lawman!"

"You get the records and bring them to me at the school in Lake Mine, day after tomorrow, by noon. If those records aren't there by then, I'll get a warrant for your arrest."

"Everybody in town knows the man is gone, and I am telling you that I don't know nothing about no shooting."

"You said, lead message."

"That was what you call a theoretical; I coulda said rhubarb message, but I'm an outfitter, and I think in terms of man-goods and woods. How the heck would I know you was shot?"

"I don't know. You just said so? I never told you I was shot."

Egerd looked increasingly panicky. "You're a difficult and confounding man to talk to. I don't know nothing about *nobody* getting shot in the back."

Bapcat leaned forward, thumped the butt plate of the Krag on the wooden counter. "You're sinking deeper. You didn't know somebody got shot in the *back*. Is that theoretical, too?"

"I guess I just naturally think that way," Egerd said.

Bapcat said. "Time for truth. It won't hurt. You know who shot me?"

"Nuh-uh, Deputy. I don't know nothin' about no such thing."

"But you do. You just said so, didn't he, Jimjim?"

Fra Goodman nodded and tapped the grip of his .32. "I'm certain I heard those words, and would so attest with my hand on the Bible in front of a magistrate."

"Attempted murder. You have any idea what the penalty is for that?" Bapcat pressed Egerd.

"*Stinkmouth!*" Egerd blurted, almost shouting. "But that sumbitch is long gone missing too."

Bapcat looked to Fra Goodman, who said, "Stinkmouth—works some for Archibald. Well-known town roisterer, does odd jobs here and there."

"Including bushwhacking?"

"Would not surprise me an iota," Jimjim said.

Bapcat returned his attention to the businessman. "How do you *know* this? Truth, or else."

"Heard him brag on it."

"Where and when?"

"Pig and Bird Saloon, month or so back."

"Where's your sheriff?"

"Ain't got one."

"Acting, then."

"Hoke Desque? He's drunk every day over to the Pig."

"You tell him what this Stinkmouth claimed?"

"Thought it was just talk, and tell *Hoke Desque*? Why?"

Bapcat pointed a finger at the man. "Don't leave town or I will hunt you down."

"Given how you done with Mackley, that don't 'zackly shake the feet in my boots," Egerd said belligerently.

Bapcat gave the man one of his smiles that Zakov once said made him look like a lunatic. "Try me."

"I ain't going nowhere," the man said, holding up his hands.

"Mackley's sales records, day after tomorrow by noon, at the school in Lake Mine. All sales to him, ever."

Bapcat and Jimjim stood in the street. "Stinkmouth first, then the acting sheriff. Where's this Stinkmouth live?"

"Heard some time back he's got a loaner shack behind Archibald's business establishment."

"People around here sure are different."

"Most're normal folks, just tryin' to make their way."

"By backshooting strangers?"

Jimjim stopped and poked him. "Listen, a game warden's never a stranger. Everybody sees him as a threat to stopping them from doing all the things they think living up here gives them the right to do. Game warden is an impediment."

"Game wardens are not impediments." Another word whose meaning he was uncertain of.

"You're a game warden and you don't know this? Up in this county every soul here knows who the game warden is, and where he lives, and when he's in his house and when he's out and about. People here make a point of keeping track of the local game warden."

"Not this time," Bapcat said. "Here he is gone, and everybody seems to know that fact, and nobody, including his wife, seems to really care where to, or why. That don't strike you as odd?"

"I guess I didn't think of it that way. My point is, they all know he's gone."

"But that doesn't feel like quite enough, does it, given all the town interest in my kind? What's your take on Archibald?"

"Seems to me everything with that man is about money, and how to do anything that will get him more."

"*Anything*?" Bapcat asked.

Jimjim squinted up. "I meant more in the line of lying and cheating—using untruth to get what he wants."

"Shoot men in the back?"

"Archibald would never do that himself."

"He'd send someone else, maybe?"

Jimjim said, "I guess I'd be surprised. If he did that and got exposed, he could lose both his money and the freedom to chase more of it."

Bapcat regrouped, said, "My being shot isn't relevant right now. All we care about is finding Mackley."

"Mackley is to you what money is to Archibald."

"I guess you could put it that way."

"So we ain't interested in Stinkmouth?"

"I didn't say that."

# CHAPTER 15

## *Ontonagon*

### FRIDAY, JULY 3

There was a neat, orderly row of little painted cabins behind Romney Archibald's Livery, the sign out front proclaiming "Boarding—Feeding—Equine Supplies—Buy—Sell—Rent By the Day—All Things Horses." Red, white, and blue bunting was strung across the main street, and all the nearby taverns were sporting patriotic ribbons and signs.

"Regular jack-of-all-trades," Bapcat said as he and Jimjim walked past Archibald's. His first look at the small cabins caught him by surprise: Flower boxes under windows, fresh paint, good roofs, the whole effect different than the town proper, which had a lot of buildings, many of them built of new lumber, few of them painted or finished. Despite the fine appearance of the cabins, Bapcat saw in his mind a Mathew Brady photograph of slave quarters. Colonel Roosevelt had shown it to him in his days in the Dakotas, and it had stuck in his mind. It was one thing to go from range shack to range shack when you were working and moving cows, but living so close permanently—it just didn't seem normal.

A tall, elegant man with a massive sweep of silver hair met them in front of one of the cabins, advancing with a crooked yet welcoming grin and a hand held out, triggered for handshaking like he and Jimjim were a couple of long-lost and much-loved kinfolk.

"By golly!" the man proclaimed, with a mouth of shiny white and perfectly even teeth. "I'll bet you'd be that Deputy State Warden Bappat people are saying so many fine things about."

The deputy said, "It's Bap*cat*, and I wasn't aware that Mormons countenance wagers. You are Mr. Archibald, I presume?"

The greeting slowed the man, but stopped neither him nor his grin, and Bapcat heard Jimjim chuckling behind him.

"I am so very sorry we could not connect earlier today, sir, but if you had made an appointment, as is customary in the business community, we could have saved trouble and met at a set time of profit to both of us, which is the heart of business, is it not?"

"I'm not here to do your business," Bapcat said, ignoring the man's waiting hand. "We're looking for Stinkmouth."

Archibald looked befuddled. "There must be some mistake. There's no Stinkmouth here, neither in these abodes nor in my employ."

"The Kraut, Willard Schlueter," Jimjim said.

"Ah," Archibald said, nodding. "Willard—God-fearing, hardworking, a fellow of many God-given talents, but little self-direction." Bapcat watched the silver-haired man clasp his hands in front of him. "Alas, Mr. Schlueter has left our employ, without leaving a forwarding address or plans. It seems many men these days are pulling up stakes and heading south to Mr. Ford's Dearborn, and the promise of top pay. Yes, there are surely good days ahead for the horseless carriage and all who manufacture and sell them. It's a business that tempts even a settled businessman such as myself."

"Stinkmouth," Bapcat repeated.

Archibald looked at him, blinking furiously. "I'm sorry, but I have never heard that name applied to Mr. Schlueter."

"Foulest mouth in the county," Jimjim said. "Most profane man I ever heard carry on."

"I'll take your word on that. I won't countenance profanity in my presence," Archibald said, "but what they do outside my presence is beyond my control, as is no doubt self-evident."

"When did he leave?" Bapcat asked.

"To answer that inquiry I would have to confer with my personnel and payroll master. He sees to the details of all such things."

"We'll wait," Bapcat said.

Archibald grinned nervously. "I did not mean today. There will, of course, have to be an appointment made. This sort of request cannot be granted without forethought and preparation."

"These ain't your regular circumstances," Bapcat said, "so fetch your man, and do it quick. I ain't in the mood this day for no games. I'm conducting a legal criminal investigation, and I'm in a hurry."

Archibald moved away, quickly running a hand through his hair, not looking back.

"You a believer in coincidence?" Jimjim asked the deputy.

"Not in my line of work. I don't believe in miracles neither. You believe this Stinkmouth just took off? Seems sort of odd to me."

"What I know is people here say he was born and raised and spent his whole life right here in this town. I guess he could've lit out for Detroit if he was an ambitious man, which I hear he ain't never been."

Archibald returned with a harried-looking middle-aged man in tow, underarm sweat rings on his shirt not hidden by his green vest. "This is Mr. Hulbert Tyler. He oversees the hiring, payroll, and dismissals of all Archibald Enterprises employees and contracts."

"Stinkmouth got dismissed?" Bapcat asked, arching a brow.

"Nobody said that," Archibald responded, clearly annoyed.

"Nobody mentioned dismissal 'til you said your man Tyler here takes care of such things, so it just seems odd you'd say that, unless it might be in your mind and on the tip of your tongue. Sometimes when we talk, we say a lot more than we think, sometimes even when we think we're not talking. All you said was the man left your employ, but not when or under what circumstances. You seem the type to hold your cards real tight, Archibald, so while your Mr. Tyler might do the dirty work, I can't see no details slipping past you."

Tyler intervened. "He appears to have departed on or around June tenth. That's our last record."

"You have his employment records?"

"He's not a permanent man, just temporary and part-time, paid day-cash."

"But you let him use a company house, and you pay him?"

"From petty cash," Tyler said. "And yes, he used the house as part of our arrangement. He was free to work for others as long as he worked for us when we needed him."

"Doing what?"

"Odd jobs."

"*How* odd?" Bapcat asked.

"I don't understand," Tyler said.

"And no notion why he departed?"

"None, but it must have been a fast and impetuous decision, because he left without collecting his last pay. If you see him, tell him that. We always treat our people fair and square."

"Was the county sheriff told?" Bapcat asked.

Tyler yipped, "Absolutely *not!*"

Archibald added, "Men leave here all the time for any number of reasons, some logical, and some not."

"How many of the men leave without drawing their last pay?"

"Few, but this man is one of them," Tyler said, "and now, if this business is concluded, I have actual work awaiting my attention."

"There you have it," Archibald said, clapping his hands together. "Mr. Schlueter is no longer with us."

"Them words make him sound dead," Bapcat said.

Archibald's jaw dropped, his face flushed red, and he strode away.

"You have an interesting way of going about things," Jimjim said.

"Time to visit the acting sheriff," Bapcat announced. *Something ain't right here. I get shot on June eighth, and two days later this Stinkmouth is gone?*

"Archibald knew you were coming today," Jimjim said. "All the city's leading citizens have telephones. They're like a murder of crows; one sees something and alerts the rest of them."

"Damn interesting way of putting that," Bapcat said. "Ain't it?" *And another reason to dislike Mr. Bell's confounded invention.* The deputy warden didn't think of himself as one to think too deeply about things, but he saw a recurring pattern where people with money and power could get new devices and machines to help them be more powerful, and when law enforcement caught up, those same people would take the next step—meaning, law enforcement would never get ahead and mostly be playing catch-up. Such thoughts did not make him happy.

Jimjim led them to a saloon called the Pig and Bird, which featured a huge red silhouette of a pig with the word bird painted on it in white letters.

"Pig and Bird?" Bapcat asked.

"Was supposed to be the silhouette of a great bird in flight, and the owner paid one of his regulars in nightly whiskeys to make the sign. Man brought back a pig instead of an avian, and the owner said to hell with it, had it repainted and the word embossed in it. Most people don't even notice."

The interior of the saloon was crowded, loud, and reeked of sweat and stale beer. The clientele, Bapcat saw, consisted of a motley crew of mustachioed river hogs, sailors, loggers, miners, and old men, most of them well into their next drunk.

"Corner to the left," Jimjim said as they walked through and everyone gawked at them.

One man sitting alone at a poker table with a faded brown felt top.

"Wanting a game?" the man asked with slurred words, not looking up.

Bapcat flashed his badge past the man's face, grabbed him by his shirt collar and belt, and frog-marched him through the bar, his boot toes scuffing the sanded wooden floor. The other patrons sat silently, watching.

The state deputy dumped the man in a large barrel of rainwater, and when the man surfaced, spitting, spluttering, and coughing, Bapcat pushed him under again and held him down until Jimjim tapped him and held up a firearm. "He dropped this."

Bapcat took the .38, which looked like one of the cheap ones mine owners had given their so-called deputies during last year's strike. Bapcat dropped it into the barrel and yanked Desque up to the air, where he gulped and gagged theatrically.

"I'm Bapcat, deputy state game warden, and you are a damn disgrace to all lawmen."

The man exploded upward, punching wildly. "You miserable dog! You assaulted and attacked a peace officer!"

Bapcat pushed him under again, and brought him back up. "My intention is to drown you if you don't snap to, and fast."

"I ain't never done nothing to youse," the man said with a whine.

"Who said something got done to me?" Bapcat said.

"People talk."

"If so, one of them is guilty. You want to give me some names?"

"Wun't be good, professionally speaking," the man said, pressing the heels of his hands into his eye sockets.

Bapcat dunked the man again and held him down, despite strong resistance, and relented only when Jimjim touched his sleeve. "You ain't God."

"This is goddamn wrong," the man sputtered.

Bapcat grabbed the man by the hair again and Desque took a swing, but Bapcat easily deflected it to the side, slapped the man's face with a report so loud that a few drunks stumbled onto the wooden sidewalk to see who just got shot.

"Names, damn you!" Bapcat said, snarling.

"Stinkmouth," the man said, gagging.

"Willard Schlueter?" Bapcat said.

"Who the fuck is that?" Desque said.

The deputy game warden let go and slapped the man one more time. "Tell your masters you kept the stories straight this time, or next round you may find the waterworks even more severe."

Bapcat shoved the man under and walked away. "We're leaving," he said.

"Can we grab some grub first?" Jimjim asked, trotting to keep up with the game warden's long strides.

"I've got sandwiches in my saddlebag."

"Dry and stale as dust, I bet. You could have drowned that fool."

"Maybe I should have," Bapcat said. "When you accept a badge, you swear a sacred oath."

"Not all lawmen feel as strongly as you," his companion said.

"They better, if they want to work with me." Bapcat stopped and pointed at Jimjim. "And don't go blabbing to Jone about what happened here today."

"Won't have to. She'll know everything before we get outside the town limits."

# CHAPTER 16

## Lake Mine

### SUNDAY, JULY 5

For reasons she didn't share, Jone Gleann didn't come to examine his wound or talk to him again until almost Sunday noon, not long before Egerd's deadline for bringing his sales records for goods sold to Deputy Mackley.

"I see you've overdone it," Gleann said from behind him. His shirt was off and he was sitting on the table in the small cabin, his shadow McIlrath right outside the door, eternally ready to plunge into action on his behalf.

"It feels fine," Bapcat said. "I'm fine and ready to move out."

Her voice dripped with sarcasm. "To where, exactly? I'd be interested to know."

"I'm working on that."

"Yes, I've heard about your work. Drowning people usually leads one to a state penitentiary, I believe," she said, tapping his shoulder as a signal to put his shirt back on.

"All you hear are reports of what, not why, and what you're getting ain't much use without the thinking behind what I do."

"There's thinking in stirring the town pot?"

"I believe there is."

"Well, that certainly allays any fears I harbored that you were just charging around to physically and verbally rough people up for the sheer fun of it."

She departed with no further word and he went out onto the porch. Scale then joined him, as did Jimjim and the boy, Mac. "Some musketeers you are," he said, "leaving me alone with the likes of her."

"I thought there was three musketeers," the boy said, bewilderment in his young voice.

"That's your first lesson in grown-up misdirection," Bapcat said. "Somebody calls his book *The Three Musketeers*, then writes about four." He was still frosted over discovering this when he'd first read the story. "And all the damn names in the book are French and real hard to pronounce and stretch your brain until it hurts, because somebody else took the story and made that French talk into American, and didn't have the brains or courtesy to make the names American, too. Grown-up people don't make a lot of sense, Mac."

"You'd think they woulda fixed the title when they done that," the boy said.

"Got no answer for you. Me and books ain't the easiest of friends. I like them, but sometimes they don't seem to like me."

"I like books," the boy volunteered.

McIlrath was an interesting boy. "Good for you. Let's hope they like you back better than they do me," the game warden grumped.

"You got to practice," the boy told the deputy.

"I want your advice, I'll ask for it."

Come noon, Egerd hadn't shown, and Bapcat couldn't hide his irritation. Soon afterward, Mac, who had disappeared after the book discussion, came flying around the corner of the school, his skinny arms and legs windmilling and kicking up tiny dust devils. "They been seen!" the boy announced breathlessly, pointing behind him.

"Who?" Bapcat asked.

"Some little fella with four armed outriders, front, back, and sides—they got him pinned in the middle like a hot pepper in a big Eyetalian sandwich."

Bapcat leaned toward Jimjim. "Seems like a lot of guns for a simple mail delivery."

"Considering what happened to you on that same road, Egerd may want to avoid a tragic repeat."

"I guess that might smack of some knowledge beyond the obvious," Bapcat said.

"Had a similar thought," the dwarf said.

"No number of outriders gon' stop a man got but one thought in his head," Scale offered.

"Especially if that one thing is killing somebody," Bapcat said.

Scale nodded, said, "Yassuh, 'zackly so."

Bapcat remained seated on the porch like an imperial potentate as the Ontonagon outfitter rode slowly up with his four companions. Egerd stopped in front of the deputy, fished papers out of a saddlebag, and waved them like a fan.

"Don't make me get up and come fetch them things," Bapcat said. "You're late, and I don't like late. Fact is, I *hate* late."

"I'm sorry, but it's a long ride up here."

"Seems like you had plenty of company to pass the time with," Bapcat said with a nod toward the other men.

"Weren't a trip predicated on social exchange or chummy conversation. We come all this way on serious business," Egerd said, dismounting and handing the reins to one of his deadpan companions. "Think a man could get a drink?" the outfitter asked, rubbing his sleeve over his mouth, "to clear away the trail dust and such."

"There's a rainwater barrel over there," Jimjim said, pointing. "Help yourselves, one at a time."

Egerd handed the paperwork to Bapcat and went to drink from a wooden ladle hanging on the drinking water barrel.

Bapcat read: 12-gauge and .30-30 ammo, guns, tents, prepared and canned foods . . . The list was long and detailed. "You call this the *usual* stuff?" Bapcat said, thrusting the papers at Egerd.

"Quite usual in my business," the man said, nervously slapping at a fly on his cheek.

"You know the best way to pick up a turd?" Bapcat asked.

"Sir?"

"Grab hold of the clean part."

"There ain't no clean part of a turd," Egerd said.

"You get my meaning. These papers are worthless."

"But they're what you asked for," the man contended.

"I wanted records to tell me a story," Bapcat said, "not something to put a bookkeeper to sleep."

The deputy warden slapped the paperwork on his leg. "How'd he pay? These records don't say cash, nor bank draft, nor line of credit. These papers don't say nothing."

Egerd said, "If it ain't remarked, it be a cash transaction, my preferred way of doing business."

"Sure, cash is preferred. How come there ain't a total on here, and why don't they say the bill's been paid in full, in part, or is on credit?"

"Just an oversight."

"I bet," Bapcat said, and started calculating out loud. "Three sixteen-by-twenty-foot, twelve-ounce Duck half pyramid tents at sixty dollars each, which came to one eighty. Eight ten-by-twelve-by-seven-foot wall tents, also twelve Duck, twenty-four fifty each, round it off to twenty-five to make it easier to figure, call those tents two hundred, which makes the tents alone come to three eighty. All the damn numbers are making me foggy. My head ain't big enough to do this inside it. Mac, do you know your math?"

"Yessir."

"Add and divide?"

"I can."

"Go fetch pencil and paper."

"Yes, Master," the boy said, smiling brightly.

"Don't be calling no man 'Master,' boy," Scale yelped, clearly annoyed. "We all equals, boy. Only our Maker is our master."

"*Master* is what they call a teacher in Scotland," McIlrath said.

"Says who?"

"Says Jone."

"That don't make it right," Scale grumbled. "And don't be sassin' me."

The boy came back with pencil and paper and sat at Bapcat's feet. "Speak, Master."

Bapcat said, "I'm with Scale on this one—cut out that 'Master' crap and write and cipher. Forty quarts of Margaux claret at two hundred total; what're we up to now?"

"Five hundred and eighty," the boy said.

Bapcat kept reading aloud: "Cocoa, jams, jellies, teas, coffee, Russian caviar, English biscuits, tinned beef, Axminster carpets, bed frames, mattresses, bread and cake knives . . ." Bapcat looked up at Egerd. "*Cake knives?*"

The man looked away as Bapcat read on. "Two hundred rounds of thirty-thirty ammo—hell, that alone is two hundred. Six Webley double-barrel shotguns, breech load, right barrel half-choke, left barrel full-choke, thirty-inch length, each one ninety dollars."

"Five sixty," Mac said. "Takes us up to eleven forty, but you ain't give me no prices on jellies and beds and whatnots."

Bapcat ignored the boy, tapped his paperwork on his leg. "Sheets, pillows, towels, linen table napkins, knives and forks for forty-eight, dishes, pots and pans . . . A whole damn US army regiment wouldn't need all this gear and froufery," he hissed at Egerd. "How much here, three, four thousand, and you say he paid cash and you *forgot* to mark that on the record? You are stretching my patience real thin, Egerd."

"I can't explain a simple mistake," the man said in his own defense.

"Can't, or won't—especially if it ain't a mistake? No wonder you was so nerved-up over showing these records to the law. Mackley say what he intended for all these goods?"

"No, sir, I don't believe that he did."

"Even when you sold him two dozen Newhouse bear and wolf traps for two hundred and forty dollars—that didn't set you to thinking what he might be up to?"

"Up to one thousand, three hundred and eighty dollars," Mac reported.

"That's enough, Mac. You done good." Bapcat handed the papers to the boy. "Add it all up—quietly." Bapcat looked back to the outfitter. "Traps didn't suggest nothing to you?"

"Well, he may have mentioned bear country," Egerd said.

"Where might that be?"

"I'm no trapper."

"So Mackley told you he was going trapping?"

"Not in them words, and it seemed unlikely, pelts being what they are in summer."

"Maybe he was not looking for pelts," Bapcat said.

"I would not know such confidences."

Mac elbowed Bapcat's leg. "I come up with just under five thousand. I never seen that much money," the clearly astonished boy added.

Bapcat looked at Egerd. "Was you, I'd take the long way home."

"Sir?"

"We detained a suspicious fella with a thirty-thirty along your road just before you fellas come along now. There might be others out there, but I can't say for sure."

"Who was he looking for?"

"He ain't said," Bapcat said quietly. "Yet."

"The long way, eh?" Egerd said.

"I were you. Mackley paid you cash for all that?"

"Cash got paid," Egerd said, turning to leave.

Bapcat had a thought and ran over to grab the reins of the man's horse, stopping it. "You said cash was paid for Mackley's order, but you didn't specifically say Mackley was the one who forked over the cash. Was it him?"

Egerd looked off in the distance. "In a manner of speaking."

"You better put a name on your lips, Egerd, or you're coming off that horse and not much gonna enjoy what follows."

"You can't threaten citizens," the man said.

"A name!"

"Mrs. Mackley," Egerd said.

"His wife paid his bill?"

"She did. Every red cent."

"That ever happen before?"

"No."

"How did it come to be?"

"I dropped by her place and made her aware of the standing bill, and she paid on the spot."

"Without discussion?"

"No, but she was smiling some."

"Goods were paid for. Were they delivered?"

"They were."

"To the Mackleys' house?"

"To Mr. Archibald's warehouse."

*Mrs. Mackley paid the bill and the goods were delivered to Archibald?* Bapcat bounced this around in his head and couldn't get it to settle. *Was Jone's hunch about Mackley's reliability right? Or was it more than a hunch?*

Jone Gleann came out of the cabin as the men rode away. Bapcat had no idea when she had gone inside, or how long she had been there. "The long way?" she asked.

"He brought along his protectors, so I thought I'd give them something to think on. Mackley buying bear and wolf traps going into summer—that sound sensible to you? I used to trap, and I can tell you, it ain't sensible or logical in my book. You buy supplies, you wait till fall so you don't have to carry them on the books so long."

"Leg-hold traps aren't best for live specimens," she said. "But the box-trap models you saw would work fine, I'm thinking."

"I guess knowing where the trap-maker plans to make delivery might be good information to have."

"It might indeed," she said.

"I guess I'll take the train up to Houghton to see Mr. Beaumont Clewd at North Country Iron Works and Machines," he said.

"Don't you have a partner up there?"

Bapcat looked at her.

"I have my own telephone," she said. "No need to trek anywhere. You'll have your privacy here. With so few people, I would think you game wardens would think of more ways to be efficient, to do more with less; otherwise, you'll end up spending all your time running around and getting nothing done."

Her point was a good one—if more than a little irritating.

"Movement alone isn't progress," she told him, and this struck a chord he would never forget. "The right direction trumps speed."

"How does that Nick Vedder fit into Archibald's business?"

"Purchasing clerk in a department that reports to Hulbert Tyler."

"Huh," Bapcat said. "Might've helped to know that when you first showed me that cage toy."

"I thought it was obvious," she said. "Who else would know the details about such an order, except the purchasing clerk? That training of yours didn't include deductive and inductive reasoning?"

"We skimmed through some of that stuff pretty fast."

"You might want to revisit it and spend a bit more time."

"I know if all the premises are true, inductive reasoning can still plop you down on a false conclusion."

"You continue to astonish me, Deputy. Care to bathe?"

"Ain't dark yet, and there ain't many skeeters out right now."

She stared at him. "What is your point?"

"Dunno; guess I drew the conclusion you enjoy being miserable."

"Based on previous bath times?"

"Yes, ma'am."

Jone Gleann smiled. "Evidence of your earlier declaration of false conclusions based on solid premises?"

"You don't hate skeets?"

"What sane person doesn't? But I prefer my privacy more."

"To hide all your scars?"

"I can hide only those that show," she said, "but yes, and I assume you want to know about them."

"Only if it pleases you to talk. Me, I've seen a lot of scars, and how they come about ain't usually so pretty, nor even worth recalling."

"I never took you to be a philosopher," she said.

"I ain't," he said. *What I am,* he reminded himself, *is a game warden, and still a pretty darn green one at that.*

Bapcat said, "Mackley ran up a huge bill with Egerd and never paid, and when Egerd went to Mrs. Mackley, she paid cash for her husband's debt, but had the goods delivered to Archibald's warehouse. He in the storage business?"

"Not that I heard of, but he's got his hands in a lot of things."

"Was afraid of that," he said quietly. "Looks like you might've been on the right track in this thing."

"Thank you. What do you propose to do about it?"

"Got to find Mackley—otherwise there ain't nothing to hold on to except speculation, which ain't worth spit in a court of law."

# CHAPTER 17

## *Bruce Crossing*

### TUESDAY, JULY 7

"You're leaving tomorrow," Jone Gleann had told him the day before as they'd sat by the creek in bright afternoon sunlight she draped in a towel, he in his long johns. He had been getting ready to ask about her scars, but her statement had snapped him out of his reverie. "To the mountains?"

"The circus," she said. "It may prove more informative if we start there."

"You and me are going to the circus?"

"Neither I, nor we, just you—though I suppose you should take that scamp McIlrath with you. Don't let him see the naked ladies; he's already got too big an interest down those lines."

"The circus has naked ladies?"

She looked at him. "Have you never been to a circus?"

He shook his head.

"Even better than I could hope for," Gleann said. She stood momentarily in a sunspot, which made her leg scars flame magenta, stepped into trousers, yanked them up, twirled a towel around her shoulders like a tape, tied it off, and marched away.

• • •

The circus had come to Bruce Crossing in its own small train, now parked on a siding. It was eventually bound for Wisconsin and Minnesota, Jimjim offered. The dwarf had come along on his own, as had Scales, and both men were as excited as children. They came upon a yellow tent and near it, three smaller, longer ones, like Indian sweat lodges, a sign declaring "Pellerin's Traveling Showmen & World Menagerie of Beasts." Painted in red letters on a white canvas banner, the sign stretched across an entrance arch. The small-est of the three tents promoted "Raree Show—Nature's Geeks and Freaks Galore," and the other canvas structure had signs proclaiming "Ferocious

Man-Eating Beasts, Still Wild & Untamed." The last tent advertised "Exotic Dancers" in bright red-and-gold letters, five feet high.

Jimjim said, "Stick close by me" to Scale as they neared the raree tent.

"You a'fearin'?" Scale asked.

Jimjim said, "Little folk like me sometimes get pressed into service by the likes of these, and are never seen again."

"Ain't nothin' ta be feared of, if a man got Jesus in his heart," Scale said. "I personally seen fields awash in guts and blood, and crows and vultures playing tug-of-war with men's chitlins."

"Our fears are each our own," the dwarf said quietly. "Leave me to mine and you can have yours."

"Ain't nothin' rankles or peeves me. I seen the elephant more'n I can count. You little fellas sure are touchy."

"Call me Master," Jimjim said.

Scale bristled immediately. "*Damned* if I will," the Negro said, puffing up.

Jimjim grinned. "Seems we little fellas ain't alone in the touchies."

"What's a raree freak?" young McIlrath asked, staring up at the sign which showed a bearded woman.

"Depends on who's lookin' and who's bein' looked at," Jimjim said. "I'd say it's mostly in the eye of the beholder."

Bapcat steered the lot of them to the Beast tent, paid their admission, and took them inside. Four cages were lined up end to end: a mountain lion in one, a timber wolf in another, a fox in the third, and a crowd of open-mouth gawkers in front of the fourth cage with a sign that read "Sultan the Bear."

The deputy game warden pushed through the crowd, using his rifle as a lever, and finally got to the iron bars. There were three men around a prone black bear.

"I done kilt thet monster dead with my magic killin' stick," a boy of no more than eight declared to the gathering, his little chest puffed out.

One of the men, on his knees by the animal, looked up and grinned. He wore a clown suit, but no greasepaint. "Hey, kid, maybe we ought to get the boss to hire you as our bear killer."

The boy looked pleased. "What's it pay?"

The crowd laughed and applauded, patted the boy's head.

"What happened?" Bapcat asked through the bars. The reek of shit and blood was on the floor, pulling in wedges of hungry flies.

"Ain't your business, Larry," the man in the clown suit said.

"I know some things about animals."

"Go on and beat it," the man said.

But Bapcat went to the back of the cage, slid into the open door, and flashed his rifle. The three men took a step back. "I think it's illegal to kill a bear with a stick around here."

"That kid didn't kill *nothin'*," Clown Suit said, making a twirling motion with his forefinger near his temple. "Little booger's daft."

"Did *too* kill it," the boy yelped and whimpered in his own defense. "Was a fierce and bloody fight. See the blood for yourselfs."

No doubt about the blood. *Big hemorrhage*, Bapcat thought.

Jimjim stood by the boy. "It's your story, son. Tell it how you like."

Bapcat looked at Clown Suit. "What happened?"

"Started pukin' blood outten his mouth, shittin' all over ever'thing, keeled over dead."

Bapcat stepped closer. Clown Suit said, "That ain't allowed."

The deputy warden ignored the man and squatted beside the dead animal, a male. He looked at the animal's head, opened its mouth. All the canine teeth were gone, the rest, mere yellow nubs. There were huge amounts of scar tissue all over the animal's body. "How old is he?"

Clown Suit again: "No idea, chum. He come aboard to perform with us two seasons back. What's it matter now?"

"Perform how?" Bapcat asked.

"Dance, balance tricks, the old make-the-kiddies-laugh-and-piss-their-pants routine."

"So many scars."

"Guess he was just a clumsy kind of bear," one of the men said.

Bapcat saw that the animal's claws were gone and lifted one large front paw. There were burns all over the pads, bad ones, scarred over. Same on the other paw. He looked at Clown Suit for an explanation.

"Gotta find a way to make them mind," the man said, shrugging. "Tell 'em to stand up, they damn well better stand up."

"He loved kids," one of the men said. "Until today."

"So much scarring," Bapcat said again. "Gotta be better ways."

"In this racket, the fastest way is the cheapest way, and cheapest is always best," Clown Suit said. "Quick results, and move on."

"This bear fight others?"

"We're just cirkies," one of the men said, "not performers. You got questions, take 'em to Paul."

"Who is he?"

"Paul Pellerin, the bossman."

"In the big tent?"

"The big tent is called the Big Top, buddy. It's more likely he's in the backyard in the red wagon, getting dressed."

"He has an act?"

Clown Suit spoke. "Ringmaster. Owners can do what they want, I reckon. America, right?"

Bapcat left his companions at the entrance to the raree tent, caught a lot of hard stares as he carried his rifle through the maze of wagons. Pellerin's trailer was the only one painted red and the door was open. A girl in tights that barely qualified as a costume, much less clothing, was vigorously brushing a man's thick, wiry hair.

"Pellerin?" Bapcat asked.

"I don't know you," the man said, not bothering to look at the door.

"I go by Lute."

"I got a show to do here. You want work, come back after. You got skills?"

"Big animals."

Pellerin turned in his chair, squinted out into the light, and pushed away the girl's hand and brush. "Such as? And kindly enumerate."

"Bear, buffalo, elk, deer, some big cats."

"Bears. Trick or scrap?"

Assuming *scrap* meant fighting, Bapcat said, "Whatever's needed."

"Luke, right?" Pellerin said.

"Lute."

"Right—Lute. Come back after the show." He slapped the girl on the behind.

"Babs, baby, I gotta see John Robinson, so make sure this fine fella gets it free, okay?"

"But Paul . . . ?" she said in a questioning tone.

"That ain't no request, baby. Take care of the man. The whole thing."

"You mean . . . ?" she asked, pouting.

"Are you deaf? You know what I mean. Go on now, git."

The woman took Bapcat's arm and tried to lead him away, but he balked. "Is the bear supposed to fight today?" he asked the big boss.

"Nah, that's for other times and other places, you know, special events out in the gauze. Babsy, get him moving." Pellerin suddenly stood up. "Wait! You know anybody can lay hands quick on a live bear? Word is there's lots of them up in the high country."

"Depends," Bapcat said. "Scrap, or something else?"

"All of it, I hope."

"Trained then, not untrained."

"Word's raw, pal. We got the guy here can teach it what it needs to do."

"Who's that?"

Pellerin turned away, said over his shoulder, "Ain't got the job yet. Go with Babs—it's on me. She's clean as soap, just had her doc check yesterday. I won't tolerate no social problems in my troupe."

The woman took Bapcat's arm again. "I got a tent," she said. "It ain't no caravan, but I keep it clean, and I reckon it's nice enough to roll around."

"I'm with friends," Bapcat said, stopping.

The woman studied him. "If the boss says it's on him, bring them, too. Chava for one, chava for all."

Bapcat did not know the word, but had no problem figuring out the meaning. "One's a kid."

"How old?" she asked.

"Not nearly old enough," Bapcat said.

"What do I tell the boss?"

"The truth: that I politely declined."

"Mister, ain't nobody ever politely declined my pussy."

"Tell him you gave me all I wanted and I went to see the show."

"Thanks," she said. "I sure could use me a break."

"Tell me something," Bapcat said. "Who is Pellerin's animal trainer?"

"Himself. He's too damn cheap to pay anyone else."

• • •

Bapcat rejoined the others and Jimjim asked, "Saw you were over by the circus boss's joint. You thinking about a new job?"

"It's always good to keep an open mind," Bapcat said.

"The people in this outfit breaking any laws?" the little man asked.

"Don't know," Bapcat said, which was true, but the burn scars on the bear's footpads were disturbing, which came as a surprise to him. He'd killed countless animals over the years, bears included, but he had never felt this way before. He supposed this meant something, though at this point he couldn't say exactly what.

Over the past year he had worked quite a bit with Houghton County assistant prosecutor Roland Echo, and a friendship had developed. Echo was prosecutor Tony Lucas's lifelong friend, and what Judge O'Brien once called a real backroom, keep-his-mug-out-of-the-newspaper type. Echo was the real legal brain in the county office, and what he didn't know, he would dig like a hungry dog to find.

"Hey!" Mac yelped, pointing at a sign: "EXOTIC DANCERS—ADULTS ONLY."

"You're too dang young to ogle kootch, boy," Scale said.

"Kootch?" the boy asked.

"You make my point for me," Scale said, smiling slightly. "Kootch is pussy."

"*Please*," the boy entreated.

Jimjim said, "Happens sooner or later for all of us."

Bapcat shrugged. Jimjim was right. They all paid and went inside. The boy's presence was unremarked upon, much less challenged.

There were three women on a foot-high stage, and they performed one at a time. The last one was the youngest of the three, and the most animated by far, though all of them had wiggled and jiggled until they sweated their skins to a bright red glow.

The boy said nothing until they were back outside. "I like that last kootchie's *things* the best," he announced.

"Things?" Bapcat asked.

"Like Sister Jone's, only hers are a whole lot bigger!"

Bapcat thumped the top of the boy's skull with his forefinger. "How do you know *that*?"

"All us boys like to watch you two in the stream."

"I'd better not catch you," Bapcat said finger-thumping the boy one more time.

"We ain't seen no circus yet," the boy complained, changing subjects.

"I guess you've seen more than enough," Bapcat proclaimed. "See too much stuff like that, and your brain becomes oatmeal."

"No it don't," the boy insisted.

"Where do you think all them freaks you seen today come from?" Jim-jim asked.

"The bearded lady and melted-face man?" the boy asked.

"Whole dang lot of them," Bapcat said.

Bapcat sent his company back to Lake Mine, and with them gone, found himself a place to sit in the shade and think, the rifle across his lap keeping people away. There were few patrons, which reinforced his earlier curiosity about why the circus would stop at such a drip-drop burg as Bruce Crossing, when Bergland was said to be much larger, more level, and just up the tracks.

• • •

Back at the red wagon, show over, Bapcat was greeted by Pellerin and another woman, this one the youngest from the kootchie show. Pellerin said, "Babs says you're queer, which is jake by me. You like that flavor, we can find some around here. Seems like it's everywhere these days."

"The job," Bapcat said.

"You got bona fides?" the boss asked.

"I ain't sure," Bapcat confessed.

"Means experience."

"Trapper, miner, soldier, cowboy."

"All laudable, but I refer to cirky work. The rest ain't worth squat."

"Just animals," Bapcat said.

"Live or dead?"

"Both."

"Bears, specifically?"

"Both alive and dead," Bapcat said.

"How you catch 'em alive and whole—pits and nets?"

"Business secret."

Pellerin smiled. "You got a price?"

"Depends on what you want."

"A big-ass bear is what I got to have. If it ain't tamed enough to go out in the ring, fine by me, but he's gotta hate dogs the way a Mick hates Prods. Am I making myself clear here?"

Bapcat nodded. "There ain't a wild bear alive that *likes* dogs."

"Good to hear. So how much, and, more to the point, how soon?"

"Rut season right now," Bapcat explained. "Boars are cranky and looking for sows. Makes them cover a lot more ground in their search, which makes them a lot harder to catch now than in the fall, when all they got on their minds is food."

"Sort of like us," Pellerin said, "pussy overriding all else." He tickled the kootch and she laughed out loud. "I need me that bear *now*," he said.

"No can do," Bapcat said. "Where'd you get your last one?"

"Boughten off some ghillies in Texas, who said they got him from a fella up in north Arkansas. Told me he was ten and I could expect maybe twenty working years out of him."

"Not ten," Bapcat said. "Much older. What teeth haven't been pulled are ground down to stubs. What *did* you feed it, rocks?"

Pellerin grinned. "How the hell I know what bears eat? I'm the boss, not no damn bear hand. See here, I got a problem; are you gonna help me solve it?"

"I'm trying, but fall's the best I can do."

"Ain't good enough, and you still ain't given me no price to mull."

"What did you pay for the dead one?"

"Paid five hundred, and I was fucked."

"You ever buy from a zoo?"

"Where you think Sultan come from? Zoo in Fort Worth."

"And they said they got it up in Arkansas?"

"As a cub, they claimed, a prevarication I now suspect, like his age. Point is, I got to have me a bear before we roll into Wisconsin. Bears are big draws up here in the North Country."

"What'll you do without one?"

"Don't know for sure," Pellerin said. "Ask around, I guess. Was you serious about fall?"

"I can be for a thousand."

"A head?"

"Two fifty a foot," Bapcat joked. "The head's free. How many you want?"

"Get me two or three?"

"Sure."

"Discount for volume?"

"I don't catch 'em in volume, just one by one, and the danger and work is the same every time."

"How about we say nine hundred each for a brace of bears? This ain't your big show like The Two B's, Barnum and Bailey."

"I *guess* I might do that," Bapcat said after pretending to think about it.

The men shook hands, and Pellerin gave him a gaudy business card. "Send me a telegram in Minnie Polis. We hit there for a September first show."

"After that?"

"We make our way south and barn out the winter in Cool Pepper, Texas, just east of Dallas."

On impulse, Bapcat said, "What will you do with the bear carcass, Pellerin?"

"Dump it."

"Okay if I take it?"

"Pelt's no damn good, but sure, go ahead and help yourself. It's one less thing for us to bother with."

Babsy came over to him outside the red wagon. "I know you ain't queer," she said, "but I had to tell him something. He wants specifics when he puts me with other fellas."

"Got to do what you got to do," Bapcat said. She peeled away from him before he got the bear carcass, found it in the grass outside the animal wagon tent. He made a travois he could haul with his hands, dragging it behind him like a litter. The bear's head was huge, but there wasn't much to it other than that. It was a good twenty miles uphill to Lake Mine, and he figured he could do it in six hours, maybe eight, depending on how winded he got.

One mile up the trail he came upon his companions. "You think we'd let you go all the way alone?" Jimjim asked.

"We been talking about kootch," McIlrath announced.

"You have, huh?" Bapcat said, glaring at the adults.

"There a reason you hauling that smelly old bear?" Jimjim asked.

"To give it a decent burial," Bapcat said.

"You people sure got some odd notions," Scale remarked.

"Wanna talk more kootch?" Mac asked.

"While we dig a grave," Bapcat said.

"Ain't got no shovel," the boy said.

"That's what God made hands for."

Bapcat lay the animal's back against a slight slope and gutted it, letting gravity help him peel out the innards. Then he quickly skinned the animal. Its head was so huge, it was out of proportion. He left the guts and tied the carcass to the travois and started north with his retinue following along, exchanging views about and experiences with various kootch.

# CHAPTER 18

## *Lake Mine*

### WEDNESDAY, JULY 8

"What did you want me to learn from that circus?" Lute Bapcat asked.

Jone Gleann countered brusquely, "More to the point, I should think, is what *did* you learn?"

"You couldn't have known in advance that the show's bear would die, unless of course you had a hand in it, which would make you a witch, a schemer, or both."

"Ludicrous," she said, smirking. "I saw that animal last year when the show stopped in Bruce, saw its condition, understood what I was seeing. I'm astonished that it survived the winter with that rabble."

"Understood how?" Bapcat asked.

"Bucharest, Romania," she said. "They tame and train and fight the beasts there, and have for hundreds of years, probably since Roman times."

"You were in this Ramonia place?" He'd never heard the word before, didn't even want to say it and look like a fool, but took a stab.

"Aye. You took the carcass, the lads tell me. For legal evidence, I presume."

"Evidence of what? All things die, us people included. I took the carcass to give the animal a decent burial."

"A decent burial for a mere beast?"

"Don't start. You are not so far in the know as you think."

"I'm not?" she said.

"All your precious schoolboys have been sneaking looks at their nekkid teacher."

"Those scamps," she said, blushing, with the hint of a grin.

"McIlrath told us you're better endowed than a kootch he saw at the circus."

"Did he now?"

"Sure did. Made quite a story of it, too."

"Perhaps I should take the willow to young McIlrath's behind."

Bapcat felt heat on his neck. He had been beaten mercilessly and relentlessly at St. Cazimer's. "No beatings. Use shame; it lasts longer, and doesn't leave scars."

"You have some experience down that line, I presume."

"You presume too dang much," he said.

"And your own view of this matter?" she asked.

"What matter would that be?"

"McIlrath's value judgment."

"Don't have one," Bapcat said.

Jone Gleann raised a brow. "Truly?"

Bapcat stared at the ground. "I reckon he had a point," he admitted after a long pause.

"I shall take that as a compliment," she declared, "and thank you."

*Why is she thanking me? And how did we get on this subject?*

"I expect you might have noticed that the adult males in these surrounds don't lean much toward compliments of female qualities. Honestly, I expected no more from you, but now I wonder."

*What the devil is she going on about now? At least she hasn't taken me to task for letting Mac see the kootchie show.*

"You know, of course, that the boy should not have been there," Jone Gleann said. "Looking at those women will only fan carnal flames."

"They didn't stop him from going in," Bapcat argued.

"A circus side show wouldn't stop a newborn if someone bought it a ticket. You should rest, Deputy. Your jaunt appears to have left you with a weary look in your eyes."

"I guess I feel better on the inside than I look on the outside. I need to use your telephone, and I may want to talk to Mr. Nick Vedder."

"Better, I think, if I do that. You know where the telephone is. Shall I arrange a meeting for us with Mr. Vedder?"

"Rather I do that myself."

"I insist on this. When do you want to meet him?"

"I don't know—maybe after I talk to my partner, which is why I want the telephone."

She pointed the way.

Zakov answered, "Game warden."

"Have a chance to visit North Country Iron Works?"

"Jordy is fine, Jaquelle is as delicious and ravishing as ever—and deeply missing you. Your copper tub is on order, and the widow instructed me to inform you that should she find your hands harvesting another distaff field, there will be a reckoning of epic proportions."

"I have no idea what any of that means."

"She is, as foretold, jealous and suspicious of your motives."

"She ain't got no reason."

"Women *always* have a reason."

"Ain't a dang thing I can do about how Jaquelle feels."

"The fact that you would declare this verifies the statement as both fact and sad truth."

"I didn't call to gab about such," Bapcat said. "What about Beaumont Clewd?"

"There is nothing specific on bears in *Tiffany's*, as anticipated, but I talked to our fine colleague Roland Echo, and he believes that a New York law passed soon after your Civil War and was later adopted in Michigan. The New York statute made all forms of animal fighting illegal, and they specifically included bulls, bears, dogs, and cocks. It is equally unlawful and illegal to keep such fighting animals, or organize, manage, or patronize such activities and events."

"Okay, but what about *here*, in Michigan?"

"There is a statute, he assured me, which is seldom enforced and largely ignored by the regular constabulary; in fact, in places like Detroit, police officers are actually thought to be impresarios in such endeavors."

"But the law stands here, and statewide?"

"It does indeed. I find it interesting that according to Assistant Prosecutor Echo, knowing how regular police might be somewhat ambivalent about such matters, the writers of the New York laws gave specific police and enforcement power for such crimes to the American Society for the Prevention of Cruelty to Animals, not to the regular police. The Michigan law makes no such special provision for the ASPCA, and thus enforcement here is solely in the domain of peace officers of various jurisdictions."

Bapcat tried to process what he was hearing, but Zakov kept talking.

"Our good friend Roland Echo believes rather strongly that deputy state game wardens should consider this law to be in our purview and portfolio."

"Rollie thinks we could enforce the law?"

"*Should*, not could, and it is a misdemeanor; however, if the number of counts or severity warrant, it can be increased to a felony."

"Thinks ain't the same as how it is," Bapcat said. "What about Clewd?"

"Ah, yes, Beaumont Clewd, gentleman by declaration, but it seems he's rather a thug by nature. The Roman god Mercury was the patron of merchants, and thieves, an odd yet somehow suitable coupling. I quickly found where his men repair to for their post-labor libations, and there I myself listened, and the barmaid, I would add, volunteered to assist me. The organization is indeed building the devices you inquired about, and they are openly referring to them as bear-catchers," the Russian said. "Knowing this, I went to see Mr. Clewd and showed him my badge, whereupon he attacked me with a cane, which I quickly relieved him of, holding him on the floor outside his gaudy office with my boot on this throat.

"His people summoned Cruse's minions, who ordered me to release the man, and Big Jim himself came along in full puff and threatened me with arrest for harassment and trespass if there was a repeat of the incident. Interestingly, when we got outside, he put his fat arm around my shoulders and said, 'Find a way to do your job that don't piss off the city's leading citizens, and you might tell that to your partner, too.' And then he waddled away."

"Clewd—traps?"

"He stated his company's business in plain terms, and I quote: 'Ain't nobody's bloody concern but the owners,' of which there is but one—Himself. I'm quite sure he capitalizes the H."

"How'd you read that?"

"The trap manufacture is a fact, but the man will never talk about it unless compelled by a law and a court, and even then I suspect he will resist and fight by all legal means."

"You had your boot on his neck, really?"

"Like most ruffians, he is unschooled and under the false impression that bluster will override skill, which it will not, and did not. You should call the Widow Frei and smooth any ruffled feathers."

"Why should her feathers be ruffled? You're the one making her threats at *me*. I will thank you to keep your own counsel. That's how you'd put it to me, right?"

"Accurate and succinct, as always," the Russian said.

"The barmaid who volunteered. Care to explain those circumstances a bit more?"

"I decline with courtesy," Zakov said.

"She one of them flesh barmaids with double employment, one downstairs and another upstairs?"

"Very possibly; in fact, quite probably. Your acumen in logic is sharpening."

Deputy State Game Warden Pinkhus Sergeyevich Zakov had a taste for what he called a certain class of professional women.

"Thank you," Bapcat said. "Let Rollie Echo know we would appreciate his taking a deeper look at the law, and see if he can pin down what game wardens might and ought to do when they come up against such situations."

"*Is* such a case under consideration?" Zakov asked.

"It could be if I can figure out how to put all the pieces together." Knowing who was to get the cages, and where and when, seemed to him to be the most critical things to know now in order to weigh any future actions. He wondered, too, if Deputy Warden Farrell Mackley would turn up in this thing once it all got sorted and lined up. Finding him was, after all, the original goal in this complicated mess.

Bapcat told Jone Gleann what he had learned and she beamed happily. "Aha! There *are* laws to prevent cruelty to animals," she said.

"There's a law preventing animal fighting, but I ain't seen it, and don't know exactly what it means or says, or if there's more than fighting in it. People who write laws are real vague at times—on purpose, I'm guessing."

"It's a start," the woman said. "It even somewhat refreshes my faith in our lawmaking system."

"I need to talk to Nick Vedder," he reminded her. "Soon."

"Already arranged for the day after tomorrow. Perhaps you can ride Joe, to test your back muscles. Shall we bathe?"

He was shocked. "So them boys can *watch*?"

"Well, I am a teacher," she said with a gleam in her eye. "What a lesson we might impart, eh?"

"I ain't imparting nothing," Bapcat said, remembering Zakov's vivid description of Jaquelle Frei's mood.

# PART II: TRAP HILLS

This is a queer country, and a stumbling block to world-makers. Its features and construction would almost warrant the belief that it was made by another hand from the rest of the common footstool, and that the Evil One had a hand in the matter. Anyway, it is a cold, sterile region . . . and the country is bleak, barren and savage without any signs of civilization or cultivation except bed-bugs and whiskey; rats and cockroaches have not yet come up but are expected. It is the land of dirty shirts and long beards. Everyone tries to look as wild and boorish as possible, and far more than is in any way agreeable.

This country is undoubtedly immensely rich in mineral treasure. All the statements you have seen in the newspapers are true, and yet nineteen-twentieths of the whole speculation will be a total failure. Further, there is no doubt but that a small part of the valuable deposits is all that has yet been seen by mortal eyes, covered as it is with drift and the most impenetrable growth of cedar, spruce and tamarac [sic]. Nothing short of clairvoyance will discover it. . . . There is not a spear of grass on a whole eternity of country, and an ox or an ass, turned out, would starve, unless he could feed on pine shadows and moss.
—*1846 letter to editor of* Buffalo *(New York)* Morning Express

CHAPTER 19

*Flintsteel River*

FRIDAY, JULY 10

"We'll make an early start," the woman had told him last night.

"We?"

"Vedder's edgy, and having second thoughts about what he told me in confidence."

"Where's the meet?"

"He has a fishing cabin camp where Monehan Creek flows into the Flintsteel."

"That's too general. Tell me where, exactly."

"I can show you," she said.

"Tell me anyways," he came back. "I like to know details. My mind needs maps."

She sighed dramatically. "If you follow the road you came out on from Ontonagon, you will cross a bridge. It was wood until four years ago when it was replaced with cement. That construction work opened the area to a number of trails around there. The trestle is built where the river bends like the bottom of a nose in profile, and the Monehan dumps into a nostril, an eighth of a mile upstream. Is that specific enough for your needs?"

"Where's the source water for the creek?"

"North of the Ontonagon Road, about two miles southeast of the road you'll use to cross it, but the easiest way to Vedder's camp is to climb down at the trestle and walk the good trail upriver."

"Any maps?"

This time she gave a squinty, questioning look, but answered, "Yes."

"Mind if I take a look?"

"As I said, there's no need. I know the way."

"Still, I would like to look at that map myself," he said.

She fetched it and he'd spread it out. The mining outfit called Bohemian had created the map before the century's turn, and someone had penciled in some changes since. "This scale trustworthy?" he asked.

"Yes."

"Which creek is Monehan?"

She pointed with her pinkie.

"Five miles northwest of Greenland," he said, calculating it was farther if he followed Monehan directly and came to the man's camp from above rather than from below. "Have you seen the camp?"

"I have. We take the children there to fish on occasion."

"Vedder selected the meeting place?"

"Indeed he did."

"Describe Vedder for me."

She sighed again. "Fastidious and orderly, bachelor, Episcopalian, thinker, planner, prim and proper, and an enthusiastic angler of the fly. He has a beard as thick and black as a bear's fur."

"You two are friends?"

"What are you getting at?"

"Friends?"

"He has no children, but helps pay subscriptions because he believes in the power of schooling."

"You won't be going," he announced. "There's no need."

"Reality and maps often differ dramatically," she said. "We have an agreement."

"You may know the hills, but finding people in the woods is what we wardens do."

"I doubt he will talk without me there," she said.

"I guess I'll chance it."

She had neither agreed nor disagreed. She had simply walked away from him and he had taken off on foot right after midnight. By first light he had a watching place in boulders above the camp, which was no more than a crudely built trapper's shack, a lean-to against the side of the hill, directly beneath him. It had a rusted metal roof, which blended into the brown pine duff that littered the steep ground.

Situated where it was on the east bank of the river, Bapcat guessed the sun would reach it just before noon. But early on, two men came out of the cabin. He could smell smoke, imagined bacon too, wanted hot coffee in the worst way, but pushed away his cravings. When he had to, he could go days without eating, and he was surprised the Russian was the same. Zakov loved good food, but he had the inner means to starve with a purpose.

*Two men, not one, and the creek and river both still high from snowmelt.* The game warden's wary mind churned with possibilities. Both men carried sidearms and talked little. After a while, one man stepped down to the river, crossed to the far side, and waded slowly upstream, unfurling his fly line and beginning the silent, rhythmic casting motion that Bapcat had always found beautiful, as near to art as his mind ever stretched.

The second man, with the long black beard, stepped down to the river and remained there, looking around. Vedder, he guessed. He wished he could have gotten a better look at the other man, but he was apparently not the stand-and-watch sort that many fly men tended to be.

Bapcat snaked his way downhill through the rocks and downed logs and got behind the man, who had yet to cast.

"Mr. Vedder?"

The man turned slowly, his face expressionless. "I am, and who be you?"

"Deputy State Game Warden Bapcat."

"Pleasure," the man said. "I expected Miss Jone."

"School business," Bapcat lied. "She sends her apologies."

"None needed," the man said. "I didn't expect a meeting until midday— hoped to entertain you with a meal of fresh squaretail."

"I don't want to interfere with your fishing."

"Morning is rarely a hatch time, but I watch and hope. I expect that's the core of an angler, watching and hoping."

"There's nothing like fishing alone for trout," Bapcat said.

"Might you be an angler of the fly?"

"Upstream, and dries only," he said, which was true in intent, if not fact. He rarely got to fish, with flies or by any other means.

"Yes, simplicity is purity, our gift from our Maker have we the sense to recognize it. Familiar with these waters?"

"No, sir."

"Fine brook trout, occasional fat rainbows, a bounty for man's judicious use and pleasure. God gave us all of this and instructed us to use it wisely. I'm certain a legitimate game warden understands that finer point."

"Do you know Farrell Mackley?"

"Only in town, never out here. In fact, none of my brother anglers report seeing him on this river—or any river, for that matter. Is that normal for your kind?"

"Every county is different," Bapcat said candidly, "though this is a little odd."

"*Irresponsible* is the word that comes into my mind," Vedder said.

*Time for business.* "You came to Miss Jone with certain information."

"I provided her a prototype, if you will."

"Jone says you've gone squeamish on this."

"It ebbs and flows as I weigh loyalty to my employer against loyalty to my profession. Do you understand the fine line I am attempting to delineate?"

"Game wardens feel something like that nearly every day."

Vedder stared hard at him. "I take your words as heartfelt truth."

"Yes, sir."

"Natural-colored flies?" the man asked.

"Yarn mostly, with a small feather post on top. I can't see very well without the feather."

"A feather post," the man said. "Very interesting. Different color than the yarn?"

"Sometimes, but it ain't necessary. It's the profile my eye needs."

"You have profound knowledge," the man said. In truth Bapcat's knowledge was close to exhausted.

"Natural hatch man myself," Vedder said.

*He's testing me, feeling me out. Why? Time to turn it around.*

"You said you're here alone?"

Vedder looked away. "I assume you know differently," the man said. "My clerk Brimley shares my passion and avocation. I respect your professionalism, Deputy, your restraint. One of your forerunners was not so discerning in social contacts or graces."

"I'm sorry to hear that." *It's real odd how all you need to get people talking is to give them a little time and silence.*

"No need to be sorry; he wasn't fit for either the time or the place. Half-Indian called Gray Lark. Lived carnally with four wanton squaws, two of them white women. Public servants and business leaders are honor-bound to respectability, to putting appearance and reality into proper order and harmony."

"Game wardens don't like to come into anything blind," Bapcat said. "We like to look first, then act."

"A sound operating principle."

"The traps are being made in Houghton?"

"Yes. I myself placed the initial purchase order with specifications."

"Including delivery date?"

"No," Vedder said. "I placed the order, but Mr. Archibald subsequently took over the project."

"Any idea when or where the traps will be delivered?"

"Only Archibald knows."

"If you hear a date, could you get in touch with me through Miss Jone?"

"You may count on it. Would you care for coffee? I predict no hatch this morning."

Bapcat made a sniffing sound. "No thanks on the coffee. Warmer, heavier air will bring the hatches."

"Indeed it will. Contact you directly?" the man asked.

"I'm out and about. Miss Jone will know my whereabouts."

"It shall be done," the man declared, and Bapcat had no reason to disbelieve him.

The game warden made a point of departing upriver, but quickly climbed up and circled the camp to the downriver side where he descended when he was beyond Vedder's sight. He moved through the woods until he saw a man in the river, netting a fish and releasing it.

"Is it Elphinstone or is it Brimley?" Bapcat called over from shore, giving the man a start.

"Where did *you* come from?"

"Came out of the vapor."

The man smiled. "As regards name, both or either, depending on circumstances."

"With me?"

"Elphinstone, if you please. Better, Phin."

"Why not that name all the time?"

"Never warn the enemy an attack is at hand. Surprise is essential, don't you know."

*Is the man balmy? He's wearing a helmet of the kind Colonel Roosevelt called a* topee, *which the Colonel classified as tosh, or foolishness in most circumstances.* "You are Mr. Vedder's clerk."

"His *clark indeed*, as befits a proper Britisher, but I'm here in the Colonies, and 'major factotum' would be more accurate, both here on the river, and at my place of employment."

"Vedder tells me Archibald had him place an order for special large animal traps."

"Yes, I prepared the papers myself."

"But without a delivery date, and now Archibald handles the details."

"What Mr. Archibald knows, so too does his clerk, Mr. Brimley."

"Mr. Brimley knows when and where said traps will be delivered?"

"Knows indeed, at least in part. The delivery is to be in Silver City at the mouth of the Iron River, by watercraft."

"When in Silver City?"

"Alas, that detail is in reserve for later."

"Is there a way to find out?"

"Brimley is ethically constrained from such activity."

"Nary a constraint," the curious man said. "Are you still at the school in Lake Mine?"

"I am for now."

"When secured, I will come to you with the details."

"When might that be?"

"I lack the credentials for seer or oracle. It will be as soon as it can be, and not a moment later."

"A week?"

"Only God knows."

Bapcat climbed his way back to the road and returned to the school, where he saw Jone Gleann that night.

"Success?" she asked.

"Depends on your definition" is all he said.

# CHAPTER 20

*Lake Mine*

TUESDAY, JULY 14

Bapcat had been off talking to Mac, who was regaling him with all sorts of stories about people in surrounding towns. Jone Gleann brought him a message she said was urgent. Roland Echo needed Bapcat to call him back. She showed him to the room with the telephone.

When he finally got through, a voice answered, "Echo."

"Lute calling."

"Thanks for calling back so quickly. I talked at some length with the attorney general's office in Lansing. They confirm that animal fighting is illegal and a misdemeanor, which can be increased to a felony, depending on the situation. They also told me that anyone involved, including spectators, may and should be arrested. As for the sale of wildlife, the AG's men promise to look into that, and asked me to tell you that you have raised an interesting and intriguing legal question, deserving of serious study."

"Good."

"Listen to me, Lute: I know that you're on a mission over there, to find that missing deputy, but the attorney general just called me and told me that the state is going to appoint you as a special AG investigator. The AG told me of a man named Heinrich Junger, also known as Henry Young and—."

"Hank the Shank," Bapcat said, wondering how it was that old history never lay dead, somehow always seemed to turn up at the worst times. Back in his army days he had made an enemy of a Rough Rider sergeant named Frankus Fish, whom he had thrashed when the NCO threatened a soldier with a skinning knife. Last year, a decade after those events, Fish had shown up in the Keweenaw as a strike-breaking detective, and had been killed by an unlikely shot from a small-caliber pistol wielded by one of the main strike-fighters among mining company men. Fish and two other men had been in the process—thankfully, not completed—of eliminating the man who had triggered the Italian Hall disaster, apparently as a prank done on mine operators' orders, or manipulation.

*Now Hank the Shank? Is this how my future will be?*

Echo paused. "Uh, yes, but my note says he's Hank the Shank—that's the name I wrote down. The AG has reason to believe you and this man were together as boys at St. Cazimer's."

They had been, and it was anything but a pleasant memory. "I knew him."

"Good; excellent. Mr. Junger apparently left St. Cazimer's soon after your own departure. The AG told me his office has incontrovertible evidence of the man's involvement in at least one murder during the recent strike."

"I haven't seen him since the orphanage, Rollie. I haven't even heard his name until today, and for sure not during the strike." The red-haired Young had been called Shank because he invariably carried a knife. He bullied younger children and more than a few adults, and was forever starting fights and fires, and torturing animals. Bapcat had been nine when he came upon Young dousing puppies with kerosene and setting them on fire. His anger had exploded. He had grabbed an oak stave and broken both of the boy's arms and was moving in on his head when other kids from the institution pulled him away and disarmed him. He couldn't abide anyone abusing someone or something with little power. Henry never came near him again.

"Junger was here briefly as a hired gun, but left the state before the strike ended. It appears that he winters in far southwest Ontario near Fort St. Francis, and has put together a gang of thugs there. They steal as many furs as they trap for themselves, and are wanted for murders, robberies, arsons, and rapes in Canada, Minnesota, and Wisconsin. And now this murderer is thought to be in Michigan. The AG calls his intelligence 'extremely reliable,' and this source claims Junger spends some summers cavorting somewhere up in the Porkies. By all accounts, lawmen over that way have shown less than minimal enthusiasm for pursuing or confronting him."

Bapcat felt his stomach tightening.

"The AG orders you to find and arrest the man and any associates with him, and to deliver said prisoners to the Gogebic County sheriff in Ironwood, from where said prisoners will be extradited to Minnesota for prosecution. This order takes precedence over your Conservation Department mission. The AG will authorize you and provide funds to retain a posse for this purpose. Judge Maxim Edson in Ironwood will swear you in by telephone, and empower you to appoint deputies. Am I making this clear?"

"You are, and I ain't liking it one damn bit. I don't work for the attorney general."

"You do now, at least temporarily, and your own leadership has signed off on this. They will formally notify you in due course to alter your assignment. Lute, Junger is extremely dangerous, and you are authorized to use any and all force necessary in order to apprehend. Understand?"

"Yes."

"I'm sorry to be the one to drop this on your shoulders. Questions?"

"Where the hell in the Porkies is he supposed to be? This area is pretty damn big, Rollie."

"The AG has confidence in your ability to find the man and do your duty for the people of the State of Michigan."

"Hell, Rollie, I ain't even found a lead to Farrell Mackley yet."

"You will, Lute. Get a pencil for Judge Edson's number and call him this afternoon. He's waiting by the telephone with his Bible in hand."

Bapcat took down the number and called the judge in Ironwood. "Deputy State Game Warden Bapcat, calling as instructed, Your Honor."

"You clear on your assignment, Bapcat?"

"Yes, sir."

"Excellent. Now repeat after me . . ."

His next act was to dictate a telegram to his supervisor, Horri Harju. He wrote carefully and quickly, read it aloud, and gave it to his dogsbody, with instructions to get it on the wire fast. Mac took off like a hound on a rabbit's ass.

Bapcat then placed a call to Zakov and brought him up to date.

"You want me down there?" the Russian asked immediately.

"I sent a telegram to Horri telling him I'm pulling you down to help me."

"What happens if we are both gone from our territory?"

"We report to Horri, which makes it his problem to solve."

Jone Gleann came into the room as he hung up. "Are you all right?"

"I ain't at all sure," he confessed.

"Need someone to talk to?"

"Only if he's got a crystal ball in his lap."

"May I recommend you try God?"

"That's never much worked for me."

"Don't give up," she said.

*Find Mackley and Hank the Shank? Where? It would be almost laughable if it wasn't so daunting. Junger was the kind of man who had lifelong get-evens tattooed inside his tiny brain.*

Bapcat looked at the woman, shook his head, and grimaced.

# CHAPTER 21

## Lake Mine

### WEDNESDAY, JULY 22

Roland Echo had been calling every day and not hiding his anxieties. "I am sending twenty AG special investigator badges to you by messenger on a train."

"Rollie, I don't need more than a few—a half-dozen at the most."

"Junger's outfit is estimated at twenty to forty guns."

"Force size matters only if your people and the force itself are well trained, and regularly. A few skilled men can always manage a poorly trained or untrained larger crowd."

The Houghton man said, "I don't know, Lute—twenty to forty guns sounds like a lot of firepower to me."

"Can be if it's coordinated, but not so much without discipline." Which they had plenty of on the San Juan Heights. "Why're you so dang jumpy, Rollie?"

"I'm not jumpy; I'm just exercising due caution, and here I would remark most emphatically that this is a military mission with top political support, and so forth."

"Dammit, Rollie, this *ain't* a military mission; it's strictly *civilian* law enforcement. See, if this were military, we'd be in uniforms, and the other side—well, those jamokes would be in their costumes, and a war would be declared, legal and proper. Our countries being legally and morally at war, we'd each side be required to attempt to kill everyone in the enemy's uniform—on sight. We could tell each other apart with no more than a glance, and because we were officially at war, we could commence to killing each other as soon as our eyeballs locked on the other side.

"Policemen can't do that, Rollie. We ain't at war. We're carrying a court warrant for one name, and we've got to find and identify that fellow, and if he gets owly or uncooperative, well, it could get rough and bloody, I'll grant you that. Point is, police can't go wading in like soldiers with guns blazing."

"I recognize and accept the distinction. I do not have to like it," the lawyer said.

"Nobody likes it but the bad guys. However, the law's the law, and that's what we swear to uphold."

"Off the record, Lute—way off it—if you happen to bring Junger in folded over a saddle, there ain't gonna be many questions asked."

Bapcat couldn't believe what he was hearing. "The AG ordered me to arrest the man, Rollie, not execute him."

"I wouldn't be so sure about that, Lute. I think more than anything, the AG wants shed of the problem, and however said erasure transpires he will not parse facts with much precision or enthusiasm, much less interest."

"I ain't traipsing way up in them woods to kill that man, Rollie. Hell, chances of us even finding him ain't spit in a cattle trough."

"Just take care of yourself and that Russian. He get there yet?"

"Come in last night riding a brown horse looks stole from a glue factory."

Echo laughed and hung up.

Zakov was sitting across from him and said, "My steed's feelings are bruised by your commentary."

"That horse looks like he'd run from a butterfly."

"Prince is stout of heart."

"You named that pathetic nag Prince?"

"You named yours Joe. How pathetic and plebian is *that*," Zakov countered before shifting to a more serious tone. "Have we a host here, or have you commandeered the school for the State?"

"Woman runs the school and still does. We're her guests."

"Ah," the Russian said, "a hostess at our beck and call."

"Schoolmarm, not one of your professional kootches. Further, she will be going with us," Bapcat added.

The Russian seemed startled. "To what end if not a camp follower?"

"Scout—and until we find Mackley and/or Junger, she will be, in fact, the expedition leader."

"I must protest," the Russian said. "Her field skills cannot possibly equal ours."

"Could be hers are better, and, more to the point, she knows the ground."

Zakov exhaled dramatically. "I bow to your judgment," he said. "Is she at least pleasing to look at?"

"Some would say so," Jone Gleann said, stepping into the room, "but I leave meaningless evaluations to men. I am Jone."

"Pinkhus Sergeyevich Zakov," the Russian said, standing and bowing dramatically.

"Bapcat here assured me that despite your foppish manner, you are a competent and serious individual. From first impressions I cannot possibly see how this can be true, but I will defer to Deputy Bapcat until I can see and verify for myself."

"You will not be disappointed, madam," Zakov told her.

"Nor shall you be, sir," the woman said.

"Surly and combative, and prideful—all fine qualities in a fighting man," Zakov said when she was gone. "And quite easy on the eyes, as well."

"She's a woman, not a fighting man."

"When the guns fire she becomes a fighting man by definition and presence. Do we have the slightest notion where our quarry might be?"

"Not a drop of an idea."

"This woman, you and me—this constitutes our force?"

"Jimjim and Scale give us five, and there might be a sixth, but we'll call us five at the starting line."

"Facing?"

"An estimated twenty to forty."

"Sounds reasonable," Zakov said.

"We're intending to bring back two prisoners, alive."

"Even Mr. Farrell Mackley, our erstwhile colleague?"

"If we find him and he can convince us he has had a good reason for being lost so long, he can join up with us. If not, he goes along in restraints, same as Junger."

"Does a colleague not deserve the so-called benefit of the doubt?" Zakov asked.

"If either of us had even met the man, I might allow you've got a point, but from what I've gathered so far from folks hereabouts, the man wasn't much at doing the job the State paid him to do."

"The situation regarding the traps—how stands that thread?"

"I have a source trying to get us the delivery date and such."

"When do we commence this epic sortie?"

"I guess when Jone says."

"Even if your source has not yet provided critical information?"

"Even if."

"But our main objective is Junger."

"Until we know where he is, we stay with Jone Gleann. She knows the bush better than anyone here, I'm told. If Junger's out there and making trouble, I expect we'll hear, one way or another."

# CHAPTER 22

## *Finn Town*

### THURSDAY, JULY 23

Most of the hills had been denuded by mining companies' insatiable need for timber shoring, and the sharply angled hillsides were dotted with clusters of mining buildings and superstructures, which reminded Bapcat of drawings of castles he'd seen as a kid.

The area here looked no different than it did from their cabin in Allouez on Bumbletown Hill, where he and his Russian partner lived on a bedrock mound, just east of a steep cliff. Down below was one of the last stands of mature trees in the area. No doubt the mines would take those trees one day, as well.

The desolation brought by so-called progress made the deputy game warden wonder what kind of future life he'd be leading. Telephones were replacing telegraphs and letter writing. Wagons and horses were being replaced by gasoline-powered motorcars and trucks. And kerosene and candles were being made useless by electricity, especially in towns. Here in Ontonagon County, with the future of mines somewhat doubtful because of deposits out west, farmers were coming in and taking down trees the mine companies had missed in order to make fields in which to plant crops, which struck Bapcat as strange. What the hell could grow up here in such a short growing season? Look at this year; it was still snowing in June.

But the rate of change seemed unstoppable and unending. Bapcat tried not to dwell on such things because it was all too much for him to process, and he needed to stay focused. In this job, a drifting mind could get you seriously hurt, or killed. Yet, he wondered, did change always mean better? Somehow he doubted it.

He had no ideas, and pulled his mind back to the job at hand.

McIlrath and several other children had appeared to see them off as the group departed from the school before first light. The Russian had said to the boy, "Do your father and mother not care where you are?"

"Not when they don't know," the boy said. "They've got eight of us at home, so they ain't so petic'lar about watchin' any one of us all that close." Mac lifted his hand and waved. "See youse soon!"

Zakov asked his partner, "What does he mean by soon?"

"Nothing; it's just an American saying."

The column skirted Mass City and angled downhill and southwest, paralleling the Mining Road up on the high ridge, where most of the mines were dug, their superstructures a silhouette against a blue sky.

Riding in column reminded Bapcat of his cavalry days, long, twisting columns of sweating troopers and stinking horses, strung out over the trail, equipment clicking and clacking and leather moaning, saddles groaning under their weight and the mounts' movements, a hubbub of snorts and neighs, men and animals farting and hacking from dust, and mules braying and the searing stench of fresh plops pinching all nostrils, and all around them the aggressive buzz of fly armadas following in swarms so large they made black clouds.

Gleann had them ford the Ontonagon River south of Rockland, and turn back to the northwest to climb back to the heights, drifting eventually past the village and mine of Victoria, and walking on to the west into Finn Town, a village of perhaps a hundred stubborn wood-frame houses and one whitewashed public bathhouse, the town sauna, which Jimjim pointed out as they passed through because almost all the signs were in Finnish, an alphabet and language Bapcat couldn't easily identify, much less translate.

"Are you certain you are up to this?" Zakov asked Jimjim.

"Is that a remark on my size?" the dwarf yelled back, bristling.

"I refer to the thirty-two you carry. Are you expecting the opposition to be rats and cats?"

"A thirty-two round in an elephant's eye is as lethal as a cannon."

"This contention is purely speculative, and I harbor doubts of its verisimilitude," the Russian said.

"You can't speak proper American English, get one of them interpreters."

"That *is* proper English," Zakov said.

"Not to me it ain't," the dwarf retorted.

"You ever notice how some folks won't let silence be?" Scale asked Bapcat.

"Ain't you the one just broke the silence we had?" Bapcat challenged.

Scale sputtered, then sulked.

Jone Gleann halted and looked back at Bapcat. "Girls are sometimes women and women are sometimes little girls, but men are forever little boys. Do you not find that a curious phenomenon, psychologically?"

"I guess I ain't never give much thought on it," Bapcat admitted, which was true, and was not about to change. Out on the trail he liked to keep his mind clear for the business at hand, not foolish speculations and building air castles and other such nonsense.

"And likely won't think about it hereafter either," Zakov chimed in.

"Why Finn Town?" Bapcat asked their sortie leader.

"A good livery here. The next town is ten or twelve miles on, and it's mostly vertical from here to there. The mules and horses and their riders will all be tested. If we need to replace mounts, we'll know by Gleason Creek Falls, and, if necessary, I will come back here for replacement mounts and return by a flatter route to the south to catch up with the group in Norwich."

Each of them had more than one animal. Bapcat had his mules; Zakov rode a horse and led a mule. Scale had two horses, Jimjim rode a pony and led a small mule, and Jone rode a mule and led six pack mules loaded with gear, including two with wooden panniers filled with canvas foldable buckets, but when asked their purpose, she smiled and kept riding.

Fifteen animals in all, eleven of them mules, and on this first day they had all been cooperative and steady, which was all one could hope for. Back in the Dakotas during his army days, Bapcat had ridden many a horse that would panic at the sight of a yellow butterfly, or the sounds of the voices in the animal's thick head, and immediately shift to all-out, no-holds-barred panic run or bucking spree. It seemed all horses had damn demons in their heads or hearts because all of them were prone to unpredictable behavior. Mules were a lot calmer and more predictable. And, unlike horses, they were thinkers, which made them safer. Even Colonel Roosevelt in his ranch days sometimes turned glassy-eyed when the boys gave him a new cayuse to mount.

Gleann directed them to the base of a precipice west of the village and they set up camp. Bapcat kept looking up, wondering if it was as bad as it looked. As darkness fell and they were settling into their bedrolls and saddle pillows, a blonde woman rode loudly into camp and dismounted, raining a cloud of dust on everyone. Well over six feet tall, wide-faced, young, her hair shorn short like a man's, and brushed over with a sweep. She wore denim overalls and knee-high leather hunting boots.

"Horses over there," Jone Gleann told the new arrival. "Bed wherever you want. Gentlemen, meet Rinka Isohultamaki. She is joining the expedition."

Both Scale and Jimjim muttered drowsy greetings and she nodded, unsaddled, put her mount and pack horse with the others, and spread her bedroll and saddle near Bapcat.

"I'm no talker," she told him, settling in.

"Me neither," he said.

She sat up. "My remark did not require acknowledgment. Are you *thick*?" she said peckishly.

"Probably," Bapcat answered.

"Jone, what is the man's problem?"

"Thick, as you surmise."

"How do you make it stop talking?" the new arrival asked.

"Just ignore it," Jone said.

"For the record," Bapcat said softly, "you're the one doing most of the talking."

Which caused her to relocate nearer to the Russian, and the camp finally settled down, save the usual sounds of night animals and a robust snore from Scale.

Gleann had not mentioned the Isohultamaki woman. She looked to be twenty, maybe younger, and physically imposing. Reminded him of an etching he'd seen of St. Joan of Arc when he was a boy, the saint all trussed to a pole and flames licking at her legs while her face was absolute serenity. He never did figure out why the woman got herself burned, or was so dang calm about it.

The thing was, he had been surprised by Colonel Roosevelt's leadership. That is, the Colonel had never allowed his command to be surprised. He kept the men informed and up to date on everything—where they were going, when and how, and what lay ahead when they arrived. And he didn't sugarcoat problems, either. By contrast, Jone Gleann said virtually nothing, leaving all of them to their own imaginations, which in Bapcat's experience could be a lot worse than the reality ahead. But she was in charge, not Bapcat. *Is the new girl supposed to be deputized along with the others? Have to ask Jone in the morning, or during a pause on the trail.*

"Why two legs on this leg?" Bapcat whispered to Gleann.

"These particular hills are extremely steep and not so rider-friendly."

It was not an answer to his question.

"Are you two going to blabber all night?" the new girl asked with a snarl.

"She wasn't part of our agreement," Bapcat told Gleann.

"Now she is," the leader declared. "Sleep."

Bapcat found his eyes flickering and saw a reddish-brown dog walk past the campfire, just off in the distance by the dark line, but it didn't register until much later that the animal had no right hind leg.

# CHAPTER 23

## *Whiskey Holding Creek*

### FRIDAY, JULY 24

Early the next morning, as they labored all the way up to the first summit and were following the winding trail down the other side, Joe suddenly stopped and stared ahead. Bapcat leaned forward to see what the mule was looking at. It seemed the animal was considering a loose rock area that cut straight down to where the switchback trail hairpinned back directly below them. The animal snorted softly and put a foot forward. Bapcat felt his stomach roll, but Joe had shown so far that he knew best.

"Okay," he told the mule. "It's your call here."

The next thing he knew, they were sliding downhill almost vertically, and Bapcat dropped Kukla's lead to let her decide whether to follow or not. Joe had his front legs stuck stiffly out in front of him and his back legs gathered beneath them as they slid along the loose rock like it was ice.

When they approached the first trail crossing, Joe lifted his head, brayed softly, straightened his hind legs, and they settled onto the trail as easily as could be, the mule's head pointed down the next stretch of trail. Bapcat looked up to see Kukla arriving behind them in a similar slide. He dismounted, picked up her lead, and patted both animals' noses. "That's a fine hobby you two have, but give us a little more warning before we go sliding again, all right?" Joe bared his teeth in a grin, Bapcat remounted, and they moved on downward ahead of the others, who remained on the winding trail and fell behind him by several minutes.

Gleann halted the expedition at Gleason Creek Falls, announced they had come eight miles and would stop the night here. "We can slip through Norwich tomorrow morning. There's a sheer bluff face to climb first thing tomorrow. The mine's on ahead about a mile or so after we get up top. We just came down five hundred feet or so from the last peak, and this won't be quite so much climbing back up."

"Fish in this creek?" Zakov asked.

"None edible," the Finnish girl said, one of the few times she had bothered to speak all day, and this statement suggested to Bapcat that she'd been here before.

Bapcat volunteered to cook, but Gleann told him Zakov and Scale would take it tonight. The Russian and the black man seemed comfortable with each other, but their culinary skills were not. While the Russian adored eating, his cooking was on the poor side. Tonight: potatoes, beans, biscuits, coffee and tea. Scale had done most of the work.

Gleann sat with Bapcat as he scraped his tin plate. "Fine so far," she said. "The animals are solid, and that mule of yours borders on spectacular. I do believe he enjoyed his slide."

"He seemed to. Where to after Norwich?"

"We'll keep west about twelve miles or so, and angle on north for Deer Creek Falls."

"After that?"

"Rendezvous and bivouac."

"We're meeting someone? Who?"

"You'll see when we get there."

"I don't much care for how you lead," he said.

"Nor me much for how you follow," she shot back. Her voice softened. "You understand there's different ways to make love, yes?"

He stared at her. "What the heck does *that* have to do with *this*?"

"How you get where you're going isn't nearly as important as getting there."

Bapcat thought about that and decided she was right. And odd. Very, very odd, and she had a way of getting inside your head.

"You got the map?" he asked. "I want to see. We've got business, and it don't feel like we're doing much about it."

She fetched a canvas sack from her kit and rolled it out, using her pinkie as a pointer. "These here are the Trap Hills, where we are now, and they keep on for some time. Northwest and north are the Porkies. The biggest concentration of bears tends to be up here in the Elm Creek, Little Iron River area, especially in late summer and early fall. Flats there will be filled with chokecherries and several nearby hills loaded with oaks and acorns. Bears there for sure. And that, of course, may turn out to be nothing, right?"

"I've got no idea where Young might be—or Mackley either, for that matter." *And no word yet from Elphinstone,* he thought, keeping this to himself.

"Listen," she said, pointing at the map, "the way I see it, the best place to deliver the traps would be Silver City. From there it's six or so miles south to White Pine, then two miles west to the Little Iron River, and the Nonesuch Mine, which once had three hundred people and a school and now is just a shell. But it's a good place to work from—leastways, that would be my thinking if I was the one doing the planning."

"I guess that makes some sense." He *knew* that the load was likely to be landed in Silver City, so this now made even more sense. But he kept this to himself, too. He should be looking for Mackley and Young, yet his gut kept telling him to stay with his hunch on the bears—that somehow, as unlikely and preposterous as it seemed, it all fit together.

"It's a true comfort to have your blessing," Gleann said sarcastically.

"There looks to be more direct routes to that area," Bapcat said. "And flatter routes to boot."

"Deer Creek Falls first, and after that, it's all your business," she said. "We reach Deer Creek, you and the Russian might want to take a jaunt down to Bergland, see if any of the folks down there know anything about the missing deputy. You and Zakov can meet the rest of us at our destination."

Why Bergland? Did she know something he didn't? If so, it evened out because he'd not told her about Silver City.

# CHAPTER 24

## *Bergland*

SATURDAY, JULY 25

It was a relatively unchallenging eight-mile ride south to Bergland. With their pack animals left with the group, the two deputy game wardens made good time, but Lute Bapcat found himself thinking about nothing except why Jone Gleann had suggested this side trip. *Does Jone know something, after all, about Mackley's whereabouts, and if so, why is she holding back? And what? She's impossible to figure out.* It no longer puzzled him how Indian and his wife could have differing opinions of her. She was that kind of mysterious person.

Gleann told him Bergland had been a major logging town for a decade or so, but it now looked less than prosperous. For the most part there were more languages in earshot than English: Finnish, German, Swedish, Zakov reported matter-of-factly, languages being among his many specialties. Bapcat felt himself mired in the most basic English and still struggled to read, though he was feeling improvement in speed, understanding, and comfort with the printed word.

The two men went into a tavern with a sign over the entry that said "Viina." They asked where to find the local justice of the peace, and were directed to Bergstrom's Hotel, where the establishment's gaunt proprietor, Thure Bergstrom, looked ancient, but possessed a young voice and energetic eyes that contradicted his facial expression.

"Ve hat a magisrade," Bergstrom said in heavily accented English, "putt he chop tree down on iss 'ead, kill 'imself. Hat six kits, und ve try take care dose kits, eh, but his vidow, she lost sa hope and hunk herself dead. Lose hope, reach for rope, dis kind tinking no stranger up here I am tinking. Dose kitts vass splitted up, send I don't know vhere. Too bad, but Gott seem sometimes play mitt pipples like cats mitt mouse, I tink. Now Bergstrom got dem JP jop too."

"Did you have any dealings with Deputy State Game Warden Mackley?"

"I guess ve don't see no demm came varden over here since I come ten year beck. Ve alvays vonder vhy dat is da vay, no came varden come, by Gott." The man chopped one hand with the edge of the other. "By Gott," he repeated.

"What about the Gogebic game warden—you know, from Gogebic County?"

"No came varden, by Gott, not from no demm county. You fellas come pick up dat circus fella vee god upstairs?"

"What circus fella might that be?" Bapcat inquired.

"Da von wat come here, got drunked, hat beek fight, stab Ole Stengel, who said circus don't treat animals so good. Circus guy cuts off Ole's ear, *och*, den Ole cut off da fella's ear, tooth for tooth, eye for eye, *och*, I guess it follow ear for ear too, by Gott! Da poys jump in, break up dat fight 'fore dose two lunkaticks cut off udder's ears, noses, who knows vat else, by Gott. Ole, he went back oop Norwich, and we got dat circus fella up dere, room six."

"Does the acting sheriff know?"

"Ve don't need dat fool down here, *och*, Herr Justice Swoon, he send telegram, say tell game vardens ven dey coom."

Bapcat was at a loss. *How could JP Teedy Swoon know where they were? Gleann said she had told no one. Did she know about this before they departed and not tell him?*

"We're not regular lawmen," Bapcat said.

"Ole say dis man hurt animals, *och*. Dat's not so right no, by Gott?"

"It's not what I like, but it's also not against the law," Bapcat told the Swede.

"Den it shoot be, by Gott," the JP-proprietor said. "Vat ve do vit dis circus fella, den?"

"Let him go, I guess. Does Mr. Ste—"

"Ole Stengel."

"Does Mr. Stengel want to press charges?"

"No, I don't tink so; he yust vant dat circus not hurt dose animals no more."

Bapcat tried to think before speaking. "Where's the circus now?"

"Hass picked up and headed vest, I tink. Got some blont koontch tell everbody vat to do and dey jump to her vord, by Gott!"

"Would you want me to talk to this circus fella?"

"*Uff da*! Ya, sure, you betcha. Got him room six, up *och* to right, Dagmar Vollmer, she sit in hall outside da room. Tell her Swoon said okay you fellas go in dere."

Bergstrom solemnly thrust a key at the game warden, and said no more.

Vollmer was a tiny woman, leaning her chair against the wall, and Bapcat found himself staring at the business end of a double-barrel shotgun as he topped the landing.

"Easy, we're the law. Swoon wants us to talk to the prisoner."

The two men showed their badges. The woman eyed him a long time before moving the gun away.

"Youse fellas gon' take this circus fella? Bergstrom's a damn cheapskate, don't pay me much ta do this job, and it's cuttin' into my earnings."

"What do you do?" Zakov asked.

Dagmar Vollmer smiled. "Whatever an agent will pay for," she said. "Got something special in mind?"

Bapcat turned away from his partner and unlocked the door to room six. It was dark, and stank inside. He announced himself, "Deputy game warden," held out his badge, stepped inside, and found himself eye to eye with Paul Pellerin, who said, "I sure never figured you for the law. Guess you won't be getting me that replacement bear."

"I don't know yet. Things like that can be arranged for the right price, but I'd guess it's a bit on the hard slog to manage a circus from a hotel room."

"Babsy's waiting for me. She knows how to ramrod the outfit. Thank God it's you. I've got to get out of here."

"Your show left town," Bapcat said.

"The hell you say!"

"The justice of the peace told me some blonde moved the outfit west."

Pellerin had a bandage covering the left side of his head, and there was dried blood on his shirt collar. "I ain't lettin' no crooked cunt whore steal my property," Pellerin growled through clenched teeth. "I catch up, she gon' get a lesson she won't soon forget."

"Temper put you in this room. You want it to keep you here, or worse?"

"I want out is what I want."

Bapcat said, "Just hold your horses. Out is possible, I think, if you don't tear out after Babs, and if you raise the price you'll pay for bears to twelve hundred each."

"This is nothing but goddamn thievery, and it ain't neither fair, nor sportin'."

"I still have to capture the animals, and now I have to make sure the locals are happy to let you loose. My expenses just went up because of you and your temper. Understand?"

Pellerin stared at him, breathing hard, obviously trying for emotional control. He was sweating, and nervously running his hand through his long black hair. "I should probably thank her. If she had followed my orders and stayed, we'd have missed our Bessemer dates, and that might have broke us financially."

Words and feigned reason aside, Bapcat could see that Pellerin was still hot, fire deep in his eyes.

"So, what's all this about, the bandage and such?"

"I don't know, and that's the God's honest truth. Man jumped in my face about bear guts and how I beat an animal to death, and if God didn't punish me, he'd do it himself. He was crazy!"

"Guts where?"

"Guy's from Norwich."

"Has the circus been to Norwich?"

"Hell no, ain't no way to get up there. So this little Kraut, he sticks his finger in my face and I wave my blade at him, you know, just to make some space. Only the fool quick-steps me, which I did not expect, and off come his damn ear, and quick as that his blade was out and my ear was gone! I don't mind telling you I thought that Kraut and me were about to butcher each other over a damn pile of bear guts, and I remember thinking, Ain't this a stupid damn way to die, chopped up by a German in Bergland. When do I get out?" Pellerin asked.

"Don't know," Bapcat said. "That's up to the law."

"Thought you *were* the law."

"Not for this I ain't."

"I'll be," the man said, but Bapcat left the room before Pellerin could say more.

Zakov and the guard were in some kind of deep discussion, and the woman's skirt was riding up, showing almost all of her leg. Bapcat ignored them and went downstairs to talk to Bergstrom.

"Your prisoner just threatened bodily harm to another circus person. I think it's just talk and he'll settle down. Were me, I'd keep him here another couple of days before I let him loose."

"Who gon' to pay da bill, by Gott?"

"Send the bill to the assistant prosecutor up in Houghton. Name is Echo. He'll make sure you're paid, and while you're at it, pay your guard what she usually earns."

"I don't know how much curl like dat she charge all dose tings she do."

"Ask her."

"My Gott, den she tink I vant pye dat service she does."

"Figure it out," Bapcat said. "Stengel—where can I find him?"

"Schoolteacher up to Norwich."

Bapcat sat outside the hotel to smoke, and eventually the Russian came ambling along. "Delightful creature," he announced, sitting down beside his partner.

"Money talks," Bapcat said.

"Don't be so quick to assume I lack the ability to attract gratis distaff attention."

"Did money change hands, or not?"

"It did indeed, and a good thing, because that poor gal's earnings were being crushed by that cheapskate Swede who runs the place."

"You did this solely to help the woman's financial situation?"

"As stated previously, she is delightful, and may I add at this juncture, exceptionally talented."

"We're heading to Norwich."

"This is your total reaction to my exquisite encounter? And more to the point, isn't Norwich taking us backward, directionally speaking?"

Bapcat walked away to fetch Joe, the Russian sputtering along behind him, mostly to himself.

# CHAPTER 25

## *Norwich*

SATURDAY, JULY 25

Stengel was easy enough to identify, being that he wore a bandage identical to Pellerin's. And it was on the same left side. As Bapcat watched the man he realized he was left-handed, whereas the circus boss was right-handed. Wouldn't a right-hander's swipe naturally take the left ear off a man facing him? By the same token, a left-hander should take a right ear, but both men's left ears were gone, which suggested that Pellerin's story of the man taking an unexpected step might be true.

"Esteemed colleague, Herr Stengel is ready to answer your questions, and you seem distracted," Zakov said, breaking through to Bapcat.

The man's head was tilted like a curious dog's.

"Sorry, Mr. Stengel. We heard about your brouhaha with the circus man. Could you explain to us exactly what happened?"

"My brother and me found a bear gut pile just up the road from where the circus show come."

"Around here?"

"No, this was over north of Bruce Crossing. Me and Karl-Heinz were on our way to Gem where we got kin, and we come upon that pile. See, last year, me and my brother went to the circus and saw a bear and what bad shape he was in, so we figured this must be the same bear, and me and Karl-Heinz went down to Bruce Crossing, only the people there said the circus moved on to Bergland, and that the show's bear died during a show. Me and Karl-Heinz was both fuming, you know? We don't hold with people hurting dumb animals, even big strong ones, nor dumb people, either. Violence don't solve nothing for the world. I guess I got over-full on righteousness, and the circus was right up the road, so me and Karl-Heinz went to find that damn owner and talk to him. I introduced myself politely, and he pulled a knife and told me, 'Don't let the door hit your ass on the way out, Kraut.'"

The man hung his head. "I guess I pulled my knife and he slashed at me, and I slashed on him, and then people broke us up and went to work stopping all the blood we made, and me and my brother come on home."

"Are you saying he assaulted you?"

"I guess he scared me some with his knife and I just wanted to defend myself."

"But he struck first?"

"Yes, sir. But it don't matter. If I wasn't there, none of that stuff would've happened, so him and me is square in my mind, and I guess we're both at fault."

"That gut pile," Bapcat said. "That's probably the one I put there when I took the skin, but if not that one, it could have been a bear somebody else legally shot."

"I know, I know; I think about all that stuff since this happened. I've had a bad temper since I was a little boy, and now look—I got one less ear. That bear was worthless; why'd youse want it?"

"Not worthless to me," the game warden said, but offered no more. He'd had in mind its potential as evidence, and he'd not thought it through, as was often the case for him. And now it dawned on him that the pelt was evidence, just as Jone had suggested, and instead of burying it, the kids led by Mac had tacked it up on boards, poured on the salt, and were cleaning the hide, which meant the skin could still serve as evidence.

"Who killed that bear?" Stengel asked.

"That is not at all certain," Bapcat said. "It seems it collapsed as the show started and died in its cage."

"No wonder—all the beatings that poor thing musta took over the years."

"That's contention, not fact," Bapcat said.

Stengel frowned. "You can split hairs. I know what I seen."

"There's no law says a man can't kill a bear any way he likes," Bapcat explained.

"Well, there damn well ought be," the man said. "Got laws to protect everything that don't need protection, like mine owners, bankers, and such." The man stopped. "How come the law lets kids go tramping around in the woods without no grown-ups to look over them?"

*Kids?* "I don't know," a suddenly weary Bapcat said. "I would have to know all the circumstances in order to answer that." He was trying his best to be cooperative and genial.

"Come yesterday morning, early, Karl-Heinz meets twenty-five tykes marchin' up the north bank of the West Branch, sticks over their shoulders, kits in a cloth ball on the end, like little soldiers marching off to war, or little hobos up to no good."

"Local children?" Zakov asked.

"Karl-Heinz never seen 'em before, and asked their leader, who refused to say. All the boy would say was that they had been ordered not to talk to strangers, and away those kids marched."

"Westward?" Zakov asked. "Is there a town in that direction?"

"Ain't nothin' but way-wild up this way," Stengel said. "I doubt they'll last without firearms, luck, or the intervention of our Lord Jesus. Karl-Heinz and I fear for children led by a boy who sounds so much like a wild turkey it makes you look around when he lets loose a yell."

*Mac*, Bapcat thought. "Do you think your brother would be so kind as to show us where he met these children?"

"*Ja wohl*—of course!"

The brother did as asked, showing the game wardens the path, and they quickly read the sign. "There are hoofprints. We thought they were just on foot."

"The leader has an ugly horse that walks behind him like a dog."

The two men mounted and headed west, Bapcat close to his partner.

"No pearls of wisdom to impart?"

"We do not take the risk to children lightly," Bapcat said, knowing full well this was mostly his personal opinion, because the miners and loggers and others in Copper Country tended to use kids without a second thought for their safety. "This doesn't happen in your country?"

The Russian said, "It happens in every country. Births are celebrated, young lives declared gifts, and sacred, and then the children are used as fodder and slaves by adults. It disgusts me."

"Two days is a long lead in this terrain," Bapcat said, "and even on horseback we can barely make walking time."

"God will decide," the Russian said.

"You suddenly believe in the Almighty?"

"No, but whether any of us believe in Him, He will do as He damn well pleases. There are times when I think He must have a special revulsion for children."

Bapcat found the Russian's words unnerving, and kept his eyes on the tracks in front of them. Why would McIlrath be leading children into the wilderness? It made no damn sense. As usual, many questions and no answers. The one good thing: A blind man could follow the horseshoe prints. The shoes were marked with deep cross-hatched etchings, like mats of straw.

# CHAPTER 26

## *White Deer Creek*

### SUNDAY, JULY 26

The children's trail led almost all the way back to Jone Gleann's camp, but when the game wardens rode in, the camp was empty, a haze of smoke lazing low over the area, and the animals pastured nearby, grazing. There were no lingering campfires, but Bapcat slid off his saddle and felt the coals. Barely warm. Neither man spoke. Over their nearly two years together they had learned to read each other in the woods, no language needed—only eyes and thoughts and a few simple hand signals.

Zakov dismounted and walked around, finally looking at Bapcat and pointing north along a low ridge. Bapcat rubbed Joe's nose, twirled his reins around a low cedar branch, and followed his partner.

The trail along the ridge passed a trickle of waterfall and descended into a small valley covered with pools of the blackest water, a damp morning dew leaving reindeer lichen soft underfoot. The two game wardens moved silently along until the trail spilled down between two huge boulders, like a V, and the two men descended again, this time emerging onto a flat area of grass hummocks and carpets of sphagnum moss, which bounced and undulated under their weight.

Clothes were scattered all over the flat area beside the swamp pond bank, as if those who had worn them had suddenly turned to vapor. There was a gelatinous fog over the black water that seemed to swirl languidly as if thinking about lifting.

Zakov touched split fingers to his eyes, pointed, and gave an exaggerated squint.

Bapcat felt a tremendous sense of foreboding, something dreadfully wrong, found himself trembling. Before he could start posing unanswerable questions, pale blue wraiths seemed to be moving from the fog toward the embankment. The smaller phantoms were led by two larger ones, who crawled out of the water on hands and knees: Jone Gleann and the

Isohultamaki woman, then Scale and Jimjim, followed by an angled line of children, all of them naked from the waists down and covered with writhing small black ribbons.

Bapcat stepped speechlessly toward the others and saw the ribbons moving and wriggling. He grabbed Jone Gleann by her shoulders and began yanking at the leeches to pull them off. They were earthen green with lines of red-orange spots and stuck to the woman's legs and buttocks and stomach, dozens of them, all over her white skin. It was disgusting.

Gleann shivered and slapped his hand away. "Don't, Lute!" she ordered, pushing hard on Bapcat's chest to back him off. "Everyone out now, children, everyone out and to your buckets. Don't pull the leeches. Scale will come to you and apply drops of tobacco juice and they will let go all on their own. Pick up each one and put it in your bucket. Fra Goodman will come around and you will give him your number for the tally. All right, out—let's move."

Bapcat watched as the children calmly and dispassionately did as they were told. The fog began to lift in earnest, revealing a beautiful morning, the sun's rays ricocheting off the eastern basalt ridgetops. The sun would soon peek over the ridges and light their swamp.

He could contain himself no longer. "What in the name of hell is going on?" Bapcat shouted angrily at Jone Gleann, who was applying some sort of cloth poultice to the green ribbons on her flesh, causing them to release, and picking each up and placing it in a bucket of water, where it entered soundlessly. The woman looked over at him, said *Shhhh*, and continued her work as Rinka Isohultamaki stood beside her, doing the same. Both women had blood trails all over their exposed skin.

Bapcat couldn't stop himself from shaking, and without thinking, pointed the rifle upward and jerked a shot and screamed "Stop!" The report of the heavy .30-40 reverberated from rock wall to rock wall across the small valley.

"Lute," Jone Gleann said calmly and quietly. "This is not the time. We need to safely harvest this batch and get back into the water."

"This is not right! This is wrong, and nobody, least of all them kids, is getting back into no damn water!" he said with a snarl, shaking his rifle at her. "These are babies, and you are—hell, I don't know who you are, or what the hell this is."

"That's correct, you don't know. Do you trust me?"

"Right now, probably not; in fact, no, I sure as hell don't!"

"Listen to me," she said calmly. "We sell each of these leeches for a dollar and a quarter. Each student gets a quarter from each sale, and the school takes a dollar. We have only ten days to do the harvest—ten days before water temperatures turn unfavorable, and the creatures dive deep and dark for the summer. It's now or never. One window opens briefly, once a year. This is the school's lifeline."

*Sell?* "Who the hell would buy these damn things? All they're good for is fish bait."

"There is a large hospital in St. Louis that serves large German and French communities, whose people continue to believe in the medical value of bleeding treatments. If you want to help us, leave us be, or join us. If you won't help, please be quiet and don't interfere. Time here is important. I want the children to remain calm. They are learning not only to help their families and their school by their own actions, but also to help overcome irrational fears. There is no pain in this, Lute, except in your head. You are confusing other feelings with safety, and they aren't the same."

"Goddammit, you're bleeding, Jone."

She smiled thinly. "It's nothing. There is no pain, and it will eventually stop."

Bapcat heard a rustling beside him and looked over to see Zakov undressing. When his trousers fell, he went to Isohultamaki, who smiled at the Russian and whispered, "If they attach themselves to places they should not, I will kiss it and make it better."

Jone Gleann clapped her hands. "Jimjim?"

"Average seventeen each, four fifty-nine total—more than five hundred dollars."

Gleann said, "Well done, children! If you feel weak, talk to Jimjim or Scale, and when you are all right again, please get back into the water. Where in the pond is not important, but shallow is best, above your knees. The leeches are everywhere in the shallows now, and looking for hosts."

The children cheered with muted enthusiasm, and began to slowly slide back into the water.

Bapcat was shaking all over, his brain working in starts and fits, finding nothing to connect to except raw emotion. There were no protests, no reluctance, as everyone got back into the black water. For reasons he knew he would probably never be able to explain, even to himself, Deputy Warden

Lute Bapcat did as his partner had done: stood on the water's edge, the sphagnum rising and falling like there was a heart buried inside. He was naked from the waist down, and looked to see Jone's hand held out to him, to help him descend, and he took it and joined her in the ink.

The water was frigid at first. For a while he felt things bumping his flesh, and then he went numb. He tried to send his mind away and steady his breathing as he had done growing up when he was afraid, but this time it refused to obey, and he felt chills, and then the presence of Jone Gleann pressing against him. "No pain, Lute; temporary discomfort for the individual, for the long-term benefit of the group. Isn't this the highest value in social life, to sacrifice for each other?"

"Your scars," he said, understanding.

"Yes," was all she said, and continued to hold his hand. Bapcat slid his free hand down and felt leeches against his flesh and imagined their small teeth opening holes, and he felt dizzy and disgusted with all these people, with Zakov, with himself, for everybody's sheeplike behavior, something he had both feared and loathed his whole life, but the woman's grip was solid and held tight as his resolve strengthened.

"You won't be sorry," she whispered.

He already was.

• • •

The camp was quiet at midday, lunches eaten, everyone resting for what Gleann called the evening session. Bapcat recognized some, but not all, of the children, saw blood on their legs and felt revulsion. He was torn by urges—one of them to gather all the children and take them away, another to scream at all the adults and put them under arrest for mistreating children—but he was not a full peace officer, and had no idea what sort of protection children actually had under the law, if any. Worse, he had taken part, which made him guilty as well.

Surely the boy Jordy he had taken in and who now lived with Jaquelle had been totally ignored and beaten repeatedly by his father, and nobody had stepped in or even raised an eyebrow. Random beatings had been commonplace at St. Cazimer's, and nothing was ever said of them, good or bad. They just *were*, a naked fact to be faced and accepted.

Mostly he stayed to himself to avoid acting without thinking, and while the camp rested, he finally made his way over to Jone Gleann and sat beside her.

"Coffee?" she asked, pointing at the pot in the coals of a campfire. "You're unhappy," she said.

"Honestly, I don't know what I am. This thing turns my stomach."

"Do you want to talk?"

"Yes. And no."

"Do the leeches bother you?"

"Not the leeches themselves; I guess they're just part of life out here. It's the children."

"What exactly about the children?"

He had to think about the question. "They marched all the way here with just Mac to protect them, and then you strip the clothes off them and use them to let those creatures suck their blood!"

"Are you a fisherman?" she asked, her voice even and soft.

"Sometimes."

"And you use bait?"

"Can't catch much without it."

"This is the same thing. Leeches require a host; usually they attach to fish, frogs, or the legs of snapping turtles, and around farms they like the legs of cows and horses, but when they get the chance, the warm blood of a human is best of all. We are bait."

"You're still bleeding," he pointed out again.

"It eventually stops," she said. "It has always been so."

"Your legs and all those scars. You've done this before."

"Yes, but then I was a slave; now I am free, and the children and the rest of us are partners."

"Children are children, not much more than babies. They can't be partners under the law until they grow up."

"Nonsense. You besmirch Mac's good reputation and name. That boy is a born leader, a rare thing to encounter."

"He's ten, if that."

"Why are you so focused on irrelevant numbers? McIlrath has uncommon common sense, the equivalent of most adults, and he has high intelligence as well. The other children naturally follow his lead, even those who are older than him."

"It don't seem . . . *moral*," he told her.

"Moral? Every child is here because he or she wants to be here, to be part of this, and they are limited to doing this for only four seasons so that permanent scarring is limited. They lose some blood, yes, but there is no pain, and they return home with money for their families."

"Life isn't about money," he insisted. The Widow Frei might disagree, but he had his own strong opinion.

"True—if you happen to be one of the fortunate who has enough. With few exceptions these children live on the thin margin between life and death. School offers a way out, a route to a better future. The other towns, their schools are little factories and nothing more, paid for by the mines and intended only to keep young folk around long enough for the operators to put them to work at the age of thirteen or so."

"What's wrong with the mines paying?"

"You went through the strike, and *dare* ask me this? Maybe you *are* thick."

"You make the children pay for the school, so what makes you different than the mine operators?"

Her answer was a sharp slap to his face, and it left his cheek on fire.

When they went back into the water in the evening, Zakov said, "My surgeons carried leeches to assist in amputations. They have some way of helping to clear infection and clean living flesh. Army surgeons rarely use things that do not. Warfare always advances the practice of medicine."

"How many of your soldiers were children?"

Zakov smiled and shook his head and went back into the water next to the Finnish girl.

Bapcat also went back into the water and stood near Jone Gleann.

"I probably overreacted," she said.

"I probably deserved it," he said. "Why did you send us to Bergland?"

"Honestly? I couldn't think how else to get rid of you. I wanted us to get started and use all the time we have and not be interrupted by what just happened. You accept what we do?"

"No, I don't think so."

"And still you participate?"

"I figure an adult has more skin than a kid."

"Your logic is not at all clear."

"I know," he said, wishing it was. All he could do was mentally shrug, and try not to think about the striped green leeches in the black water.

# CHAPTER 27

## Jack Spur, Gogebic County

### FRIDAY, AUGUST 7

Bapcat found himself in a thick mental fog that had been clinging to him for two weeks and he had no idea why. This morning when Gleann helped launch Mac and Rinka Isohultamaki on their trek eastward, he found himself listless, speechless, and powerless to object. The terrain between here and Lake Mine was more than thirty miles of pure up-down misery and wild. He thought one of the men should go along to provide protection, but instead stood silent, ashamed and not able to explain to himself exactly why he felt the way he did.

Mac, followed by his ugly nag, Rinka on her animal, and twenty-four children optimistically marched east, strung out in single file. It was still two hours to early dawn.

An hour later the adults were a-horse and headed west, eight huge canvas bags hanging from panniers. With every step of the mules, they could hear water sloshing; Bapcat wondered how more than two thousand green leeches could possibly survive. He had questioned Jone Gleann about this, but she had said not a single word about the leeches, or their intended destination.

"Won't you lose a lot of the creatures?" he had asked her.

"Most will live," was all she said.

Zakov pulled alongside. "I should have insisted I accompany the children."

"You mean keep company with that girl."

"She's hardly a girl," the Russian said. "She is an enchanting woman in full flower."

"I hope she ain't had that flower plucked," Bapcat said.

"It is entirely a platonic relationship."

"I ain't entirely sure what that means," Bapcat said.

"It means . . . the opposite of the relationship you have with the Widow Frei."

"Platonic, eh?" Was this the sort of bond he and Jone Gleann were making—for surely there was something forming, even if it was twisted and against some things he thought he believed in. It was impossible for him to describe what he felt, even to himself, only that he felt something that rubbed him wrong, yet right, and totally frustrated him. This was very different from what he shared with Jaquelle; both had good and bad attached to them, though this one seemed to have more bad than good.

"Rinka will see to the safety of the children," Zakov proclaimed.

"I guess Mac might be just fine all on his own," Bapcat said. "He got them here alone, after all."

"I meant no insult to our young friend McIlrath."

The route took them around the base of a peak and eventually struck a fair path, which four hours later put them at a lake with a small clear river flowing north out of it. Gleann forded them just to the north, swerving the column south along the slightly elevated banks of the lake until they passed another lake to their west, and beyond that, a massive long ridge of dark green and an occasional stony massif.

Shortly thereafter, Bapcat spied a follower paralleling them to the east and uphill a bit, but he said nothing of the single rider, only gave a nod to the Russian, who acknowledged with a fist by the side of his leg.

Just south of the two lakes the group hit another trail, this one more worn, and flatter than anything they had been on in a long while.

Three hours south, they crossed and rounded the west end of a swayback hill and descended in a straight line for an hour to an east-west railroad bed and track. Bapcat saw the shiny tops of the rails and knew these tracks were in regular use.

Standing at the tracks they tipped drinks of water from their canteens and water bags and Gleann dismounted and wiped perspiration off her head. The day was steamy and uncomfortable, the horses sweating and antsy.

"This is our place," she pronounced, before going back to one of her pack mules, removing a six-foot aspen pole, tying a large red cloth to it, and sticking it in a mound of dirt three feet off the tracks.

"This place is not teeming with humanity," the Russian observed.

"Teeming humanity is not our objective," Jone Gleann said tersely.

"Well, it lacks any sense of a place for a serendipitous rendezvous," Zakov said.

"There's no serendipity in any of my undertakings," Jone Gleann told him coolly.

The Russian said, "Some people would surely characterize that as a sad condition, a life without whimsy and serendipity."

Her face contorted in the rictus of a predator about to pounce. "I'm not *some* people. I'm me, and I know what I'm about."

"How will the train know you're here?" Bapcat asked, guessing at what she had in mind, and trying to break the growing tension between the woman and his partner.

Jone Gleann said, "Engine, coal car, and a baggage car—a special run. This happens the same day every year."

"Same time and place?" the Russian asked.

"Of course not. Do you take me for stupid?"

They had been riding for almost eleven hours and emotions were strained. "The animals need a break," Bapcat said.

"We won't camp here," she said, and promptly led them up a small rise to a thick stand of paper birch. "There is a grass field right behind us," she said, jumping off and cutting through the birches back to the front, looking out over the tracks before eventually sitting down.

Bapcat could sense a tightness in her. Nerves? Fear?

"This will happen quickly," she explained, "and as soon as it is done, we'll go back to the north and camp where we came across the back of that ridge a mile or so from here. There are springs and small creeks there for the stock, and good grass."

"I might not do that," Bapcat said.

"You're not in charge," she said wearily. "This is old ground."

"I'm not trying to take over," he said, "but the Russian and me seen we got us a shadow since we come between them two lakes back some."

Jone Gleann glared at him. "But you never said anything."

"And you never told any of us what you want us to do. We don't read minds."

"You're experienced men on the trail. I wouldn't think I'd have to tell you what to do."

"You should rethink your thinking," Zakov said softly, joining them. "One mounted man. He has a telescope. I saw a glint of the glass when the sun got lower in the west."

"That doesn't mean anything."

"I guess me and the Russian know a thing or two about following and getting followed," Bapcat said in his partner's defense.

She tried to shrug it off. "There are strange people with crackbrains in the mountains, poor for social company, but often rife with curiosity."

"Same day, every year," Bapcat said. "The easiest person to surprise is the regular person, the one you can predict."

"Explain," she said.

"I'm guessing money is about to change hands."

She nodded.

"I wouldn't rule out trouble," Bapcat said.

Jone Gleann looked behind her and asked sourly, "What do *you* think we should do?"

Bapcat said, "I would send Pinkhus Sergeyevich and let him confront this shadow-watcher of ours."

Gleann dispatched the Russian with a flick of her hand.

"What exactly is going to happen here?" Bapcat asked.

"The special train will stop at our flag. We'll hurry down and move the canvas sacks from the mules to the baggage car. The bags will be loaded into large glass jars, designed for this purpose. They will count the leeches, pay us in cash, and depart immediately."

"Who is *they*?" Bapcat asked.

"Dr. Marcella Tourant of St. Louis Catholic Hospital and Sanatorium."

"It's always this same doctor you deal with?"

"Always."

"How long has this gone on?"

"My sixth year. I discovered the leeches seven summers back, made contact with Dr. Tourant, and we established this arrangement."

"The special train, cash for the leeches—this seems like a lot of money for the doctor to pay. There're leeches everywhere in this country."

"Not like these. This is a species much like those favored in Europe, and they are very, very rare, especially this far north. Dr. Tourant uses them in therapy and in her research. She is a woman of science."

"Who in Lake Mine knows about this?"

When she failed to answer immediately, he quickly pressed. "Not everybody over that way is your supporter."

"The children know," she said, "and their parents, and those children who've made the trek know of the swamp and what we do there. Only Scale, Jimjim, and I meet the train, always the same day, but always at a different time and location. When I meet Dr. Tourant today, she and I will look at a railroad map and decide on next year's location."

"Scale and Jimjim?"

"Just she and I will know the specifics."

"Where's the money go?"

"The Ontonagon bank."

Bapcat looked at her. "How long after you get it does the money get to the bank?"

"A week to ten days."

"And then?"

"Scale, Jimjim, and I go back into the mountains until September."

"For what?"

She shrugged. "Whatever moves us," she said. "Gathering, hunting, looking around."

"The bank's people know you put a lot of cash into an account every year about the same time," he pointed out.

"I don't want to believe what you are intimating."

"I ain't saying nothing for sure. I'm only telling you that the way you done this has left a clear trail to follow, should one get such a notion. It don't take much to backtrack," he added.

"Nobody followed us," she declared.

"This is true," he said, "but you did not see our watcher today, and the children could have been followed."

"They would follow children?"

"Possibly, or take one aside and threaten his family, or promise him rewards. Children are human."

"Your mind is twisted, your view of the world dark."

"I guess a bullet in the back helps shape a man's thinking," he told her.

"Life can be beautiful," she told him, "if you allow it."

"I am who I am," he said.

"I can see that now, but nothing's happened in all these years."

"Nothing in the past don't mean nothing in the future," he said. "Point is to live so you don't make nothing easy for nobody, never."

"I will allow that I am a guarded person, but you are a fortress."

Minutes later the train hove into sight and began slowing for the marker flat. The entire stop, transfer, count, and payoff lasted less than thirty minutes, and when the train pulled out, heading west, they had two saddlebags filled with cash, two thousand four hundred leeches bringing in three thousand crisp dollars. The group mounted and rode back up into the birches to await the Russian's return, but he was already there, with a prisoner on a brown horse, trussed with rope and a black canvas bucket over his head.

"I believe this individual to be mentally deranged and incapable of basic human communication," Zakov said, greeting them. "I gave deep consideration to putting a bullet in his brain, to save anguish and pain, the way I would dispatch an injured horse, but the man's tears made it impossible, and now I present him to you."

The Russian lifted the canvas bucket.

"*Phin*?" Bapcat said.

"General Wellington Trafalgar Smith-Jones Elphinstone, reporting as ordered, if in a somewhat irregular manner made necessary by circumstance. Your man is to be congratulated for his extreme stealth, but needs remediation in his emotional control. A few tears is all it took to get what I wanted, which was to be brought to you."

"Dammit," Lute Bapcat said to the man. "What the hell is going on?"

"Far-reaching question, that. The Germans are at war with the Russians and the French, and the Bosch have moved to occupy Belgium, which caused Great Britain to declare war on the Hun. You can safely wager that the Austro-Hungarian blokes will soon opt for war with Russia, and the Serbs will no doubt declare against Germany."

Zakov asked, "The world is at war?"

Phin said, "All but America, it seems. Your eloquent and loquacious President Wilson has gone mum."

"He can't keep the country out forever," Zakov said.

"I guess we'll see," the old Brit said. "Always wondered how long forever is."

"Never mind all that malarkey!" Bapcat said. "What the hell is going on with you following us?"

"Easily explained, dear boy. Got your information, you see, followed the children, watched your camp, and came along looking for an appropriate time to announce myself. No magic here, my boy. I myself gave McIlrath that horse he so dearly loves, shod it myself with shoes specially made to leave distinctive prints. Like Hansel and Gretel, I imagine, wot."

"You might've been shot!"

"*C'est la guerre*, dear fellow, luck of the draw and all that. Silver City, I say again: Silver City, October the first, Mr. Archibald, his ducks 'imself, to take personal possession of said delivery."

"You are Nick Vedder's clerk," Jone Gleann said.

"*Was*, madam, was. Bit uncomfortable with this business. A respite from these bindings would be most welcome, wot."

Bapcat nodded to Zakov, who cut loose the prisoner.

"Are you out of your mind?" Bapcat asked.

"One clearly hopes not," the General said. "But how can any one of us pathetic and frail creatures ever know what's real and what's just our own notion of real? Mr. Nicholas Vedder is to order materiel for a camp to be established one mile west of White Pine, on the west bank of the Big Iron River. A Frenchy called Pierre Malyotte is to set up said camp and organize it for the arrival of the traps from Silver City to Nonesuch.

"Malyotte and sons run a hotel and general store in Nonesuch and guide hunters and anglers, mainly city sports wanting to buy themselves an adventure in the great North Woods. Malyotte is reputedly a good and honest man. It would behoove us to find a way to confer with him. I doubt he knows the details of what lies ahead with Mr. Archibald."

"You've gone from not knowing much to knowing a heap, General."

"As ordered, and as it happens, a pattern in my life, which is driven as much by pure serendipity as hard logic and intent. It turns out, you see, Monsieur Malyotte's integrity in business aside, the old Frenchy dabs it up with a part-time blowen called *Les Trois Tetons*, for which she is quite deservedly if merely locally famous."

"This . . . whatever she is, just happened to drop all this information in your lap."

"For a fee, sir," the General declared. "It may be a tawdry business, her line, but a business it surely is, one of the oldest in recorded history, wot, and there are protocols extant. Wouldn't have it any other way."

Bapcat looked at his partner, who said only, "He's a raving lunatic."

"He brought us information," Bapcat said.

"No doubt worthless."

Bapcat did not agree. "We're going north to make camp, General."

"Capital notion. I haven't eaten anything but raw rat in two days, and it is quite salty, I must report."

Zakov grunted loudly and Phin said, "English humor, old boy, humor. You Russkies are all too bleeding serious. Haven't you read your Gogol?"

"He was Ukrainian, not Russian," Zakov said gloomily.

# CHAPTER 28

## Ironwood, Gogebic County

### WEDNESDAY, AUGUST 12

They camped north of the rendezvous point for several days, and Bapcat—never happy to be idle when he could be moving and doing—was exceedingly antsy. Moreover, the pile of cash in Jone Gleann's saddlebags added to his edginess. While the animals enjoyed the break and grazed, they all caught large, fat brook trout from Cherry Creek until they were tired of eating fish.

With the General now part of the sortie, and Rinka Isohultamaki possibly returning, the expedition needed more supplies. When Bapcat pressed Gleann, she told him, "We'll go to Sullivan and Coumbe in Ironwood. They sell groceries and supplies to most of the area iron mines, and have the best prices around. Most businessmen are robbers and will charge you all they can get."

Bapcat pulled her aside after her announcement and stumbled at making his point. "I don't know for sure—probably the Ontonagon bank is fine. But if we're going to be in Ironwood, why not put the cash in a bank there? You can always have it wired later, and Ironwood's closer to your annual rendezvous place than Ontonagon. You might even meet the doctor in Ironwood. It's a bigger town, and you'd both be invisible strangers there."

"The woodsman is suddenly a finance expert?" she said.

"I just think you ought to get that cash into a safe place."

"I'll give it some thought," she said, and walked away.

Though no decision on the money was forthcoming, their leader decided they would head to Ironwood for supplies.

Ironwood lay about twenty or so miles west, on the banks of the Montreal River, which was also the border with Wisconsin. Zakov and Jimjim immediately decided that the expedition should detour to Silver Street in Hurley, on the Wisconsin side, to visit the famous red-light district and partake of its various amusements and entertainments.

"Suppose you'll be joining the men," Jone Gleann said to Bapcat.

"No, I ain't much for such sport."

"I thought drinking and women were every man's sport," the teacher said.

"Could be, I guess. Just not mine."

Bapcat had traversed the area years before and it had been an affront to his eyes then. Now it was far worse, mine location after location, starting south of Bessemer with Ramsay and on through Anvil, Yale, Puritan, Bonnie, Jessieville, Aurora, and Norrie, and eventually into Ironwood itself, fifteen thousand people strong, supported by two major mines inside the city limits, a trolley line to move people around, and a lot of languages, of which English was not even the most often heard. For some reason, iron mining seemed far dirtier and more destructive than other kinds, especially open pit sites where they gouged out the ground and no doubt would leave it that way when they had finished taking what they wanted.

It was, in fact, Bapcat thought, like moving through different countries, each one's political borders marked by hundred-foot-high ridges of red iron ore, the air choked with swirling red dust and smoke, and sometimes around sundown, the low rays of the sun illuminated the air like the Devil's forge in the fires of Hell itself. The clank and clunk of equipment was relentless at all times of day and night.

Last night they had camped south of Ramsay on the Black River, and this morning steadily made their way ten miles to Ironwood, where they found a traveler's hotel called Delmer's House, and a livery for their stock. The men repaired to a public bath run by Finns and Bapcat used the hotel telephone to call Roland Echo.

"We're in Ironwood," he told the assistant prosecutor in Houghton.

"Bit off your usual trapline."

"We need the name of a trustworthy banker here," the deputy game warden said.

Echo paused. "Now that's a tall order anywhere," the man said, "but I'd seek out Hugo Plinlimon of First National. He grew up here, went to school in Ann Arbor, and has a law degree, but married a lovely lady of means and took to banking when her father-in-law went to the Great Vault in the Sky. You can trust Hugo. Feel free to prominently use my name."

Bapcat thanked his friend and he and Gleann went to the bank, a stately Jacobsville sandstone monolith on the town's main drag, the bank's red stone not suffering much from the red dust in the air. Bapcat wondered if that had been an accident or intentional.

"Appointment with Hugo?" a male greeter asked.

"No, sir, but Roland Echo of Houghton said we should see him."

The man excused himself and went away. Bapcat decided this was the first banker he had ever met whose employees referred to him by his given name.

Ten minutes later they were seated in the banker's office, which was more of a space carved out among other white-shirt employees. Bapcat expected a banker big shot to have his own big office, not a rabbit's warren.

"How's Roland? Still tilting at windmills?"

"He still comes to work early and stays late," Bapcat answered. The allusion to windmills had no meaning to Bapcat whatsoever, and he ignored it.

"Needs a good woman in his life," the banker said with a twinkle in his eye.

"Or a naughty one," Jone Gleann said, and Plinlimon exploded with laughter.

"I take your point," the banker said when the laughing fit subsided.

"She needs an account for savings," Bapcat said, driving directly to their reason for being there.

"I'll want to draw from it," Gleann added.

"You're local, ma'am?"

"Lake Mine near Mass and Greenland, or thereabouts," she said.

"First National is pleased to accommodate you."

Bapcat plopped the saddlebags on the banker's desk and unbuckled the straps.

The banker stared. "That's a *lot* of cash."

"Three thousand," Jone Gleann said. "Even."

"You won't be offended if we re-count it before deposit?" the banker asked.

"No, sir," the teacher said. "I'd do the very same."

Plinlimon took the bags into another room and came back with a clutch of papers. "We want to make business with us easy," the man said, "but there are laws and procedures." He laid the papers on his desk, handed the woman a pen.

Bapcat went outside to the street for a smoke and the banker joined him in his shirtsleeves, waving to passersby, calling many by their first names, and using several languages to exchange comments.

Lute Bapcat showed the man his badge.

"Your colleague Napoleol Gunt is a good customer," the banker said. "You know him?"

"Not well. We met at training last year over in the Soo."

"Long time in this community, carried over from the old patronage system, widely respected and narrowly feared by those who have ample reason for it."

"You know where he lives?"

"As it happens, I do. He has a cabin four miles north of town where Spring Creek meets the Montreal."

Bapcat thanked Plinlimon and they both went back inside, where Jone Gleann had finished filling out the paperwork. The banker looked over the papers, went into the other room, came back, and handed her a piece of paper and an envelope. "Your receipt for three thousand dollars and your new bankbook is in the envelope. Thank you for your business."

Back in the street, Gleann told him, "I guess we ought to see to our supplies."

"I'll be back tonight," Bapcat told her, offering no explanation for going his own way.

• • •

A brisk walk of just more than an hour took him to a cabin not much improved over what he had once used as a trapper out on the tip of the Keweenaw, and it struck him ironically that his cabin and Gunt's were both on the banks of a Montreal River. He found Gunt outside, shirtless, and driving a splitting wedge with the heel of a Swedish bighead ax. Bapcat noticed the man also carried a holstered Colt .45 on his hip.

Gunt looked up. "You lost, Deputy Bapcat?"

"I guess there'd be some spirited debate over that particular point."

Gunt grinned. "Where's your Russian chum?"

"Hurley, I suspect."

"Both of you out of your territory when we've got all this damn animal survey stuff to do? Not work enough to enforce the law, now we got to gather facts for Lansing? Ain't no good comes from Silver Street," the Gogebic County deputy state warden added. "The sheriff across the river is Roebuck, a real galoot. Just use my name if the need arises."

"What about the sheriff on this side of the river?"

"Terrence Torrance, once known as Terry the Terror. Had the badge only since last fall. He scares hell out of people who need scaring, and lots more who don't. Even money if he'll last out his term. The iron mine bigwigs ain't fans, and claim he picks on their people, which amounts to no more than a bag of hot air."

"I've been thinking on the Five Rules," Bapcat said.

"Don't hurt to do so," his colleague said, putting down the ax. "Drink of rainwater?"

The two men sat on either side of a barrel and shared the ladle. "Harju told me rumor's the fuel of law enforcement," Bapcat said.

"Tells everybody that because it's true. His rules are: Rumors lead to possible informants," Gunt recounted, "informants lead to suspects, suspects take you to investigations, which can lead to arrests, the cascade of all falling in a nice neat line, *if* the rumors bear fruit."

"The circus came through here," Bapcat said.

"Every year, but I take no note. Too much to do in the real world to pay attention to all that folderol."

"Deputy Farrell Mackley."

"Hired after our gathering in the Soo. I got a letter from Harju, but never heard from him, nor seen him, nor even heard no words about the man, good or otherwise."

"He's been missing since March. I'm supposed to find him."

"Better you than me; I got enough to do. But that's a long time missing."

"Tell me about Judge Maxim Edson."

"Max? What about him?"

"He swore me in as a special investigator for the attorney general down in Lansing. I've been ordered to find and arrest a man named Heinrich Junger, or Henry Young. The AG wants me to bring him here and give him over to Minnesota officials."

"Not heard a thing of the man or your deputization. Just you?"

"No, I got Zakov."

"Who did Horri get to take care of your counties?"

"He's never said, and I ain't never asked. Your sheriff hasn't mentioned this Junger character?"

"Nope; the judge probably didn't tell him, and me and the sheriff don't see much of each other. His job's in town and mine's not."

"I think I need to talk to your sheriff and the man in Wisconsin. I've got two runabouts and no real leads on either man."

"Not even a general location?" Gunt asked.

"Some claim Junger could be in the Porkies, but nothing so far on Mackley."

"The Porkies can mean anything from here almost to Baraga," Gunt said, shaking his head, "but it's true, them hills seem to attract a right snarly assortment of social misfits and downright criminals."

"Chance you can get me a meet with the two sheriffs?"

"When?"

"Tomorrow, I'd hope, mid-morning?"

"Probably can do—say eleven, at Chalk House?"

"I owe you."

"Yes, you will, but that's the nature of the badge beast, ain't it? Few as we are, we got to stick close, as and when we can. What's this Junger fella done?"

"Murder, robbery, rape—you name it. Supposed to lead a gang of twenty guns, maybe twice that."

"Be good if he is in a fat company. Can't hide a big crowd, even in the woods. Numbers could make them easier to follow, even if the leader is try-ing to be secretive. It's hard to miss a mob like that."

*Clandestine . . . was that a word for secret?* "My thought, too."

"I know people all along the south shore of the big lake, from Little Girl Point over to Pinkerton Creek. I can put out the word. Where can you be found?"

"Not sure yet; we're on the move. Will probably make a camp southwest side of the mountains."

"Good bear country up that way," Gunt said. "Hang your grub high, or those pests will be into it every chance they get."

"Heard that."

"Bears in this stew you're cooking up?"

"Could be, I guess; don't know for sure yet."

"That area's rich enough in said critters. Heard a Kraut trapper name of Pippig used to trap up that way, had a cabin, I heard, nearly a homestead. Don't know if he be dead or alive these days, but anybody in his reach of tra-plines, the German would know about it. Last I heard, his camp was way up the headwaters of Bush Creek, up the side of a hill, just south of a side creek that runs on down into the Little Carp."

"Pippig got a first name?"

"Ludger Arnd—a double-barrel name for a real hermit type."

"Your name open doors with him?"

"I guess that depends on the man's mood and his state of sobriety. The old German is somewhat wed to strong spirits and few words."

• • •

Midnight in Marheine's Palace on Silver Street, Bapcat with Gleann, answering a late-night summons from Hurley gendarmes. Scale, Jimjim, Zakov, and the General looked a bit flushed and ragged, and also relieved.

Sheriff Thurgood Roebuck met them at the sporting-house door. "What the hell were you thinking, sending a nigger, a runt, a Russian, and a crazy old man into an establishment like this? I can't see nothing but trouble in that."

"They weren't *sent*," Bapcat said.

"Put it how you like. They claim to be your boys," the sheriff told Bapcat.

"They are *mine*," Jone Gleann said coldly. "Why are we here?"

"They took over the establishment, forced all the patrons upstairs, and that old man pulled out a sword five feet long and I had to tell him I'd shoot him if he didn't give it up, and he told me he's a general." Roebuck looked at Bapcat. "When, in old George Washington's army?"

"We'll pay any damages," Jone Gleann said.

"Well, I guess there ain't none to speak of, 'cept them upstairs couldn't reach the swill down here all the time they was barricaded up there in Heaven. 'Course, they did have access to the local talent, so I guess some money mebbe changed hands, tradewise. Just take 'em and leave us be. We've got a rough image to uphold, but to be held hostage by this lot? We'll never get past it."

The trip back to Delmer's House was subdued.

"Don't care to hear the facts?" Jimjim asked.

Jone Gleann turned and shook her fist at the men. "*His* boys?"

## CHAPTER 29

### *Ironwood*

#### THURSDAY, AUGUST 13

Waves of emotion were surging through Bapcat, leaving him feeling helpless and worthless, feelings so strong he was tempted to quit. He was crashing through one of those waves now, on the verge of walking away out of honor and a sense of self-loathing, born of what he felt was his own incompetence, so far unseen by the people around him. How long until reality exposed him and all of his weaknesses?

Last year it had been the violent strike, the most complex thing he had ever been caught up in, including the war in Cuba, which had been easy by comparison, his role then one of simply carrying out orders. During the strike he was trapped into thinking and planning and guiding the actions of others without any counsel from above to help him. It had been awful.

Now this, whatever this was, which was anything but clear. He still found himself swelling with pride when he remembered that Colonel Teddy Roosevelt himself had recommended him for this job, but the Colonel, great as he was, finally was only a man, and subject to flaws just as all men are. Even in his second year, and with the strike mostly behind them, Bapcat sometimes felt unworthy of the badge and lacking in what the job required. Thank the stars he had the Russian. Zakov was smart, educated, and calm in the face of impending disaster. But why the hell had he gone off to the meat houses in Hurley? Truth: Pinkhus Sergeyevich had a weakness for a certain flavor of flesh.

Jone Gleann was in a silent snit over who-knew-what, the drunk revelers were sleeping it off, and Bapcat lay in his room, arms crossed like a corpse laid out by an undertaker, staring up at the black ceiling, wishing he was outdoors, *anywhere* but in this room. The animal survey issue lay heavily on him, mostly because he and Zakov had not done anything resembling a thorough job last year. Never mind that there were legitimate reasons and excuses, he lectured himself; you didn't do what your bosses wanted, and that's failure.

Rolling this around in his head from endless angles, he suddenly found himself sitting up in the bed. *Could it be that Chief Warden Oates shares my own concerns about animals? If not, why ask your small force of deputies to spend so much of their time and energy making a count of the state's animals?* Bapcat felt a surge of optimism: *Was the big boss's interest solely political, or was there tobacco in that pipe? Was the man truly concerned about animals disappearing? No way to know, but what if?*

Bapcat put his feet on the floor and rubbed his eyes. *Does Oates really know I've been deputized and ordered to find Junger? Has Oates heard my questions about bears as State property?* Until now he had been tempted to see Lansing as his foe. *But what if Chief Oates is really more of an ally? Oates, after all, told me of the coming beaver-trapping bans when he offered me the job. He'd said, "Leave beaves for a few years; let them recover their numbers." If the boss is concerned for beavers, why not for bears, too?*

These were good questions for which he had no answers, which in his mind was yet more evidence of his unsuitability for this work. Long-term, this just wasn't going to work out. He wasn't good enough.

Bapcat's head sometimes throbbed from so much thinking and worrying, and there, on top of it, he felt a near-overwhelming longing for Jaquelle Frei and their ward Jordy. Yet, and this made his gut ache, he kept hearing Jone Gleann's voice calling him to her, and his brain kept trying to shut it off as improper at best, and a possible betrayal of Jaquelle and Jordy at worst.

• • •

It had been a terrible night filled with worry and little sleep. Chalk House was lit with electric bulbs and painted bright white, the effect one that made him want to put his arm in front of his eyes, but he looked down to avoid the brilliance and saw a table, Napoleol Gunt sitting with three other men, one more than he had asked for. Bapcat thought he recognized Sheriff Roebuck from the night before, but the other two faces weren't familiar.

One of the men had slicked-back blond hair and gave off the perfumed scent of Brilliantine. The man's teeth were as white and gleaming as the room, and he wore a tailored white suit, freshly and crisply pressed.

"Special Investigator Bapcat," the man greeted him, and raised his hand. "I'm Judge Edson. Our Wisconsin colleague has been regaling us with a tale of your, dare I employ the term, posse?" The judge was not smiling and kept his hand held out. Bapcat wondered if he wanted it shaken or kissed, decided against both, and sat down.

Edson said, "Why the AG wants a *fool* for this assignment escapes me, it truly does, you who sent a nigger, a dwarf, a Russian, and a crazy old man into a sporting house, and didn't foresee a problem? Makes me question your judgment, Special Investigator Bapcat, and, dare I say, my opinion of Attorney General Grant Fellows as well."

There was nothing to be gained from an argument here. The Colonel had taught him to pick his fights. "Sorry, Your Honor."

"I've known AG Fellows a long time, and how a man of such physical frailty could be so damn stubborn is beyond me. Could drown that man in an inkwell, but here's the thing I also know: Grant is a thinker of the deepest order, and what he'll do is follow the chain of command until he concludes it's not working, and then he'll do the thinking and deciding for himself, which is how I assume you got dragged into what should be no more than a routine criminal matter. There's got to be something about this desperado we are not privy to."

"Your Honor," Deputy Napoleol Gunt said to the judge.

"Right, I'm just the addition here, not the main speaker."

Gunt looked at Bapcat and made eye contact, and said, "I believe you've met Iron County sheriff Thurgood Roebuck from Hurley."

The sheriff gave a peremptory nod to Bapcat.

Gunt turned to the third man, who had black hair and was unshaven, with eyes as black and shiny as coal. "Sheriff Torrance."

"Get on with this, Deputy," the judge said. "I've got court at one, and a fine lunch to eat before that."

Bapcat launched into his tale of Heinrich Junger and the Henry Young he'd known in his early days at St. Cazimer's, then on to the missing deputy, and finally the circus and the whole quandary in his mind concerning bears as valuable state property, and without thinking, he'd added, "Comes down to it—all fish and trees and animals in this state belong to all the people, and we who work for the State are sworn to take care of the people's property, which I'd think applies not just to bears, but to all the animals and birds and fishes we got. And over in Wisconsin, too."

Judge Edson listened with his mouth hanging open. "Damn, son, your head and your plate's both over-full and about to spill the goods."

Bapcat made a plea for them to help funnel rumors to him, with the hope that rumors might take him to some real leads he could follow. He finished by saying, "Over where I'm assigned, regular people don't make a habit of willingly talking to game wardens."

The men all smiled. "*All* instruments of the law," Judge Edson said. "Damn masses want nothing to do with us until they need us, and then the song lyrics change."

Sheriff Torrance spoke. "The Porkies are damn big. How many people you have deputized?"

"Six including me, and maybe a seventh later."

Torrance shook his head. "A sizable army could hide out up in those hills and gullies and live a long time off the land alone."

"The thing is," Bapcat said, "if Junger's gang is as big as we've been told, they won't be able to hide that easy, especially if someone who knows what they're doing is looking for them and tracking. One man could hide forever, but twenty to forty—that just can't be done."

The judge said, "All you're asking for is information on larger groups passing through the county or area? What if Junger's a smart cookie, and don't keep his personnel in close proximity, but leaves them elsewhere as individuals and just calls them into a group when he needs a force?"

Bapcat had not considered this possibility.

The judge went on, "I know a fella way down south, a fellow jurist, once told me this is how nigger lynchings get done down that way. A group assembles out of nowhere, a neck gets stretched, and the killers disperse back into the local woodwork. Classic guerrilla tactics from the Quantrill days, hit and run, and hide, Indian-style."

"Knowing the kind of people likely to be mixed up in murder and all that," the Gogebic County sheriff said, "I can't picture such riffraff keeping such marauding to theirselfs. This Junger is here, somebody around here will know, and know who and what he is. I'll see what I can scrape off my hoi polloi."

"Will do the same on my side of the river," Roebuck said. "Some of our many sporting-night ladies in Hurley possess considerable information about goings-on hereabouts."

"Don't be sampling the wares," the judge quipped.

"I'm a churchman," Roebuck said indignantly.

"Some of them girls make a good living off leading citizens, especially good churchmen," the judge countered.

Roebuck seemed to ignore him. "I'll pass the word to other sheriffs in the northern counties. If your man comes straight across from Minnesota, he'll have to pass this way. Someone may hear."

"Unless he comes by boat from Duluth," the judge said, "in which case nobody would know."

Boats, Indians, gangs on call . . . Bapcat had considered none of this, and hearing it now and seeing how obvious it was, it made him feel even worse than he'd felt last night.

"How do we get information to you?" the judge asked.

Bapcat could muster only a blank look as he realized once again he'd not adequately thought this through, but he hated to admit it, so he said only, "Napoleol will know, and he can pass it along." Bapcat looked at his colleague, who nodded.

The judge slapped the table, got up without eating, and departed.

Roebuck stared at Bapcat. "That Russian of yours has the hardest eyes I've ever seen."

"You read him good, Sheriff. That posse you saw might look and act strange, but they are all hard and tried men, and none of them will willingly kowtow to the threat of force."

"Then I hope you got what it takes to handle them," Roebuck said, standing and stretching.

Bapcat thought, *If only he could see Jone Gleann in full force.*

Napoleol Gunt said, "Lute, you gotta have a better plan. I make it a point of not being easy to find, and by the time information gets to me we could all be a lot older, and way behind. Why don't you think more modern, let so-called technology help you do the job?"

"I'll think on it," Bapcat said. Did he mean telephones, or something else?

Jone Gleann pounced on him as soon as he walked into Delmer's House. "You and I need to talk . . . *now*," she said, greeting him in the foyer. He followed her outside and into a dark alley. "You are trying to usurp my authority," she barked at him, and banged a fist on his chest. "*Your* men!?"

"Why're you so worked up over one dang word?" he wanted to know.

"Try being a woman," she shot back. "Then you'd know."

"Well, that ain't likely to happen," he said. "We are what we are, and I guess exceptions and those who are questionable end up in circus sideshows."

She struck his chest again. "That's it—make a joke of it. This is serious!"

"Was a fact, not no joke," he said.

Jone Gleann sucked in a breath. "Am I or am I not in charge?"

"Nothing's changed."

"I want to be deputized," she said. "Officially."

"That's a different chicken," he said, taken by surprise.

"You talked to Scale and Jimjim as if it's a foregone conclusion they'll be badged, but not me."

"I ain't deputized or badged nobody yet," he said, "and I don't see no need until we get a plan and corner the opposition."

"I want pay as a deputy," she said, "equal with the men, not less."

"You already got free labor from me and Zakov. Is money all you think about?"

"I think about some fifty kids, and the only way I can do right by them is money."

"I guess that makes some sense, but what if I ain't ready to hand out any badges?"

She stared him down, forced him to look off into the distance, and he knew she'd won this little battle, though he had no idea why all this was coming up now.

"We have differences," the woman said, "you and me, but you have no doubts about what's the right thing to do, not in your head, but in your heart. I've not figured you out yet, but that much I know. You have a sense of honor, and you value it."

"Badges and oaths tonight," he said. "Do you want to know what I've been doing?"

"Shouldn't the leader be in on the thinking that leads to the doing— *while* the thinking's going on, and not after the fact?"

"Maybe you ought to look at how *you* lead," he shot back. "You don't never tell nobody nothing."

She seemed to be on the verge of saying something, but remained silent. "Who is in charge, you or me?"

"Have we reached that point yet?"

"Not by a long shot."

"Then who leads now?"

"*You*, I just said."

"Was that so difficult?" she asked.

"Was what?"

"Admitting I'm the boss."

"I already done that," he said.

"It never hurts to be explicit when delegating authority," she told him.

"You just lost me," he said. Her language and attitude made his head hurt.

"Don't worry," she said. "You're not lost. I know where we're going. All you have to do is follow me."

"Where?"

"I guess I won't know exactly until you share what you've been up to."

"So you want to know what I've been doing?"

"Are you not listening? That's another thing a woman can tell you about—being ignored."

"I'm thinking if I was ignoring you, we wouldn't be standing here, would we?"

She banged his chest again with the heel of her hand. "I *am* listening, but *you* are not hearing."

"Why do you keep smacking me?"

"Because I want your full attention when I talk."

"You got that."

"*All* the time," she said in a voice that stopped him.

"Are we still talking about leading?" he asked.

"Mostly," she said in an odd voice, then, "Of course—what else *would* we be talking about?"

"If you don't know, I sure don't," Bapcat said.

"You were saying?" she said.

"I was?"

"About what you've been doing."

He laid out everything for her, and she kept quiet until he was finished.

"So you set it up so this information might come to us, but not how or when?"

"It doesn't sound so good put that way, but I guess that's the meat in the stew."

"I guess we'd better think some and talk about it," she said, "figure it out together."

"You *and* me?" he asked.

"Is anybody else here?"

Lute Bapcat shook his head. *If she's such a pain, why can't I stop thinking about her?*

# CHAPTER 30

## Jessieville, Gogebic County

### SATURDAY, AUGUST 15

Scale and the other Negro engaged in a one-minute stare-down, with no clear winner that Bapcat could determine.

"Scale, this here is Mr. Bowdler," the deputy game warden said. "Head telegrapher for Jessieville Western Union."

"I ain't good enough be put with a white man?" Scale challenged.

"I guess you good enough be put with the top hand in upper Michigan and Wisconsin," Bowdler boasted. "Don't be puttin' no mouth on me, boy. I earned my way to this. What *you* do?"

Scale huffed but kept silent and Bapcat intervened. "He's a veteran," the deputy said. "Michigan Volunteer Infantry. I guess he earned his way, too."

"Not ever-body got the chance ta run off, shirk responsibility, play dress-up soldier-boy and all," the man said.

"Ain't no play in killin' men," Scale said on his own behalf as Bapcat watched Bowdler shrink back.

Bapcat said, "Deputy Warden Gunt has arranged for us to keep a man on the premises to bring messages. Something comes in, you bring it to camp. You get there, somebody else will head back here in your place." He and Jone Gleann had worked out this scheme yesterday, and this morning he had gotten ahold of Gunt, who recommended Bowdler and Jessieville without even a slight hesitation.

Bapcat's first move was to send identical telegrams to Echo, Harju, and State Game Warden Oates. The wire read:

DEPLOYING PORKIES SOUTHWEST SOON. STOP. CAMP THERE. STOP. ALL WIRES TO HERE FOR DELIVERY TO CAMP. STOP. TO DATE, NO PROGRESS ON MACKLEY OR JUNGER. STOP. ADVISE ON BEAR OWNERSHIP. STOP. BAPCAT.

"Where's Sister Jone's name?" Scale asked. "It ain't there."

"Her leadership is for the mountains, not legal matters. She told me to take care of things, and I didn't argue."

Scale gave the hint of a grin. "Here I thought you don't know swirls from squirrels, but maybe you'll learn."

"What kind of name is Scale?" the Western Union man asked.

"Term of affection among men who seen the elephant, which clearly you ain't."

"I object," Bowdler said.

Scale said, "Man don't object; he act. What you gon' *do*?"

Bowdler glanced at Bapcat. "Is your man always so intolerant and abrasive?"

"First, he ain't my 'man,' and if you mean he comes across like a sharp stick up the arse, he is."

"I descend from warriors," Scale said haughtily. "My tribal name is Quashi Ojnab."

"Well, la-di-da," Bowdler said. "Nigger with a pedigree. You got paper on that stuff, or is it all hand-me-down hot-air talk?"

Scale seemed to study the man. "Guess you could grow a backbone after all. I don't mix with men got no backbone." Scale looked at Bapcat. "Okay, I can work with this clerk, but don't leave me too long or I'll start usin' words like *abrasive* and *intolerant*, and strut around like some damn po-fessor."

"Name's Thomas," Bowdler said, extending his hand.

• • •

Walking out of the Western Union office, Jimjim said, "That man in there won't never be the same when Scale's done with him. I guess I'll be the one who swaps with Scale when the telegraphs start to talk."

"*If* Isohultamaki doesn't come back. Your pony can't move like a full-size animal."

Jimjim poked his ribs. "You know how it feels to have your size thrown at you from every imaginable angle?"

"I know what it is to be a bastard and thought dumb," Bapcat volunteered.

Jimjim puffed up his cheeks and exhaled loudly. "I guess that's close enough."

"You're really a priest?" Bapcat asked.

"Seminary of Christ the King, East Aurora, New York—top of my class, diploma and all, but never deployed to save souls. My Franciscan brothers harbored unspoken concerns about my lack of size degrading the image of the order, and Jesus as well. What they told me was that they feared for my personal safety, but that was truth with a big twist, and I decided 'Enough,' and left," the man said. "Christ, he learned to rub shoulders with the hoi polloi, so why not me? Our Savior preferred the company of the low, and so, too, do I, not that I would ever liken myself to the Son of God. Questions?"

Lute Bapcat said, "Do you take confessions?"

"I do indeed, one of the great offerings of a deeply flawed church, a chance to cleanse guilt in private. Are you in need, my son?"

"Nope."

"Pity," Jimjim said. "I'm a bit out of practice."

"Are you Jone's priest?"

Jimjim laughed. "As in her confessor? Never. Our dear Jone does not subscribe to dogma, or even to earthly morality. She believes God put us here to be who we are and do what we do; she doesn't see guilt riding on every human act."

"You agree with that?"

"I've got no role in right or wrong for others, so I guess I do."

The dwarf suddenly snapped his head in Bapcat's direction. "You hurt that woman and you'll get a thirty-two in the eye."

"They teach shooting in seminary?"

"The church prefers stealth, political ambush, and a sneaky metaphorical knife in the opposition's back rather than a bullet someone just might see coming, and duck."

"If I ever need to confess, you'll be my choice," Bapcat said.

"So you're Roman Catholic?"

"I ain't of no flavor of church, nor politics."

"Fate has thrown us together."

"That the same as God?"

"Well, He made the whole thing, natural forces included, so I guess it's close; in some minds there's no difference at all."

"I guess He done all right with what He made," Bapcat said.

"And if He turns out to be a She?" Jimjim asked.

"Might explain a whole lot," Bapcat said, which sent the priest into a laughing fit.

"The church in Rome actually expects priests to go without a woman their whole lives?"

"Some do, especially them that favor boys and men more."

Bapcat was befuddled. "You mean?"

"Do you need me to draw a more detailed picture?" the priest asked.

Bapcat muttered, "Nuh-uh."

# CHAPTER 31

## *Tula, Gogebic County*

### TUESDAY, AUGUST 18

Bapcat decided group size was a double-edged sword, and if Junger had the notion to spread his people out to wait for recall later, then Gleann and the four men and their pack animals had suddenly become the more-visible group. Their assumed advantage was potentially gone. The Henry Young he knew had been an impulsive sort, not a thinker, so while he doubted the boy had grown into a think-ahead man, the possibility still had to be considered.

The two game wardens talked to Gleann about their concerns, and she agreed to take the group north behind the cover of a ten-mile-long series of high peaks and ridges. Once above them, they could swing around at the northern extreme and aim southeast at the vicinity of the German's camp.

We need maps, Bapcat told himself. Good, accurate maps. They had learned in training that the United States Geological Survey had decided on a country-wide topographical mapping plan more than a decade ago, but so far less than half of Michigan had been mapped, and none of the Upper Peninsula. Maps meant less wasted time and more safety, and being without them annoyed Bapcat every time he thought about it.

If there was a trapper up there, and if he had been there a long time, he might very well know about local goings on better than anyone. Hopefully he was sane, not always the case with such antisocials.

"I don't know a German trapper named Pippig," Jone Gleann told them yet again. "And I have been all through that country many, many times."

Bapcat knew from experience how one man could get quite close to invisibility, and he didn't argue with her. Before leaving Ironwood, Gleann sent a wire to Isohultamaki, ordering her to the Jessieville Western Union Office where she would receive further instructions. Scale would meet her and pass along an envelope containing directions to a camp in the Porkies.

Today they stopped in the developing lumber town called Tula, which had a new hotel, general store, post office, small school, and sawmill. There were mountains of lumber piles around by the rail siding, awaiting shipment. A sign on the one street proclaimed "Tula Lumber Company, Founded 1910."

A new company town, and like company towns in the Keweenaw, it was overly organized and controlled, built on a swampy creek by the same name. The creek dumped into the Presque Isle River a mile north of the town. The company had its own currency in the form of tokens and scrip for employees and families to spend at the company-owned store, the only such emporium in the village.

Bapcat went into the store with Zakov while the General and Jimjim stayed outside. Bapcat saw that as soon as he started walking down the aisles, the store clerk started reversing price cards. When Bapcat picked up one, he saw the prices for nonemployees were three times higher.

Zakov leaned close and whispered, "There is a town twenty miles from Moscow, same name as this, same thieving personality, gouging customers for the God Profit. I *spit* on all Tulas!"

Bapcat chuckled. His mostly rational partner was prone to some very irrational and funny moments when his temper and sense of righteousness got the better of him. "How many people in this town?" Bapcat asked the clerk, who followed like a dog.

"Almost a hundred already. We're gonna be *big*."

*Air castles*, Bapcat told himself as he walked out. Every American businessman seemed convinced he would become big, rich, and powerful.

The four men found Jone Gleann north of town. She had balked at going in and sent them instead, with no explanation, of course. As they moved north, Bapcat saw a lot of deer sign and wondered if Gunt patrolled over this far east, so close to the Ontonagon County border. The counties in the Upper Peninsula were huge swaths of geography, and it took a lot of time to move around. With only one or two deputies in some counties, there were sections that never saw a game warden. Bapcat wondered how Lansing felt about this flaw, or whether Oates even knew.

"You do not like towns?" Zakov asked Jone as they headed for a ford in the Presque Isle River.

"More like some towns aren't so fond of me," the woman said.

"You have a history back there?"

"You ask too many questions," she said, and hurried to put distance between them. The two game wardens looked at each other and shrugged.

"Our leader," Zakov said sullenly.

The season's immense snowpack and late snowmelt was close to finished, and rivers were becoming more manageable by the day, but there was naked bedrock at this crossing and a lot of loose cobble, a dangerous combination. The party members took turns leading pack animals across, and it was slow going.

"You know this north trail?" Bapcat asked the woman as they waited for the others.

"Marker trees," Jone Gleann said. "The Ojibwa make maple sugar here near Tula, and use this trail back to their summer grounds and winter hunt camps on the big lake. There are a lot of trappers in Tula. The locals call them shackers, and refuse to mix with them."

"Reasons?"

"Towns like rules; trappers don't."

*How does she know this?* "I trapped for some years," he said, "out on the Keweenaw."

"You aren't like the lot in Tula," she said.

No explanation, just a flat statement. *Again.* It was a pain to deal with her, but he reminded himself to let it be and leave well enough alone. "Do you think you can find the German's camp?"

She turned and glared at him. "There is no German—at least where your game warden thinks there is. I know this for a fact. I know the land there like the back of my hand."

*Change the subject.* "Did you learn the trail from the Indians?"

"I learned it by seeing it," she said. "On my own, the way I do most things."

"How far until the north end of the trail?"

"It ends at the shore of Lake Superior."

They weren't going that far, and her remark was intended as an insult. He amended the question: "How far until we swing eastward?"

"Twelve miles crow, twenty the way we have to go, but there are no major rivers after we get across there. Two full days," she concluded. "Without pushing."

It was late afternoon when they stopped where two creeks joined, just east and uphill of the Presque Isle, which they had paralleled all day. Gleann called the creeks Ledge and Canyon. Bapcat asked to see her crude map again; she gave it to him, and he spread it out and used his memory of everything Gunt had told him to make an overlay in his mind. He felt bad about a lot of his mental capabilities, but his ability with maps and directions was second to none. "I could cut northeast here, follow Canyon Creek to the top, then strike north for the Buck Creek headwaters from there."

"I suppose," she said. "But why?"

"One fewer in the group makes us harder to detect," he said. "If I can find the Pippig fellow Gunt talked about, I'll intercept you when you make the swing to the east."

"There's nothing to find. You're wasting your time, but go if you want. Take your pack mule?"

"No, Kukla will stay with Zakov."

"It's steep and dangerous up that way," Jone Gleann said.

"You've been to the top?"

"No need. I can recognize steep without testing it."

Bapcat pulled the Russian aside and told him what he intended.

"Tonight?"

"First light. Joe may do all right in the dark on a mountain, but I don't."

"You think this German is real?" Zakov asked. "Our Jone thinks differently."

"We won't know until I take a look. What I can do when I get up high is find myself the side of the northernmost peak and look east and north from there to see if I can spot any smoke. It's hard to hide a campfire, especially from someone holding the high ground over you. Even a small Indian fire will show up if you know what to look for." Indians favored tiny fires made in openings or holes in the ground and away from trees to avoid reflection from distances, especially at night.

"See you tomorrow night?"

"More likely the next day. She'll camp again tomorrow night. She's in no hurry."

"How will you survive a day alone without her silent leadership?"

"I guess I'll manage. I might even sing a song or two."

"You have no musical ear or acumen. You are a coarse barbarian in such matters."

"I'll pretend I'm a Finnish logger, warble 'Tula Tullalla.'"

"That's real?"

"Tune is. I once heard Mac singing it, but couldn't make out a single word."

"A child's song," the Russian said, shaking his head and making a clucking sound. "You are too long without your woman. Your mind begins to separate."

"I wonder which part I'll keep?"

## CHAPTER 32

### *Buck Creek Ridge*

WEDNESDAY, AUGUST 19

In Bapcat's mind there was no sense hurrying when they didn't know exactly who they were after, and a lot of what they knew to lay ahead, rested on Elphinstone, which meant slow and deliberate was the sensible way to proceed, especially in such unforgiving terrain. It had been a nerve-racking vertical day, and even Joe seemed at wit's end by late afternoon as they snaked their way along a sharp ridge that seemed to connect two rocky peaks, about three miles apart. The climb up Canyon Creek had been easy enough, but the sharp turn northward was a different proposition entirely, every step a challenge as he and the mule picked their way deliberately and carefully.

But now the effort seemed to have paid off. They were safely up, and he had a long promontory from which to examine the countryside. There was even a decent patch of graze for Joe. He hobbled the mule and sat on a rocky ledge, glassing the forests and undulating layers of verdure a thousand feet below. From up here the world looked to be an impenetrable green, but he had spent time in the mountains in the Dakotas and again in Cuba, and he knew that while a high vista had some real advantages, it could also paint false impressions. What mattered was down on ground level, not what you imagined from on high, and he wondered if God knew this, or even cared.

At Roosevelt's ranch there was a Northern Cheyenne called Tooth, and Bapcat remembered how the old man was so deliberate that everything he did looked painful. Most cowhands shunned the Indian, but Bapcat found him interesting, and after a while they began to spend a lot of time in each other's company. Tooth was interesting to work with and knew a lot. Eventually they went everywhere together, including as guides on Roosevelt's beloved big game hunts in the hills. Tooth never talked about his past, but Bapcat noticed other Indians gave him a wide berth, like he was dangerous, or unpredictable, or haunted—something. Who knew with Indians?

One day the old man was sitting with him as they scouted a hunt. "Most men," Tooth said, "are blind."

"That's a darn shame," Bapcat said.

"They choose blindness," the Indian said.

"They do? Why would they do that?"

"Lazy; impossible to say. Takes much effort and work to be Not-Blind."

"Am I blind?"

The Indian nodded.

"I swear I never knew," the much younger Bapcat had said. "Here I thought I could see pretty darn good."

"Only the Not-Blind know. Not many Not-Blind among white men."

"Roosevelt?"

"Four-eyes? He's Not-Blind; sees everything around him."

"Indians are blind, too?"

"Chinaman, red man, black man—most of them, all blind."

"How do I get to be Not-Blind?"

"I can teach you, but once you are Not-Blind, you must not let yourself become blind again."

"That can happen?"

"Many times," Tooth said. "And them usually dies when it happens."

"Why's that?"

"It's one thing for a man to not-see and not-know, but once he can see and knows he can see, and then lets himself go blind again, the dark is darker, and he becomes lost because he has forgotten the ways of the blind, who go about in the dark all their days."

"Just how hard is it to stay Not-Blind?"

"Not so hard. Just do what I tell you every day."

"What is it I do?"

"Look straight ahead. What do you see?"

"Woods on a hillside."

"No, *what* trees in those woods, and tell me about the hill."

"I guess it's steep, and the woods is mostly birch, but I see some pin oak behind them and a couple of them birches is bent like loaded bows, so I'm guessing most of the wind comes from the northwest."

"Good," Tooth said. "You missed an eagle and a lark, and there was a jackrabbit. Now, your left."

"You didn't say nothing about animals," Bapcat said in his own defense.

"Did you see them?"

Bapcat nodded.

"You said nothing," Tooth told him, "like you were blind. Now, your left."

This went on for hours, a demand for an instant detailed inventory not only of everything in sight, but what its behavior might mean; for example, a mule deer who had their wind but kept looking to its right when they were to its left suggested a more-pressing concern was over to the animal's right. It was a plain and obvious sign to be read for those who could see it. The Indian taught him to look left and right, front and back, and after months Bapcat asked, "Am I Not-Blind yet?"

"Not for me to say," Tooth told him. "You looked everywhere?"

"Ahead, left, right, behind—that seems like everywhere."

"Still blind."

Bapcat mulled this over for several days and went over to Tooth one morning and looked up and said, "Three bone-pickers overhead."

"Now you're Not-Blind," the old Indian said, smiling. "Practice or lose it."

This time of year dark came late and sunrises early. He had practice. Not-Blind virtually every day since then, everywhere he went, and even now, sitting on the ledge near the top of the ridge, he turned his upper body and looked up, and after a moment spied a diaphanous tendril of smoke curling from a fissure in the rocks higher up. It was no more than a smudge, but he knew it was a fire. Had he been further away, or down below, or not looked up even though he was so high, he would have missed it.

Not-Blind, he thought, smiling.

## CHAPTER 33

### Little Porcupine Peak

### THURSDAY, AUGUST 20

Whoever owned the smoke was obviously not of a social bent. In Bapcat's experience men of this kind could be dangerous, fly down on you without warning. The day had worn out his mule and him, and he wanted nothing more than to eat a little and sleep, but he guessed this night would bring neither.

The stranger in his high redoubt was likely to be looking downhill a lot, searching for possible threats, so Bapcat built a large campfire that was kicking out smoke, grabbed pemmican and water, left Joe to his grass, and ascended the rocky crags as dark came down, finishing his climb in a fissure above where he had seen the wisps of smoke. Once above, he eased his way down the slope until the smell was clear and directly below him. Tooth had taught him that Not-Blind required the use of sight, hearing, and smell, all of this together, and the Indian had added, "This too?" and pounded his fist on his chest. Bapcat had no idea what that meant, but guessed it referred to guts, or heart.

It was pretty unlikely the man in the mountain would ignore smoke so close; close meant an immediate threat. The same fire down in the valley below would be no more than a curiosity, an oddity to be watched, noted, and forgotten.

The challenge would be to catch the man between his shelter and the open fire. Men who lived alone like this tended to move like animals, unseen and unheard, but those same men also often had a weakness. Most were not fond of bathing and carried with them a fusty cloud that, like a bear or fox, often announced their presence.

"*Ach*, hands raised up high to *Gott!*" a voice barked beside him, and Bapcat immediately recognized his mistake. Like most humans, sometimes subject to hubris and a desire to remain Not-Blind, Bapcat forgot you had to use all of your senses *and* your brain. Being so pleased with himself, he had forgotten how many times he had heard that Germans, unlike many other European people, bordered on fanatical when it came to personal hygiene. Blind again. Dumb. Disgusted with himself. Embarrassed by his own failure.

"I could shoot you for trespassing on my mountain," the voice said, with only the slightest hitch of accent.

"It's not *your* mountain," Bapcat said. "This is State land, meaning it belongs to all citizens."

"This shotgun is on you, and I say it is mine."

"I carry a badge and say differently."

"What I care, this bedge? My mountains, my little country here up high, we don't got no bedges up here."

"You do now."

"I just shoot you, leave you for wolfs."

"A shot will bring attention you won't welcome."

The man laughed. "*Ja*, all those scaffengers on the mountain think it's a call to dinner!"

"You really think I came up here alone?" Bapcat guessed the man was on his way to investigate the fire when he'd stumbled upon the game warden, meaning he'd not yet been below and didn't know the reality for certain.

"How many you got?" the man asked.

"Squeeze the trigger and find out. You're Pippig, right?"

"I don't know you."

"Heard about you from the Gogebic County game warden, Napoleol Gunt."

"This Gunt I heard of, but don't know him neither. What do you want here on my mountain?"

"To talk."

The man coughed. "You think I live way up here because there's lots of people to talk to?"

"No. I used to be a trapper, and like you, I lived alone in the wayback, and I liked being alone just fine."

"Where you trapped?"

"Beavers, Keweenaw County, but not no more. Not a lot of beaves around. I ain't your competition. I just want help."

"What kind of help you mean?"

"Maybe you seen a large group of armed men moving through this country?"

"If I did, why I tell you this?"

"That answer tells me you have seen such a gang."

"*Ach*, I said nothing like that!"

"But I can tell differently. Game wardens get special training."

"From who, witches? *Ach, mein* name *ist Hase, ich weis von nichts.*"

Bapcat knew a handful of German words. "Your name is Hase—is that what you said?"

"*Nein, ja*—I say I don't know nothing about no gang riding out there over to east."

"I never said anything about east."

The man waved the barrel of the shotgun. "*Mach die fliege*—you go away now!"

"I thought you were going to shoot me."

"Catrich she cost money; I don't waste none. *Hau ab*—get lost."

"All right, but when I find that gang, I'll have to tell them Pippig told me how to find them."

"This is a gottdemm lie!" the German yipped. "What is wanted with this men I have never seen?"

"I have a warrant to arrest their leader for several murders, and a lot more."

"*Morde wollte*—several murders? This has nothing to do me. I live on this mountain, trap down there, that's all. I see no gang, *nein* gang. Go now." The man wiggled his scrawny hand dismissively.

All the while they were talking, Bapcat had inched his way closer to the old man until the barrel was in easy reach. He guessed the man's age as eighty or older, and though his voice was young, his body was thin and bent. Bapcat swept the Krag hard, knocking the shotgun away, and stepped close to drive his elbow into the old trapper's face. The shotgun went off and the old man slumped heavily and Bapcat quickly knelt with his knee in the man's back, pinning him against the rocks. "I'm going to handcuff you. Don't fight me."

"I don't know no gottdemm gang, I tell you. I am not a criminal."

"Not yet, but you just lied to me about seeing a gang, and that now makes you guilty of conspiracy to prevent a peace officer from pursuing his lawful duty. That can be a felony. You know what that means?"

"*Ja*, I know this word. But I ain't done nothing," the man said. "I am *not* a criminal. Pippig is trapper, that's it."

"Pippig, eh? Why didn't you say so when I asked?"

"I don't know you," the man said glumly.

"Gang or no gang?" Bapcat asked, pressing the man's face against the rocks.

The answer was a series of gagging sounds, and Bapcat rolled the man over and found his face covered with blood. The game warden pulled the man to his feet and gave him a cloth for his face.

"Gang or no gang?"

"Just that woman *und* those three poor boys," the man said. "I had shack over upper Blowdown Creek, *ja*, saw her bury them over there, terrible thing I seen."

Bapcat's mind had been on a large gang, not this, and the information caught him by surprise.

"A woman and three boys? *Her* children? What woman?"

"Don't know. I built my camp up here on the mountain after that."

"When was this?"

"Three year back, I guess."

"Did you know these people?"

"*Nein*, I never see before."

"What did she look like?"

"She wear a bandanna over face because of the stink, so no face to see, but I saw those scars, I did," Pippig said. "All over her legs. Horrible to see, so many scars she had."

# CHAPTER 34

## *Greenstone Falls*

### FRIDAY, AUGUST 21

Bapcat made Pippig come with him and at first light helped him swing up behind him on Joe, who took the burden of an extra passenger without complaint. A woman burying three boys, supposedly a woman with horribly scarred legs; how many women with scarred legs frequented this country? For that matter, *any* country? He was left with a lot of doubt and questions and only one very ugly possible conclusion he tried not to think about.

They intercepted the others watering their stock in the Little Carp River, at the base of scenic falls cascading over moss-and-lichen-covered boulders.

The group stared at him and his passenger.

"That woman?" Bapcat asked Pippig, pointing at Jone Gleann.

"I was never so close, *ja*. I don't know," the man said.

Jone Gleann walked over. "Who is this?"

Bapcat said, "Pippig, the German trapper who doesn't exist."

"I never saw a camp," Gleann said.

"He saw a woman and three dead boys. He watched the woman bury them. He moved his camp because of this. Three years ago."

"I wasn't in this area three years ago," Jone Gleann said.

"The woman he saw had badly scarred legs."

"I am not baring my legs for the likes of some German," she said angrily. "Do you think I am the only woman who has scars?"

"I think there's not many women coming this far up into these mountains is what I think," Bapcat countered. "Did you or did you not bury three children?"

Jone Gleann stared him in the eye. "That is none of your damn business."

"You've got to talk to us, Jone."

"I've done nothing wrong, and I am not obliged to explain myself to anyone."

"You're the leader. You can't be tainted."

She hissed at him. "I don't concern myself with so-called taint. We are all soiled or tainted in some way, and I have my own values and conscience to guide me, thank you."

Bapcat was almost at a loss. There had to be a reasonable explanation. "Why won't you talk about this?" he pressed her.

"My life is my life. I owe no explanation to anyone—and what business is it of yours? You're a game warden, not a policeman."

"Three dead children," Bapcat said. "That's everybody's concern, and it should be yours too."

He looked at the German, said, "Take a good, close look at her."

"I have looked, and I cannot say. There was a bandanna, and she was not so close, *ja?*"

"Tell us about the bodies."

"They was wrapped in blankets, gray ones."

"Was the woman on a mule or a horse?"

"On foot; I didn't see no animal."

"Did you see her carry the bodies?"

The man pondered this. "No, I seen them on the ground there, and I seen her dig graves and put them boys in those holes."

"Did you ever see the actual bodies?"

Pippig said, "What else there be in those blankets?"

"But you *didn't* actually see them?"

"*Nein,*" the trapper said, "but I know what they was."

"How could you know they were dead boys?"

"What would little girls be doing this far in the big woods?"

Zakov was suddenly beside Joe and flooded the air with waves of loud and guttural German and a lot of angry grunts and facial expressions and hand gestures, and the two men barked at each other like snarling dogs for several minutes.

The Russian said, "Those boys were around here for several days, and the German saw them. About this time he also saw a large group of men pass through on horseback, and the next day he saw the woman and the blankets and concluded she had done something to them, or the men had, and she was cleaning up after them; his mind is a bit jumbled, and what he believes is not entirely clear."

Bapcat dismounted and stood beside Jone Gleann. "Tell us, Jone. We need to know about this."

She refused to look at him. "They had been tortured, their throats cut, what remained of them tied to trees and left there for animals to feed on. I untied them, wrapped them, and put them in the ground."

*Why hadn't she just told him this when he'd asked?* "Dead how long?"

"Days," she said, "not hours. The stench was bad, and rigor mortis past. I did the decent thing," she said. "As you did, with the circus bear."

Bapcat didn't tell her he'd cured the skin and not buried it. "What sort of sign was there—how many people, horses—anything readable?"

"I was preoccupied with the dead children. It was all I could do to hold myself together to do what had to be done. I came back to Lake Mine early that year. I needed to be out of the mountains and all that's out here."

Bapcat looked back at the German. "Armed men. I asked you about them on the mountain, and you lied! Don't lie to me again. How many of these men were there?"

"Twenty, I count, got rifle, shotguns, many pack animals. A small army, *ja?*"

"What about the group's leader?"

"Impossible to tell who led. I was not so close. They were quiet like soldiers, taking their time, moving slowly."

"Like soldiers?

"*Ja*, nervous, careful."

"In a formation?"

"*Ja*, I see them spread out in the middle, with riders left and right, away from the main group."

"Where did you see them?"

"South of the boys' camp, day before I seen the woman."

"That's the only time you saw them?"

Pippig nodded.

Back to Jone Gleann. "Say again how long you thought they were dead."

"Days."

"And you never saw the large group?"

"No."

Bapcat wondered if a doctor or medical examiner could make something of remains that had been in the ground for three years. He wished he knew, took his lack of knowing as another personal flaw.

"If Pippig saw the gang the day before you found the bodies, a day later, and they had been dead for days, it's likely they were already dead by the time the German saw that group come through."

So many questions lingered in his head. Bapcat looked at the German trapper. "You said the person you saw with the bundles wore a mask. How could you even know it was a woman?"

"*Grose dinger*," Pippig said sheepishly.

"Big things," Zakov translated, and gestured to his chest.

That also described Jone Gleann, as did the leg scars.

The woman's eyes were glazed over. Bapcat took her by the shoulders. "You have to help us, Jone," he said. "Show us where the children are buried."

"I can't remember."

Pippig said, "*Ja*, I show you this place. But then I go," he added.

The woman never raised her eyes. Bapcat watched her mount up and knew there were questions he had missed, a familiar pattern. If he was lucky, they would pop into his head later, usually when his mind was on something entirely different. He hoped that would be the case this time.

# CHAPTER 35

## Blowdown Creek

### FRIDAY, AUGUST 21

Jone Gleann was listless as the trekkers made their way through severely chopped-up terrain filled with boulders, small rivulets from seeps, slash and blowdowns of every description, and detritus left by melting snow that grew spring rills into rivers for a month or more.

The German was on a spare mount and looked entirely uncomfortable on a horse. A man used to using his feet, not a saddle, Bapcat thought.

"He lied about the group at his camp," the game warden told Zakov.

"Jone was there and not forthcoming right away, either, but we know by her own admission that she *was* there, and that the trapper saw her. What is your plan if we miraculously locate the alleged bodies in this labyrinth?"

"I don't know. See what we can see."

"And then?"

"We'll decide that when we need to."

Pippig halted them two hours later, in what had once been a tightly packed cedar grove, the trees now all uprooted, showing only their upturned shallow root-balls. Even so the trees weren't entirely dead. Bapcat noticed clusters of tiny yellow pinecones. The German stared up a rocky creek bed and hill. "Here," Pippig said.

"You're certain?"

"*Ja.* I make a mark there."

Bapcat followed the man's finger to a gray rock etched with a small cross. "You said you never got very close."

"I come down after woman is gone, saw graves."

"Where are they?" Bapcat couldn't see anything obvious.

The man picked up stones and sticks and placed one each on three different places. "Stick is in direction of the grave," he said.

"There are no indentations, no signs."

"They sink and settle," Pippig said.

"Ground's too hard for that," Bapcat said.

"Only all stone is too hard for settling. Come, I show you."

The old man led him up fifteen feet or so and pointed down. "See?"

Bapcat saw vague depressions; the markers the old man had placed were right on them.

"They are deep," the trapper said, "beyond reach of beasts."

The exhumation of the first body took almost an hour. The blanket it had been wrapped in was in tatters, but there was a small fragment with the letters "TLC."

Bapcat thought for a moment and looked at Jone Gleann. "You avoided Tula. These are the letters of the lumber company there. What's going on?"

"Those letters could mean anything," she countered dismissively, but her shoulders slumped and Bapcat thought she was going to fall. "There were traps," she said. "I buried them. Over there." Bapcat saw where she pointed but didn't look.

The body was missing a foot and an entire leg, one hand and an arm. Bapcat looked for an explanation from Jone Gleann, who seemed to be mentally elsewhere.

Zakov and the General stood nearby. "Seen this before," Elphinstone said. "Never pretty, but entirely human in desperation."

Zakov nodded, "Always a leg is missing. They start there because of the muscle."

Jimjim knelt by the remains and made the sign of the cross. "You want all of them out of the ground?" the priest asked over his shoulder.

Bapcat talked to the woman. "Are they all like this, Jone?"

She nodded.

"Show us exactly where the traps are," he said.

Jimjim and the General started digging where she indicated.

The traps were not as deep as the bodies, and were wrapped in heavy canvas that had survived its time in the ground better than the wool blankets.

"Your canvas?" Bapcat asked the woman.

"No, it was here."

"Was this a camp?"

"No," she said.

Bapcat fingered the canvas. "Twelve-ounce duck, heavy and real expensive."

He picked up one of the traps which had rusted where the parts had been exposed outside the canvas wrappings. There were five traps. "New-house; not cheap," the game warden said. "Were there sets here?" he asked. "I don't see clamps." Clamps were viselike devices used to anchor traps, to keep animals from dragging them away.

"No sets," she said. "The traps were in a pile, over by the rocks."

"Where were the children?"

"Look on that cedar. It wasn't uprooted then." She pointed. "Crucified," she added in a whisper.

The tree was tipped at 45 degrees, its root-ball standing like a plate beneath it.

"How do you know this is the tree?"

She showed him a scar in the bark, a long, deep slash.

"Yours?"

"Yes."

It seemed clear that she had not panicked that day, had managed to keep her wits about her. He wondered how calm he would have been as he sur-veyed the area of the graves, and saw small piles of dried debris, just hints, but definitely nothing that grew on the rocks. It hit him what he was seeing. "You've been coming back here," he said, "leaving wildflowers."

She gave him a hard look. He asked, "Did you see it happen?"

"No, after. I found them."

"Only you were here?"

"Just me."

He heard something in her voice, a catch in tone, something. "But you did see someone else, yes?"

"Three days later, after I buried the children."

"Let me guess," Bapcat said. "You tracked them, east of here to the Elm Creek area." His eyes were closed, studying the maps she had drawn and shown him, not locked in his mind forever.

"They trap bears, sell skins, or make coats for winter. They are animals."

"How many of them?"

"Just three."

"Not an armed band of twenty?"

"The three talked about that, laughed, said this time they beat the Big Red to the prizes."

*The Big Red? Prizes?* "You never reported this," he said.

"For what happens up here, justice should be done up here—not in some damn town."

"We have laws."

"These animals follow no laws except force."

"You took this job thinking we might stumble onto them and a certain violent nature might show itself. Is that why you agreed to lead?"

"They deserve to die," she said.

"If a jury says so," he reminded her. "Only then."

"No capital punishment in this state since before the Civil War," Zakov said.

"How do you know *that*?"

"It is in *Tiffany's*. Everything is in that wonderful volume."

Of course it was in the book, and of course he had read only the parts relating to game wardens and fish and game laws. Damn.

"The law is wrong," Jone Gleann said. "Not all murders are equal."

"It doesn't matter," Bapcat said. "Law is law."

She leered at him. "Except when a certain game warden decides it no longer applies, as happened last year during the strike?"

*That again.* "Murder and deer laws are not equal," he told her.

"Right," she said. "There is always a hierarchy in misbehavior. The killers of children are not equal to other murderers. They are heinous and deserve to die."

"I have no opinion of these things," Pippig said nervously. "I am going now; thank you for horse rides."

"Stay where you are," Bapcat snarled at the man. "You lied to me at least once, and I'm thinking there's more you know and haven't told us."

"There is suddenly law against lies?" the German whined. "If this is true, all jails will soon be full."

"You're staying with us. You threatened a peace officer."

"You hid to ambush *me*!"

"I was the one who got ambushed."

"I should have shot you; then none of this would be happening."

"It's that attitude that's keeping you here, Pippig."

His temper loose, Bapcat turned to Jone Gleann. "You tried to use us."

"You came begging me, not the other way around, and you make it sound like using you is a difficult thing. All people use each other, by consent or not. It is the nature of civilization."

"You're going to lead us to the trappers' camp," he said solemnly.

"Why would I do that?" she came back.

"I bring you here. The woman doesn't do this," Pippig said. "I go now."

"Shut up!" Bapcat yelled at the German.

To Jone, "Who is the Big Red they talked about?"

"I don't know," she said with a defiant look.

"Leader of the twenty," the German said.

Bapcat yelled at him. "You swore you couldn't identify a leader! Another damn lie!"

"It now comes into my mind, *ja*, and now I will be going. *Danke*."

"Stay where you are!"

"You do not want to confront these men," the German said.

"No?"

"Berserks," Pippig whispered.

"A myth," Zakov commented.

"*Nein, nein*, here is real," Pippig said. "The leader's hair is red. He wears the fur of a bear, and all of his men, the heads and skins of *die wolfe*."

"Wolves led by this Red Hair?" Bapcat said.

"He is a monster, sir, sent by *der Teufel selbst*," the German said. "I have now said all I know, and it is time for Pippig to go. I thank you very much. *Auf wiedersehen*."

"For the last time, you are staying with us," Bapcat said, remembering Mac taunting little girls with a tale of Red Hair. More disturbingly, he remembered a boy from St. Cazimer's whose hair seemed to get redder when violence and anger erupted.

"The Red Hair will kill us all," Pippig said quietly.

Bapcat knew *Teufel* meant "Devil." "I don't believe in *der Teufel*," Bapcat said.

The German pointed a crooked finger at him. "This is to invite him into our presence. Now we are doomed. You have killed us all!"

Bapcat looked over at Jimjim, who raised an eyebrow. "He's not alone in such beliefs."

"You too?"

"We'll soon see who is right," the little man said.

# CHAPTER 36

## North of Jack Spur

MONDAY, AUGUST 24

"I don't care what your laws say—those men deserve to die," Jone Gleann said. It had taken considerable cajoling and near-bullying to get her to move south. Bapcat had in mind to push into Tula to make a public show, if Gogebic sheriff Torrance would agree.

Bapcat said evenly but sternly, "Jone, you didn't *see* those three men *do* anything."

"You don't know what I saw," she snapped back at him.

"This case is circumstantial," Zakov offered, and Gleann scowled at him as well.

Bapcat was doing his best to remain calm in the face of her continued obstinacy. "I'll explain all this to Sheriff Torrance. It will be his call what happens next."

She shook a finger at him. "I am not going to identify anyone, and I don't give a damn what some sheriff, you, or anybody else thinks."

"Without identification there can be no prosecution," Zakov said.

"Good," the woman said.

"They will be free," Zakov added.

"Only until the reckoning," the woman said.

Bapcat understood what she intended. "You can't go after them. If you do, it will be you who ends up behind bars."

Jone Gleann said through clenched teeth, "You. Did. Not. See. What. I. Saw. Lute, you did not see what I saw."

"I know I didn't. But you also didn't actually see those men do anything."

"I buried the results, followed their trail to their camp, heard them talk."

"But they didn't talk about killing kids."

"They talked about Red Hair not getting the prizes this time."

"*What* prizes? That could mean anything. Tell me."

She looked away. "I know what I know."

Zakov said, "More to the point, you don't know what you don't know. It's up to the sheriff to find out."

She raised her hands in obvious frustration and stalked stiffly away.

Bapcat looked over at Jimjim. "Is she capable of killing?"

"I can't say she isn't," the priest said.

"I can go now, *ja*?" Pippig the trapper chimed in.

Bapcat looked at Elphinstone. "If that man says anything like that even one more time, put a bullet in his knee."

"*Ach*," the trapper said, "you tell the woman not to kill, but is okay to shoot me? Nothing wrong I've done."

"You lied to me," Bapcat said. "And you annoy me."

"So I will not be leaving now?" the German said.

Bapcat said, "General."

Elphinstone unholstered a large-bore revolver and clicked the hammer back. The trapper slumped to the ground and said, "*Ja*, I have no more to say."

# CHAPTER 37

*Ramsay, Gogebic County*

TUESDAY, AUGUST 25

Bapcat rode into the mining town to find a telephone to call Sheriff Torrance, who was not available. The person on the other end asked if there was a message. Telephones, Bapcat knew from Horri Harju, were not exactly private; others could listen in, which forced callers to be circumspect. "Tell the sheriff this is Bapcat, and I'm in Ramsay. I need to have a talk that concerns him, not game wardens."

"Where in Ramsay?" the calm male voice asked.

"You know a place?"

"Anvil Mine has a tavern called Irondale Red Ironman. Food's eatable, beer's cheap."

"Who am I talking to?"

"Deputy Bresnahan. The sheriff should be back anytime now, sir."

"I'll wait for him at the Red Ironman."

"Shall I tell him it's urgent?"

"I guess it is at that, thanks."

It struck Bapcat after hanging up that the telephone had potentially just saved a lot of travel and time. Maybe he shouldn't be so quick to condemn these new devices.

Torrance arrived late in the afternoon, covered with red dust and sweat, and ordered two large glasses of Pabst on the way to Bapcat's table.

"You've been here long enough to sink roots," the sheriff asked. "These ironmen will chew off your ear soon as they get a beer down the hatch."

"Not if you show them your badge as an introduction," Bapcat said.

The sheriff grinned and shook his head. "Most people abide by regular laws and backslap the sheriffs they elect, figuring if a wrong step gets took down the line, their ol' pal sheriff will look the other way, and I'm sure that might happen in some places. But you game wardens get put here by Lansing, and that scares hell out of the locals, because they see fish and game as all theirs. Any law stopping them from doing what they want is an imposition and interference from the foreign government downstate, which might as well be in China, far as Lansing is from these parts.

"Sorry you had to wait so long, Bapcat. The Electric's supposed to extend to Bessemer by next year, but it ain't so now, and I had to ride my horse all the way. He don't travel like he once did. A dozen or more people stopped me along the way to bend my ear and lament some imaginary wrongdoing they've suffered and want righted by my supposed magic wand. Bresnahan told me this is urgent."

The beer came, and Bapcat let the man drain his first Pabst before relating the sad tale of the three dead children in the mountains.

Torrance sighed. "Ought to hang bastards who do that sort of thing, or worse—and out in public so all can bear witness and let it serve as a public warning. The truth of the matter is that these kinds of cases are damn hard to deal with. We've got so many kids up here, there ain't no real way to keep track of them. Some go to school some of the time, and some never go. People up here reproduce like rabbits, and if one dies, they just make themselves another. Children are going missing all the time, and usually show up after a decent interval. I know one woman who's a regular biblical begat. She has fifteen brats from nine men, and she couldn't tell you her kids' names if she had a week to think on it. I'd guess most runaways just want out and on to what they dream will be better lives. Some get killed trying."

"Do people ever report their missing kids?" Bapcat asked.

"Some do, some don't. My boys and me can look through what records we've got, but I've only been in the office a few months, and the fella before me didn't think much of records and paperwork except as related to prisoners, trials, and his pay. Three kids, three years ago? I'm gonna guess we'll be out of luck. You got the bodies?"

"Only dug up one and put it back."

"I guess I'll have to send someone up in them hills and fetch them all back to Ironwood."

"You might want to consider setting up a temporary place in Tula," Bapcat suggested. "There's some chance the kids were from there."

"Why would you think that?"

"The woman who took us to the bodies refused to go into Tula before we found out about the bodies. I wondered why then, but later it hit me: She might have been scared she'd run into one or more of the men."

"But you said she refuses to identify anyone."

"That's true, but if we put those remains in town so all can see, it just might touch some nerves, and get us something. The blanket on the one body was marked 'TLC.'"

Torrance looked at him and nodded. "TLC, you say? That's a top-shelf idea, and I think we'll do just that. I'll need you to guide my people to the bodies. There'll have to be autopsies. I think I'll send Doc Minturn up there into the hills to dig up those poor boys; do her good, get her out of the bloody morgue and see how bodies and remains get to her. Prissy little thing. Never could understand why such a handsome woman wants to doctor the dead."

"Minturn?" Bapcat asked.

"Her given name is Pembina, but what she's called by her friends I can't say, because I can't say I know any who'd fit that category. My late mother always entreated us Torrances to speak kindly of folks, but I don't see much to work with as regards Coroner Minturn."

"Medical doctor?"

"Trained, but not quite graduated is how I heard it. Lot of us figure she killed so many patients with her sour puss that they farmed her downstairs to the cadaver ward. You know, Bapcat, there ain't exactly no evidence of a crime here, and won't be unless Minturn can figure something out through whatever process she uses."

Bapcat said, "I know."

"You ain't said the name of the accuser; there a reason for that?"

"You know much about Italians?"

"More than I want."

"It's like the Spaghettis say, 'An informer is like an honest woman, faithful to only one man.'"

"She don't care to sing in another church, is that it?"

"Something like that, but I'm working on her. Her name is Jone Gleann, the schoolteacher from Lake Mine. She runs a subscription school there."

Torrance said, "Makes me wonder what business a schoolmarm has galvanating around Nowhereburg."

"You'd have to know her."

Torrance asked, "What do you make of all that nonsense about Red Hair and prizes?"

"Not much, I guess." Bapcat had not shared the German's ranting about Berserkers and bear- and wolf skins and all that.

"Well, this may mean nothing, but it's a helluva coincidence if it don't. We have a hot-tempered fool in our jail who swears he was approached by a traveling whore in Hurley who wanted him to join a gang that works the Porkies every summer, hunting and sporting around. They even carry a half-dozen game gals along. Durkee Bitche swears the woman said he'd have a time he'd never forget—how her crowd runs around with wolf skins over their heads and follows a hard-nose fella they call Red Hair. You think all this might be related to what you heard?"

"Why's the man in jail?"

"Well, mainly he's a certified imbecile. Every time he takes offense at something someone does or says and puts him on the peeve, he cuts the throats of all that person's stock and pets. He's as big as a rich man's privy door, and every time we arrest him, it takes six of us to hog-tie his gigantic arse, and none of us comes out looking too good. This time it was two milk cows of a farmer named Langlois, and don't it figure the farmer's got new-born twins at home depending on them dead bovines."

"Bitche is one of your regulars?"

"Not quite, but he's an incurable idiot. Every year or so he gets thrown into the clink, does his time, acts contrite, apologizes, and goes out and does it all over again. This time is different because he says he doesn't want out—that if that strumpet finds out he's free, she'll either force him into the mountains or see him quartered alive."

"What exactly does 'quartered alive' mean?" Bapcat asked.

"No idea, but Bitche's a drooler, and I'm guessing this time the court will send him over to the state hospital in Newberry. He ain't gonna get better, that's for sure."

"He's still in your jail?"

"Indeed he is."

"Think he'd talk to me?"

Torrance laughed. "That fool talks to everyone and anyone, most of all himself. When?"

"Soon as possible, I guess. You want to sit in with me?"

"Sure, it ought to be entertaining if nothing else. How about tomorrow?"

"Tomorrow works."

"I'll arrange it so you can talk to him before the prisoners get their morning swill. He's a man wed to habit, and any small variation puts him off the wall, so he may be more focused than normal this way, feeling a little pressure to please us in order to get his vittles. Afterwards we'll make arrangements for Tula. Could be your informant's heart will soften if she sees a display of the remains and public grief in Tula."

"Maybe," Bapcat allowed. "If your prisoner's an imbecile, why listen to him at all?"

"That mention of Red Hair. Probably this is a waste of time, but this work is sometimes about grasping at straws, even imaginary ones. Can you be there before seven a.m.? Not eating on time will tip him over the mental cliff and might just loosen his tongue."

"Well, I guess we've got trouble enough right here. I'm glad old Woodrow declared us neutral in that scrap across the ocean," Torrance said.

"Woodrow?"

"President Wilson."

"What war?"

"The one brewing in Europe. Ain't you following the news?"

"Ain't no papers in the deep woods," Bapcat said.

Bapcat didn't want to hear about war declarations. The sheriff was right. They had a plateful of trouble right in front of them. "I'll be there in the morning," he said.

# CHAPTER 38

## *Ramsay, Gogebic County*

### WEDNESDAY, AUGUST 26

Bapcat was at the jail at the appointed time, and Torrance met him outside.

"That damn fool hung himself during the night."

The deputy game warden was immediately suspicious. "Did he know I was coming?"

"Only person who knew was Bresnahan, and I've got him in mind to be my senior deputy."

"Is he here?"

Torrance smiled. "He lives right here—bachelor man. His room is in the old jail wing in a former cell, and if there are any problems, the jailers call him first. He gets the room free, eats with prisoners, and I don't have to be running down here on fool's errands all the time."

A quick check found Bresnahan's cell empty, his clothes gone, the place picked clean.

"Maybe he got a house and forgot to tell me," the sheriff offered weakly.

Bapcat's gut said differently.

"You might want to call your coroner on the suicide," Bapcat suggested.

"You've got an expansive imagination this morning."

"I add one and one, I like to be sure I get two, and not another sum."

"Sounds reasonable," Torrance said. "I guess you'll get to meet Dr. Pembina Minturn a little sooner than expected."

• • •

Minturn was as the sheriff described her: tiny and attractive, with a high-strung air. Bapcat noticed she picked up the belt the man hung himself with, and quickly dropped it.

"Move this body to the morgue immediately, Sheriff."

"What's the hurry? He ain't going nowhere soon."

The woman left, saying nothing more.

"Seems like you made quite the impression," Torrance said.

"She didn't even look at me."

"And don't think I didn't notice," the sheriff said.

• • •

Late that night, in the saddle, Bapcat was headed east, and tired. The autopsy revealed water in the man's lungs and brought a preliminary finding of homicide. The man had drowned before being hung; how was anybody's guess. And no one had seen Deputy Bresnahan since late last night when he'd unexpectedly gone into Bitche's cell for an unscheduled visit.

Before leaving Ironwood, Bapcat arranged to meet Torrance's people at Jack Spur midday on Friday. They would head north the next morning, give them a good part of the day at the burial site.

He wondered how Jone Gleann would react to all that was happening, and guessed not well . . . not well at all.

# CHAPTER 39

## Upper Blowdown Creek

### SATURDAY, AUGUST 29

Coroner Pembina Minturn wore a long riding dress and fancy leather boots, and she had come into camp the day before on an English saddle atop a skittish, high-stepping roan with ankles as thin as a deer's and a wild look in its eyes. Life itself may have been a total nightmare for the creature, and the rider looked like she'd ridden directly off the pages of some Eastern city catalog, instead of Ironwood.

The doctor showed not a whit of recognition when introduced to Bapcat again, and he wondered if he'd known her somewhere along the line and run afoul of her for reasons he couldn't remember. Truth, he sure didn't remember her, and she had a look one wasn't likely to ever forget, as if her face had been finely sculpted of the smoothest porcelain and somehow glued to her skull. She wasn't the type to be mislaid in even the mustiest of memories.

The doctor had three assistants, all women, and none of them particularly friendly, except to Jimjim in his hooded brown cassock, which he rarely wore.

The group had made the ride north with little comment and no complaints, and when told to do something, got right to it without delay. Finally reaching the burial site, Bapcat took Sheriff Torrance and Dr. Minturn up where the German had taken him before. He pointed down at the graves.

The doctor climbed down immediately and talked with her assistants, who went to their lone pack animal to fetch shovels. When the General and Zakov stepped forward to get the tools, the women ignored the men, got the shovels themselves, and went to where the doctor pointed and started digging. Zakov said, "The general and I would be pleased to perform such beast work for such fine ladies."

The doctor said, "Shoo," and waved them away from the work, leaving the Russian with a disapproving look.

Bapcat kept looking down—not at the grave excavations, but at the spot where the traps had been. Who left such expensive harvesting gear behind? The three men, Jone Gleann claimed, were trappers. Wouldn't they have taken the traps with them, even if they weren't theirs? It didn't make any sense. Trappers who managed to turn a profit (these were rare birds) didn't do so with profligate habits.

"You see something?" the sheriff asked.

"I have a habit of taking some long hikes inside my head."

"Nothing wrong with that, long as you pop back out where you started."

Actually, the deputy game warden hoped such journeys would bring him out at places different than where he'd started, which was the whole point of such trips. The trap thing rubbed him wrong.

He went to find Jone Gleann and found her downstream, sitting by a placid black pool watching small trout swimming in circles, looking for food.

"Jone, I need your help," he said.

"We've been over this ground," she said. "And my mind's the same."

"Not the men, the traps. They were in a pile at the base of the big boulder?"

"I showed you where."

"And you think these men were trappers, only you ain't said why."

"Not think," she said. "Know."

"How?"

"I saw their camp."

"Saw what there?"

"Three bears chained up."

"And the traps?"

"Traps were hanging in trees. There was a wind that day, and I heard them before I saw them."

"Any sign that the traps here were used on the boys, or used at all—blood, hair . . . you know?"

She looked up at him. "Can't you simply resign yourself to the fact that what you see is what you see?"

"I guess I might have, if I'd seen something with my own eyes. Could be they weren't their traps."

Jone recoiled. "Are you calling me a liar?"

"No, ma'am, but we're all different, and each of us can look at the same scene and see it our own way, which might be similar to how others might see, or not even close."

"In a pile," she said, "where I showed you. I didn't examine them for blood, even when I buried them."

"Why did you bury them?"

"I wanted the murderers to know they'd been found out if for some reason they came back."

"But the traps might not have belonged to them."

"Of course they belonged to them," she said.

No point arguing with her, her thinking being nailed in place. "How do you think them boys got took?"

"I have no idea. They were dead and mutilated when I came on the scene."

He didn't know if Dr. Minturn would want to talk to Gleann, but he wanted the doctor to try to clarify if it was possible to figure out how long the victims might have been dead when Jone found them. He didn't know if such a determination was even possible. And how had she come upon the scene? She'd never said.

"Jone, you told us you found the victims, but you ain't told us how it happened you come upon them. You mind telling me?"

She didn't answer right away, and sensed she was suspicious of his motive. "Just simple facts," he said, "about how you came to be here in this place at that time."

"I don't see that it matters," she said.

"Which it probably don't, but I need more time to chew on things than most folks."

"I was on foot, climbing up Blowdown. I didn't know its source and wanted to see for myself, and check for leech ponds in the headwaters. I was just about to this place when I heard a voice, so I went to cover and stayed put. After a while I crawled out and went to look."

"And you saw?"

She nodded, her eyes misting with tears.

"You heard a man's voice," he said.

"I never said it was a man's voice."

"A woman, then?"

"It was just a voice, through some trees. Could have been a man, or a woman. I didn't care, and didn't want to be found."

"How long did you hide?"

"An hour? I don't know."

"You came upon the site and seen them poor children, and then what did you do?"

"Cocked my rifle. I saw the blood and carnage right off, so I stayed back and looked around to make sure I was alone. Then I checked each boy's pulse to be sure some miracle wasn't taking place that would let one of them live. But they were all dead and cold."

"Flies?"

She nodded.

"You bury them right off?"

Another nod for an answer.

"Bear traps?"

"Didn't notice them until later, after I was done with the burials."

"Then?"

"Found tracks."

"Three sets?"

"I wasn't certain, so I followed what I found to where they had left their mounts."

"How many animals?"

"The tracks told me four."

"Three to ride and a pack animal?"

"I suppose; I don't know."

"Why only one pack horse for three of them?"

"They never said, but I saw six pack horses at their camp."

Bapcat leaned toward her. "That fourth animal might not have been theirs. That's possible, right?"

"I doubt it, Lute."

"But it *is* possible."

"Yes, just about anything is possible—but not probable. Why do you sound like a prosecutor?"

"I don't mean to," he said. "You know there's a state law that requires all dead bodies to be reported to the authorities. It's a misdemeanor to not report."

"I don't *care*, Lute."

"How'd you find where their horses were?"

"Boot tracks."

"Anything special?"

"Boots are boots."

"Corks, heels, anything?"

"Just boots."

"Sizes?"

"I didn't notice."

"How many boots?"

"I don't know. It's rocky, can't you see that? I picked one and followed it."

"How far?"

"Crow? Less than a quarter-mile."

"Easy going?"

"Nothing's easy in this watershed. You can't see that?"

"Seems like a long way to be wandering," he offered.

"I guess I thought they took those boys up there to kill them."

"You see any small boot prints?"

This seemed to catch her off guard. "Just one."

"The tracks didn't tell you if the boys were with them when they climbed the hill?"

"Too rocky and rough, and I don't know if they went in the way they came out. I didn't."

"The answer is no?"

"No, I couldn't tell, but this is three years since; questions are damn easy to ask, answers, a lot harder. It would be different if you were staring at fresh carnage."

Bapcat felt for the first time that she was finally thinking rationally and carefully. "The coroner will want to talk to you."

"About what?"

"You know I ain't no doctor," he said. "I guess she'll talk about whatever it is people like her get paid to talk about."

"You ever met a female coroner before?" she asked him.

"No."

"She must be a remarkable woman to win a position over all-male competition."

"Maybe she's the only one who wanted the job," he said.

"There's a practical, no-nonsense, unromantic streak in you I sometimes find particularly exasperating and irritating."

"I been told that before," he said.

She said, "I'll be right here when the doctor wants me."

• • •

Late in the day Torrance and Bapcat decided it would be better to spend the night in the woods, and ride south in the morning. Torrance had a stop-flag to halt trains. With that he could stop a freight, load the remains, and run the whole lot into Tula.

"The doctor agreed to Tula?" Bapcat asked the sheriff.

"It weren't put as a choice, and she took it neither happily nor easily. I don't think she likes being outside her morgue. One of these nights I'm gonna go take a look and see if she lives and sleeps there. Never seen her anywhere else in town. Nobody has."

"Timing of the deaths?" Bapcat asked.

Dr. Minturn had sat almost an hour with Jone Gleann. "Impossible to say; she says it was for sure more than twenty-four hours, based on what your girl told her, but how much more ain't certain at all, and all bets are off on the exact time."

"I've been thinking," Bapcat told the sheriff.

"You seem more prone to that than some."

"The woman who approached Bitche—have you gone back down that trail?"

"Ain't had the time, nor the people with that no-count Bresnahan having tooken off."

"You mind if I take a run at it?"

"Lord, no. I hate them whore halls over to Hurley. Can feel the clap bugs hanging up in the air like dang blackflies. They're all yours, and don't let temptation cloud your judgment. Peckers ain't known for clear thinking. The thing is, whores come and go all the time over the river."

"Did Bitche describe her at all?"

"Said only that she drew the eyes of every man in range, so that narrows it some. Most of them girls over to Hurley have turned into cows from their work, loose ways, and too much rotten firewater. You need help over there, call Sheriff Thurgood Roebuck. He's a Baptist preacher on the side, and likes nothing better than steering lost ewes back onto the Lord's One True Path, which I hear ain't first choice of most professional girls."

# CHAPTER 40

## *Hurley, Wisconsin*

### MONDAY, AUGUST 31

The bodies were on display in Tula in the company schoolhouse.

While Bapcat couldn't be sure that seeing the remains would cause any information to break loose, it seemed worth a try, even if all they got were the names of the kids, even just one. Sheriff Torrance stayed with the bodies, assisted by Jimjim and the General. Jone Gleann still refused to go into the town, and Zakov stayed with her at their campsite north of Jack Spur.

The coroner and two of her three assistants went back to Ironwood, leaving one assistant behind. Bapcat rode with Minturn and the others, who all acted like he was invisible.

Bapcat checked with Scale in Jessieville and took a room near the Western Union. No word from Echo, Harju, Oates, Isohultamaki, or anyone else. Scale was bored and antsy, and Bapcat enlisted him to help burrow into Hurley's Silver Street pleasure swamp.

The establishments themselves had little to offer other than their lineups of loose women, most of whom seemed to be at the bottom of a long fall from decency, but one house, Auntie White's Club for Men, seemed a cut above the competition, the women cleaner-looking, better-smelling, and far better dressed than those in nearby bawdy houses, which Scale called "ill reps," short for ill repute.

"I go in a place like this down south, even just so far as Indiana, my body be soon dancing from an oak tree branch. Women up here is a lot more accommodatin' of colored men, and the men up here don't seem nearly so quick with ropes, fast hangin's, and such."

"You sound like you've been down this road before," Bapcat said.

"Ain't all men my color?" The Negro looked over at him. "How a man get your age, ain't never poked no pay gals before?"

The deputy game warden had no answer other than the fact that all towns seemed equally inhospitable and anything they offered therefore irrelevant.

"Hope you ain't one o' them cowboy sheep fellas," Scale said.

"That's a damn myth, just like all the damn things get said about men of a certain hue."

Scale perked up. "Things such as *what*?"

"I don't know. I just write off that crap as untrue, like cowboys and sheep."

Scale grunted.

Bapcat said, "Now, if you want to talk about cowboys and fillies, that's a whole 'nuther tale to tell."

Scale laughed out loud.

It was Monday night, the business brisk but subdued in Auntie White's. Madam Patricia, the place's namesake, was holding court for a half-dozen gents redolent of bad whiskey, stale sweat, money-driven hope, and man-fumes, the latter being Scale's word and observation.

Bapcat and Scale joined Madam's audience and ordered drinks from hostesses, none of whom looked more than fourteen. The madam pontificated, "Customers ought to get all they pay for, and leave the house like they were coming out of a Shakespeare play that left their heads wobble-legged and full of merry wonderment at the beauty of the human condition. This is a place where men come for fun," she said, smiling. "Or for enlightenment, if you prefer. Once my girls light the wick of your candle, you won't go nowhere else for a match."

The men all laughed.

The deputy game warden held up his badge so just Madam Patricia could see and she said, "Excuse me, gents, I have to see to a priority here." She stepped over to Bapcat, crooked her arm like a teacup handle, and led him through the crowd, which opened before them the way the Red Sea parted in Bible telling.

She took him into an impressive office with floor-to-ceiling bookcases, a huge desk, and a curvy little daybed that looked designed for fancy dallying. Madam leaned against the corner of her desk, took his drink, and poured it into a planter with a flourish. "My private visitors don't imbibe forty-rod; only genuine quality is allowed inside my private sanctum. I can't say that badge you flashed is one I've seen before."

"Game warden," he said. "Michigan."

She grinned. "Well, I guess I've had one helluva lot of men hunt for me," she said, "but I can't recall ever being classified formally as game before. Has a certain cachet to it, though, don't you think? Are you a reader, sir, a consumer of provender for the fine and discerning mind?"

"I ain't sure what you're asking. My name's State Deputy Game Warden Bapcat."

"Your name is Bapcat, and all the rest of that is your job; these are never the same, Deputy."

"No, ma'am, and I ain't much of a book reader, if that's what you're asking."

"Sad," she said, "and us just past the end of the canicular days. I'm guessing you aren't in possession of a working foundation of the master tongue, which is obviously Latin. You did have Latin in school, yes?"

"No, ma'am, I sure didn't." *Talk about strange birds.*

"Pity, she said. "We all benefit from the Romans. The term 'canicular' refers to the period between July third and the eleventh day of August, the so-called and just-passed dog days of summer, which in my business is aptly named. Come fall, we do a far better trade as the cold comes in and the leaves start falling off. Somehow this change seems to drive the male need for intercourse with the opposite gender—and by intercourse, let me assure you that I also include polite and engaging conversation right along with old-fashioned and traditional pump-and-hump body couplings. For some men, it seems, talk would appear to be enough; although I surely don't understand it, I recognize it and accept it. Now, is this *your* interest, or are you a red-blooded, drop-your-drawers-and-make-it-roar kind of fella?"

"I'm here to get information," he said.

"No chance of something more . . . physical?"

"Probably not," Bapcat said.

"Wifed up, are you?"

"No, ma'am."

"So that ain't no impediment."

"I guess not."

"A steady girl then?"

"I got one, I guess."

"You don't know?"

"I guess I know."

"Well, good—all that business is mostly settled. What can Madam Patricia do for the badge who wants only palaver?"

"I'm looking for someone in your line of work."

"Madam or working girl?"

"A girl who might have worked for you."

"You got some kind of history with this woman? I don't like getting in between, unless it's a sandwich for cash, if you take my meaning."

"No, ma'am, I never even met her before."

The woman smiled. "Aha! You're thinkin' of trying something different than you and your regular gal sport at, and you've had your eye on one of my beauties."

"Not that neither," Bapcat said. "I never met nor seen her, and I don't even have a name. All I know is she was in town sometime recent and made acquaintance with a fella name of Durkee Bitche."

"That drooler fella who hung himself over to the Ironwood jail?"

"I guess that's him."

"She turned him down and he couldn't take the rejection. Suicide's a poor choice—that is, a permanent solution for a very temporary condition. She turns him down and he strings himself up. Downright sad, but he wasn't too bright, and he had him a nasty temper to boot, which is a terrible combination in a man."

"No, ma'am, we heard he turned *her* down."

Madam Patricia took a green cheroot out of an enameled box, flicked a wooden match with her fingernail, lit up, inhaled, and exhaled. "So you don't know this girl's name?"

"No. That's why I wanted to talk to you."

The woman paused, pushed a loose strand of hair off her forehead. "She goes by the handle of Min the Miraculous—claims she knows carnal tricks that date back thousands of years, to Cleopatra and the Egypterites, but I say, honey, when you get a fella's pants off, it's *all* old tricks."

"She works here?"

"Never did. Tried to freelance from here, which did not sit well with yours truly. Have to give credit where credit is due. She's a looker, that one, in a class all her own, but I run her off—told her she's either in my stable with my rules, or she needs to shoe-leather it down the road, looking for other prospects."

"When was this?"

"Couple of weeks back, months, it all runs together I reckon. But not officially."

"Local gal?"

"Drifted in from Minnesota, I'm told."

"You remember who?"

"I honestly don't. I got men and women whispering in my ears all the day long, and most of what I hear don't float. And that which don't float, I don't bother to think on anymore."

"Think you could describe her?"

"Good God, yes. Damn tall, red hair, and scars all over her legs such as I never beheld before, nor could imagine. I asked her what they was from and she laughed and said, 'We all got our own special needs, don't we?' See, the thing for a business like this is that a freelancer is like cancer. Here we are in a fine little town, all the houses and all the girls in them in *stasis*—that's Latin for 'balance'—and in comes this new talent with a flair for self-promotion and independent ways, and she upsets the whole apple cart. A girl's got to get along, or just plain git—you follow my logic here?"

"Yes, ma'am, I do. Did you hear what she was proposing to men?"

"You mean, other than what most men want, present company apparently excepted—and I ain't making no value judgment in declaring that so indelicately. God made us all in His image, which is a damn scary thought when you look around and sit a minute in contemplation."

"Other than the regular," he said.

"She give a cloud of smoke about runnin' nekkid and wild up in the Michigan mountains with some jamoke they call Red Hair. That what you're looking for?"

"Yes, ma'am, I believe it is."

"This ain't the first eye-turning kootch come to town spinning that yarn. Seems to happen every year come June or July."

"Always the same woman?"

"Sometimes, but usually they ain't the same. We usually see them once and that's it."

"This Min was from Minnesota," Bapcat said.

"Seems like they all was, now that I think on it. Makes one wonder what rotgut them Minnesota Scandihoovians is imbibing these days. And now that you mention it, I believe I remember this same Min passing through two or three summers back. She's the kind of woman not easily forgotten."

*Interesting time reference.* "Any other talk of a Red Hair being in the mountains?"

Madam Patricia shook her head and took a puff on her cheroot. "You ought to talk to our sheriff. I hear he has some interests down that line."

"Sheriff Roebuck?"

"Our revered sheriff himself. You seem a fine smart fella, and if you was in the mood, I'd be happy to oblige with one on the house. Believe me, this ain't an offer that gets put on the table—or the bed—all that often."

"Roebuck has some interests down what line?" Bapcat asked.

"Women," Patricia said. "Allegedly saving them. My offer still stands."

"No, thank you," he said.

Bapcat went through the bar and found Scale with a woman hanging on his arm. Bapcat disconnected the floozy and directed his companion outside.

"Me and that fine girl in there was just gettin' the shells off'n the pistachios," Scale complained.

"Well, go ahead back inside. I'm heading for my room."

"We ain't working?"

"Not any more tonight, anyways."

"I'm at the office eight sharp in the morning."

"I'll see you later in the day."

"What you got lined up?"

"Thinking I'll be mining a mind."

Scale grinned. "Never heard it put that way before."

# CHAPTER 41

## Hurley, Wisconsin

### TUESDAY, SEPTEMBER 1

Thurgood Roebuck lived at the end of a row of mining houses on a treeless hill in north Hurley. He met Bapcat at his front door looking haggard.

"Is this a bad time?" the game warden asked the sheriff.

"It is never a bad time after I've been in spirited conversation with our Lord and Savior."

Bapcat caught himself blinking. "I'm not quite sure how to put this . . . but I've heard that you take a special interest in a certain group of women in town."

"Falling angels," the sheriff said. "It's no secret. You're free to say the words out loud. Our Lord endorses what I do in his name. The female race, as we all know, carries Satan's mark, and while some may resist temptation, there are others who dive headlong into the sin-fire. I am appointed to go into the flames and pull them back to the loving safety of His all-embracing arms."

"You're a preacher, I hear."

"My true vocation. Law enforcement is no more than an expedient and temporary job to enable and allow proximity to those who are falling."

"Where do you find falling angels?"

"Silver Street, mainly, but there are bars and temptresses in all mining towns, this state and yours."

"You hunt for them?"

"It's not like still-hunting for deer. I have a web of supporters, and their word of a falling angel travels to me, wherever she may be."

"Any luck in saving them?" Bapcat asked.

"Quite good. Both the Lord and I are pleased, but neither of us believe in numbers for substantiation. One save justifies my crusade."

Bapcat guessed saves were rare, if at all. The reverend-sheriff's eyes were glazed with fanaticism, and something that suggested only he knew right from wrong. The man stood with his hands folded prayerfully in front of him.

"Any particular kind of girl more difficult to rescue than another?"

"God's grace knows no boundaries or limits," the man said.

"How well do you do with girls out of Minnesota?"

Roebuck frowned. "I loathe circuitous paths. Please make your point, Deputy, or I shall bid you good day."

"I'm told the latest girl from Minnesota is called Min the Miraculous," Bapcat said, "apparently the most recent in a long series of drifters from over that way."

Roebuck exhaled forcefully. "They pass through here en route to join Satan, who is everywhere on this imperfect Earth."

"I heard mostly they're looking for a gang leader called Red Hair."

"A name Satan travels with, just one of many—to wit: Abaddon, Beelzebub, Devil, Lucifer, Mammon, Perdition. There are countless more in the Good Book."

"What I'm told is that the girls believe Red Hair is up in the Porcupine Mountains."

"Satan is everywhere, all around us, all of the time."

"Like God, right?"

"You dare *compare* them?"

"No, sir, just making conversation. Did you meet this woman called Min?"

"I had verbal intercourse with her."

Bapcat awaited amplification, but none was forthcoming. "Were you able to save her?"

"Not in so many words, or in a time frame you would understand, but I surely planted the Lord's seed, and now must trust in Him to take hold of her soul and grow within it."

The game warden watched the sheriff for a long time, trying to sort out and process what he had just heard. "Planted the Lord's seed? How do you mean that?"

"As one plants any enduring seed. Words alone are fine, but often inadequate for this kind of work. One must put healthy seed into the ground in order to lead them away from carnal sin. You plant the seed, then pray, as the Lord specifies."

Bapcat couldn't believe what he was hearing. "You call that the *Lord's* work?"

"Wouldn't you? To beat the Devil, one must use his own tools and ways."

The game warden ignored the question. "What happens after the seed is planted?"

"They go on their way."

"Falling further?"

"One prays not, but I assume that's possible. It is inexact work, and the Lord and I can't save them all."

"Go on their way to Red Hair?"

Roebuck raised his hands. "There is no way to know where. I trust in God and the power of prayer."

Bapcat rested the barrel of his .30-40 Krag on the man's chest, and pushed sharply. "That's *all* you know?" Roebuck stepped back warily and tried to push the rifle away, but Bapcat held firm. "You'd better hope I don't learn otherwise," the game warden said.

"Armand," the reverend-sheriff said. "Armandville, Gusville, Flemtown—many names, but they're all the same place."

"This Armand is a person?"

"Flemish. He has a place on an island in the Presque Isle River, just above where the Copper Creek comes in."

"You know this fellow?"

"Only by reputation. He and I seek similar ends by different methods."

"Meaning?"

"Those who visit Armand tend to remain there."

"By choice?"

Roebuck shrugged. "There are competing theories."

"Such as?"

"I do not engage in speculation, rumor, or gossip, sir."

"Have you ever considered going into the Porkies to find Red Hair and rescue the falling angels?"

Sheriff Roebuck grinned demonically. "The Lord has not yet called me to martyrdom, and I ain't like some Mooslim looking for it, neither."

"But if you know Red Hair is the Devil, what's the threat? You operate with God's protection."

The man shook his head. "To confront the beast on his own territory is to invite and seal a bad outcome with certainty. Think of Custer invading Sitting Bull."

"Sitting Bull was the Devil?"

"I think Custer would not dispute that, sir."

# CHAPTER 42

## *Armandville, Gogebic County*

WEDNESDAY, SEPTEMBER 2

Bapcat was surprised to find Rinka Isohultamaki sitting with Scale in the Western Union Office in Jessieville. After a short discussion, Scale decided his superior telegraphy skills made him the right choice to remain as the one to receive messages. Isohultamaki could go with Bapcat to rejoin the group in the mountains.

"The next message you get from Echo, Harju, or Oates, bring it directly to us. But wire them all, let them know it could be a while before we can get any further wires."

Scale nodded and walked along as they rode to the outfitter to pick up a week's light supplies before heading out.

"How long until we reach Jone and the others?" the woman asked.

"We're not going there for a while," he told her.

"Where then?"

"Armandville."

She scratched her face and tossed her hair. "Never heard of it."

Bapcat guessed few had, but said nothing.

"How far?" the girl asked.

"As near as I can estimate, a dozen or so miles north of Ramsay. It's an island in the Presque Isle, above Copper Creek."

The woman acknowledged him with a nod, keeping her eyes riveted straight ahead.

They reached the island around noon. The water was deep, black and coursing on the west bank. The east bank seemed too far from the rocky lump to make an approach from that direction, even if there was a place to cross. They neither saw nor smelled any sign of human activity. Bapcat told her about Roebuck and the falling angels and Min the Miraculous and Red Hair.

"That sheriff needs to be stopped," the girl said. "With a bullet."

"Law won't allow it."

"Who needs law for such a creature?"

He couldn't disagree, and said nothing. In fact, he had entertained a similar thought.

They dismounted and walked the banks, looking for any sign of human traffic back and forth from the island to the mainland, an old trail, anything, but it was hopeless. Each time Bapcat looked at the Finnish girl, she appeared focused, tense.

The closest distance from the mainland to the island was twenty feet.

Isohultamaki wandered upstream and returned. "I can jump across this."

"On horseback?"

"On foot."

"It's too far," he said, looking at the river gap.

"Not here," she said. "Upstream of here."

He followed her up the bank. "Here," she said.

"Looks even wider," he said.

"Yes, but here I can get a longer run, and it is easily ten feet higher than the other side. The height will give me greater distance." She immediately knelt and drew a diagram in the dirt. "You see," she said, looking up. "By gathering speed with my run, I get greater distance before gravity can grab me. Jone taught us geometry and trigonometry."

"Trigger—"

"Trigonometry," she said in a voice he imagined she reserved for the very young and the old and feeble. *So many things I don't know, all of which might help me,* he lamented.

"Shall I jump it?" the Finnish girl asked.

"What if you break a leg, or worse?"

"Don't be so gloomy. Think of me soaring across and settling as lightly as a seagull."

He was thinking of a wild turkey's barely controlled crash landing, such as he had seen in his Dakota days.

The deputy game warden was deep in thought. The island was nearly a half-mile long by more than a hundred yards wide, like a razorback surrounded by water spumes and riffles, and a hundred-foot-plus cliff face in the middle. If people lived here, which was doubtful, they had to have a way to come and go, unless they waited for freeze-up, which seemed unlikely. He guessed the water was too deep and fast to freeze here except in the most extreme years. There had to be something they were missing, or this was no more than an attempt by Roebuck to get rid of him. Would the reverend-sheriff do that in good conscience? Possible, but not probable, which led him to think that Roebuck legitimately believed there was something here.

"Do you want me to jump, or not?" Isohultamaki asked. "The sooner we get over there, the sooner we can find out what's going on."

*Unassailable logic, along with "Never split your force"—but he had already done the latter.*

"Deputy?"

"Go ahead, but leave your guns. Too much weight."

"A knife is all right?"

"A small one."

Isohultamaki grinned, showing her perfect, gleaming-white teeth.

"What?"

"You men always assume the woman wants big ones," she said, laughing even harder.

*She's a very queer bird.*

Five minutes later the bird easily and gracefully soared across the gap of roaring black water and landed lightly on her feet like a cat. She looked around, back at Bapcat, pointed at her ear, and disappeared into the boulders.

"You there," a voice called from the island.

Bapcat looked to see a man at the top of a boulder. He wore a black robe, had a cleanly shaved head and a long white beard, cut square along the bottom.

"Identify yourself!" the man demanded in a stentorian voice.

"Bapcat, State Deputy Fish, Game and Forestry Warden."

"Certainly got enough in all that to keep a soul busy. Why are you on my private property?"

"This ain't private. This is the State's land."

"It's clearly marked 'private' in my mind, and you are trespassing," the man said. "We will give you one minute to depart."

"We?"

"Do you expect us to make a public display of our strength?" the man said, chuckling.

"I'm here to see Armand."

"Armand who?"

"Armand is all I know. Sheriff Roebuck sent me to see Armand."

The man glanced behind him. "Do we know a Roebuck?" He nodded and looked back at Bapcat. "What country is this Roebuck?"

"He's a person, in a state, not a country."

"We are each a country," the man said. "Armandville is in my country, and I am Armandville, which is *my* country; it's not *in* another country."

Bapcat said, "You can't be your own country. You are part of Michigan, which is part of the United States."

"But we are," the man said. "Like the Indians, who have their own countries."

"They have reservations, on land the United States gave them. Who gave this land to you?"

"We settled it," the man said. "On our own."

"I want to talk to Armand."

"You mean First Arm, our discoverer and founder?"

"Armand, the one in charge."

"That's me."

"You don't look old enough to have discovered this place."

"Excellent observation and analysis. You said nothing of discovering, only that I'm in charge. First came First Arm, who found this place, then his son, Second Arm, and then me, Third Arm. First and Second have gone to God, and I have assumed the title and work of First Arm."

"Then I guess I'll talk to you."

"About what?"

"Falling angels."

"Go away," First Arm said.

"Not until we talk."

"You're leaving me no recourse but to forcefully remove you from our country."

Rinka Isohultamaki appeared, held a knife to the man's throat, and said, "Like the boss says, it's time to talk."

Bapcat saw the air go out of the man. "How many over there?" he yelled across to her.

Isohultamaki said, "Don't know. There's a maze of caves and paths all through and around the island."

"How do they cross to here?"

"There's a canoe beneath an underhang near where I jumped. I can see it from here."

*One boat on this side. Did this mean one of their people was over here?*

Bapcat looked around. There had been no sign anywhere.

Isohultamaki made the man climb down to Bapcat's level and walked him south until she said, "The canoe is almost under your feet. Look for a crack in the boulders to your right."

Bapcat found the gap, squeezed through onto a small sandbar, and knelt. The canoe was an old birch-bark, yellowed with age. "Who is off the island?" he yelled across the roaring water.

"Almost all mankind," First Arm said.

Bapcat slung the rifles across his chest, knelt in the canoe, picked up the paddle, and pushed into the current, which shot him downstream with alarming speed. He quickly saw an opening between some rocks and slid the bow neatly into it, using the paddle to glide up on a gravel bank. Isohultamaki and her prisoner came down to meet him.

"Finally we meet in person," Bapcat told the man, causing Isohultamaki to break a smile. "Tell me about Roebuck."

"Never met the man."

"But you know him."

"Of him—and I don't care for what I do know."

"Like him, you rescue falling angels."

"I rescue them, and he does the unspeakable in the name of the Lord."

"How do you know that?"

"The angels come to me."

"For salvation?"

"Don't be petty; they come for temporal protection. Only God can save souls."

"They come here, and then what happens?"

"We do our best to return them to health and send them on to where they can have new lives."

"With old skills and habits?"

"They don't come here unless they want to change, and that's what it takes."

"As with Min the Miraculous?"

"No; that one came and threatened us with annihilation, unless."

"Unless what?"

"Unless I gave her Second Son."

Bapcat thought quickly. "Your son, you being First."

The man nodded. "I think it's important for him to learn the ways of the other country for when he replaces me."

"The canoe was over here. Your son, too?"

"We assume. We have not seen him."

"And his name is?"

"Armand—Second Arm. Our angels sometimes call him Manny."

"You think she may have him?"

"We pray not, but don't know. He's a clever boy, and headstrong."

"How old is Manny?"

"Fourteen."

"If she has him, is she taking him to Red Hair?"

"This seems most probable. Why do you seek this woman?"

"I don't. It's Red Hair I want—for crimes in several states. The woman might lead me to him."

"You think to capture him?"

"I do. Are you like Roebuck, thinking he's the Devil?"

"Roebuck is a devil deceiver. Red Hair is earthly dirt."

"You've had experience with him?"

"Three years back he and the same Min came here to extract our angels."

"Did they?"

"He got only fusillades of lead and moved on."

"How many with him?"

"Twenty and some; we never counted. They were disciplined, trained to obey."

"Did any of them get to the island?"

"No, we shot them in the water, trying to swim their horses across."

"Just that one time?"

"It was enough," First Arm said, "but almost every year since then, an angel appears and tries to draw others to Red Hair."

"Successfully?"

"Not so far."

"Same temptress every time?"

"Some come more than once, others just one time."

Bapcat considered what he had heard. Based on the man's account, it sounded like the traveling angels were under some kind of instructions, which had to have been given before they reached his area—unless Red Hair had an agent in place. Bresnahan's name popped into his mind. "How long since Min the Miraculous came through this time?"

"Three weeks and four days."

"And your son?"

"Not seen since."

"But you doubt she has him?"

"Oh, I think he's with her, but not in the way you may think. I believe he's following her with the intention of wreaking vengeance on Red Hair."

"At fourteen?"

"The Bible puts no age limit on an eye for an eye. He's more man than boy, and possesses a man's resolve. He has not yet fully accepted our Lord into his heart. If you find him, you'll help steer him back to us?"

"Yes, sir, I'll talk to him. That's all I can promise."

"He must feel so terribly alone," the father said.

His early days on the run flashed back to Bapcat. "I'd guess he's probably all puffed up with his grand adventure."

"How could you know that?"

"Ran from an orphanage when I was twelve."

"How far?"

"Keweenaw to the Dakotas."

"Lord help and protect him," the man said. "Will you and your woman break bread with us?"

"I ain't *his* woman, or any man's woman," Isohultamaki said with a growl, "but I sure could eat."

The island, Bapcat saw, was a remarkable place with a dozen scraggly inhabitants, only one of which was First Arm's acknowledged blood kin. Some of them had been there more than twenty years, and there were no children save the man's missing son. It seemed clear that the people in Armandville were on the island to embrace the next life, not this one, and Bapcat found the whole notion somewhere between appalling and depressing.

# CHAPTER 43

## *Jessieville*

### THURSDAY, SEPTEMBER 3

Everywhere he went, it seemed, Bapcat found more trouble, and more strands than in a rag picker's bag, none of which seemed connected in any obvious way. It all seemed so formless and disconnected as to be lighter than air, and circumstantial at best. He knew his Russian partner would declare, "Too speculative." Yet his gut was telling him to keep at it—that there was something here that would sooner or later be revealed.

They were headed to Western Union to see Scale. Rinka Isohultamaki said, "I intend to become a peace officer."

Bapcat glanced at her. "I don't think women get hired for such positions."

"You're deputizing me," she came back. "And Jone—that's *two* women."

Posse work and full-time law enforcement were only loosely connected in substance or skills, but he chose to remain silent. Who was he to say her deputization would not earn her an appointment somewhere? Who would have thought he would be wearing the badge of a state game warden. Life took some strange twists.

The young woman's statement forced him to think about her. She sure did not seem cowed by anyone, and seemed more than competent and comfortable in the woods. Bapcat forced himself to focus on other things. He needed time to think; seemed like he always needed more time than others to sort things out in his head.

The facts, such as they were, seemed scant. A woman called Min had propositioned an imbecile named Bitche, who ended up in jail and was murdered there. Sheriff Roebuck over in Hurley, Wisconsin, had heard the so-called Red Hair story, *and* met the woman called Min—probably the same woman who had propositioned the dead man in Ironwood's lockup, but this was speculative and not certain at all.

The Gogebic County deputy sheriff Bresnahan was missing, and alleged to be the last person to have seen the suicide victim in jail. Bapcat found himself wondering why suicides were called victims. Didn't they willingly kill themselves? Victims were such not by choice. Why were things never straightforward? Bresnahan, who actually lived in the Gogebic County jail, had cleared out in the wake of the suicide. Suspicious, yes, but still circumstantial. It was all circumstantial.

So-called First Arm on the island said a woman named Min had approached them three weeks and four—no, five—days ago. He knew this because his son had been missing that long.

The timing of all this seemed to fit Bitche's arrest. That is, one didn't cancel out the other. The island boy went by the name of Manny. Had he gone in pursuit of the so-called Red Hair? Bresnahan, Gogebic County Sheriff Torrance insisted, was the only person to know that Bapcat had wanted to talk to Bitche in his cell. Apparent suicide to start, but the autopsy report came back with water in the suicide's lungs—ergo, which meant murder, not suicide. Why kill Bitche? And who?

Bapcat's gut continued to tell him he had cut a trail, but the thing remained muddled in his mind.

Scale seemed glad to see them, held out two telegram envelopes with messages from Rollie Echo and Bapcat's big boss, Oates, which he opened first.

Oates wrote:

ARREST, DETAIN ANY, ALL INDIVIDUALS CAUGHT INFLICTING PAIN ON ANY ANIMALS, BEARS INCLUDED. STOP. ATTORNEY GENERAL PRELIMINARILY OPINES BEAR CAPTURE IS LAW VIOLATION, EVEN IF SALE INTENDED TO LEGITIMATE AND LEGAL ZOOS. STOP. STATE HAS OTHER FIDUCIARY STATUTES GOVERNING SALE OF THE PEOPLE'S PROPERTY. STOP. BE SAFE. STOP. BUT PRESS BOTH OF YOUR MISSIONS. STOP. OATES.

The second telegram was from Houghton County assistant prosecutor Echo:

ARREST BEAR-TRAPPERS, ORDER CONFIRMED BOTH BY STATE AG AND YOUR CONSERVATION CHAIN OF COMMAND. STOP. HERE IF YOU NEED BACKROOM HELP, SUPPORT. STOP. BEST, ROLAND.

Bapcat rubbed his mouth.

Scale asked, "Good news?"

"I guess that depends," Bapcat said.

"On what?"

"Won't know until it happens," the game warden said.

"That don't make sense," Scale told him.

"Welcome to the fog of law," Bapcat said.

"Laws is always wrote down," Scale announced, "which means they's black and white, cut and dry."

"Cut maybe," Bapcat said, "but far from dry." What he was learning was that the so-called law was like a swamp that never seemed to dry out, remaining pestiferous and annoying to all involved, especially those trying to enforce what sometimes amounted to some vague statutes.

"We got us a plan?" Scale asked.

"Gather your gear and your mount. We don't need an outrider waiting for any more telegrams."

Isohultamaki looked at Bapcat. "Me?"

"All three of us are headed to Tula, and from there, up into the hills."

"Do we have a destination in the high country?" the woman asked.

"Bear country," Bapcat said.

"That's pretty much everywhere up there," Rinka Isohultamaki said.

"Jone thinks there's one place better than others. She means us to bivouac there."

The Finnish woman nodded resolutely and patted his arm. "Don't worry," she said.

"About what?"

"Anything."

"Why not?"

"We have a strong woman in charge. We are making history."

Scale raised an eyebrow and chuckled. "Put me in charge and we really change that history you talkin' about."

Scale and the woman laughed.

Bapcat cringed, wondered if his surrendering leadership to Gleann in return for guiding him would come back to bite him. He also wondered if Jordy and Widow Frei were missing him, and it gave him a pang of guilt to know that he had been so lost in his own troubles and challenges, he'd made no time to think about them. Truth was, he missed them badly, but he told himself he'd just have to suffer with the feelings. No time to let your mind wander. Need to keep it focused on the job.

# PART III: *KAG-WADJ-KIW* (CROUCHED PORCUPINE)

We traveled on foot the last five miles over points of mountains from one to three hundred feet high, separated every few rods by deep ravines, the bottoms of which were bogs and which by thick underbrush were rendered impervious to the rays of the sun.
—George F. Porter, Assistant Secretary to General Lewis Cass, 1826

# CHAPTER 44

## Tula

FRIDAY, SEPTEMBER 4

Sheriff Torrance had a room in the town's boardinghouse for loggers and drummers, close to the town's school, which looked new. The weather was nasty with stickiness, the sheriff's first words on seeing Bapcat, "The remains has gone ripe, even with nothing much for worms to get holt of. Minturn's girl is befuddled and perplexed by this development and has threatened many times to resign, or at least to decamp. She says she didn't sign up to have so much social congress with the public."

"Any leads?"

"One. Woman by the name of O'Quinn said she remembers three boys come through town three years or so back, when the town was a lot smaller and not even an actual town yet. She fed them and asked them where they were heading, but they weren't talkative and only pointed north. Mrs. O'Quinn says she told them it wasn't safe in the highlands, and they told her they were men and guessed they could handle anything that might come their way. They'd come this far, hadn't they?"

"This far?"

"How she remembers it," Torrance said. "Insists she pressed them on this point, but their lips was buttoned tight."

"Not locals then," Bapcat said.

"Looks like," the sheriff said. "But had we not fetched these stinking remains down here we'd never have known that, I guess. Time to close up here, I'm thinking, bury these little fellows decently."

"Here?"

"Got a better idea?" Torrance asked.

"I guess the dirt in one place is as good as dirt in another."

The sheriff grinned. "'Zackly how I see it. I even got us a preacher man standing by."

"Not Roebuck, I hope."

"You seen Hurley. Man's got to be a bit bent to want such a job. Few show even the slightest interest, and finally it comes down to polite folk not much caring what goes on between whores and drunks, long as it stays out of their drawing rooms and churches. The preacher I got can do this job pronto, and we even got three nice holes already dug over to the graveyard

"They have such a place?"

"The boys will be first among the unclaimed and unmourned."

"But they'll be prayed over properly?" Bapcat asked.

"Well, hell yes, they will," the sheriff said. "You don't strike me as a church fella, and most of us ain't barbarians over this way. You and your people attend?"

"Never intended to mark you as a barbarian, Sheriff. Some of us will be there, and no, I ain't the churchy type. Guess I ain't found the right flavor yet."

"You ain't alone," the sheriff said.

Jone Gleann was still north in the woods, and Bapcat wondered why in the dickens she was so dead-set against coming into Tula. It now appeared that the boys were not local. Were there assailants she could identify, or them her, and what hadn't she disclosed yet about what had happened up in the mountains?

The burial services were abbreviated, the preacher a stutterer who moved his head left to right like he was pecking typewriter keys with his nose, and all the time spraying spit into the air like a fine mist, backing up the mourners several steps, including some locals who had no relation to the dead and apparently considered funerals a fine pastime for accumulating some theoretical favor points with the Almighty.

Bapcat gave little thought to the dead, preferring to focus on those still aboveground. As he watched the town mourners, he noticed a reddish-brown dog behind some gravestones, and watched as the dog circled the ceremony. *No back right leg. Seen that fella before,* he told himself. *Norwich for sure, but maybe another time as well.* He touched Isohultamaki's arm.

"See that dog?" he said.

"Shall I dispatch it?"

"Dammit, no. But I want you to follow it—find out where it lives, and who it belongs to."

"A stray cur knows no master," she said.

"It's your job to figure out *if* it's a stray."

"How long?"

"Two days if it just hangs around unattached, and however long it takes if it moves on with someone."

"I don't like open ends," she complained.

"Welcome to the world of investigations."

Scale said in a low growl, "Hush, girl; I can't hear that preacher. You got a job, now go do it."

Bapcat started to thank the man, but Scale had his hands joined piously in prayer, his face uplifted and eyes closed.

The game warden did the same, and hoped an omen would soon be forthcoming.

# CHAPTER 45

## *Following a Dog*

### SATURDAY, SEPTEMBER 5

Less than two hours after Isohultamaki left, she returned, flushed in the face.

"The dog belongs to Ernst Nixon," she said. "He's a trapper from Norwich, and he's been around Tula for the past three weeks."

"Doing what?"

"Nobody knows for sure."

"That's roughly the time we got to these parts. Are you sure?"

"Nixon's said to be a dour man of bad temper. The dog, however, is much loved, and goes wherever its master goes, but always at a distance. This has captured the town's interest."

"You learned this how?"

"Men such as Nixon are seldom forward and therefore quite easy to learn about. People cannot abide a vacuum and will fill it, even if they are not entirely accurate."

"How old are you?"

"Twenty," she said. "Very nearly."

At times she seemed much older than her years; her approach to this Nixon fellow was quite the way a peace officer might have gone about it. "Where's Nixon now?"

"Camped east of town."

"Alone?"

"Yes, the dog and him."

"You saw the camp?"

"I did. I found a boy watching the camp and I startled him. He admitted to feeling great sympathy for the dog and its attachment to such a nasty person. The boy was waiting for an opportunity to liberate the creature."

"Steal it?"

"Give it a better home, is how the boy put it to me."

Bapcat could tell she had more.

"Nixon will leave in the morning. There was a woman of ill repute at his camp today, and the watcher-boy heard them talking."

"Just talking?"

"There was apparently much more, which is not relevant to this report or our interests."

He was impressed.

"Shall I follow Nixon?" she asked.

The game warden made a snap decision. "Show the camp to me and I'll follow. You stay with Jone and the others. She'll need help."

"Do you think I lack competence to track?"

"I never said that."

"But you no doubt thought it, otherwise the tracking would be my task."

Bapcat closed his eyes, made another snap decision. "We'll track him together. Four eyes beat two." He had learned this fact years ago in the Dakotas, and later in the army.

"I have excellent eyesight," she said indignantly.

"I didn't say you don't."

"Yes, you did."

"Do you want to go with me, or not?"

"I want to go alone, without you."

"With me, or with Jone and the others," Bapcat said. "These are your choices."

"With you," she said with a pout.

Now it was a day later, and Nixon continued traveling into the night, not stopping to cook food, rest, or take care of his animal. His progress was slow, steady, relentless, unhurried.

Bapcat considered sending Rinka Isohultamaki ahead to Norwich to see what she could learn about the man, but he rejected this because it might lead to spooking the man. Suddenly he closed his eyes, felt the bullet slap his back, just as it had months ago, but this time he was unhurt, and in his mind's eye he saw the large reddish-brown dog with three legs.

"Nixon may be the one who shot me," the game warden told his companion.

"How can you know that? You were shot in the back."

"I saw the dog seconds before I was hit."

"Nixon's dog?"

"I think so. He was ahead of me on the trail."

Neither of them talked for a long time. "Nixon is dangerous," the girl said.

"Maybe," Bapcat said, "but we'll assume so. The bullet came from far off. I'm not sure the shooter actually meant to hit me."

"But you *were* hit."

"You ever sleep in the saddle?" he asked her.

"I have no wish to fall off and break my neck."

"You can lash yourself in."

"But why? If you must sleep, get off and sleep."

She was difficult to talk to.

"Will you kill Nixon?" she asked, "if he is the guilty one?"

"No. I'll try my best to arrest him."

"But you may have to shoot him."

"That's possible, but I will do my best to avoid it."

# CHAPTER 46

## Norwich

### SUNDAY, SEPTEMBER 6

Nixon never showed any indication of knowing he was being followed, and the dog, if it knew, showed no sign of tipping off its master. Bapcat used his spyglass for a closer look at their quarry. The man showed no concern, and kept his head and horse pointed straight east, either lost in thought and oblivious, or the sort of person who could focus on only one thing at a time. The stock of a long gun protruded from a saddle scabbard, but there was no way to tell if it was a scattergun or a rifle.

Isohultamaki rode close behind him, and when Nixon stopped and dismounted, the followers stopped. They were somewhere north of Matchwood.

Nixon left his horse and scuttled down a narrow defile with a slow-running stream at the bottom. Bapcat followed the man and watched him check a trap that was set alongside an impressive beaver dam.

"He's trapping all right," he told his companion as their slow-follow ground forward again.

"Can you tell what he's after?" she asked.

"Standard number thirty-four Hawley and Norton, set for beaves," he said. "Used them myself."

"Beaver trapping is allowed? I thought it was closed," she said.

*Impressed she knows such a thing.* "You're right. There's a three-year ban to allow the population to recover," he explained.

"State law?"

"State regulation," he said, which triggered some thoughts.

Oates had questioned him about beaver populations at the meeting where he had been hired. The boss had made the point then, that if there weren't enough animals, you stopped the activity and let them come back. Would Lansing do the same if hunted animals were in question, and how would you know such control was needed? Only then did he again remember the animal and fish survey Lansing had wanted game wardens to conduct.

It would provide a sort of rough count. Either Oates or others at the top seemed to have a strong interest in using their intelligence to manage game population. The answer from Oates about bears seemed to fit this overall concern, which told him that some men down there had a pretty good big picture of what ought to be going on.

"Winchester," Isohultamaki said, interrupting his thoughts. "Forty eighty-two caliber."

"What is?"

"Nixon's rifle."

"How do you know that?"

"While you followed him, I went to his horse and looked," she said proudly.

"The horse could have spooked, or the dog could have barked," he told her.

"But they didn't. What's wrong?"

"You shouldn't have," he said.

"He could have seen *you* when you followed him. Do you want a partner with initiative, or not?"

"Yes," he conceded. "Initiative is good."

"All right, then," Isohultamaki said. "The rifle has a twenty-six-inch, octagonal barrel—a fine weapon. What caliber struck you?"

"Something between forty seventy-two and forty eighty-two," he told her.

"Ah," she said.

"There are Winchesters everywhere," he reminded her.

"Will we talk to Mr. Nixon? We have reason because of the beaver trapping, right?"

"Yes, we have cause, but I'm not sure yet."

"When will you reach certainty?"

"When I do."

"Do you want a partner who wants to learn?"

"Learning's fine," he said.

# CHAPTER 47

*Norwich*

MONDAY, SEPTEMBER 7

They hovered around the man's cabin all night. No light showed from inside, no smoke rose from the chimney, but it was humid, and there was no reason for a fire. They needed to be invisible, and they had provisions that didn't need cooking. Hot food made the mind stronger, but security came before comfort. Even so, Bapcat became suspicious, and had to force himself to sit tight until the first hints of dawn, when they crept closer to the man's cabin. The camp was situated a half-mile west of the mine, on the south side of a hill overlooking a valley, the West Branch of the Ontonagon River a few hundred yards south of them.

No dog, no man, no sound, no light inside, no smoke, no nothing. Bapcat considered knocking on the door and confronting the man about the beaver trapping. Taking beaves was illegal now, and what sort of trapper took beavers in summer when their pelts were sparse and ratty? As for the rifle and his being shot, suspicion alone wouldn't get a warrant, and in any event, they were too far from anywhere or anyone to seek any sort of timely legal counsel.

Isohultamaki went behind the cabin and came back thirty minutes later. "He has a rabbit hole, a tunnel south. He left it uncovered, otherwise I wouldn't have found it."

Typical trapper behavior, to have alternate ways in and out. But trapping beaver in August and forgetting to cover his escape hole was unlike any trapper behavior Bapcat had ever witnessed.

"I guess he left in a hurry" was the best he could manage.

"Why?"

He had no answer for a while, but as they sat, he sniffed at her.

"Why are you doing that?" she demanded.

"Your scent," he said.

"I smell clean," she said. "I bathe regularly."

"Exactly. I caught a whiff of you when you were coming back to join me from behind the cabin. You smelled clean."

"He smelled me because I'm clean?"

"People who live alone in the woods develop abilities to hear and smell better than town people. They have to if they want to survive."

"I live alone," she said defensively.

"You are a woman, and you bathe."

"Are you telling me this to eliminate me from wearing a badge?" she asked.

"No," he said, trying to soothe her and not sure why. "Maybe you can specialize in clean criminals."

"There are such creatures?"

"There's always hope," he said.

"And prayer," she added. They laughed. Nervously.

The man's horse was pastured west of the cabin.

"He's on foot," Bapcat said, looking at Nixon's boot tracks, which pointed due south at the river. As he expected, the trail led not just to the river, but to an area of almost solid rock and stone.

"We can find where he gets off the rocks on the other side," Isohultamaki offered.

"I doubt it," Bapcat said. "The way he came right to this rocky section tells me he's spooked bad and wants to disappear. We can check the edges here, but I'm assuming he crossed the river, and if you look over there, the rocks go on forever. He can probably travel miles without leaving sign."

"So we just let him go?"

"He's already gone, and all we have is a possible misdemeanor on beaver trapping," he said.

"And now?" Isohultamaki asked.

"We'll find the others and join up."

"We haven't seen the three-legged dog," she said.

"It's probably with Nixon," he said, although he could not understand why any living creature would attach itself to another who seemed not to care if it lived or died.

"I like that," Isohultamaki said.

"Like what?"

"You have used the word 'we' twice to refer to us. I like that very much."

"Think about important things," he said.

"I always do," the girl said.

## CHAPTER 48

*Little Trap Falls, Ontonagon County*

TUESDAY, SEPTEMBER 8

The trails west were up and down and twisted around, through narrow gaps and over sharp rocky ridges, through littered forests and what seemed like an endless series of marshes, swamps, and pestilential streams. But Bapcat kept them moving steadily, the way he had learned from his Northern Cheyenne friend. The great advantage of a horse was the expanded range it provided over a man on foot, and the Sioux, Cheyenne, and Comanche had perfected this tactical advantage over enemies who wanted to fight on foot rather than on mounts. It had taken a long time for the US Army to adopt Indian tactics, and when they did, the cavalry's firepower had finally put an end to the so-called Indian troubles on the Plains and in the Southwest.

"Do you never feel hunger?" Isohultamaki asked early that morning.

"I feel it."

"It is a comfort to know you have human needs."

"I keep pemmican in the saddlebags."

"As do I, but if you can go without, so can I."

He looked at her. "This is not a contest."

She shrugged. "To you, perhaps."

"We're sort of a split force right now," he told her, but she just shook her head.

They paused on an old game trail on the side of a steep and irregular hill, and Bapcat arched up in his saddle. "I hear waterfalls," he said, turning up a creek bed and eventually coming to the cataract. Here they paused to allow the animals to drink. The creek was skinny but clear, and quite cold. Joe lapped water greedily. Later they could stop to let the animals graze. "I don't believe my scent caused Nixon to run," Isohultamaki said.

"That's not important now," he told her.

"Then why did you say that?"

"Why can't you let it go?" he said, and tuned her out. The temperature was dropping and fog was forming in the trees, a turn of events that concerned him more than her protestations. Heavy fog could be dangerous for the animals, and with scattered iron deposits causing his compass to find false readings, navigation would soon become a serious challenge.

## CHAPTER 49

## *South of White Pine*

### WEDNESDAY, SEPTEMBER 9

The fog that finally settled in was a milky froth, causing Joe to advance more cautiously than usual. Rinka Isohultamaki rode close behind him.

"You are lost," she said.

"And you aren't?" he said.

She had actually laughed out loud, and he was glad that the heavy air kept her banshee-like voice from carrying too far. He was trying to head due west, but sensed they had drifted somewhat north toward White Pine. He cursed their lack of a good map. Someday, perhaps, game wardens would have detailed maps to help them do their jobs, rather than leaving their travel to luck and skill with a compass.

As usual, it was one creek crossing after another, either muck bottoms or sharp rock cobble and shards, and almost all of them with tag alders forming thick walls along the banksides. Rotting slash flopped helter-skelter across the streambeds, forcing them too often to have to try several approaches in order to find their way across. Despite the suddenly cool temperature, it was sweaty, nerve-racking work. Bapcat had calculated a destination six or seven miles west of the Nonesuch Mine, which he had seen on Jone Gleann's map, but her map was crude and showed none of the streams they had crossed, leaving him with a lot of guesswork.

After struggling west he decided they would be better off ascending to a high point, sitting until the fog burned off, and finding a vista to help them figure out where they were. It was not that he was totally disoriented; he was pretty sure that if they struck due south they would eventually strike east-west railroad tracks, and if they went far enough north, they would undoubtedly hit the shoreline of Lake Superior. Knowing they were somewhere between the two extremes meant they weren't technically lost, but he would be hard-pressed to say exactly where they were.

Reading the terrain angle, he turned Joe back to the southeast and found another game trail which led them steeply upward. Once it was clear they were going high, he resolved to get to the top and sit there until morning came and the fog lifted.

By the time he decided to call a halt, he guessed they had climbed up four or five hundred feet, but there was no way to know this for sure. They had stayed in trees the whole way, and once he had dismounted and moved to his left, outside the trees, he saw they were paralleling a cliff.

Eventually he stopped, patted Joe's neck, and dismounted.

"What?" his companion asked.

"We'll stay here until we have light. No fire," he added.

"Are you afraid of something?"

"I'm always afraid when I don't know exactly where I am, can't see, and don't know who or what else is close by."

"Game wardens harbor fear?"

"It helps to keep us alive," he said. "Do *you* have any idea where we are?"

"No, but I am not the one leading us," she said.

"Even followers have to pitch in with what they know," he told her.

"I have no idea where we are," she admitted.

They found a small clearing and hobbled their mounts. Bapcat cut balsam boughs, lay them on the ground, and placed canvas on top. They then sat on the boughs with their backs to the trees. "Sleep," he said. "I'll take first watch."

Sitting like this was always a challenge. How to stay alert and awake, the two states not being exactly the same thing. When on guard, his practice was to close his eyes and push all of his energy into his ears and nose.

It was a short time later when he thought he felt a thump. Felt more than heard. Then another, a thump for sure, both of them south of their position and lower, though it was hard sometimes in the woods to know for sure. He lightly touched Isohultamaki's hand.

"I heard," she whispered. "What is it?"

"Not sure yet."

More thumps ensued, then intermittent series of distant, shrill screeches, howls, yelps and squeals, squeaks and squawks, such as he had never before heard in one place at one time. He found it disorienting. Then a loud, deep thump resonated again and was repeated solidly for several minutes. He leaned over to Isohultamaki and whispered, "Drum," and added, "Indians, maybe."

"Indians have huge drums?"

"Yes. Several braves sit around one, thumping it."

"But this one sounds like it is moving," she pointed out.

"Yes, it's moving."

"Do we go look?" she asked.

"The sound is coming toward us," he told her.

"Should we move out of the way?"

"In this fog?"

"I don't like just waiting," she told him.

"It's a choice," he said. "If you want to go, go."

"No, I am with you. We are we, and we will go or stay together."

The sounds were closer now, but low and seeming not to come up any higher.

"I think the fog is lifting," Isohultamaki said.

"They're not coming up," Bapcat said. "They're below us, and moving south."

"Who are they?"

"I have no idea," he told her.

"We'll follow them, then?"

"No. We'll look down from afar, get our bearings, and make for our group."

The cacophony erupted again in the distance and kept receding. The fog was indeed lifting a little, and Bapcat got up and went to the precipice on the southeast face. A sheer drop of two hundred feet fell to a cloudy mattress of fog. Sheer drop, probably deeper than the distance to the clouds below. He felt Isohultamaki beside him. She seemed tentative along the edge. In the gloaming, he was compelled to look at his compass. "I want to backtrack down, toward the falls where we watered the horses, and strike due west from there."

"But what about all that we've heard?"

"Some mysteries must remain so," Bapcat said.

The howling began anew in the distance, rising and falling, sharp and ragged, barks and snarls, a virtual menagerie of lifelike sounds, and Isohultamaki, standing beside him, said, "Ah—wolves."

*Not wolves*, Bapcat realized. It was men, trying to sound like wolves.

"Let's go," he said. "When we get lower and farther west, we'll find a place for the animals to feed."

# CHAPTER 50

## Sleepy Pond, Ontonagon County

### THURSDAY, SEPTEMBER 10

They descended the hill slowly, almost as the fog lifted in front of them. It seemed to Bapcat as if they were pushing away the shroud to welcome the sun, which soon began to show. When they reached the bottom of their descent, Bapcat turned Joe eastward.

"We are now walking into the rising sun," Isohultamaki pointed out.

"Your sense of direction survived the night," Bapcat said sharply.

"You said we were going to make our way west," she reminded him.

"Your memory is as solid as your sense of direction," he said.

"You make jokes at my expense?" she asked, not hiding her irritation.

"Be quiet," he said. "The wolves are no doubt sleeping now."

"Wolves?"

"You yourself identified them not long ago."

"Am I to understand we are attempting to *find* sleeping wolves?"

"Possibly."

"Won't waking them make them angry?"

"Wolves are light sleepers," he said. "Their biggest threat is from others of their kind, *especially* their own kin."

"This makes no sense to me," Isohultamaki said. "You don't fear sleeping wolves?"

"I respect all wolves, awake or asleep."

"You respect them, yet you want to awaken them?"

"You need to listen better, Rinka. I said possibly we would find sleeping wolves, and you assumed we would wake them."

"So, we will *not* wake them?"

"There is a good chance we will not even find them. Have you ever seen a sleeping wolf?"

Silence followed him. "You're not curious why we're doing this?" he asked her.

"You are being smug, and I do not like this trait in you."

"What we heard," he said. "It wasn't wolves."

Long pause. "I *know* I heard wolves."

"You heard men *imitating* wolves," he told her.

"*I* heard wolves," she insisted.

"Which is the intent of imitation." The Cheyenne could make a call so real your spine would shake. "In some places men use wolf calls to talk to each other."

"To what end?"

"To guide members of the group, to navigate true to course, to build group morale, and loyalty—many reasons."

"In this instance?"

"Perhaps we will learn today," he said. "Or not."

"Answer me," she said with a groan.

"I am only stating the obvious."

"If it is, as you contend, obvious, it needs not be stated. Obvious means self-evident."

"Obviously *not* to everyone," he said.

"Are you telling me I can't see what is obvious?"

"I am saying only that there were no wolves, only men trying to sound like wolves."

"I *know* I heard wolves," she insisted, almost in a whisper.

"We shall see," he said.

"And if they *are* wolves?"

"They will no doubt run from us."

"Wolves don't run," she countered.

"Wolves, Indians, bears—they almost always run when given a chance."

"All right. Let us say for discussion purposes that we find men, not wolves."

"We will watch them."

"Will men run?"

"That depends on who they are and what they are doing."

"They could be doing anything," she said.

"True."

"Or they could be wolves," she added.

"Not likely, but it's possible," he granted.

"Then I would be right, and you wrong."

"True," he said.

"Good," she said. "I like it that we will establish right from wrong."

"It's more likely we will find nothing at all," he said.

"This change of direction, then, will have been a waste of our time," she pointed out.

"Without doubt," he said. "But it is a beautiful country, and we are in fine company."

"You make jokes," she said.

"No, I mean what I say."

"Do you find me irritating?" she asked.

"Yes, sometimes."

"Are you always so frank?"

"With a partner, yes. Each must speak his mind, then do everything in his power to support the decision which is made."

"Even if you don't agree?"

"Even then."

"I like the word 'partner,'" she told him.

Bapcat had seen tracks two miles back, and suddenly they were descending onto softer ground, the tracks more distinct and easier to read. He stopped, looked back at his partner, and pointed down. He watched her lean forward in her saddle and look up at him.

"Wolves," she said.

"Look closer. There is an indentation behind the wolf track. Most are slight, but some are clear and distinct. Look at the shapes. They are left by boot heels."

She studied the ground and nodded.

Soon he smelled smoke dregs and pointed at his nose and she nodded again.

Only one horse. Most of the wolf men were on foot. Probably just the leader riding, a less-than-formidable mounted force. The trail led to a precipitously narrow defile, down to a runoff creek, with seeps down the sides and some pools still in place from melted winter snows, and eventually a steady trickle over a sand and mud and rock bottom, to the sides, evidence of black mud he knew as loon shit. This alone told him there was a watery marsh ahead, and that they could get bogged down.

He aimed Joe up the side of the creek bed and Isohultamaki followed. They moved forward and slightly upward, searching for a look-down, which they came to an hour later.

Bapcat dismounted inside the trees again and slung Joe's reins around a branch. Isohultamaki emulated his action. He crept on all fours to a viewing point, and she crawled right beside him. Bapcat studied the area below with his brass spyglass. There was a dark-water pool, ringed by sphagnum tussocks and niggard black spruce and pools of standing water atop what he guessed was bottomless black muck. The only dry hump was directly below them, and on it he saw a blackened area and smoldering coals. Smoke hung in the air. There was a large pine near the place, stripped of branches, and something strapped to the main trunk, though his angle made it impossible to tell what. What he could see were the naked legs of men, and beside their prone bodies, wolf pelts and heads, the men unmoving. Were they passed out drunk? He had seen this in Indian camps in the Dakotas. No sign of a horse. He gave her the spyglass, heard her gasp, and took it back from her.

"Stay," he told her, sliding to his right to find a better angle. When he did he saw a white horse grazing, farther to his right, and then something that stirred rage within him.

The game warden returned to his partner, his stomach roiled, and pointed at the tree line behind them. They crawled back to cover, stood up, mounted, and started back the way they had come.

"Are we retreating?" she asked

"Yes."

"May I know the reason?"

"We are badly outnumbered. How many did you count?"

"Wolves? Thirteen, an unlucky number."

"Not wolves, Rinka. Men."

"I *saw* wolves," she insisted.

"There is a boy's body lashed to a tree down there, Rinka. Have your wolves learned to tie knots?

"I'm sorry," she mumbled.

"Don't be. Sometimes we see what we hope most to see, not what is actually there—understand?"

"I'm sorry," she said again.

"No need for apologies. Learn, absorb the lesson, apply it, and move on. We have all done this."

"Even you?"

"Especially me," he said. "We all have to learn to see, which is different than looking."

"Why do they have the boy?" she asked.

"He is dead," Bapcat said.

"Why don't they bury him?"

"Perhaps they will when they are done."

"Done with what?"

He turned to her and made a sweeping, scooping gesture with his hand to his mouth. He saw her slump heavily, and when she looked up, her eyes were wet, but her jaw set.

"We should attack them," she said.

"Bad odds," he said, and continued riding until he found ground to the west, aiming Joe onto the rocks to hide their passing.

# CHAPTER 51

*Elm Creek, Ontonagon County*

MONDAY, SEPTEMBER 14

Under his lead, they struck the Big Iron River after five difficult miles and Isohultamaki suddenly became animated. "This is where Jone comes every summer," she said. "Ahead is the West Branch of the Ontonagon River. It is in a steep, rocky canyon, but there is a ravine with a gradual descent to a ford that leads us up an equally gentle climb on the other side. Once on top we will stay west until we skirt a side canyon, then swing north and east to Elm Creek, which will be within two miles. Do you want me to tell you the way?"

"Show me, don't tell me. You take the lead. If you know this area so well, why not the rest of the region?"

"Where we just came from?"

Bapcat nodded.

"Jone has always insisted we follow her directions in the hills, her routes and only hers. You would never know it, but she is a worrier," Isohultamaki confided.

"About what?"

"Everything," the Finnish girl said, dramatically throwing up her hands.

What interested him more than Gleann's worrisome nature were the specifics of what drove her worries.

When Isohultamaki led him to a gentle trail down to the West Branch, his confidence in her soared, and when they found Gleann's camp on Elm Creek where it joined with another tributary, he was pleased to be challenged by Jimjim, brandishing a small rifle. When he learned Scale was a sleeping party of one with animals, he was elated.

As soon as he saw Zakov, Bapcat said, "We should put another person with Scale."

"Expecting trouble?" the Russian asked.

"Always."

"This was my intention when I am done here," Zakov said. "It's been a long time."

"Food, coffee, and we'll talk. Where's Jone?"

"She and the General are camp cooks."

Bapcat and Isohultamaki unsaddled their mounts and took care of the animals' needs before their own. Joe was especially pleased to be shed of his burden and wiggled around, enjoying his freedom.

"We expected you sooner," Gleann said when she saw him.

"There was a dog to be followed," Rinka Isohultamaki said. "It led us to Norwich."

Gleann stood with crossed arms while Bapcat and Rinka dipped food from an iron pot onto tin plates. Isohultamaki sat cross-legged on the ground, shoveling food into her mouth and telling their story. "We saw a dog in Tula, and it occurred to Bapcat that he had seen this dog at least once before, and very probably twice before, including just seconds before being shot."

Gleann looked at Bapcat, who nodded.

"A 'certain' dog?"

"Reddish-brown with a missing right rear leg," Isohultamaki said. "The animal belongs to one Ernst Nixon, and we followed him to Norwich."

Bapcat took over. "But something spooked him from his cabin."

"What exactly?"

"Could have been anything," Bapcat said. "We don't know. The point is, he ran."

"That proves nothing," Jone Gleann said.

"He carries a Winchester forty eighty-two," Isohultamaki said.

Zakov piped up, "How can you be certain?"

Bapcat explained: "The man stopped to check beaver sets and I followed him. Rinka checked his rifle while I watched the man."

Zakov grunted. "Trapping beaver in August? He's a fool, or an amateur. When did he flee?"

"Later, in the night. No idea why, but he left his horse behind."

"Suspicious behavior," Zakov said.

"We were probably no different in our day," Bapcat reminded his friend. They had both been trappers, both exemplary in their eccentricities. "Forty eight-two is a common enough caliber. When we have time for it, we can look more closely at Nixon, but now there are more immediate concerns."

He told them about the wolf men and the dead boy. Elphinstone crept into the group and said, "Red Hair rides a white stallion, and he and his men costume themselves as wolves."

"They wear wolf paws attached to their boots," Bapcat said.

"Part of their theater," Elphinstone said.

"How far?" Jone Gleann asked, fetching her crude map. Bapcat perused it, pointed to where there was a prominent peak north of Bergland. Only now did he realize they were not as far north as he'd thought they had been, and if they had stumbled on in the fog, they would not have seen the wolf men. He pointed north of the mountain. "I believe they came from up toward White Pine."

"Less than ten miles from here," Jone Gleann said. "The General wants to go to Silver City to await the trap delivery, and Archibald."

"I think it's probably too early," Bapcat said. "Better later, closer to the expected delivery time."

"I'm expert at blending in," Elphinstone said.

"I agree with Lute," Jone Gleann said. "We need everyone here to help secure us."

Later, when it was just the two of them, he asked her point-blank: "What's Red Hair's role in all this?"

"None that I know of."

"But you *knew* he was up here." Not a question.

She chewed her lip and he pressed her again. "You still think trappers in Tula killed those children?"

"Until evidence proves otherwise," she said, avoiding eye contact.

"That makes Red Hair a wild card in this, and wild cards always change the game."

"What do *you* suggest?" she asked.

He shook his head, wishing he was a better thinker. So many elements seemed to be spinning around them, and each other. If all of them collided, he was not at all sure what sort of result to expect, other than disaster. And where was Farrell Mackley; how the hell did the missing game warden fit into any of this, if at all? He had allegedly designed the bear traps, which proved nothing.

There were times when Bapcat felt sorry that Colonel Roosevelt had put him forward for this job, and this was one of them.

# CHAPTER 52

## *Elm Creek*

### WEDNESDAY, SEPTEMBER 16

It was just Bapcat and Elphinstone, and for privacy they were at some remove from the others. They stood in the morning shadows of volcanic traps taller than either of them. Bapcat got right to the point. "When I first heard your voice, I was out of my head a bit, not sure you were real."

"Real enough," the man said. "Had limited time in which to assess you, old boy, and I wanted to be reasonably sure it was true when I heard a game warden had been bushwhacked."

"I didn't know I was public talk," Bapcat said.

"Hardly that, Deputy. Only a few knew of the event."

"*Jone* told you?"

"Truth front and center, 'twas dear old Jimjim, not her presumed ladyship."

"Why would the priest want *you* to know?"

"One might call it professional courtesy."

"A priest . . . and what exactly are *you*?"

"Special investigator for the Federal Bureau of Biological Survey."

Bapcat shook his head. "Never heard of it."

"Puts you in the unlearned majority of our countrymen. Our main concern is preventing avian damage to farms and crops, and to keep track of our country's mammalian populations and their relative health."

"Avian means birds, and bears are mammals," Bapcat said, hoping he was right. "Why talk to me?"

"Our jobs coincide, in a sense. So why this secret chat today?"

"I need to sort out some things," Bapcat said.

"Things, as in people?" Phin asked.

"People top my list. You just didn't seem real when I thought back on your sneaking into the caravan, and likewise, Jimjim tips the scales heavily toward odd."

"Ah, Jimjim let me in and made sure we weren't interrupted."

"Why would he do that?"

Elphinstone said in a conspiratorial whisper, "Jimjim's been sent by the great State of Minnesota, dispatched by their attorney general to find and deal with Red Hair."

"Deal with?"

"You see how serious he is with that thirty-two of his?"

"Deal with, as in outside the law?"

"I believe his orders are suitably vague so as to be interpreted in the vernacular as *whatever it takes*."

*Minnesota? Feds?* "How did you two make contact?"

"The oldest, surest way: voice to ear. His supervision talked to mine, and both made their revelations. To prevent us working at cross-purposes, they sent word to me."

"Who told the priest?"

"Another messenger."

"Seems unlikely that a state would send a priest to do 'whatever it takes.'"

"Indeed, but the priest is a pose. Our Jimjim's a pure copper."

"Huh," Bapcat said. It had never occurred to him that Jimjim was anything other than a priest. "So explain exactly who *you* are."

"Elphinstone is real. Some call me Harry the Elephant, me possessing a prodigious memory for the most minute of things, wot. British-born, true enough, hardly royalty or military genius; I served in the ranks, but Americans like some sort of motley continental history behind a British accent. Like you, I am a proud citizen—and for goodness' sake, call me Phin."

"At some point I think you told me that 'the game lies ahead,'" Bapcat said. "First time you came to me; I was in and out of reality."

"Exquisite recall on your part, Deputy. Were my exact words now to be amended, I'd change them to 'the game is now afoot.' Read Conan Doyle, have you?"

"Who?"

"Sherlock Holmes, man, scientific detective, the greatest deductive copper in the Empire, be he mere fiction. Surely you've read of Sherlock."

"Not much of a reader," the game warden confessed sheepishly, certain that this divide between himself and educated folks would render his life more and more difficult if he didn't do something about it.

"Never mind that," Elphinstone said, taking out a badge and showing it to his colleague.

"How long have you been here?" Bapcat asked.

"Since last autumn. I arrived during the strike, though it seems things were considerably more bloody up your way."

"Exactly why *are* you here?"

"To investigate rumors of Red Hair—stop him if legally justified."

"Stop him from what?"

"Capturing bears for paying clients. Very lucrative little scheme he has going for him."

"There are federal laws governing bears?" Bapcat asked.

"None whatsoever, sir, but perhaps one day. Now, to our collective shame, there remain none."

"You're telling me Red Hair is mixed up in this bear thing?"

"I am indeed. Apparently done similar and worse over the border in Ontario, and the Mounties would love to have him back."

"Did you meet Deputy Mackley in the fall?"

"Can't say I did, though I have seen quite a bit of his handsome missus flitting about town with self-importance."

Bapcat was having a hard time following the man. "Do you think Mackley made the model traps for Archibald?"

"No reason to disbelieve that fact, Deputy. That's the hushed word they use in Romney Archibald's most inner sanctum."

"You're that far inside to know that?"

"Not me, but my superior, Mr. Nick Vedder, whom you've met, and who knoweth not how to keepeth a secret, secret. Pity, as he has many other fine qualities."

"But the bear-capture-and-sell plan is real?"

"Substantial money's been invested and expended in this undertaking, which means Mr. Archibald believes in it most fervently. The man doesn't do anything without first gauging potential profits against inherent risks."

"But he's not doing anything illegal by state or federal law," Bapcat said.

"True enough, but Red Hair's wanted for multiple homicides and all sort of bloody barbarian behavior. The point is to get him out of circulation and take Archibald with him—conspiracy, you see?"

"Put Archibald in jail?"

"If possible, and if not, a box in the ground will surely suffice."

"And Red Hair?"

"Jail or grave, however it turns out."

"This is Jimjim's view?"

"Yes, whatever the job requires. He ain't of squeamish stock, our Fra Goodman."

Bapcat paused to think. "Are you sending progress reports to your bosses?"

"Not I, and I can't speak for Mr. Goodman. I have seen myself immersed in hostile waters, all alone, until encountering Jimjim, and now you, it seems. A triumvirate."

"But you never had contact with Mackley?"

"The man was nowhere to be seen, and nobody had seen him for some time, it seems. Then you arrived, a new state game warden, and I calculated, more hoped, you might be here in the matter of bear commerce, in Mackley's well-known and obvious prolonged absence. Very quickly you seemed to ruffle some local feathers, and were sent a lead message for your trouble."

"I didn't know anything about the bears—only that Mackley was missing, and I was sent to find him, or learn what happened to him. I talked to Mackley's wife and JP Tecumseh Swoon."

"Pitiful creature, His Honor. Self-interested, with judicial credentials to provide leverage. He belongs to Archibald, directly or indirectly. People in town doubt he makes a move without Archibald's approval, and that includes visits to the hollyhock house."

Bapcat smiled inwardly. Hollyhock was code for outhouse. "That's a serious charge."

"Knowingly repeated as speculative by his various colleagues and chums."

"So you carry that badge with you all the time?" Bapcat asked.

"When not out like this. Here I am the exemplar of incognito. You wish to verify my credentials and identity?" Elphinstone asked, grinning.

"I guess I might," Bapcat admitted. "For peace of mind."

"Not being one for intuition and the like."

"Probably not," Bapcat admitted.

"Got nothing to offer, old boy. You think the JP or the erstwhile widow-in-waiting had a role in your being shot?"

"I'm still trying to figure out what to do about you."

"Best way to learn to swim is to jump into the deepest water, wot."

"Something in me says the JP and lady are directly involved, but I'm not sure exactly how."

"That's called the gut, Deputy. Gut's the heart of us in this line of work. Put another way, here we are; what exactly are your options? For the record, I should be in Silver City to verify trap delivery and follow them from there."

"After that?"

"Hope Red Hair is looming in the somewhere-soon."

"Big if."

"As stated before, what are your alternatives?"

"I want Jimjim with us," Bapcat said.

Ten minutes later the dwarf stood there, smiling.

"He knows," Elphinstone announced.

Fra Goodman's expression did not change. "Knows what?"

"Your assignment, old boy."

"Bloody loose-mouthed Brit," the little man said in a hiss.

"He's our natural ally," Elphinstone offered.

"I work alone," Jimjim said.

"Your boss and mine are of a different mind-set," Elphinstone said. "Otherwise, why point us toward each other?"

"We all want the same things," Bapcat said. "Red Hair in jail, our game warden found, the bear plan spoiled, and those behind the plan arrested and prosecuted."

"Michigan will prosecute?" Jimjim asked.

"I'm ordered to arrest and hold all involved."

"On what charges?"

"Attempted theft and the intention to profit from the illegal sale of State property. And I'm to arrest Red Hair and turn him over to Minnesota law enforcement."

"Bloody brilliant," Jimjim said. "You have warrants?"

"Telegram authorization from the state attorney general."

The priest beamed and rubbed his hands together. "Now all we need is for Red Hair to walk into our trap."

Bapcat thought about the valley he and Rinka Isohultamaki had seen, the dead boy lashed to the tree, the sleeping wolves, a white horse. "I don't need Red Hair in order to discharge one part of my assignment."

"You'd ignore some of your charge?"

"No, but I don't quite understand how Archibald's plan connects to Red Hair."

"Archibald needs trappers. That's the link," Jimjim said. "He needs bear men, which Red Hair and his lot are."

Bapcat stared into the woods for a long time. Their numbers were limited. Splitting would make them vulnerable, unless they pushed apart and stood ready to rush back together at the right time. A plan began to form in his mind. "We have to find Red Hair and follow him to Archibald."

"No need to complicate it," Jimjim said. "If we find Red Hair, we move on him. No reason to risk losing him."

"I want to get all of them," Bapcat said. "All of them at once."

"That leaves your missing colleague as a loose end," Elphinstone said.

"Possibly," Bapcat said, "but if he made the models of those traps, he's connected somewhere in all this. When we arrest Archibald, we may be able to trade dropped minor charges for information, for what he knows."

"He may not know anything," the Brit said.

"I'll take that chance."

Elphinstone said, "Settled, then. By your leave, I'm off to Silver City."

"Not alone; take Scale."

"A nigger in Silver City is as welcome as a black snake in Eden."

"Take Isohultamaki," Bapcat said.

"Your Russian mate?" Jimjim asked.

"Zakov stays with Jone, the German trapper, and Scale."

"That leaves you and me for Red Hair," Jimjim said.

Bapcat nodded grimly. It felt like he was in an all-or-nothing moment, and he did not like the feeling.

# CHAPTER 53

## *South of White Pine*

### WEDNESDAY, SEPTEMBER 16

Bapcat waited until later in the afternoon to call them together, and even then, cognizant of the importance of their mounts, held the meeting close to the livestock. "Raise your right hands," he told them, with an aside to the German. "You, too."

"I just want to go home," Pippig said.

Bapcat repeated. "Raise your right hand." The German trapper complied with obvious reluctance.

The game warden swore them in as state deputies under the order and authority of the state attorney general, asked if there were questions, and was answered by blank stares. "Jone, Zakov, Scale, and the German will go to the trapper's camp and sit tight."

Still no comments.

"The General and Rinka will go to Silver City and follow the trap shipment to its final destination, then return to us here."

More silence.

"Jimjim and I will be together."

"To what ends?" Jone Gleann asked. "*Any* of this?"

"Jimjim and I will follow Red Hair," Bapcat said. "The General and Rinka will track bear traps and stay with them to whatever destination they have."

"And the rest of us?" Jone Gleann asked.

"Wait at the Blowdown Creek area and keep watch on the valleys over there."

"Watch for whom?" the woman pressed. "The bears are *here*."

"*Whomever* shows up," Bapcat said, aping her, then looked at his partner. "Do your best to get rid of any sign we were ever here."

"This is where they will come for bears," Gleann said.

Bapcat had little doubt she was right. The area abounded with signs and promise, thick stands of beech and oaks laden with nuts and acorns, massive spreads of chokecherries, some with branches already broken by climbing, greedy animals. Scat piles showed berries, and there were several old bear trees where boars had marked their territories by dragging their sharp claws from a spot on the trunk above a man's head to the ground. One set of marks reached up almost eight feet.

"I know you're right about this place," Bapcat told the woman, "but we want them to be busy with bears and not spooked by us. Good trappers will read ground as easily as civilized folk read the newspaper."

"You give these people too much credit," Jone Gleann said.

"Always overestimate the other side," Bapcat said. "Hope for the best and plan for the worst."

"He is right," Zakov said, chiming in.

"We'll never get rejoined," Gleann complained. "Too much area."

"Possible," Bapcat said, "but I suspect our two lines will, as you predict, lead here, so this is where we will rendezvous when the time comes."

"How will we know?"

"We are in pairs, one a follower and tracker, the other a messenger as needed."

"How does this help find Deputy Mackley?" the woman pressed.

"I don't know; maybe it doesn't. But Red Hair is our first concern because he's the most dangerous. If we can get the bear thing as well, that's ideal, but arresting and stopping Red Hair is a must, the bears second, and Mackley a distant third."

"Do we have any notion of when these so-called lines might actually connect?" Gleann asked.

"No, ma'am," Bapcat said, "but not till after October first, if the General is right." Bapcat turned to Phin, Rinka, and Jimjim. "Light rations for the four of us. The rest of our supplies go with Zakov and Jone."

The Russian nodded. "You're certain you and your companion can handle Red Hair?"

"Jimjim is a lawman from Minnesota and we are the two most directly charged with capturing the men, and, in any event, I doubt there will be much chance of a confrontation until Red Hair joins with Archibald. Until then our job is to locate, follow, watch, and learn. When it comes time to form up one group, Rinka will bring word and lay out our plan."

Jone Gleann stared at the ground and said nothing.

"All right, let's get to it," Bapcat said.

Jone Gleann grabbed his arm and held it a long while. "Jimjim and you are *most directly* charged. Why am I just learning this?" she asked indignantly.

Bapcat undid her grip. "Talk to Jimjim about that."

Rinka came over while he was saddling Joe. "I can trust this man you send me with?"

"He talks funny, but he's true," the game warden said, hoping his gut was right.

"Do you think this will end in bloodshed?" Isohultamaki asked.

Bapcat looked her in the eye. "I sure hope not," he said, sensing by her look that this was not the kind of end she was hoping for.

Zakov pushed his hat back. "The dog you and Rinka talked about—I think I saw that animal this morning."

Bapcat turned to his friend. "Where?"

Zakov pointed upstream from camp.

"Doing what?"

The Russian said, "It was stretched out most comfortably on a flat rock, staring west."

"Did the dog see you?"

"Not at all. I had the wind, and the animal seemed far more focused on the other direction."

"Describe the dog."

Zakov told him and the coloring seemed to fit. "Missing leg?"

"Could not tell from my angle or distance. But I wonder—if by chance this is the same animal, why is it here? This is too odd for coincidence."

Bapcat had no answer, but had reached a similar conclusion. He and Isohultamaki had last seen the animal at its master's cabin near Norwich, a grueling twenty miles southeast of their present location.

"Proceed as we planned," Bapcat said. "Saddle the livestock, clean away all sign."

"Then what?" Jone Gleann asked.

"Nothing, I hope," Bapcat said, and told them all, "We can't safely ignore that dog."

"Assuming the worst?" Zakov asked.

Bapcat sighed, nodded, got down from Joe, and began to assemble a figure of cloth and rags to replace him in the big mule's saddle. He crowned the creation with his Rough Rider hat.

Zakov said, "'Sui generis,' of its own kind."

"The dummy?" Bapcat asked as he stood beside Kukla.

"It and its maker," the Russian said.

## CHAPTER 54

## Elm Creek

### WEDNESDAY, SEPTEMBER 16

When the shot came, Bapcat lurched involuntarily and saw Jimjim gesticulating north toward a tree-covered ridge ahead of him. The head of the dummy lashed to the saddle had evaporated into a cloth mist when the bullet crashed through it, and Joe had bucked ahead with the effigy flopping around on top of him.

Scale, the General, Rinka, and Zakov were quickly converging on the hill the priest had pointed to after the report.

Zakov's sighting of the dog had weighed on Bapcat so much that he'd gathered them all together. It took very little time to conclude that while they didn't know why, the dog's owner might very well be following him, or them, he wasn't sure which; he had no idea why this might be so, but it seemed prudent to assume Nixon was near, armed, and up to no good. Was he on his own, or part of something else? Once again, so many questions.

Jone Gleann had thrown his own words back at him: "Plan for the worst, hope for the best."

The dummy had been a sop to the worst, and the rifle shot, which he supposed he had half expected, confirmed the reality. A second rifle report included a ricochet that sounded nearly musical, and with this the dog had come scampering to the game warden's feet, where it curled up, shivering, staring at the hill the priest was pointing to.

"Not sure I should thank you, or kick your behind," Bapcat told the dog.

Thirty minutes later a bloody-faced man stood before him, propped up by Rinka and the Russian.

Zakov said, "There should be a sign around this woman's neck declaring her dangerous. Mr. Nixon initiated fisticuffs, and you see before you the result. No contest."

"I have brothers," Rinka Isohultamaki said sheepishly. "Fists before words."

"You're certain this is Ernst Nixon?" Bapcat asked. He had gotten only one look at the man when he was checking a trap, and the view had not been all that clear.

Rinka said, "This is the man I saw in Tula. There is no doubt."

"Nixon?" Bapcat said to the man.

"I have nothing to say to the likes of you," the man mumbled.

Zakov leaned over the man. "We are an army in the field, sir. Justice is here with us, the process ours, followed by sentencing, and immediate punishment, including execution. You have attempted murder here in front of all these witnesses," the Russian added. "This is the same as murder under such conditions."

"You can't prove nothing," the man said.

"We don't have to. We are not the State. Are you not listening? Your life and fate now reside in our hands, not with a jury in a town. *We* are the judge and the jury."

"There is no capital punishment here," the man said officiously. "It ain't allowed."

Bapcat said, "True enough if we were in a town, but as Deputy Zakov says, we aren't. What we are is a moving unit of law in pursuit of known felons."

"We take no prisoners," Zakov added, "and we have you in custody. Thus, what happens next is almost entirely up to you. I advise you to do your best to please us."

"I don't understand," the man said with a whine.

Rinka slapped his face. "You are a lying, bushwhacking pig."

Zakov said with a smile, "This is simple. Sing like a nightingale or die."

"I kill nobody here."

"You tried," Bapcat said. "Twice."

The man glared at Bapcat, and Jone Gleann said, "I know this Nixon. He does all the dirty work for a mine captain at Norwich, name of Eustice Pled. He was deputized by the mines during the strike."

"Honest man, honest work; I follow the damn rules," Ernst Nixon insisted. "And orders."

"Rules?" Zakov said.

"I am a man of law and order," Nixon said. "God's rules, the mine's rules, this great country's rules—all of them."

"You were shooting at me today," Bapcat said, "*and* back in June."

A morose Nixon said, "I got nothing to say."

"Talk or you'll be in the ground," Jimjim said, cocking his .32 and holding it to the man's eye.

"I know this is just *ein bildnis* I shoot, *ein vogelscheuche*—you call scarecrow or dummy, yes? Only this I shoot, I swear to *Gott*. You got no charges that can stick," Nixon said, almost spitting at them.

"No charges needed," Jimjim said, making the sign of the cross with his left hand as he held his gun barrel to the man's head with his right. "Talk or die. Now. Your choice."

"This ain't damn right, I think, what you do, breaking rules when you want," Nixon said, glaring at Bapcat. "You breaked all rules during strike—everybody know game wardens take the side of those damn strikers. You got no right, change rules like you done, you and rest of those damn game wardens."

"This is about the strike and deer rules?" Bapcat asked incredulously.

"Not right we gotta follow rules and you don't, and you got that badge to hide behind, I think."

"You shot me."

"I shoot damn dummy."

Zakov pointed out, "You didn't know it was a dummy until after you shot."

"There wasn't a dummy back in June," Bapcat said angrily.

"Was accident that time," the man said. "We want you to know you don't get to bend no rules in Ontonagon County."

"*We*? Who the hell is *we*?"

"Just me, but others sure feel same way as me, I think."

"How'd you know back in June I was a game warden?"

"I guess there's ways," the man said. "I ain't saying no more until I see my lawyer."

"Shoot the bastard," Jimjim said, but Bapcat pushed his gun away from the man's head.

"Likely to be a very long time before you see a lawyer," Bapcat said, "if ever," and smashed the man in the side of the head with his rifle, dropping him to the ground. "Take him to the trapper's place," he told Zakov. "Tie his arms and legs and keep him miserable and uncomfortable. I want to know who he means by 'we,' and what the whole story is. Pippig can stay with him."

"Are you certain you don't want to invest more time in an inquiry now?"

"No time," Bapcat said. "We need to clear this area, but keep squeezing and pressuring him. Jimjim?"

The priest mounted his pony and handed Joe's reins to Bapcat. The general had already stripped off the effigy. "Make sure that damn thing disappears," he told Elphinstone as he and Jimjim prepared to ride west before they turned south and east again.

"That was another long shot today," Jimjim said, "and he hit his target. I'm of a mind that the first time was no warning. The bullet caught a gust of wind, I'm thinking, or you'd be dead."

Lute Bapcat had reached the same conclusion.

# CHAPTER 55

## *South of White Pine*

### THURSDAY, SEPTEMBER 17

Bapcat intended to keep to the route he and Rinka Isohultamaki had followed to catch up with the others, but not two miles away from the main group, the deputy game warden announced to his current companion, "I don't like all your fake priest stuff."

Jimjim laughed. "But it's all true, Lute; the collar and badge are legitimate, and real as winter snow."

"The church allows this?"

"The church allows almost anything it judges will give it an advantage. Let's just say it doesn't encourage me. Any idea how many embezzlers and priest-cheats there are? Rome abhors cheating as much as it hates lost souls, the latter being at least theoretically retrievable in the church's estimation, but not so money lost—the cardinal sin of cardinal sins."

"Does Jone know?"

"The lady is of the sort who knows what they want, and what they want to know, and practice selective memory as seems both practical and temperate."

"I want to take Red Hair alive," Bapcat declared.

"*You* want?"

"My state."

"I won't argue the jurisdiction, but I'll wager I know far more than you about our quarry."

"You may know more," Bapcat said after a pause, "but I'm thinking he and I did time in the same orphanage together." He had suspected for some-time this was the boy he had known, but now his gut told him his first intuition had been right. There was no evidence, just an overpowering sense of the situation.

"One does not *do time* in an orphanage," the priest said.

"I guess you weren't there to know, were you?"

• • •

It was many hours later before they spoke again of anything other than route choices and ways around trail obstructions.

"Truly, you know Red Hair?" Jimjim asked.

"Heinrich Junger was called Henry Young, or Hank the Shank by us. I knew him well enough and long enough to not be surprised by what he is now."

"Bad blood, is there?"

"Briefly, a long, long time ago."

Jimjim said, "As a priest and as an investigator, I have seen bad blood endure for decades. Some people are incapable of letting go of slights, real or imagined, large or small, and now that I know you have a history with Red Hair, I feel a bloody ending is most likely, never mind your intentions."

"It *could* end like that," Bapcat said. "But I want to arrest him."

"Your jurisdiction, your command; I will likewise do my best," the priest said.

They slept curled up on the ground near their animals with less than two hours of darkness remaining.

# CHAPTER 56

## South of White Pine

FRIDAY, SEPTEMBER 18

When the sun came up the next morning, they mounted and moved on toward the place where Bapcat and Isohultamaki had seen Red Hair's wolf men.

"This is the place," Bapcat announced many hours later, as he steered Joe into a clearing below the cliff. It was late afternoon, the sun falling.

"Shouldn't we be tracking while the light is still good?"

"Not yet." Bapcat dismounted and walked the ground for several minutes before looking for a higher vantage point. When reached, he quickly saw the amorphous outlines of a hole, and pointed. He dug with a hatchet and a knife and got down a couple of feet before a stench emerged with vengeance.

Bapcat continued to dig until he had located part of a small arm, with blackened, rotten meat, and worms. He tipped it up for Jimjim, who grimaced. The deputy game warden reburied the arm. "Wanted to be sure what I saw was real," he explained to his traveling partner.

"Monsters deserve no justice," Jimjim declared, hurrying ahead of Bapcat to get out of the awful place.

"Henry Young," Bapcat said when he caught up. "It sounds so plain and harmless." Yet he reminded himself that while he'd seen a white horse that day, he hadn't actually seen Young.

Fra Goodman blessed himself and seemed to say a silent prayer. Bapcat didn't ask him what he was praying for.

Once they were out of the valley and climbing into the higher elevations of the Trap Hills, Bapcat led them to the familiar falls where he and Rinka had stopped.

"We'll stay here tonight, and we'll try to cut the trail in the morning," Bapcat said.

Jimjim asked no questions about fire, instead, dug into his saddlebag for pemmican, bit off a chew, and began to grind it between his teeth as night descended. Joe and Fra Goodman's mount were hobbled near them, and Bapcat insisted they keep a rope connection in case they needed to mount fast, an old Indian trick. On foot against a force like Red Hair's was likely a death sentence.

# CHAPTER 57

## Big Iron River, North of White Pine

MONDAY, SEPTEMBER 21

It had been three grueling days of unseasonably cold winds howling in from Canada. The two trackers were speechless when the trail showed that Red Hair had taken his group right through the town of White Pine, as if he and his gang enjoyed immunity there.

Red Hair might move unchallenged through a populated area, but Bapcat didn't want to risk being seen and having word sent to their quarry. The pair skirted east past the mine, and eventually angled due west looking to cut trails, which they finally did that morning. Even now Bapcat knew they were close to Silver City, but he couldn't be certain how far south. He wondered if Red Hair was moving north to Silver City to meet the trap shipment, a possibility he played off the priest, who shrugged at the suggestion.

"Don't like this," Bapcat said. "Too damn cozy to go through that town, and so close to the mine. If we don't get fresher sign soon, we could lose them to the east or the west."

"East and north is Ontonagon," Jimjim said. "West makes more sense, up in the mountains—cover, terrain advantages, all of that."

Despite finding sign of the larger group that morning, the damn trail seemed to keep changing. Bapcat couldn't read it, and wondered if somehow he had missed the sign that some riders had peeled off on their own. As it was, the sign they kept to zigzagged the way cavalry men sometimes did when fearing an ambush or like ships did when maneuvering into a defensive posture. Was Red Hair leaving a rearguard with messengers? Did Henry Young know he was being followed, or did he always assume this posture near towns?

As usual, questions without answers.

The crisscrossing trail led them to a bedrock step-waterfall that stretched all the way across the river, a series of brown stone layers with orange water cascades. It was easily a hundred yards to the far bank, during which they would be vulnerable to an attack.

"Take Joe," Bapcat said, handing the reins to the priest. "I'll find a narrow place to cross and come back down the far bank, see what's over there, make sure we aren't walking into a surprise."

Wading quickly with his rifle over his head and an unstable cobble bottom under his boots, Bapcat crossed and darted up into the woods on the west side and started north, moving quickly but cautiously. Clear. Bapcat signaled Jimjim to cross, and once he'd done so, remounted Joe. The new tracks led west to a small river with a reddish-gray bottom, the orange-brown waters tinged by tannin and iron. The trail led south along the river until it reached a place where two streams joined and then continued up the middle onto higher land between the creeks.

Bapcat racked his brain to recall the rough copy of Jone's map he had hurriedly sketched in his mind. "If they keep south, they'll hit Nonesuch."

"Perfect name," Jimjim said. "It means 'unrivaled,' and was the name of Henry the Eighth's first palace, though his was spelled without the e in the middle. If memory serves, he never got to live there."

"Henry the Eighth?"

"Monster in his own right. Six wives, and he split Rome from England because the pope refused to grant him either an annulment or divorce from his first spouse."

"How do you keep all that in your head?"

"My church thinks of all the past as present, and takes special efforts to mete out its justice for old hurts and grudges. The pope excommunicated poor old Henry, which had no effect, as it seldom does. Dear Henry happily fucked his way through his subjects in hopes of creating a male heir, and died at fifty-five, unrepentant, I might add."

"Jone told us all this would lead through Nonesuch," Bapcat said. "Large place?"

"No idea. I know it's way past its prime, and I'll wager the operations today are marginal, and minimal at best."

"But possibly friendly to Red Hair," Bapcat pointed out.

"One must presume so, out of prudence if nothing else."

"Tomorrow is soon enough to push closer," Bapcat said.

"May I state for the record that I am sick of cold food?" the priest said.

"Me too." They somehow needed to make contact with Pierre Malyotte, who Phin reported would set up Archibald's camp and then meet with Phin to guide him from Silver City.

• • •

The temperature continued to drop, and the humidity seemed to hang high. Bapcat wondered if more snow was coming. He dug out his black oilskin pants and coat and sou'wester hat, hacked some boughs for ground insulation, and took two seven-by-seven-foot oilskin tarps off his saddle, tossing one to the priest. "You've got rain gear?"

"In my bags."

"Better get it on. I smell snow or rain coming in."

"Ah, the excitement of the chase. Heaven-sent moisture and no hot food—what more could a man want?"

Thunder began rumbling within an hour, and to the north they could see purplish-blue lightning bolts out over Lake Superior, but neither rain nor snow fell. It hailed instead, marble-size pieces bouncing through tree branches and hitting rocks in the open areas, falling so heavily they looked like giant snowflakes until they struck something solid and bounced. Bapcat and his partner released their animals, which immediately came over and stood by them, seeking protection and company. Joe let drop a stinking wet flop nearby that made Bapcat's eyes water.

"I thought that mule was perfection," the priest chided.

"Ain't nothing perfect," Bapcat said. At least they were relatively dry and warm. He'd spent many a night when neither condition applied.

"God included," Jimjim said. "Made the pitiful likes of us, didn't he?"

"And Joe," Bapcat added.

"I'd have to say your Joe probably stands a level above run-of-the-mill mankind."

"Are you allowed to say such things?"

"Rome is far, far away, and I don't see you as the informing type."

"I ain't, but I guess I don't understand why you kick at your own church. Seems to me it would be better to leave it if it's so bad."

"Physical leaving is easy; emotional departure is not. I grew up with it, am indoctrinated, marked for life and death."

"Sounds like you've been branded."

"Indeed," the priest said with a steady expression. "Got a large crucifix tattooed on my arse. All priests do."

Bapcat considered this for a moment. "That's a joke."

"Albeit poor, and a gallant attempt."

More hail crumpled down on them, and Bapcat withdrew into himself to think for a moment.

"Red Hair—do you hear about things he does in confessions?" Bapcat asked the priest.

"That kind of creature don't know there's a right from a wrong, which tells them they got nothing to confess."

"Would God forgive him?"

"Only through my intercession," Jimjim said.

"But you have to, right?"

"Technically and theoretically, but as a wise man of science once proclaimed, 'In practice the theory is different.' Now let me ask you if you would let the man go unpunished if the court finds him not guilty, or drops the prosecution?"

"That couldn't happen . . . could it?"

"The court is at best a roll of the dice. I assume you know there are thirty-six possible combinations when one spills the bones."

"No."

"Even more variation in court outcomes, there being so many different combinations of laws and how they get interpreted. The few that might be considered supportive of pure justice or lawmen are quite limited. 'Innocent until proven guilty' has proven a huge barrier to prosecution in front of juries, and I'm thinking it will only get worse."

"Guess I don't know what I'd do," Bapcat admitted.

"Oh, I think you know in your heart, Lute, and let me say quickly I would be the first to absolve your sins. It ain't a sin to murder a murderer or snuff out a monster."

"I'm not Catholic."

"All but the world's Red Hairs are catholic when it comes to sin and guilt in this life. They just go at it differently."

Bapcat felt sleepy and edgy. "I ain't much on all this think-talk."

"The seed's planted," Jimjim said. "Let it grow. Good-night, partner."

# CHAPTER 58

## *Nonesuch*

### TUESDAY, SEPTEMBER 22

Hail became gushing rain, which came in sheets that engulfed all sound and took their oilskins to their limits, a fault of fate, not a test of manufacturing. When the downpour finally tapered off, they found themselves dry in the core, with soggy edges, and trees around laden with peanut-size droplets that dislodged with the slightest provocation. Both Joe and the pony looked miserable, but neither had tried to find better cover.

Intense slivers of yellow-pink morning light knifed through the trees. Bapcat looked over at his partner. "I guess we ain't drowned."

The priest stared up at the canopy of trees. "One of His meaningless tests. You'd think such a grand Creator would have better things to occupy his time than annoying his puny creations."

"Maybe He just made the weather, not how it moves."

"Hair-splitting nonsense, and small consolation," Jimjim said. "I never imagined you as an optimist."

"I've got all I can handle with what *is* without fretting over what could be better, or worse. What is, is, and that alone leaves my plate full."

"A pragmatist to the marrow. Perhaps we should offer a prayer to help us find tracks."

"Do what pleases you. Me, I'll look to luck and good eyes. The last tracks we saw seemed aimed at Nonesuch. I'm thinking we should have us a look up there, and if we don't see them, we can double back to this spot and try to re-cut their trail. With all this dang rock up here, it will be a trick, even without the rain."

"Once we find Red Hair?" the dwarf asked.

"Watch him."

"How long? Cage traps aren't due for more than a week, and we can't go indefinitely without hot food, real sleep, and letting our animals graze. There's not enough oats in our saddle bags."

"Once we figure out what's happening, we might withdraw to another place. One man on them, one man in our camp, swap places every day."

"You're not concerned that regular coming and going might attract attention?"

"Won't be regular in timing or route," Bapcat said. "We'll watch their routine before deciding, try to bend ourselves to what they do, when."

"Anything about the trail we had earlier strike you?" Jimjim asked.

"They walk more than they ride."

"Why would that be?"

He had no idea. "We'll need to figure that out."

• • •

It was disconcerting to discover the probable northern approach of the gang led to a large, open, stump-filled field and a road maybe fifty acres across, or more, with fourteen log houses on either side of a rocky dirt lane. Around the perimeter he saw numerous giant stacks of timber ready for burning or underground shoring. The houses were made of logs, not like the newer wood-siding places mines built for their people around Red Jacket. These looked old and not in such good condition. Different structures, but the standard fifty-by-one-hundred-foot allotment of land was the same.

As in White Pine they'd come right in the front door. Fourteen houses, and at least two dozen other buildings he could see, most of them, he assumed, used in mining. Mining companies didn't waste money on anything that didn't contribute to bringing copper into the light.

The two searchers skirted wide to the east of the houses and hobbled their mounts in the woods, which Bapcat assumed would be gone in a few years. Mines had an insatiable need for logs, and every year more forests disappeared.

Bapcat left the priest and went alone on foot. The few people who were out and about wore miners' coveralls and helmets. This in itself was odd, because most miners at other mines hung their clothes in a dry house and changed into aboveground clothing. Not here. He had no idea what this might mean.

The game warden worked his way south to the river, which flowed almost due east, but downhill of the houses and other buildings. He crossed the orange-brown water and gray rock below the closest building, in the thickest treed area he could find, and slid up into a rocky hillside with lots of cover. The river bent around a small isthmus ahead of him. A channel had been cut straight through on the north side of the shaft house. No sound of the lifts working, no black smoke from the stacks of any of the buildings. The main mine superstructure was built on what had become an island. Working his way west he looked south and saw yet another stump-mottled clearing, this one with two dozen smaller, older-looking cabins. A dirt lane led to a footbridge across the narrow river.

There was one open area he had to cross without cover, and he walked across quickly, trying not to look furtive. He heard heavy thumps west of him, and thought it might be a stamp mill, but couldn't be sure. All mines were loud and smoky and dirty, and every piece of machinery had its own sounds. But there was nobody in sight on the mine island, and nobody on the north bank. As he got closer to the slamming sound, he thought it more likely a pump in serious need of repair. No people anywhere, no sign of work or anything else. It was more than unnerving, and had all his senses on alert as he slid through the rocks moving north, finally settling into a spot where he could sit with his back to a rock wall, the embankment below him grown nearly solid with tag alder and other heavy underbrush. The vantage was good, and it was hidden.

Eventually he heard sounds and some faint voices. He moved west again to try to get a closer look, and there across the river he saw a white horse tied up and standing like a statue.

Young's horse? He hadn't actually seen Young himself on the horse, or seen him at all, for that matter. The group they'd followed had a remuda of horses, but judging by the few tracks they'd seen, the men walked more than rode. Poor mounts being saved? Inexperienced horsemen? He knew he needed to see Young and verify his presence, but the horses seemed more important at the moment. Animals could be a group's salvation or their undoing. He moved on west, staying on the military crest, just below the top so there was no silhouette for people below to see.

The river had a sluice and cofferdam built two hundred yards upstream of the mine buildings. A sizable pond had formed behind the cofferdam. The game warden found a vantage point and lay down and used his telescope to methodically study the other side of the river in some detail. Back up in the trees he located horses, estimated at least thirty animals, and saw that almost all were nags at best. Red Hair's force would mount only in the face of a challenge; if they remained afoot, they would be vulnerable to attack from horsemen. Not that he could mount a direct assault, but his people could mimic Indians, harass the enemy to sap his strength, and, if the opportunity arose, run off their horses, forcing the other side afoot.

For the moment, all he and Jimjim could do was watch and wait; he'd learned this from trapping, where patience was critical.

An hour after he'd located the horses, a dozen people came out of a mine building and built a fire. He could hear voices but not specific words. They were not dressed like miners. Red Hair's people? Hard to say, but at least he had a rough idea of how many, and where they were for the moment. Over the next hour he made mental notes of how people looked and, as he watched, he counted eight more, bringing the total to twenty. All carried various firearms, and several had axes and long spears like Plains Indians.

But no Red Hair, and no sign of the group actually being directed. Fires lit, Bapcat smelled food, and as he watched them he thought they looked as carefree as picnickers. Loud talk abounded, poor sound discipline. They felt safe in the mining village. Another potential weakness to exploit.

The game warden wanted to stay but knew he had to get back to Jimjim. He reluctantly withdrew, retracing his route back to his partner.

"Been quiet here," Jimjim said. "Like church on a Monday. You?"

"I think I found the main force and the white horse, but no Red Hair, and no obvious guards or lookouts anywhere."

"Overconfident, or stupid?"

"Not sure yet. Maybe both." *Or maybe we're missing something obvious?* he cautioned himself.

"Pull back, find us a safe haven to camp?" the priest asked. "Northwest of here?"

"I've been thinking the place Jone had us might not be bad if we pushed a bit north of there. That would put us four or five miles from here, and close to the bear-trapping area. We can come to the camp from the south and stay hidden real easy."

"Lead on," Jimjim said, smacking his lips loudly. "I can already taste hot beans."

"We'll have to see about a fire," Bapcat said.

"Are you always about business?" the other man challenged.

"Don't know how to be any other way and stay alive."

# CHAPTER 59

## *North of Elm River*

WEDNESDAY, SEPTEMBER 23

Lute Bapcat tried to think like a bear trapper, though he had never intentionally trapped a bruin. He knew bait was essential—natural foods such as beechnuts, acorns, chokecherries, and crab apples. A bear would eat just about anything, but like people, they had their own preferences, and manmade things usually ranked behind natural eats.

While game wardens didn't fear black bears, they did give them great respect and distance. The bears of the Dakotas mainly had been blackies, with a griz now and then. Griz, while dangerous, were oddly predictable. Black bears were not so easy to read or anticipate, and if they attacked it would be with killing in their minds, not some sort of territorial challenge thing. Griz charges tended to be about protecting a kill or cubs, and would be broken off if the animal felt it had won its point.

Jimjim cajoled him until he relented and allowed a fire, which they kept Indian-small, no larger than the palm of his hand. Even small, there was plenty of heat and not much smoke.

Holding a spoonful of beans in front of his mouth," Jimjim said, "Like the finest roast beef on earth, cooked to perfection, a bouquet from Heaven. A good claret would make a fine companion."

"Eat. We need to put out this fire," Bapcat said quietly. He liked the man whose small stature hid a stripe of optimism and hardness uncommon in men twice his stature. That the man was a priest and a lawman still did not set comfortably with him.

"Think we'll miss something by not being at Nonesuch tonight?" Jimjim asked.

"I hope not, but you were right about food and sleep and our animals."

"What if Red Hair's not there?" Jimjim asked.

"I've asked myself that more than once, and still can't come up with a good answer."

"I think I should get in close and have a look," the priest said.

"Probably too risky."

"If he's *not* here, why are we?"

"I've got more than one job in all this," Bapcat said.

"I don't, which is why I need to know if the man is there or not. Red Hair, Heinrich Junger, Henry Young, Hank the Shank—I don't give a hoot what his name is, as long as it's him. You realize, my fine friend, that this man is dangerous and unpredictable beyond words."

"So are we," Bapcat said. "If that's how it plays out."

"There's likely to be hostages brought into play if this is our scoundrel," Jimjim said, "which is why we need a look inside. I'm of a size that will make that easier for me."

"Not yet," Bapcat said. "If Nonesuch is where the bear traps are coming, there should be some confusion and excitement when they arrive, making that a good time to slip into the place."

"Your logic is unassailable," Goodman said. "You really knew Young?"

"I knew *a* Henry Young, and it was a long time ago."

"You are far from a social and gregarious man," the priest said.

"If that means I ain't much of a talker, you're right."

"Talk and conversation help us learn, a necessity for peace officers."

"I guess that ain't been my take on it so far."

"Shame."

*Talk to the man.* "Henry Young—bully, violent, liked to have the size advantage and numbers in his favor."

"You confronted him?"

"Once."

"Never again?"

"He stayed clear of me."

"Did it turn physical?" the priest asked.

"Might have killed him if others hadn't stepped in and pulled me away."

"Ever occur to you that there's not a lot of difference between the two of you?"

"We were nothing alike."

"You might have killed him."

"I didn't, and this is why I don't like talking," Bapcat said.

"You killed as a soldier?"

"I did."

"Did you find it difficult?"

"No." *Truth.*

"Yet you are reluctant to kill here," the priest said, pressing his argument.

"A soldier's job is to kill on sight. A lawman's job is to arrest and let the courts decide what happens."

"You're really comfortable with that distinction, even if the court would let someone like Red Hair go?"

Bapcat looked across the small fire. "You brought this up before. Are you trying to get me to change my approach? That won't happen, Jimjim. I got trained by the best of men."

"Roosevelt?"

"Knew him a long time. He's not much like most people think he is. He has passion and thinks things through, and he pitches in on the work—all of it. But he don't rush into nothing. He always thinks his way in."

"Like charging a hill in the open?"

"That day weren't as clear-cut as the newsies made it out."

"And the enemy had the high ground."

"Until we took it from them."

"You see this situation to be like that one—simple right over wrong, do what has to be done?"

"That was war, Jimjim. This ain't."

"Shooting is inevitable."

"That fact alone don't make a war."

A moment later the priest said, "I'd feel better leaving my pony here in camp days when I'm on watch."

"You can travel faster mounted than on foot."

"I can hide better on my own, and the distance from hither to yon ain't a stretch."

Bapcat preferred his mule, but understood the priest's point. "Suit yourself, I guess."

"Any reason we have to glue ourselves to one watching site?"

"What do you mean?"

"I'd like to rat my way around the perimeter and try to draw us a reasonable map."

"I already made a sketch," Bapcat said.

"I seen that, and you ain't no Fred Remington. I'll make something we can all use and read."

"I guess I'm not going to bandy at such things, but what I see sticks pretty good in my head."

"I noticed, but not all of us are as smart as you, or have that kind of natural mental order and discipline."

"Sleep," Bapcat said. *Smart?*

# CHAPTER 60

## *Nonesuch*

### WEDNESDAY, SEPTEMBER 30

They had spent eight days watching.

Jimjim's hand-drawn map was now done in exquisite detail, and the routine in the remote mining village was known and seemed predictable. But there was still no sign of Henry "Red Hair" Young, and this bothered Bapcat. The gang leader's wolf men seemed to be on holiday as they lolled about. The final head count they had was forty, including ten miners, which seemed paltry even for a small operation. The pounding water pump still throbbed like a distant heart, and the stamp mill sat silent, unused.

Bapcat and Fra Goodman had spent the past two days on a watch together, and the priest continued to press his wish—to infiltrate across the river. The game warden had a rough plan set in his own mind, however. He'd gone over it and over it and saw no reason to vary from it yet. When and if the traps arrived, there would be ample time and opportunity to give the Minnesota lawman what he wanted.

The only change they saw over the week was that the white horse got turned out in the remuda with the other animals, none of which anyone rode. And still no camp guards or lookouts to be seen anywhere. The horse's new venue was the only change, and there was no way to know if it meant anything.

What was real was that their food supplies were reduced to pemmican and some apples from wild trees, and both men were hungry all the time. Not starving, or close to it, but Bapcat felt a dull pain in his stomach and the sort of lethargy that came with not eating enough on a regular basis. Every fire eventually died without fuel.

"Trap-cages are supposed to land in Silver City tomorrow," Bapcat told his partner. "They're supposed to move them to White Pine and then to here." Phin and Rinka were following the cages. Bapcat considered trying to join them, but no rendezvous had been planned. He had given Rinka some rough ideas on Indian trail signs, and hoped she would be able to find them. Trying to make an unscheduled rendezvous seemed fraught with trouble and too many challenges to overcome. They didn't need that right now. Things were quiet, and they remained invisible to the camp.

"What if the traps get delayed?" Jimjim asked.

"They won't be."

"Care to share the basis of such iron confidence?"

Bapcat had no answer, and shrugged. Phin was eccentric, but the game warden's intuition said the odd Britisher could be trusted. Rinka Isohulta-maki was young, but solid and trustworthy, if a bit headstrong.

"I've come a long way to get Red Hair," the lawman-priest said.

"We'll get him."

"And did I mention I'm hungry?" Jimjim added.

"Too many times to count."

"I might start tearing apart old logs for grubs and such to dine on."

"Be my guest. We have water. We can go a long time without food."

"Speak for yourself, Deputy. I may be small in stature, but my appetite is that of a giant."

"So I've heard."

"Got any ideas about how the missing game warden fits into any of this?"

"Not yet."

"Do we remain doubled tonight, or should one of us go back to camp, and the animals?"

"Both of us back to camp. We need sleep, and I'm thinking there will be no traps here for three days. Arrival tomorrow in Silver City, a day to move them to White Pine, another day from there to here."

"Perhaps one of us should be in White Pine to see what happens, bring word back. If the cages don't show there, then what?"

Bapcat said, "We'll have to go into Nonesuch and find our man." But if this happened, it meant his plan to capture the bear trappers might be out. After some thought he said, "Camp tonight. You head for White Pine tomorrow, and I'll stay with Nonesuch at the watching place on the west end of the ridge."

"And Joe?"

"He can stay in camp. If you can, buy some more oats in White Pine. The graze here is unexpectedly good, but come the hard freezes, it will all be quickly gone."

"You think Red Hair is in White Pine, and that's why we've not seen him here?"

"I expect we'll find out, one way or another."

"Would surely explain his absence from here."

"Camp," Bapcat said, tired of talking and speculation and making plans with no real information to build them on. Horri Harju had always insisted, "Neither investigation nor speculation is ever glamorous. Both are boring and can lull you to sleep. But you need to be adept at both, and embrace them and the skills that go with them. Cases are often made on very small pieces of evidence. Look at it this way: Youse get paid no matter what, so there shouldn't be no beef about what might feel like wasted time."

# CHAPTER 61

## *Nonesuch*

### THURSDAY, OCTOBER 1

It was a clear-sky dawn, a bite in the air, no wind and, surprisingly, no frost yet. But that would come soon all around the Upper Peninsula, and here in the hills before elsewhere, Bapcat knew. He hoped the wind was calm in Silver City, and that the load could be safely brought ashore, but winds on the shore and ten miles away could be very different, and both were unpredictable.

Jimjim had headed east at first light on his pony, dressed in his cassock. Bapcat had watched him go, then lingered to give Joe some attention, the mule being of an affectionate nature, at least with him.

"Bored, big fella? This is the life of a game warden's mule: follow, watch, wait, watch some more. We do too much waiting, we may have to start watching your weight." The mule leaned against him as he held out an apple and felt the animal's soft lips.

Having seen to Joe, Bapcat grabbed up his ruck and rifle, and hiked to the mining town.

Not in place an hour and on the brink of dozing, he was startled awake when the morning quiet was smashed by desperate, angry screams and multiple gunshots. All the sudden action animated the remuda, and the horses started nickering and snorting and shuffling wildly.

People were running through the trees on the other side of the river, and Bapcat was about to pull back and up to a more hidden position when he saw a figure slide into the water on the far bank, just below the cofferdam. From his vantage point he could see it was a small person who swam across underwater, kicking smoothly, rising only once for air.

The figure slithered ashore with the undulant grace of an otter and ducked into the rocks, out of sight. Bapcat expected him to keep moving, but he stayed in place. Peculiar behavior with so many people on the far shore in frenzy and furor.

Bapcat made his way down stealthily until he was behind the figure, slid over the boulder, got a hand on the figure's face, and pressed him hard to the earth.

"Not a word, or I'll send you back to them with your throat cut. Understand?" He felt the head nodding under his hand. No muscles, little bulk, the figure felt almost like a small girl. Bapcat rolled him around onto his back and looked. A boy, twelve, thirteen. The game warden almost laughed. "Second Arm, I presume—Manny?"

"Who be you?" the boy whispered.

"Deputy State Game Warden Bapcat. I seen your pa at the island."

"I got no pa. I'm my own boss now."

"I guess that's what we all want, so good for you. Only right now it seems you chucked a stick into a hornet's nest."

The boy instantly brandished a dagger, double-edged, gleaming. "I stuck the both of them real good, and twice each. Kank-kank! Kank-kank!"

"Stuck both of who?" The sound the boy made perfectly mimicked that of a sturdy knife blade penetrating flesh and bone.

"Red Hair and Min, is who. I let 'em get nekkid and bounce them blankets and then I stabbed the both of them. Kank-kank! Kank-kank!"

"Why?"

"Devil's inside 'em both. See, I come along with Min to avenge the time Red Hair attacked my pa and our country, and Min said she'd help me, but she lied and give me over to that devil, and they was keeping me for kid-meat when the time come."

Bapcat was sure he knew the answer, but had to ask the question. "What's kid-meat?"

The boy grimaced. "Don't matter now. I took care of it. My yellow-back old man send you to fetch me back?"

"Your father asked only that I point you toward home. I think he believes you can find your own way."

"You bet I can, but why would I go back to that crazy old man and all them crazy old women on that damn rock?"

"He's your father."

"I never picked him."

"We don't get to pick our parents."

"Well, it ain't right," the boy said.

"You're sure you stabbed both of them?" Bapcat asked.

"She rolled off him, and I give it to her in the heart-tit and then to him in the same place. Kank-kank! Kank-kank!" The boy looked over at him. "How come you don't try to take my blade off me?"

"It's your knife, not mine."

"You're smart, mister. You'd tried, I'da stabbed you."

Bapcat wrenched the knife from the boy with one movement and held it at his throat, said, "Kank-kank," and then offered the knife back, handle first.

The boy was preternaturally calm as Bapcat told him, "You can't just stab people."

"They ain't regular people, and I guess I can after what I seen her do to them other boys."

This wasn't the time for this discussion. "Where are they, Red Hair and Min?"

"Big building up on the hill."

"They aren't out and around much."

"They don't never go out; they stay inside, and the others bring what they need."

*How to ask this?* "How did you get close to them in the big building on the hill?"

"This here place is a mine, and there's tunnels all over, right up to the place where them two stay."

"You see any other boys like you?"

"They got one over there right now, but he'll be gone and et soon, like all them others."

"How many others?"

The boy's eyes darkened. "Five since I busted loose, one already there when they brung me to camp—but he didn't last so long."

"You willingly traveled with her?"

"'Til I seen what they was up to, killing them boys, and bolted. Then I followed them everywhere they went, seen everything they done."

"Are you sure?"

"Kank-kank. I don't make no mistakes, mister."

"Men sometimes don't die all that easy, Manny."

The boy looked back with sad eyes. "I hit 'em good, the both of them."

"That doesn't mean they're dead," Bapcat told the boy. "Maybe you wanted to kill them, but couldn't do it."

"I know what I done and what I seen," the boy insisted.

The boy was trembling, looked ready to explode. Bapcat said, "They killed the boys and ate them?"

"It's Min," the boy said. "She kills 'em and eats 'em and makes some of the others, but Red Hair, he don't want nothing to do with it. He just watches. When he kills, it's just to kill. But when she does it, she wants people to hurt bad before they die."

"They've stopped looking for you," Bapcat said, scanning the north riverbank. "What's that tell you?"

"Don't know, don't care. I done God's work."

"You know them pretty well, how they do things, their routines?"

"'Speck I do at that."

"They have no guards."

"They got 'em all right, a mile out from camp. Red Hair don't want no close-in surprises."

"Like you gave them."

The boy smiled.

"They never ride their horses," Bapcat said.

"Now and again, when the hunt is on. And they eat some of them. Eating horsemeat's easier than hunting wild. They're lazy and stupid."

"Why're they in Nonesuch?"

"They don't talk much. Something about bears is all I know."

"Are they trappers?"

"I don't think they're nothing I know of."

"How many of them?"

"Fifteen men, plus Red Hair. Five women, counting Min."

"I've seen miners."

"They're separate; they go about their business, and don't bother nobody."

"What about Pierre Malyotte?"

"Runs the store and the hotel on the triangle above Mine Island, which is what they all call it. Malyotte takes care of hunters and such."

"What's between him and Red Hair?"

"Nothing I know of, but there's talk of other people coming soon."

"To see Malyotte?"

"Red Hair and Min is how I thought I heard it, but Malyotte is helping them."

"So, he's with them?"

"No, he hates them all. I heard him tell the miners that. But he wants their money."

*Hard to figure Malyotte: Was it strictly a money deal?* "Twenty-one, counting Red Hair—that's all?"

"And that boy they got, if he lasts, which he won't. Who the heck *are* you?"

"We'll talk about that when it's time. Meanwhile, you're coming with me."

"I ain't going back to Armandville—never."

"That's your choice. We need your help for something more important."

"We? I just see you here, mister."

"When it's time, there will be more."

"To do what?"

"Arrest Red Hair."

The boy grinned. "That won't never happen. I done kilt him. Ain't you listening, mister?"

Without knowing why, Bapcat doubted this was true. "How hard is it to get into the mines?"

"Ain't hard. You ever been underground?"

"Worked below for several years," Bapcat said, not adding that claustrophobia had nearly done him in. "Time comes, you'll show me?"

"I guess I might."

"Good. Let's move real slow and quiet-like. Follow me up."

## CHAPTER 62

### *North of Elm River*

SATURDAY, OCTOBER 3

Bapcat and many had watched Nonesuch by day and spent nights at their campsite. Today they came upon a determined-looking Rinka Isohultamaki just north of Elm River.

"Where's Phin?"

"He sent me ahead so he can stay with the traps. There was some large commotion in White Pine, but I couldn't wait to find out what it was. Phin says they intend to trap this country by the Elm."

*As predicted by Jone.* "How many traps?"

"Four is what we heard."

"When are they moving to Nonesuch?"

"As we speak," the young woman said. "Who is that scamp you got with you?" she asked, looking at the boy.

"Manny from Armandville."

"Second Arm," she said.

"Don't you call me that," the boy said in a whine, adding, "I stuck a knife in both of them."

Bapcat caught the woman's eye to warn her off the subject. "You were not easy to find," she told the game warden.

"I left good sign," Bapcat said, meaning various assemblies of sticks, stones, marks in the ground, and broken branches.

"I'm certain a good Indian would have less trouble reading them than me."

They made no more fires at their camping place because Bapcat was concerned Red Hair would send out scouts to reconnoiter. *He would send them if he had any sense or experience with protecting a group.* Why no guards had been posted west of the camp and town remained unexplained, and made Bapcat wonder if some of Red Hair's orders were being willfully disobeyed—or perhaps not being followed through negligence? If they were intentionally ignoring them, this might indicate trouble in the group, and it might explain their lethargy in the town. Even the loud and frantic reaction to Manny's alleged assault, or whatever it was, seemed short-lived and far from clear.

"Archibald meet the shipment?" Bapcat asked Isohultamaki.

"He did, and not alone," she said. "Eustice Pled was in tow."

"Pled, from Norwich?"

She nodded solemnly. "And Hoke Desque, too."

Archibald, Pled, and the incompetent acting sheriff of Ontonagon County, a motley assortment that made Bapcat's mind churn with possibilities, which he pushed away for the moment. There was more in this game than traps and bears. Just what it could be wasn't yet clear to him.

"How's Phin?"

"Proper, difficult, probably daft. Are you sure he's sane?"

"Not really, but I'm hoping."

She smiled. "Good; now I don't feel so disloyal. The boy here is Second Arm, yes?"

"It's him—goes by Manny. He insists he stabbed Red Hair and Min."

"Both of them—him alone?"

"What he claims."

"Claims. You doubt him?"

"Let's just say I'm not sure he can separate intent from reality."

"But Red Hair *is* in Nonesuch, yes?"

"So it seems, but this is unconfirmed, except for what the boy tells me. Jimjim and I haven't put eyes on the man."

"Where is the dwarf?" she asked.

"White Pine. He wanted to verify the traps' arrival and steal some oats for the animals and more grub for us. We pretty much ran out."

"I have plenty of both," Rinka said. "You didn't trust Phin and me to do our job?"

"It ain't about trust. It's about having two sources."

"I don't like the implication."

"We needed supplies."

"Make up your mind: two sources, or food?"

She could be difficult to deal with when she let her mind loose on stuff that didn't matter. "Both," he said. "Where's Phin now?"

"He refused to disclose his secret—said only to tell you that he is arranging for a major diversion for noon Thursday. This will give Archibald time to begin his trapping."

"What diversion? We never talked about any diversions."

"He would not disclose details—said only for you to ready the regiment for Thursday noon."

"There ain't no damn regiment," an exasperated Bapcat said.

"I believe he was speaking figuratively, but with Phin, one is often forced to guess."

*Major diversion. Thursday noon? They might have their traps out by then. Damn that old man! The regiment? Summon Jone and Zakov and Scale now? No; wait for Jimjim, and talk to him.*

The boy was hunkered down in a squat. "You want to talk now?" Bapcat asked.

"You called me a liar."

"Did no such thing, and once you help us get into Nonesuch, the facts will speak for themselves."

The boy sat silently. "If I kilt him, I'd be in trouble?"

"You could be."

"*That* don't seem fair."

"At your age a lot of things will seem that way."

"That will change when I get older?"

"Not really, but you'll be more used to the unfairness by then. The world is a lot more not fair than fair."

"That don't make me feel good."

"That's part of growing up."

"I ain't liking this talk with you," the boy said.

"Tell me about everything you've seen."

"You mean when they was nekkid?"

"Everything, but you can save that till last." *Boys. Was Jordy like this, too?*

"I seen it all," the boy declared.

"Tell me."

"Will take a long time."

"We've got plenty of that."

"Two of you is all you got, you and that big girl?"

"I am not big," Rinka said. "I'm tall, and I can box your ears, I guess."

"You're big compared to me," the boy said defiantly, but taking care to place his hands over his ears.

"Enough," Bapcat snarled at them. "More of us will be coming. Do Red Hair's people do everything he tells them to do?"

"There's some who does and some who don't, and some who're scared of him."

"Do they ignore his orders?"

"If they think he won't find out, they do as they please. Red Hair don't look kindly on shirkers, which is what he calls them who don't do what he says."

"What's he do if someone disobeys?"

"Talks honey-sweet, walks up behind them and shoots their head."

"You've seen this?"

"Yessir."

"How does he replace people, or doesn't he bother?"

"He don't have to work at it. People is coming to him all the time, trying to join up. He don't have to look hard nor long."

"Anybody who asks can join up?"

"Naw; he looks 'em over, and if he don't like 'em after a few days, he shoots ' em dead."

This seemed hard to accept, or believe. This went on in the mountains and nobody knew or talked about it? "You got any friends on the inside?"

"Just the kid-meat. I kept trying to get him to come with me, but he says he's okay and not like the others, but he is. He's just scared, and it makes his legs freeze up."

"You can get that close to the hostage?"

"I told you, it's all mines under that hill. You can move around real easy."

"Do they keep the boy with Red Hair?"

"No, they got him in the old powder house. It's got a steel cage, and he's inside that."

"Min stays with Red Hair all the time?"

"Why do you keep asking. I told you I stuck them both real good."

Bapcat took a deep breath. Humor him. "Okay, before you killed them," the deputy asked.

"She goes where she wants, when she wants. Only one he lets do that."

"He allows her to come and go when she wants?"

"He sure couldn't stop her with his leg how it was. And now they're dead, so it don't matter."

"What *about* his leg?"

"Missing one below the knee. Don't know how he got that way, but it don't break my heart none. He couldn't get around good without help, fat as he is. When he don't have his peg strapped on, he had to hop. I seen that."

"How does he get around otherwise?"

"Peg leg and a cane, and his people lifting him up and carrying him, and stuff."

*Peg leg, fat, immobile, dependent.* "He favor a revolver or a rifle?"

"Shotgun sawed off the length of a rabbit dog's leg, but he has the revolver to take care of them don't do as he says."

"Guards inside with him?"

"Mostly they is just inside his door."

"The door's closed?"

"Always. You want in, you got to knock and talk uppity."

"Uppity?"

"By your leave, say your name requests an audience with His Majesty."

*More childish imagination? The language seemed extreme and stiff and real enough.* "Then, after you knock?"

"Guards open the doors and take your weapons."

"But you got your knife by them."

"I didn't come in that way."

"Min always there when he has visitors?"

"Far as I seen."

"And the others are okay with her being with him all that time?"

"I heard some talk about it, how they don't like her highfalutin ways."

Bapcat heard Jimjim ride up and dismount. "Hoke Desque is with Archibald," were his first words.

"Pled, too. Rinka's here."

Jimjim took care of his pony and came back, dropping a saddlebag by the fire pit. "Fresh loaves of bread, made this morning, thimbleberry jam made from local berries and loaded with sugar. Glass bottle of figs, too, and two tins of Clark's ham lunch, just arrived at the store from the Hudson's Bay catalog, a feast after our starvation in the wilderness, and no fire needed." The priest tore a chunk of bread off a loaf and the boy grabbed at it.

"It's a sin to steal, boy."

"Not if you ain't got food, it ain't," the boy remarked, and the priest let him have the bread.

"Your logic's sound even if your dogma's lacking."

"You a real priest?" the boy asked, his mouth full.

"Are you in need, my son?"

"My pa says all papists is deceivers, telling people they ain't allowed to talk direct to God."

"Are you wanting to talk to God?"

"Ain't had the need," the boy said. "Ain't anybody gonna undo that jelly-jar cap?"

Bapcat and Jimjim stepped away to talk.

"The boy's been following Red Hair. They had him prisoner for a while, but he escaped and claims to know a lot about what goes on. Did you hear anything about trapping areas?" Bapcat asked.

"No, I just saw they were there, and that was enough."

"Rinka says there was some sort of commotion in town."

"Sure was. Some fool flew him a dang aeroplane right close to the rooftops and got everyone all consternated."

*Aeroplane?* Bapcat had seen a couple of them, still had trouble understanding how they could cheat the gravity thing, flying like that. Some kind of magic.

"Rinka says Jone was right—they'll set traps south of us here, just above the Elm. She also says Phin plans a major diversion for Thursday noon. He says that will afford Archibald time to begin the bear-trapping operation."

"What the hell does that mean?" the priest asked. "Diversion?"

"I don't know, but I think it's time to get Zakov and the others."

"I can go," the priest said.

"No, we'll send Rinka. You can help me talk to the boy, get all the information he has. He claims he's killed both Red Hair and Min, but I've got doubts."

"Suit yourself. I need food, and judging by that young one's appetite, you best grab some grub while it lasts."

## CHAPTER 63

## *Silver City*

MONDAY, OCTOBER 5

Rinka went east to fetch Zakov and the others. Jimjim resumed surveillance of Nonesuch. Bapcat took Manny with him, and they rode Joe to Silver City to send two telegrams, the boy riding behind the game warden. The first went to Pellerin in Minneapolis, the gist of it, in the most direct and unmistakable terms:

ATTN PELLERIN. STOP. SALE THINGS READY. STOP. AWAITING YOUR ARRIVAL SILVER CITY OCTOBER 14 STOP. BRING CASH. STOP. WILL PERSONALLY MEET YOU AT TOWN PIER. STOP. BAPCAT.

Bapcat figured the wire would be enough to get Pellerin to return so he could be arrested as soon as the transfer was made. All he had to do first was catch and cage a bear. He still harbored some doubt—no matter what Assistant Prosecutor Roland Echo had reported they were saying at the attorney general's office in Lansing—that this could work out as easily as it looked like it might.

The second telegram went to Echo in his Houghton office.

MISSING MAN REMAINS MISSING. STOP. RED HAIR IN SIGHT. STOP. ARREST ATTEMPT SET FOR THURSDAY, OCT 9. STOP. ARRESTING IN ONTY CO, NOT GOGEBIC. SUGGEST JP SWOON AND ALERT HIM. STOP. EXPECT ARRIVE ONTY, OCT 10, EARLIEST. STOP. DEPENDING ON NUMBER OF PRISONERS, CASUALTIES. STOP. ONTY ACTING SHERIFF AMONG ARREST LIKELIES. STOP. WILL SECURE ALL UNDER AG AUTHORITY. STOP. WILL NEED HELP IN ONTONAGON. STOP. ALERT AG OF TIMETABLE, EVENTS. STOP. CHEERS. STOP. BAPCAT.

"You don't need no 'stop' after the word 'cheers,'" the telegrapher said.

"Leave it in," Bapcat told the man. The "cheers" would make Echo grin. Telegrams dispatched, Bapcat went to buy more food, keeping the boy in tow.

They were in a general store call Henri-Deb's. "I won't run away," Manny told him.

"I suspect your father heard similar."

"That was different," the boy argued.

"Not from where I stand. Would you like some sweets?" Bapcat asked, pointing to rows of penny hard candy.

"No, and stop treating me like a child."

"I'm treating you like a grown-up."

"By asking me if I want sweets?"

"I want them. So, too, would Zakov if he was with us. Relax and stop thinking so much."

"I am always thinking."

"I am impressed, but suggest you save it until it matters."

Bapcat paid for the candy and supplies and noticed the boy fill two pockets with Pascall's toffee, acid drops, and fruit bounces. They loaded Joe's saddlebags and mounted the mule, the boy muttering behind him.

"Are you trying to say something with your mouth stuffed full of sweets?" Bapcat asked. "If you have something to say, say it clearly and out loud, not in a mumble. Joe likes to listen to trail talk."

"He's nothing but a damn old mule," the boy said.

"That don't mean he don't like to listen."

"Maybe I'll have to stab you too," the boy said without emotion.

"I suppose you might," Bapcat said.

"You gonna take away my blade?"

"A man needs a tool in the hills and forests."

"It's a weapon for killing, not no stupid tool."

"It *can* be that, that's true," Bapcat said.

"These ain't just threats," the boy said. "I've drawn blood."

"I know you're a serious fella. We are only having a conversation so Joe can listen."

"I don't want to talk to no damn mule," the boy said. "I told you that."

"Nor do I," Bapcat said.

They rode in silence, angling far west of their staging area, and crossed the sides of steep hills littered with slash and rotting dead trees, and no clear game trails, requiring them to zigzag continuously.

"You don't carry a compass?" the boy asked.

"Secure in my shirt pocket."

"But you never look at it."

"When I need to, I will. Until then, I know where it is."

The boy said, "I have to look at mine all the time, only I lost it when I got captured."

Bapcat halted Joe, fished in his pocket, and passed the brass compass back to the boy, who took it and said nothing for a long time.

"How will you find your way if I have your compass?" the boy finally asked.

"With my head. I have more compasses somewhere, and in the event my head won't serve, I'm certain you'll loan yours to me."

"If I don't watch my compass all the time, I get really lost," the boy said.

"It's good for a man to know his limits."

"What're your limits?" the boy asked.

"There are too many to list."

"Did you ever kill anyone?"

"I did," Bapcat said.

"Did you like it?"

"I neither liked nor disliked it; it was my job, and I did it."

"I felt kinda sick after I cut them people," the boy admitted quietly.

"I am guessing that stabbing people will not be a lifetime job for you."

"I guess, but I might have to do it from time to time, just to stay in practice."

"You might indeed, but be sure to do it in states without capital punishment."

"What's that mean?"

"I ain't exactly sure. The Russian says it has something to do with lopping off a fella's head, or hanging him by the neck 'til he's dead."

"Capital punishment means you get your head chopped off—in America?"

"It means the State kills you instead of keeping you in jail."

"They can do that?"

"If there is such a law."

"Do they stab you?"

"Hang or shoot," Bapcat said.

"That's good," the boy said. "I'd sure hate to get stabbed."

"I feel the same," Lute Bapcat said. "Very soon now I am going to ask you to lead me to Red Hair. Will you do that?"

"They're dead," Manny insisted.

"I just want you to show me where their bodies are," Bapcat said in a soft voice.

"It might be a tight fit. It's a good thing you're as skinny as a string bean."

"The priest will be with us, as will Zakov."

"Sounds like an adventure," Manny said.

It would be anything but that. "Yes, I can see how it might sound like that to you."

"Will you shoot him?"

"Why would I shoot a dead man?" Bapcat asked, catching the boy off guard.

"Oh, yeah," the boy said with a nervous twitter.

"But if he ain't dead, then you'll shoot him?"

"Only if he gives me no choice."

"How will you know what to do?"

"By what he does."

"I like to know what I'm going to do before I do it," said Manny.

"Like you going with Min?"

More silence and brooding thought. "I needed her to get me to Red Hair, and I thought it would be fine if I played along, but I was wrong," the boy said. "Sometimes a man thinks he knows what he will do, and then it don't happen that way—know what I mean?"

"Perfectly. This happens to me all the time," Bapcat said.

"I don't much like that," the boy said.

"Nor do I. Your father misses and worries about you."

"I told you, I ain't going back, not never, and I guess I made up my mind on that."

"Your mind could change," Bapcat suggested.

"I guess," the boy said. "Has Joe had enough listening, because I think I've had enough talking."

# CHAPTER 64

## *North of Elm River*

### WEDNESDAY, OCTOBER 7

"I couldn't think what to do with them," Jone Gleann confessed as soon as she met up with Bapcat. "I'm afraid he'll get in the way."

"Nixon behave himself?" Bapcat asked.

"The man is of a surly nature, but caused no special problems."

"Pippig?"

"The German reluctantly admitted to seeing a woman torture and kill the three boys, said she's crazy, that she enjoys hurting people"

"Not the three trappers you trailed?"

"No. It seems I was wrong, heard things, made bad assumptions."

Bapcat let her stew for a while in her own confessional juices. "We all make mistakes."

"This wasn't just a mistake. It's serious."

"We all make errors in judgment and what we think we see—a flaw in how we are made by God. Can we use Pippig for what lies ahead?"

She gave him a we've-been-here-before look. "I don't actually *know* what lies ahead . . . not specifically."

"Red Hair and Min"

"Will there be casualties?"

"I hope not."

"Plan for the worst, hope for the best," she said.

"Yes."

"I will be glad when all of this is over," she said.

"You set much of this in motion," he reminded her.

"Please don't say that. I find myself unfit to lead."

"You've done fine with your school." He pushed the memory of the leeches out of his mind. There had to be something less desperate for the children, but this wasn't the time to talk about it.

But she brought it up. "And the leeches?"

"I'm ignoring that," he said.

"I do not like the weight of making decisions. It is all too much *sturm und drang.*"

*No idea what she means.* "The weight of making them, or what comes afterward?"

"Both. Does experience make it easier?"

"Not that I can see," he said.

"But you do it anyway."

"Someone has to. What do you know about Eustice Pled?"

"Why?"

"He's with Archibald."

"I didn't know."

"No time to tell all to everyone. But I will, soon enough."

"Pled is a brutal man, mistreats all people equally, except for those who pay and direct him. Long time as Norwich captain. He is entrenched, and casts a long and heavy shadow."

"And uses Nixon?"

"That's what I'm told. Nixon does all of Pled's dirty work."

"And keeps his own hands clean?"

"Pled stands far away from any blood spray."

"Are he and Archibald connected?"

"So it would seem, but until now, I've never heard that said, or even intimated. You've found Red Hair?" she asked.

"He's in Nonesuch, with guards in front of him. We've not actually laid eyes on him."

"So this might all be for naught?" she said.

"Not for naught. We'll get him."

"How can you be sure?"

"I can't, but I can feel this one."

"If he's inside, how do you get to him?"

"Probably have to flush him out, but I'm still thinking about this. If he is the Henry Young of my St. Cazimer's days, I fear we'll have to dig him out."

"Rinka told me about the old man and his 'diversion.' Whatever can he be thinking?"

"Military tactics. Misdirect the other side from your side's main interest."

"How?"

"This can vary, and without talking to him, there's no way to predict specifics."

"It would take quite a spectacular diversion to capture all their attention."

"I have had similar thoughts."

*And concerns.*

• • •

They were assembled at the small campfire—all but Jimjim, who was back watching over Nonesuch. Jone, Rinka, Scale, Zakov, Manny, himself, and Pippig. Nixon was lashed securely to a tree, gagged, blindfolded, and out of earshot. The man's three-legged dog remained with him, and apparently was taking every opportunity to nip and bite him for reasons only the dog and Nixon knew. Zakov had taken the man's boots and socks, which made his feet even more vulnerable.

"Rinka will stampede their horses when the diversion happens."

"Will we be on our mounts, or on foot?" Rinka asked.

"On foot for this, like them."

"But I thought a mounted force was always superior."

"There ain't no always; circumstances dictate what has to be done. Being mounted here provides no clear advantage."

"And if there is no diversion at noon by the old man?" Rinka asked.

"One o'clock, then. Chase away their mounts and set yourself up on the west side of the camp. Detain anyone who comes that way."

Bapcat looked at the others. "Scale and Pippig are to flank the bridge between the mine island and south shore. This puts you between the two village halves. Same orders that I gave to Rinka: Detain all you encounter."

The game warden took a deep breath. "Jone, put yourself north of the northernmost houses, in the tree line where you'll have cover, same job as the others."

"What of the east?" Zakov asked.

"They avoid that direction; we don't know why. What matters is that in all this time we've watched them, not one of them has gone over that way, so we'll assume they won't this time either."

"Everyone in the village is with Red Hair?"

"We don't know. That's why we detain all; we'll have to sort it out afterward."

*If there* was *an afterward,* he reminded himself. It was not a small *if,* and anytime you were in a shooting situation, a good outcome was never certain. Certainly the diversion was a question mark that might turn the outcome one way or another. *And we're largely dependent on a boy, whose grasp on reality seems loose at times. No matter. The Colonel had always said, "Without the unknown, success would be automatic, and it never is."*

"What if they shoot?" Jone asked.

"Return fire and shoot to kill," Bapcat said. "Manny will lead Zakov and me and Jimjim underground to grab Red Hair."

"If you're all underground, how will you know if Phin has created his diversion?" Rinka asked.

*She was dead-on.* "You're right," Bapcat said. "We all go at noon, with or without Phin."

Zakov nodded, as did the others.

Bapcat took note of all the grim faces, knowing this was partly from resolve and partly from fear. Anticipation before battle was close to intolerable, but as soon as you began to move, all jangling nerves were steadied, replaced by something else: a keen, intense awareness of reality, small and large, sounds, smells, sights. Battle made normal life drab and gray and dull. No wonder some men chose soldiering and fighting for their livelihood. There was nothing like the near possibility of death to animate life leading to that moment. Even he felt the pull of it, and had to consciously calm himself.

"How do we reach Red Hair?" Bapcat asked their boy guide.

Manny said, "From beneath the pump house to the west. We climb down a ladder to the first tunnel."

"How far down?"

"I don't know—fifty feet?"

"Active mine area?" Bapcat asked.

"No, this is really old."

"Then the ladder may also be old," Zakov said.

"The ladder is metal, not wood, and age don't matter. Fifty feet down, then west to a large, deep slanted stone place."

Bapcat knew the boy was describing a structure called a *stope,* carved from solid rock and angled. It was used to move copper ore upward and out of the mine for processing. Standard in all underground copper mines.

Many continued. "From here we  got to climb up another iron ladder twenty feet or so to another tunnel, which goes only one direction. We follow that until it ends, then climb up another thirty feet to the building."

"What if they blocked it after you fled?" Bapcat asked.

"I didn't find this until after I got away and was here a while. They don't know about it, and they can't block them all."

"All what?"

"There are at least ten ways inside from the tunnel, which goes around the building."

"You can get to all ten?" Zakov asked.

The boy nodded.

Bapcat asked, "How do they open?"

"Hinges. They swing to the right."

"All of them?" the Russian asked.

"Even the high one."

"What, and where, is this high one?" Bapcat asked.

"The only one not along the lower wall. This one opens about six feet off the floor, halfway toward the door to the room."

"You entered where?" Zakov asked.

"I have watched them only through the lower doors. They didn't know I, or the doors, was there."

"Where were you when you escaped?" Zakov asked.

"In the room with them."

"How did you get out?"

"I cut them and yelled for the guards and went past them when they ran to Red Hair and Min. It was easy," he said proudly. "It was easy to disappear once I was outside."

"*I* saw you," Bapcat reminded the boy.

"That don't count, 'cause you ain't them," Manny said.

"Is there room for all of us?" Zakov asked.

"Yes, behind me," the boy said. "All of the climbs are tight, but we should make it."

"They have one bear in captivity," Zakov reported, "as of this morning. They've hauled it back to the village. Wheels on the cage make this possible. They've put it on the east side of the mine island, near water for the animal."

"Large bear?" Bapcat asked.

"Large enough. The horses all spooked when they brought the bear through, and I think they tried to find a place where its scent would not keep riling the horses."

"Guards?"

"None that I saw," the Russian said.

"Who secures the bear?" Jone Gleann asked.

Bapcat considered her question and dismissed it. "They will be too busy with us to worry about the animal."

"But a stray bullet might strike it," Rinka said.

"A chance we must take," Bapcat said. To Zakov, "You have all their traps located?"

"This was not difficult. They placed them at the intersections of the deepest, most-worn bear runs."

Bapcat exhaled dramatically. "Get some sleep," he said. "Everyone."

# CHAPTER 65

## Nonesuch

### THURSDAY, OCTOBER 8

The boy led the three men through the copper mine with only taper candles to light their way. Manny showed them the uppermost entrance, and Bapcat had the boy climb down past Jimjim, the Russian, and himself. "Whatever happens, do not come in until one of us comes for you, and uses your name," Bapcat told the boy.

Noon came. The priest opened the door, whispered back to them, "Mostly dark, little light."

Bapcat said, "Go," and the dwarf dropped into the room with the Russian close behind him. As Bapcat let himself down to the floor the room exploded with light as doors opened and men ran in, shouting. "Come, come, you have to see—they're attacking from the sky!" one of them yelled.

"*What* is attacking?" a gruff voice challenged. "Crows?"

"Guns," the messenger yelled. "Guns from the sky."

"All right, all right, goddammit, help me out of here," the gruff one said. Bapcat thought there was something in the voice he recognized: Henry Young. Older, deeper, but with the same twisted twang in the sound. The game warden felt his heartbeat quicken.

"Where is Min? Find that worthless bitch!" Young was now shouting. "Find Min and bring her to me!"

Two men, one on either side of Young, helped him hobble toward the door. Jimjim and Zakov charged the trio low, slamming the support men off their feet. Bapcat caught their leader by the collar as he teetered and held him up, surprised at how light a man he was for being so fat.

The escorts were quickly tied and rolled out of the way.

"Henry Young, you are under arrest for murder."

"How impressive to capture a dying cripple," Young retorted.

Bapcat said, "Jimjim take the door. Zakov, get more light in here."

The game warden could hear sporadic shooting outside. Young remained docile as lanterns were lit, covers taken off filthy windows.

"Bapcat?" the man said, and laughed. "My luck is truly fucked; first, stabbed by a stinking brat, and now this, and *you*, of all people! Does this feel like fate to you, Lute?"

"Anyone else might have come in shooting," Bapcat told his prisoner.

"It would be a welcome favor if you'd finish now what you started all those years ago, back at St. Cazimer's."

"That was then and this is now," Bapcat said.

"More bad luck for me," Young whispered.

"Where is the woman called Min?" Bapcat asked.

Young shrugged. "Who knows? She comes, she goes. She was another bad choice, probably the worst of them all. But unlike me, she won't be so easily cornered and taken."

"There was a boy here," Bapcat said.

"There are always boys here—her toys, not mine. I had nothing to do with any of *that*."

"Your people did," Bapcat said.

"Be that as it may, it wasn't me, and I will testify to that in court."

"If we reach a court, that will be commendable on your part."

"What do you mean, *if*?"

Bapcat heard more gunfire and occasional heavy firing from just outside the open door. "That," the game warden told Young, pushing him down into a chair and tying his wrists under his one remaining leg. The reality of Young being one-legged had still not set in.

Jimjim said, "The sound of a motor passes over, shots rain down, shots go up, the motor sound goes away, silence ensues, and it happens again. There is also some shooting to the south and west and north of us."

Bapcat exhaled. Leaving the east side unguarded seemed to be playing out in their favor, but he knew they needed to get outside, evaluate the situation, and actively take command. The first step had been capturing Young. All else flowed from that.

"Get Manny," Bapcat told Zakov, who checked the opening and said, "Come out now, Manny. We need you with us." Zakov waited, crawled up into the opening, and came back a minute later. "The boy is gone."

Quick decisions now. "We're taking you outside," Bapcat told Young. To Jimjim, "Tell his people he'll die if they don't stop shooting."

Young grinned, showing a gap in his teeth. "You mistake me for a beloved leader," he said.

As they got into the light, Bapcat saw that the man's red hair was graying, with patches falling out. "I know what you are," the game warden told the man. "If your own people shoot you, so be it."

"But I am in your custody and under your protection," the man said in a quavering voice.

"Theoretically, and loosely factual," Zakov remarked.

"You're right," Red Hair said. "What does it matter how it ends?"

"Grab him," Bapcat said.

The Russian took one side of Young and Bapcat the other.

"*Tell them*, Jimjim!"

"There is a lull at the moment, but I hear the motor approaching again. I suggest we wait."

"All right. Let's get him to the door so we can watch," Bapcat told the Russian.

The aeroplane had two wings and various thin reeds and wires, and a propeller that Bapcat could see turning, but at times it looked like it was frozen rather than moving. *The magic of flight*, he thought, as the aeroplane dived low and multiple rifle shots came from the operator, who looked like Phin, a rifle snugged by his leg and pointed down.

The plane attacked and pulled up, climbing over the forest to the north, and began to trail a wisp of dark gray, then black smoke. The craft turned east and the sound quieted before it began again, growing increasingly louder as it came in from the southeast, this time descending to land between the mining houses. The structure spit dirt and stones and ground fire from all directions as the aircraft skipped and bucked for an incredibly long time before suddenly nosing over and coming to a stop after the propeller chopped several revolutions in the dirt, spinning the frame as it did.

The craft settled with its tail up, and people began running toward the crash. Bapcat dumped Young on the ground and began firing his rifle; Zakov did the same, Jimjim popping away with his .32. The sudden assault caused the wreck chasers to turn and retreat to any cover they could find. When Bapcat stopped firing, he heard shots from the north: *Jone*. Good. Her rounds turned the attackers back, and within moments the whole camp was silent.

"What a fine end to the career of a folk hero," Young said from the ground.

"That's what you are—a folk hero?" Zakov asked.

"Yes. A modern Robin Hood."

Zakov growled, "You are the most odiferous turd in a cesspool filled with them. And Robin Hood was never real."

Jimjim, wearing his cassock, walked out into the street between the houses, one hand in the air, his revolver in the other. "We have Red Hair. The next shot from you will kill him."

Seconds passed. Silence. Then a single shot rang out and zipped past them, pounding into the stone siding of the building. All the people jumped up and began running—not toward them, but away to the west, north, and south. Jimjim shot two that passed near him, and Zakov shot a third man nearly a hundred yards away.

"Your lack of popularity condemns you," Zakov told Young.

"Yet I am still among the living. No doubt that was Min the Miraculous talking to you with her rifle. I am certain she believes that you lack the will to do what you must."

Bapcat looked at the man on the ground, his chest black and red with blood. "Are you hit?"

"By the knife, not Min. It's been a slow bleed that refuses to stop."

"You need a doctor."

"What I need is a miracle," Young said, "which I predict will not happen."

Bapcat said, "You had Min for your miracle, and she didn't work out so well."

Zakov checked the man's wound, looked up at his partner and shook his head.

"How long?" Bapcat asked.

Young mumbled, "Seconds, minutes, hours, but no more days."

They moved the dying Young back inside, and Jimjim stayed with him while Bapcat searched a barrel with mining helmets and a wooden box of teapot lamps. He checked fuel and wicks on two of the lamps and attached them to the helmets, offering one to his partner, who said, "No—we'll never find him below, and he was using only a candle."

In his day he had used candles before his employer brought in so-called sunshine lamps that looked like brass teapots and burned paraffin.

"The boy knows the way in the dark below," Zakov said. "The two of us should not be down there and out of contact. Someone must direct the forces up here."

The Russian was right. "All right. You stay and check the others. Consolidate prisoners. I'll find the boy."

"He is unfindable," Zakov said.

*So I am told*, Bapcat thought. But on the way in, when they were bunched together and the candle was with them and not ahead, he had noticed a layer of dust coating the floor—and footprints, all small. These, he figured, were the boy's. He had moved around the tunnels alone. No other tracks. Presumably the boy had fled directly. If not, his boot prints would point the way to where he had fled.

By the time he reached the lower mine level, fifty feet down, Bapcat was sure the boy had made a beeline for daylight and open country. Where, was the question. Bapcat reached the point where they had entered and carefully stashed his helmet and light in the event he might need them again.

The pump house was a short distance from the house, where the white horse had been tethered for so many days. Bapcat stood still, listening, and heard one shot to the north, then nothing. No people were in sight, and he ran for the other building, using a wall for protection. This building had windows, all of them over his head and not easily reachable.

At the end of the wall he peeked around, saw a door standing open, ran to it, peeked inside, saw nothing, and stepped in. Ten feet away there was an inner double door, cracked open, some light beyond, but dim. The noisy pump had gone silent. He knelt and waited for his heart rate to slow, to get control of his breathing, and when he felt recovered, he stood in a crouch and took one step forward.

His eyes moved constantly; he was depending on his peripheral night vision rather than direct light, and on a sense of motion or a feeling that something was there that shouldn't be.

Then, at the double door, a thin voice. "You can come in." The boy's voice. "Manny?"

"In here. It's all right, Deputy."

The game warden slid through the door, his rifle up, and saw a puddle of light. There was Min with her arm around the boy's throat. Bapcat elevated the weapon slightly, preparing to fire.

The boy ducked down in a crouch and the woman crumpled to the floor. Manny held up his knife.

"It's all right now, Thomas," Manny said. "You can come out. This is Deputy Bapcat. He's our friend."

A boy appeared, his face swollen and broken.

"This is my friend, Thomas," Manny said. "He is having trouble talking, but I know he will be all right. It's safe now, Thomas, really. She's really dead this time. It's over."

Bapcat felt for a pulse and found none. There was blood everywhere, on her and the floor. And on Manny.

The boy said calmly, "I cut her deep inside her leg, then her throat. She said only, 'Bad boy.'"

"Did she have hold of you?"

"There was a gun," Manny said.

Thomas suddenly found the gun, picked it up, pointed it at the woman's head, and squeezed off a shot. Bapcat grabbed the child's small wrist and took the revolver from him.

"Where is Red Hair?" Manny asked.

"Arrested."

"So he's alive?"

"Not for long."

"I shall have to do better next time," Manny announced.

Bapcat understood that the boy's mind was badly twisted by all that had happened, and he hoped it would not be a permanent condition.

"I'll take the knife now," Bapcat said. "To clean and polish it and hone the blade. For next time."

The boy said, "Next time," nodded, and offered the knife handle to the deputy.

"Let's find the others," Bapcat said. "Thomas, please come with Manny and me."

The boy tentatively offered his hand to the deputy. Manny took his other hand, and the three walked out into the light.

• • •

The aeroplane was painted bright yellow, and it was demolished, as was its operator, Elphinstone. Jone had him propped against a stump. One of the man's legs was bent in a direction not intended by nature, and bones protruded, gleaming pink in the midday light.

The man had a small bottle in hand and tipped it toward Bapcat and the boys. "Every day we should endeavor to learn something new, and today I learned that taking off in one of these contraptions when everything is in working order is much easier than landing one with broken parts. Let it be written thusly."

Bapcat looked at Gleann, who shook her head as she knelt by the old Britisher. "It was a great diversion, Phin. We have them all, with no known casualties on our side."

"Sorry to spoil the perfect sheet, old boy. I belong now solely to the wind, and God. Cheers." Elphinstone's head sagged forward as his chest rattled. He shuddered and died, and there was nothing Bapcat could do to change it.

Zakov came along and saw the body. "Fine plan, full surprise, less than perfect execution mixed with bad luck. A fine soldier."

"How many arrests?" Bapcat asked.

Zakov said, "Five shot dead, one alleged suicide, eight wounded, and all the horses have scattered. Eight others are detained and in custody. The priest reports his prisoner has landed in a deceased condition in Hell."

"Min is also dead," Bapcat said. "I checked the body. What about Archibald and Hoke Desque?"

"Both in custody."

"Eustice Pled?"

"Unaccounted for, and presumably at large."

"He'll probably hightail it back to Norwich," Bapcat said. "We can fetch him later. First we're going to take this lot through Silver City to meet a judge in Ontonagon."

"What about the bear?" Jone asked.

"With us, in its cage."

"There are three more cages," Zakov reminded him.

"We'll check them in the morning and release any that have been caught."

Bapcat looked at Rinka Isohultamaki. "Fetch Nixon and put him with the other prisoners."

"He may refuse."

"Change his mind, and don't be subtle."

Rinka grinned.

"Fire and food tonight?" the priest asked.

"As large a fire as you'd like."

"Praise the Lord," Jimjim said. "And *you*."

• • •

The Nonesuch mining captain was clearly relieved to be rid of the marauders. The man was found huddled with the families of his men in the southern houses, across the river.

"Bapcat," the game warden greeted the man, showing him his badge.

"Harlan Gist. You're all lawmen?"

"Sent specifically to arrest Red Hair."

"It's about damn time, him and that she-monster he runs with. We heard tales the woman was eating human flesh, and hid our children. No schoolhouse here, so they had no reason to expect kids to be around."

"They've been here before?"

"Never here in Nonesuch, but around here, seems every summer. This time they come right on in and took over. We're on a work hiatus, awaiting new equipment and orders from above. I sent most of my people away to find temporary work elsewhere, or to visit friends and kin. Unpaid, of course. Just our bad luck they came when we were at our weakest."

"Maybe they knew," Bapcat suggested.

The mine captain seemed pained by this suggestion, but allowed it was possible.

"How many are you?" Bapcat asked.

"Near thirty."

"We saw only ten."

"By design. The fewer our people we exposed, the lesser the contact and chance of trouble."

"Incidents?"

"You've seen Red Hair's lot. Can you not imagine for yourself?"

"Your people can swear charges."

"They just want to forget, get on with life and living."

"Hunkering down to avoid an enemy or threat is a poor choice," Zakov lectured the man. "It leaves the impression you are soft and weak."

"We're alive," Gist said. "That's all that matters."

Bapcat said, "We'll need the help of your people to transfer prisoners and materials to Ontonagon. The State will pay for your time. We've got eight dead so far, and five of the eight wounded are in poor shape. Can you send one of your people to fetch a doctor?"

"White Pine," Gist said.

"Wherever."

"Who will pay the doctor?"

"The State will pay for everything here."

"Shall I fetch a nurse as well?"

Money, it seemed, animated the mine captain.

"We'll need ten of your people in the morning."

"Whatever you want. Shall I keep a list of personnel and time spent on your various tasks?"

"Your choice." Bapcat imagined dollar signs in the man's head.

"Before first light," Bapcat told the group. "Zakov and me and some miners to help."

Away from the fire and without stars, it was a night where every tree and man was black.

"Improbably easy," Zakov said to his friend.

"Not done yet. Pled is still out there."

The Russian held out two helmets and teapots. "To light our way by morning," he said.

"Let there be fuel," Bapcat said.

# CHAPTER 66

## *Elm River*

### FRIDAY, OCTOBER 9

The last thing the game wardens had done the night before was to use the miners' lamps as they led Pippig to Min's body. They unwrapped the piece of canvas that covered her and looked at her legs, with all of the scarring. The old trapper said, "I seen dem ones; *ja*, she's the one tortured and killed them boys."

This morning they led ten miners to the Elm River area where the bear traps had been set, and in short order, found all three cages full—one with a gigantic animal that looked like it had been stuffed into the steel trap, and two containing smaller bears.

"Release all of them?" Zakov asked his partner.

Bapcat was in mull mode, a bit indecisive. "No, let's keep the one in Nonesuch and the biggest one here. Let the others go."

Zakov smiled. "You say it so matter-of-factly, but how exactly does one go about doing that?"

Bapcat had studied the other cage and knew he had to get on top. The trapdoor was rigged to a chain-and-pulley system; all he had to do was lift it up and the animal would no doubt jump out. The trick was not getting clawed while mounting the trap. It didn't help that the gap between the iron bars looked astonishingly wide.

But both releases went without a hitch, both animals streaking for the heaviest cover available and not looking back, and each time the mining crew cheered enthusiastically.

"All men value freedom," Zakov remarked. "Even for the great beasts. It will take the rest of today to move the large one. You're sure you want it? You already have one for your sale."

Bapcat knew he wanted it, but wasn't quite sure why yet. "I got this little voice in me that's saying, 'Keep him, keep him.'"

A new voice spoke, startling both men. "And the little voice inside me keeps telling me, 'Kill him, kill him.'" Bapcat looked up to see Eustice Pled aiming a rifle at him.

"You intending to kill me, is that it?" the game warden asked.

"It sure is."

Bapcat knelt, aimed, and fired, all in the same moment, the .30-40 Krag round striking Pled in the face, dropping him straight to the ground and spraying the area with pink mist and brain tissue. "Gon' kill a man, kill him," Bapcat muttered, his hands shaking.

The miners stared, dumbstruck by the suddenness of the violence.

"Put that trash on top of the bear cage," Bapcat told them.

"What about the bear?"

"Oh, it'll give him something to amuse himself with while he travels."

"A fine shot," Zakov said.

"The man spoke three words too many."

"A lesson we can all profit from," Zakov said. "If you had not shot him, I would have."

"He gave us no choice."

"Still," Zakov said, "one must wonder what the man was thinking."

"I'd guess he wasn't thinking much at all, stepping out into the open like that."

Pierre Malyotte appeared out of the forest as they began to move east, visibly shaken. "I wasn't part of none of that. I only showed them where to put traps."

"They hired you as their guide," Bapcat said.

"It's how I live," the man said. He had dark eyes, black hair, and a thick black mustache.

"Did they hire you to trap bears?" Bapcat asked.

"No, but ain't no law against it, right?"

"Not yet," Bapcat said. "You just tell the truth in court, and no charges will be brought against you."

The Frenchman nodded resolutely. "Pierre always tells truth."

# CHAPTER 67

## *Ontonagon*

### SUNDAY, OCTOBER 11

The mules—Joe included—were hitched to a mine-owned wagon from Nonesuch to carry the two bears in their cages. None of the horses could abide the smell of bears, and, unable to overcome their fretful tendencies, it fell to the mules to do the work—an old story.

The bodies were wrapped in canvas and folded over saddles on horses. The wounded rode on improvised litters carried by the miners. Prisoners were cuffed and roped together and walked between Rinka, as the rear guard, and Scale, who led them.

Bapcat heard Zakov talking to Scale, but couldn't make out any words until Scale spoke.

"In the man's face?"

The Russian pointed just below his nose.

"Mercy," Bapcat heard the tall Negro say.

They'd spent the previous night in Silver City, on the grounds of the American Fur Company Trading Post, and wood-tick gawkers had dawdled and ogled all night. Today, halfway to Ontonagon, they had begun to acquire more camp followers, various walkers and riders and wagons, people all wanting to see the beasts in cages, the dead bodies under canvas, and the prisoners handcuffed, or hands tied and legs hobbled, and shuffling along barefoot, most of them continuously swearing and complaining. Bapcat thought about Pellerin's circus and how people flocked to see strange sights—as if these people in canvas wraps had been killed for no other reason than to provide Sunday entertainment for citizens.

Today's follow-along crowd continued to grow even larger, but it was mostly a silent mob. Another huge collection of folks stood at the edge of town, miners and sailors and loggers and whores and church folk, all waiting patiently for their arrival, and nobody to keep them in order because Acting Sheriff Hoke Desque was among the barefoot prisoners, far and away the worst moaner and complainer, demanding rights he was hard-pressed to elucidate.

Justice of the Peace Tecumseh "Teedy" Swoon was in the vanguard of townie greeters. "Quite the haul you fellows have there," the JP said to Bapcat. "Archibald and Desque together—now that's one for the history books. I didn't know they'd been introduced. Even seeing them with my own eyes, I can't imagine the two of them together."

"We need lodging for us and our mounts, cells for prisoners, medical care for the wounded, ice for the dead until the coroner is done, and then some holes dug in the ground. They're gonna turn bad fast with the Indian Summer upon us."

"We can accommodate everything," Swoon said, handing him a telegram dated the day after Bapcat had sent his wires.

CIRCUIT COURT JUDGE DEPUTY WAGNER EN ROUTE BY TRAIN TO ONTY. STOP. WILL HELP YOU SORT CHARGES, ET AL. STOP. SHERIFF TORRANCE COMING OVER FROM IRONWOOD TO ASSIST IN MOVE OF MINNESOTA PRISONERS TO HURLEY, WHERE WISCONSIN LAW ENFORCEMENT WILL TAKE CONTROL AND MOVE THEM WEST. STOP. STATE ASSISTANT ATTORNEY GENERAL KILLANI GRINGRAS ACCOMPANYING JUDGE DEPUIS WAGNER, WILL TAKE CHARGE OF PROSECUTIONS, ALL UNDER STATE LAWS, CHARGES, ET CETERA, AB SOLUT. STOP. CHEERS. ECHO.

Bapcat looked at the JP. "Judge DePuis Wagner?"

"Known as 'Four Corners.'"

Bapcat spelled the first name out loud. "How do you say that?"

"Deepee, but he's not likely to encourage anything but 'Your Honor.' He's a flinty man in a flinty job, and one day no doubt headed for a seat in the State Supreme Court."

"He here yet?"

"Him and that slick State lawyer are being hosted by Mrs. Mackley, and she made a big deal of it before the town council."

# CHAPTER 68

*Ontonagon*

THURSDAY, OCTOBER 15

Jone Gleann and Scale returned to Lake Mine without a word. Bapcat let trapper Pippig go and he bolted, presumably for his redoubt in the mountains. Fra Goodman and Sheriff Torrance took a special train of two cars carrying Red Hair's men. Archibald, Ernst Nixon, and Hoke Desque were all in jail, with bail having been denied by Judge Wagner, who had a hangdog face and obsidian eyes that betrayed no emotion. Archibald hired a lawyer from Traverse City, name of Halmalo Gray, reputed to be somewhat of a sleaze who was attracted to clients of a similar ilk—if they had enough money. Archibald apparently qualified.

Rinka Isohultamaki remained with Zakov and Bapcat, and when Horri Harju arrived from Marquette, Bapcat took him aside and told him in no uncertain terms that he should hire her for Ontonagon County's game warden. Bapcat had expected the fact that she was a woman would cause a problem, but Harju's only comment was: "We got a woman down to TC does a bang-up job. Rather have women like her than some of the men we got."

Bapcat had told Rinka about his first meeting with Harju, advising her of the best way to greet him before he greeted her. When Bapcat introduced them, Rinka punched Harju, who managed to block most of the impact but took knuckles to the side of his head. He rubbed the spot and laughed. "Didn't dawn on me Lute might have tipped you off until the very last second. You've got a quick right, girl. I seen it coming and still barely blocked it."

This morning Bapcat had met Pellerin at the train station and walked him to where the bears were caged, with their usual crowd of onlookers. "Jesus baseball," Pellerin said. "That's the biggest bruin I ever seen. Think he'll fight dogs?"

"Will if given the chance."

Pellerin laughed. "Oh, he'll get that—and then some."

"You want both animals?"

"I do indeed. We agreed on seven hundred a head, as I remember it."

Bapcat said, "The deal was nine hundred each, but given your little gambit, I'm pushing it to one thousand even—take it or leave it."

Pellerin chuckled, took out his wallet, and counted out the money in fresh bills. "Two thousand for two bears. The traps part of the deal?"

"Make me an offer."

"Hundred per trap."

"Two fifty for each."

"You're a damn hard man, son," Pellerin said, forking over more cash.

Bapcat took the circus man by the elbow and Zakov came forward and handcuffed him, and Bapcat said, "You're under arrest for stealing State property, two felony counts of grand larceny."

Pellerin grinned. "That won't stick, son. Law ain't as clear in this state as it is elsewhere, and bears is free-market goods."

"See you in court, Ringmaster."

# CHAPTER 69

## *Ontonagon*

FRIDAY, OCTOBER 30

Bapcat would never forget Judge Depuis "Four Corners" Wagner's statement to open the trial.

Wagner began, "People like to make the law out to be a complex machine, like an internal combustion engine, but I have never shared this view. You ask me, the law is like a block, in the country or in a town; to get there from here, or here from there, you have to make sure you visit all four corners. Not one, not two, nor just three, but all four, just like a home run in a baseball game. You've got to touch all the bases in order for the runs to count. Four corners, ladies and gentlemen—the law is as simple as that."

State Assistant Attorney General Killani Gringras was acting as prosecutor, and had the witness. "Now, Mr. Pellerin, you are the sole owner and proprietor of Pellerin's traveling show known as the World Menagerie of Beasts?"

"I guess you could say I'm the head man, yes," Pellerin told the lawyer.

"Own it alone—no silent partners or anything like that?" Gringras asked.

"Just me."

"How long in the business?"

"Near ten years now."

"You know your way around—is that a fair assessment?"

"Ain't many last this long, that's for sure, so I guess you could say I know the ropes."

"What did you do before you had your own show?"

"Worked for others, different shows, some big, some dinks."

"Did you have a special skill?"

"Large animal trainer."

Gringras said, "Your show advertises man-eaters, geeks, freaks, and exotic dancers, is that right?"

"Got the best lineup of rarees around."

316

"Any of your wild animals ever eaten anyone?" the prosecutor asked.

"No, sir, not that I know of—but it wouldn't surprise me if one of the girls didn't run down that road from time to time."

The courtroom erupted in laughter, and the stern-faced judge gaveled them back to respectful silence.

Gringras followed up. "Is the court to infer that your exotic dancers are also prostitutes?"

"They certainly are not; I was just making a joke. As ringmaster, that's my job. Sorry, Your Honor."

Wagner said, "Apology noted. Bear in mind that I'm the sole ringmaster in this circus."

Gringras started again. "I see, no prostitutes. Do you engage in any sort of commercial intercourse with any of the women in your show?"

"Commercial, as in paying for it? I certainly do not, sir. It's against my principles."

"But you do—to employ a euphemism—have congress with some of your female employees?"

Pellerin said, "Ain't much sleeping involved. And it ain't commercial. It's more like what the knights used to call *droit du seigneur*."

"*Parlez-vous français?*" Gringras asked.

"I don't speak nothing but bedroom French, but I know that term, I guess."

"Would you explain to the jury precisely what *droit du seigneur* means?"

"Back in feudal knight and king times, the lord landowner got to be the first to sleep with any woman in his realm, even before her husband did. It was legal and normal back then, and nobody far as I can tell made any to-do about it. Even the church kept quiet."

"Presumably these women would be virgins?"

"That's the idea, I think. Let the boss show them the way, break them in."

"Are you the lord of your feudal empire?"

Pellerin said, "I'm owner and boss, which is the same thing, I think."

"Your employees ever complain?"

"Not one of them working for me now has ever complained."

"Because those who did don't work for you anymore?"

Pellerin grinned. "Keeps things on an even keel that way. Bad morals can cause problems in a small tent show."

"By morals, you mean *morale*?" Gringras asked.

"That's what I said, morals."

"So your special skill is large animals?"

"That's right, yessir."

"You train them yourself?"

"I do."

"Bears, cats, elephants?"

"Well, you never get no elephant ain't already trained on account of it coming from India or Malaya, or somewhere in Africa."

"You train animals as an act in the ring?"

"Yes."

"Do you also train them to fight dogs and other animals outside the circus grounds, at special events or under certain circumstances?"

Pellerin looked up at the judge. "We had a deal. I talk about animals, and you don't bring up nothing about no fighting dogs."

"I have no deal with you, Mr. Pellerin," Judge Wagner said. "Answer the questions."

"Okay, yes, sometimes they fight dogs."

"In front of an audience?" Gringras asked. "Paying customers?"

"Yes."

"With wagers on the side?"

"There might be; I don't know for sure."

"But these fights are lucrative, I understand."

"Is that a question?"

"Do you make money when your animals fight dogs?"

"Sometimes."

"A lot of money?"

"I wouldn't put it that way," Pellerin said.

"More than a regular show day."

"Yeah, sometimes."

Gringras asked. "How is the winner of a fight determined?"

Pellerin looked at the judge, who said, "Answer him."

"Depends on the kind of fight."

"Enlighten us," Gringras said, "as to the *types* of these fights."

"Either side dies or can't keep fighting, the other side wins. Sometimes, though, it ain't to the death—just a certain time period, and the winner is the one that keeps engaging."

"Do dogs ever win?"

"Not in my fights," Pellerin said, with more than a little pride.

"Would it be accurate to state that the less-than-lucrative circus side of your business is nothing more than a disguise for moving an illegal animal-fighting operation around the country?"

Pellerin's lawyer was local, stood up, and said, "Objection, Your Honor. Could be self-incriminating, and it is certainly leading."

Gringras said, "Question withdrawn, Your Honor," before the judge could rule for Pellerin's lawyer.

"How often do your animals actually fight?" Gringras asked.

"I don't know. Not that often."

"Why's that?"

"I don't know—lots of reasons."

"Share some with us, please."

"Some states got hard laws."

"Ah," Gringras said. "You wouldn't fight in a state that forbids it, you being an upstanding and law-abiding citizen."

"No."

"But laws don't stop fights, do they?"

"I hear they don't."

"Because the possibility of big money overcomes fear of legal punishment?"

"All I know is some fights pull in good money, and that's all I have to say."

"You would agree, however, that a large animal skilled at fighting is a high-value company asset?"

"That's for sure."

"For fights off premises, and for drawing a crowd to your show?"

"People come to see animals, probably for the same reason they go to zoos."

"All right, then, thank you for your candor, Mr. Pellerin. Now, Deputy Warden Bapcat testified earlier that you paid him one thousand dollars each for two bears, and another five hundred for two cages—is that right?"

"He forced me up from seven hundred apiece for the bears," Pellerin complained, "but I paid him, fair and square. Pellerin ain't no welsher, and he don't go back on no deals."

"I'm thinking you believed you would get your investment back many times over. I certainly would have made that assumption."

"Well, I would have if it wasn't for this. Hard to operate a circus from a jail cell."

"I'm curious," Gringras said. "Are bears difficult to acquire?"

"It's getting that way. Back in 1905, the Pennsylvanians made bears into so-called game animals, put in special rules to protect them. We used to get some good bears from over that way, but not no more—at least, not cheap."

"What was your thought when you heard what Pennsylvania was doing?"

"My cost of business was gonna go up if my bear died."

"Why do you think Pennsylvania and other states took such measures?"

Pellerin's lawyer waved a hand. "Objection—leading and asking for an opinion."

The prosecutor looked up at the judge. "I think Mr. Pellerin's opinion is especially relevant here, Your Honor. Laws preclude sales, yet he admits to knowing ways to buy counter to the face of the law."

"Witness will answer," Judge Wagner said.

"I guess some states see wild animals as theirs."

"As in, their bears, and their responsibility to take care of them?"

"Well, they act like they own everything else," Pellerin grumbled.

The prosecutor looked at the all-male jury. "The states own the animals and the fishes, which means the people own these creatures. The witness paid our deputy game warden Bapcat one thousand dollars each for two Michigan bears—bears that belong to you, gentlemen of the jury, and citizens of this fine county. Did Pellerin give the money to the State? No. But he gave the money to a state employee he assumed was acting illegally, but was in fact operating on orders from Lansing. That's theft by any definition."

Gringras turned back to Pellerin. "Do you keep your animals in cages?"

"Yep, good strong ones."

"Is that their natural living condition in the wild, in confined cages?"

"You know it ain't," Pellerin said.

"Would you say that's cruel, from the animal's perspective?"

"I don't know. I don't talk animal."

"Be honest, Mr. Pellerin."

"Well, being that they ain't free, I guess that could be taken for cruel."

"Your Honor," the prosecutor said, "the bear is not yet a game animal in Michigan. There are no laws to protect the species, and they are treated by some with no more respect than rats. But Your Honor, we do have strong laws forbidding animal cruelty, and I submit to the members of the jury that placing animals in cages this way is cruel punishment, and blatant violation of state law."

Pellerin's lawyer was on his feet. "Objection! My client takes good care of his animals. They are capital assets, as pointed out by my learned opponent, and it would make no sense for a man to mistreat a valued asset."

"Well," Gringras said, letting the words tumble out slowly, "may I enter something into evidence, Your Honor? We already heard how Mr. Pellerin isn't particularly good at taking care of his female employees, and they're human beings. Now the defendant just allowed that cage captivity is cruelty," Gringras said.

"What evidence?" the judge asked.

"The skin of a bear that died in Pellerin's circus when it came through Bruce Crossing this year."

"I object," Pellerin's lawyer shouted without much enthusiasm. "The condition of a bearskin don't prove how the animal was treated when it was alive," he said.

"I prefer to let the jury decide that," Gringras said. "Your Honor?"

"Seems fair to me," the judge said. "I understand the defense's objection, and were it me, I would surely also object, but I want to see what we're talking about here."

Gringras put the skin in front of the judge, who scowled and pointed. "Show the jury."

Gringras spread out the skin and walked slowly over to the jury, holding it out for them to touch and look at.

"Those are burn marks, gentlemen, and there is not a man jack here who works in the woods who doesn't know an animal been misused when he sees this skin."

"Then zoos are also cruel," the defense lawyer chirped weakly.

"They may indeed be so," Judge Wagner intervened. "But that's for another day and another case. Let's stay focused, gentlemen."

"No further questions," Gringras said.

"Your witness," the judge told Pellerin's lawyer.

"No questions, Your Honor."

Gringras said, "The prosecution rests, Your Honor."

Pellerin's lawyer stood up and looked at the jury. "My client has done nothing any different than zoos do, and we do not find them facing any criminal charges. The prosecution has not proved that my client would use the bears he bought to fight, only that the possibility exists. You can't find a man guilty of a crime on possibility alone. The defense rests its case, gentlemen of the jury, and hopes you will see the manipulations here today with a clear mind and heart. Thank you."

The jury was sequestered and given a hearty lunch. They came to a verdict on their first ballot.

Everyone reassembled in the courtroom, the bailiff handed the verdict to the judge, who read it and passed it to the jury foreman to read to the court: guilty on both counts.

Verdict in, the judge said, "Sentencing will be in abeyance until all the cases in this goat rodeo are adjudicated."

Pellerin's lawyer said, "My client has been fully cooperative; is there some possibility of bail so he can live decent while the rest of the proceedings go on?"

The judge looked at the prosecutor. "Mr. Gringras?"

"No objection, Your Honor."

The judge then set bail terms and adjourned court until the next case on Monday morning.

Bapcat sat with Roland Echo throughout the trial. "I should have waited to catch him fighting the animals."

"The verdict would have been the same. You did well."

"You think Pellerin will run?"

Roland Echo said, "Two of his gals are waiting for him. I suspect they'll keep him kind of busy for a few days."

Bapcat looked at his partner. "Why don't I feel like we done something good?"

The Russian shook his head.

# CHAPTER 70

## *Ontonagon*

### TUESDAY, NOVEMBER 3

The state's attorney had been pounding Archibald with trivia for almost an hour. There were the usual objections and rulings from both sides, and steady banter back and forth for clarification of various rules and so forth. Bapcat, who had already testified to the arrest in the lethal gun battle in Nonesuch, was feeling bored and sleepy, but Zakov was next to him, on the edge of the bench seat.

"Mr. Archibald, did you or did you not order specially designed and built traps for holding bears for commercial sale?"

"Yes, I ordered cages," Archibald said officiously.

Gringras held up one of the models and worked the tiny mechanism. "Move the bait on the trigger, and down the trapdoor comes. The bear can't get out on his own, no matter what he tries." He theatrically demonstrated the mechanism several times in front of the jury. "Yessiree, that's a trap in my book."

Archibald said dismissively, "If you have a cage, any cage, you must have a way to put the animal in and to get it out. It was my intention to capture and sell bears to American zoos. These specially made cages with wheels would make it easier for zoo operators to move animals around their facilities and parks. They would become a zoo asset for management."

Gringras said, "You're under oath, Mr. Archibald. Are you suggesting these traps aren't cruel to the animals in them?"

"That is *precisely* what I am saying, and I'm truly aware of having sworn a sacred oath, Mr. Gringras. I am sworn to tell the truth in this trumped-up, bogus legal case that is to my thinking the antithesis of truth—the antipodes, if you will."

"You deny these traps are cruel for the animals held in them?"

"I swear that while an animal may have some slight discomfort, it is not in any pain or danger in my sturdy cages. In fact, show me any mention in the records where the cages are ever referred to as anything *other* than cages."

"You hold that keeping an animal in a trap is not cruel—am I understanding you correctly on this matter?" Gringras asked.

"Zoos cage animals all the time, and so, too, does society to certain people. We call the latter jails."

Gringras looked back at Bapcat and summoned him with a finger waggle.

"You want me to do *what*?" Bapcat whispered after hearing what the lawyer wanted.

"Is it possible, is what I want to know," Gringras said.

"I guess so, but it will take a heckuva lot of work."

"Well, get to it," Gringras said, and turned away.

Bapcat called Zakov and Rinka and Harju into the corridor outside the courtroom and explained what the state's assistant attorney general wanted.

Zakov grinned. "It will be worth the effort just to see people's reactions."

"Let me know when you get back," Bapcat said, and returned to the courtroom to sit beside Rollie Echo. "Trouble?" his friend asked.

Bapcat shook his head.

"Your Honor," Gringras said, "the witness is repeatedly being evasive in all of his answers."

Judge Wagner said, "Mr. Archibald, please remain focused on answering the question, or you may find yourself held in contempt of court."

"Held in contempt by a kangaroo court?" Archibald said through a tight smile and clenched teeth. "How is that even *possible*? I am a God-fearing man who follows God's written word. God said let the land produce living creatures according to their kinds, livestock, creatures that move along the ground, and wild animals, and it was so. Genesis one twenty-four."

Gringras was quick to respond. "Exodus tells us that the reason for taking off the seventh day was to rest and refresh the animals, and the Bible further admonishes us to not treat any of His animals with contempt, domestic or wild. *Any* of His animals."

Romney Archibald said calmly, "There are no strictures on cages in the Holy Book."

"Let's look at what really happens," Gringras said. "You first take an animal accustomed to traveling many miles daily to find food, and then you confine this magnificent beast in a trap, thereby taking away almost all its movement, allowing only enough space so it can barely turn around, and you don't find that contemptuous of the creature's health and well-being?"

"There is no law in this state against cages," Archibald repeated. "Or denying the legality of trapping bears. They are pests, and any citizen may kill any bear, any time, for any reason," Archibald said confidently.

"Did your cages somehow come to contain four bears?"

"I have heard this is so, but cannot testify to seeing said number of animals in my cages with my own eyes. Furthermore, I instructed no one to use my cages for any reason except for those I approve, and I did not approve these uses. I don't know who is responsible other than the dead murderer, Young."

"You realize," the state attorney said, "that your contract with Heinrich Junger makes you a participant in the felony death of all those killed in Nonesuch."

"Show me such a contract," Archibald said confidently. "Produce it, or stop with this."

Gringras said, "Surely you saw two animals in cages when they were moved here from Nonesuch, through Silver City?"

"I assumed you were asking if I saw them elsewhere, which I did not. Yes, I sort of saw them in the places just cited, but not before, and I had no knowledge before the fact."

"How were you going to trap animals to sell to zoos?"

"That is proprietary information for my business, for a patent pending before the US government, Mr. Gringras. I assume business secrets are still honored in courtrooms here."

"Some of the survivors of the shootout in Nonesuch, *your employees*, say differently, and claim the traps were set on your orders and at your direction."

"Cages," Archibald corrected him.

"Granted, cages. Your people say you were with them on the Elm River and approved the placement of every contraption."

"Who contends this? Who tells this lie? Who soils my reputation? Let him have the intestinal fortitude to step forward and swear on a Bible, before God and me."

"You rank yourself as His equal?" Gringras shot back.

"I have the right to confront my false accuser."

"Sir, Mr. Pled is dead, as is Mr. Elphinstone, and we have subpoenaed Mr. Beaumont Clewd, who was suddenly and I might say conveniently called to Denver on unspecified emergency personal business, date of return unknown. Mr. Clewd's company built your cages—do you acknowledge that?"

"Of course; there are records of the contract."

"Built to your specifications?"

"Yes, four iron cages on wheels."

"Based on this model?" Gringras held up the model again for the jury to see.

"Yes, that model."

"Who made the model, Mr. Archibald?"

"Deputy Warden Farrell Mackley."

"And where is Deputy Mackley?"

"You'd best ask his spouse."

"We did, sir, and will get to that in a minute."

Zakov crept over to Bapcat, who went forward to the prosecutor, whispered, and then left the courtroom with the Russian.

Gringras looked at Archibald. "You maintain that the cages render an animal only slightly uncomfortable; is that a fair statement of your position?"

"It is."

"Your Honor, excuse me, but there's an exhibit the jury should see. I'm sorry for taking so long to provide this evidence, but it is only now available and ready."

"Gentlemen, approach the bench."

Gringras and Gray rose, but before they could take a step, the double doors burst open at the back of the courtroom and a wheeled cage rumbled forward, pushed by Zakov, Harju, Isohultamaki, and two others.

Someone in the gallery shouted, and people started yelling as the malodorous scent of shit, piss, and bear musk flooded the courtroom. As the noise increased, the animal grew irritated and hammered the iron bars, shaking the cage until it was thundering the wooden floor like a bass drum. The gallery grew silent.

"Now I ask you, gentlemen of the jury—does this look like slight discomfort to you?"

The bear was parked close to the jury box and obviously in great distress. Bapcat suddenly mounted the cage, reefed on the chain and pulley, and opened the trapdoor as bailiffs and others ran for cover. The trapdoor flew open, the animal let loose a terrible scream and snarl, and went out through the double doors at the back of the room, down the courthouse stairs. Even the judge ran to the window to watch the animal parting human waves as it fled down the street, desperately looking for cover.

The judge was pounding his gavel until it became an unheard white noise under all the voices and excitement. Eventually he just stopped, crossed his arms, and waited for the adrenaline to stop pumping.

"If this outbreak is over, we'll have order in my court, and I do mean now, and I do mean everyone."

When it was quiet, Judge Wagner said, "Now that the evidence has been so intimately placed before us, I could rule post facto on admissibility, but we all know you can't exactly erase certain memories. Part of me says I should declare a mistrial, but another part is urging me to push forward in the interest of justice. That bear won't be coming back in here, will it, Mr. Gringras?"

"No, sir, I don't think so, Your Honor."

"Good. Now, it's within my power to direct the jury to disregard and ignore this whole ludicrous prank, but it's one thing to tell a man to forget, and another for him to actually do that. So Mr. Gringras, what next?"

"Thank you, Your Honor. I think we could all see that the animal in that cage was clearly and unequivocally being abused, and whether we call Mr. Archibald's device a cage or a trap, its intent and effect are the same."

Gringras paused. "But we all *know* that, don't we? We just saw reality with our own eyes, and Mr. Archibald can't deny that with a straight face or without breaking his oath. So let me tell you that Mrs. Mackley will attest to certain conversations regarding her husband's fate, and Mr. Archibald's alleged role as architect of the missing warden's fate. The missing deputy is, in fact, deceased, and Mrs. Mackley will have quite a story to tell us when she testifies."

"She's not on the witness list, Your Honor!" Halmalo Gray shouted. "First the surprise bear as evidence, and now this—an unscheduled witness? Is the prosecution's case so poor that it must resort to chicanery, cheap thespian tactics, and misdirection?"

"We had the woman's testimony and a dying man's statement, as taken by deputy wardens Bapcat and Zakov, who took said statement from one Mr. Eustice Pled as he lay dying up on the Elm River."

"Is Mrs. Mackley here?" the judge asked.

"She's waiting outside at the court's pleasure, Your Honor."

Gray exploded. "Objection, objection, objection! I object! This is all irrelevant to the animal cruelty charges under indictment and this proceeding. This is nothing more than a red herring meant to confuse the jury and stink up the defense."

Archibald pulled on his lawyer's sleeve and the man sat down. The two talked quietly for almost a minute. Gray then got to his feet. "I know this is sudden, but my client wishes to change his plea from not guilty to *nolo contendere* to all cruelty charges."

Judge Wagner said, "Does your client understand that while *nolo contendere* is not a guilty plea, it is treated the same by the court?"

"He's been informed, Your Honor."

"I hope this is spontaneous, and not a preplanned and staged gambit."

"No, sir, it is my client's wish, and, of course, his right. I simply represent his wishes in my capacity as his attorney."

The judge said, "Mr. Archibald, why the sudden change?"

"Conscience, Your Honor. I have no wish to spend any further public treasure on this sham. I plead *nolo contendere*, and will take my punishment as the court so decides."

"That's quite commendable and civic minded of you, Mr. Archibald. *Nihil eminens civilis animi in civem.* You realize that you just removed the jury from this shindig?"

"Yes, Your Honor," Romney Archibald said. "I was so informed."

"So be it," Judge Wagner said. "The defendant's plea is changed from not guilty to *nolo contendere*, and it is accepted by the court and duly entered. Sentencing tomorrow at ten a.m."

The bailiff yelled, "All rise," and the judge swooped out of the courtroom to his chambers.

Bapcat looked at Rollie Echo. "What the heck just happened?"

"Archibald probably felt Mrs. Mackley could implicate him in a more serious crime. This way he pleads to something much less, which will protect him from civil suits. No doubt Mrs. Mackley is interested in filing one for a profit."

"But we don't know that she had anything to do with Farrell's disappearance."

"We have his body," Echo said. "Hoke Desque told us where to look in exchange for reduced charges."

"Where was he?"

"Up on the Elm River."

"*Did* the wife have a role in it?"

"We have no idea, but circumstantially it sure looked like she might, and we know she was involved with Archibald on the q.t., never mind his good Christian puffery."

"Was she going to testify?" Bapcat asked.

"She's not even in the courthouse. What do you think?"

"This was a bluff?"

"All Gringras wanted was to get the trapped animal into the courtroom, so the jury could see it. Any smaller animal would have been worthless for that purpose, but that monster? It was made to order."

"Did Archibald have a role in killing Mackley?"

"Probably, based on how he jumped at the new plea. The way the story came to us is that Archibald paid mine captain Eustice Pled to get rid of the game warden. We surmise he wanted the trap-cage scheme all to himself, and he knew that Mackley was planning his own enterprise with it—that is, if he could raise the capital to have the machines built. Archibald saw profit in the plan and the invention, and found out that Mackley had never filed for a patent."

"Pled had Ernst Nixon do it?"

"Nixon claims Pled ordered him to do it, and he in turn hired Stink-mouth to do the job."

"But Stinkmouth took off afterward."

"We're pretty sure that Nixon killed Stinkmouth to eliminate the trail that led to him, but he won't admit to this. He does admit to shooting at you, just to scare you, but he claims hitting you was an accident, and never intended."

"The dummy was an accident, too?"

"Both times."

"What did Archibald tell Pled that made him agree to have Mackley killed?"

"He told Pled what you and Zakov had done during the strike up north, and that Mackley was now empowered to do similar things here in contravention of mining companies and their business."

"The strike was pretty much over down here."

"Not when Mackley was killed, but it was down to a murmur. Pled feared he might bring the heat back and reinvigorate the union. Then you came to town, and Pled put Nixon after you."

A dumbfounded Bapcat said, "Farrell Mackley died because of me?"

"Well, not because of you directly, but because of the things you let happen up in the Keweenaw, and how those things boosted the union's cause."

"*Jesus*, Rollie. Jesus. I'm just a simple game warden."

"I know, Lute."

"When did everyone plan to tell me about this?"

"Only if Mrs. Mackley took the stand."

"And if not?"

"No reason for you to know anything. You didn't do anything wrong."

"I am not liking this," Bapcat said.

"*We* are not," Zakov said from beside him.

"What was Mrs. Mackley's relationship with Archibald?" the Russian asked.

"Intimate," Echo said. "Long before she married Mackley, she knew Archibald out east somewhere. She came here to join him, only to learn he was married. He spurned her at first, so she looked for other opportunities and settled in. She was the one who first got Archibald interested in the traps. Her husband went to Archibald only because she sent him there."

"How do we know this?"

"I can't tell you."

"Is she party to her husband's murder?"

"That's a long legal reach, and too far for a case."

"So, she walks free?"

"Nature of the beast of justice," Echo said. "But Archibald will be hammered with two felony counts, including fines and jail time. He will no doubt appeal, and I predict he will even get it overturned, but it will cost him dearly in time and money. Meanwhile, we have a precedent to use."

"What does the State get?"

"An entry into classifying bears as game animals and promulgating hunting regulations thereof."

"And all the deaths at Nonesuch, and the boys before that?"

"Minnesota goes first; we'll see where it all goes after that."

Zakov said, "Seems like a meager return on a costly and bloody investment."

"Things like this take time," Roland Echo said, "Great Rome not being built in a day and all that. You fellas should rejoice. You have a conviction in a bear cruelty case, and against all odds. This will open other legal doors, help provide new tools to law enforcement. Use what you have, boys; don't bemoan what you don't."

The game wardens stood outside in the crisp autumn air. "Dead because of me," Bapcat said disconsolately.

"You oversimplify, my friend. Are we free to return to Bumbletown Hill now?"

"I recommended Rinka to Horri for Ontonagon County."

"A fine choice."

"Hoke Desque will be charged with animal cruelty and dismissed from his temporary sheriff appointment. I've recommended Indian for the job."

"He will agree?"

"I'm sure his wife and Jone will shame him into it."

"The boy, Manny?"

"He has taken his friend Thomas to Armandville to live on the island."

"You are not concerned about his mental stability?"

"I am, but Rinka will visit First Arm and tell him the whole story."

"All of this for animal cruelty convictions," Zakov said, shaking his head ponderously.

"Red Hair and Min are dead. Red Hair's people are in Minnesota for trial, and other states are lined up to get at them as well," Bapcat said with a shrug. "There is sometimes more honor in taking care of animals than our fellow humans."

"A sad commentary on the world we live in," the Russian said.

# CHAPTER 71

## *Copper Harbor*

### WEDNESDAY, NOVEMBER 11

It was snowing hard, an early-season norther in the air when Bapcat walked into Widow Frei's emporium, shaking snow off his bearskin coat, the irony of wearing such a thing not escaping him, given his recent activities. The game warden stood back and watched Jaquelle talking to customers.

Jordy came in, saw Bapcat right off, flew to him and jumped up, wrapping his arms around the game warden. "We heard how some no-good sumbitch shot you. Can I see your scar? You got a scar, right? Wouldn't be right to get shot and not have a scar."

Bapcat laughed.

"You hear the whole damn world is fightin' each other?" the boy asked.

"Not Americans," Bapcat said.

The boy's hug felt wonderful, and Bapcat looked up to see Jaquelle Frei standing with her hands on her hips, grinning lasciviously. "My wayward deputy come home at last . . . Hallelujah. Jordy, please put up the 'closed' sign."

"But it ain't yet time to close, ma'am."

"It is time, Jordy. Please do as you're told." She opened her purse and gave the boy a gold piece.

"Ten dollars! You ain't never give me this much before."

"Haven't given. Go have some ice cream."

"In a blizzard? You know how much ice cream ten dollars will buy?"

"Treat your friends."

The boy took off and Bapcat walked hand in hand with Jaquelle Frei up the stairs to her front door.

Jordy came back with a three-legged dog close behind. "This is the ugliest dog I ever seen."

Bapcat said, "He's yours now. Don't hurt his feelings."

Widow Frei asked, "You get everything you went after, over there in those awful mountains?"

Bapcat nodded.

She rubbed her hand along the contour of his buttock. "I'm about to be able to say the very same," she said, opening the front door for him.

# AUTHOR'S NOTE

While this story is wholly of my own invention, our state's record with bears is quite real, and not a particularly proud or enlightened chapter in Michigan wildlife conservation history.

The Michigan legislature did not grant game animal status to bears until 1925, eleven years after this story takes place, seven years after World War I concluded, and two *decades* after Pennsylvania and other states.

Prior to 1925, people could kill bears as they pleased, the great animals considered by many to be nothing more than large pests.

Once the animals were classified as game and bear hunting began, bait was always legal to use. I used it myself, back when I was a bear hunter.

Hounds were legalized for bear hunting in 1939.

Cubs didn't get protection until 1948, three years after World War II.

The first separate bear hunting license wasn't required until 1980. And, until 1990, you could shoot a bear and a deer on your firearm deer license. Only in 1995 did it become illegal to take a sow accompanied by cubs.

I think our lives are enriched by encountering our forests' great beasts, especially bears.

As a writer is wont to do, I began to imagine that long before 1925 some of our game wardens, conservationists, and other interested parties might have begun to see the need to prevent the wanton slaughter of such magnificent animals. As these things go, I thought about Lute Bapcat and Sergey Zakov, and asked myself *what if*—knowing full well how glacially slow change can come in such important matters. But there has to be a beginning somewhere—one magic moment when an individual or individuals draw a line and set their jaws.

There always is.

Joseph Heywood
Alberta, Michigan
May 23, 2014

# ABOUT THE AUTHOR

Joseph Heywood is the author of *Covered Waters*, *The Snowfly*, *Hard Ground*, *The Berkut*, *Taxi Dancer*, and *The Domino Conspiracy*. His Grady Service Mystery Series has earned him cult status among lovers of the outdoors, law enforcement officials, and mystery devotees. In Heywood's new series—the Lute Bapcat Mystery Series—set in early twentieth-century Michigan and featuring a game-warden protagonist who once fought with Theodore Roosevelt as a Rough Rider, the novel *Red Jacket* precedes *Mountains of the Misbegotten*. Heywood splits the year between Alberta and Portage, Michigan. Visit him at josephheywood.com.

# LUTE BAPCAT SERIES

Set in 1913, Rough Rider turned game warden Lute Bapcat confronts a violent miners' strike, deadly sabotage, and the intentional destruction of wildlife.

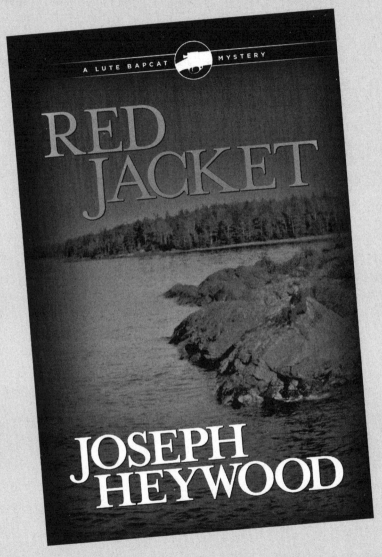

One legendary insect—enormous, white, and exceedingly rare—attracts trout of such size that they couldn't possibly exist in the world as we know it. But in Heywood's classic novel, such things can and do exist. Richly imaginative and sensual, the world of *The Snowfly* has more mystery lurking beneath the surface than our own. Or does it?

JOSEPH HEYWOOD

THE
SNOWFLY

A NOVEL

To plac                                    r to 800-820-
or ema